A NOTE.

Seaside Pointe is a fictional town set in the area of Skagit Valley, Washington. Most of the places mentioned are fictitious. However, there are very real places brought into the story too.

We are not flower farmers or real estate developers. We are writers who research and know things. Any mistakes made are either intentional for story purposes or accidental because, well, as we said, "we're just writers."

Please forgive us if we've botched something up.

— XOXO M&M

P.S. Extend some love to Floret. Erin's sites were a huge inspiration and place of reference for us. The world needs more beauty like this: https://www.instagram.com/floretflower/

D1715080

BLOSSOMS
& STEEL

Cover design © Sarah Hansen, Okay Creations
Edited by Samantha Eaton-Roberts
Proofed by Jo Pettibone

ALSO BY MINDY MICHELE

Pratt Family Stories

Paper Planes and Other Things We Lost

Subway Stops and the Places We Meet

Chasing Cars and the Lessons We Learned

The Backroads Duet

Love in C Minor, Vol one

Loss in A Major, Vol two

Nothing Compares To You, a 90s novella

ALSO BY MICHELE G. MILLER

Last Call

The Prophecy of Tyalbrook

Never Let You Fall

Never Let You Go

Never Without You

From The Wreckage Series
From The Wreckage
Out of Ruins
All That Remains
Standalone FTW spinoffs
West: A male POV Novel
Into the Fire - Dani's story
After The Fall - Austin's story (17+)
Until We Crash - Jess and Carter's story (17+)

Havenwood Falls Series
Awaken the Soul, Havenwood Falls High
Avenge the Heart, Havenwood Falls High
Co-written with R.K. Ryals:
Dark Seduction, Havenwood Falls Sin & Silk (17+)

Sign up for Michele's newsletter
http://bit.ly/MGMNews

ALSO BY MINDY HAYES

The Faylinn Series - YA Fantasy
Kaleidoscope

Ember

Luminary

Glimmer

The Willowhaven Series - Adult Romance
Me After You

Me Without You

Me To You

Individual titles

The Day That Saved Us – Coming of Age Romance

Stain - Romantic Psychological Suspense

Sign up for Mindy's newsletter

http://bit.ly/mindyhayesnews

For those who fell in love with someone
they first pretended to hate

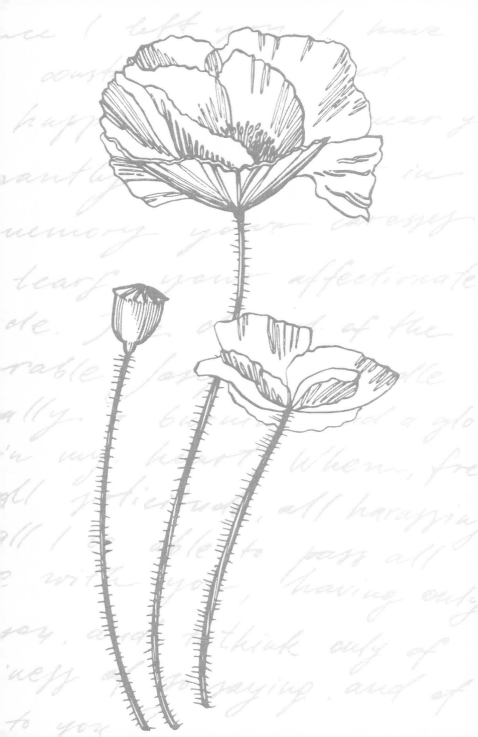

hloe

SUNRISE. My favorite time of day. Its golden light floods the vibrant fields of flowers as I stand on the back porch of my parents' house overlooking the farm and sip my morning coffee. Even though this is a sight I've woken up to every day of my life, there are times the beauty doesn't seem real. The blossoms come alive, the stems dancing in the light breeze. It's the kind of sight with the power to convince a person to believe in magic.

Surrounded by acres and acres of farmland, it's easy to hear the rumbling engines in the distance cruising down the gravel roads, the crew arriving to help deliver the first harvest of spring. Swallowing back the last of my coffee, I bring my mug inside so I can greet the crew and kick off the morning.

As I walk past the chicken coop, Mom steps out in her rubber boots and fleece jacket with her scoop for the feed in hand. "Morning, sweet pea. Did you sleep well last night?"

"I was a little restless, but nothing the flowers can't heal."

Sweeping her long, muted brown hair over her shoulder, she kisses my cheek on her way to the house. "Don't forget you have another meeting with Jordan Gardiner and Celeste Middleton this afternoon."

Cringing inwardly, I smile. "Thanks, Mom." Hopefully they'll approve of the changes we need to make to their wedding flowers, otherwise we'll lose the account. I can arrange something beautiful, but if it's not what they want, there's only so much I can do.

WITH THE RISING sun pouring over the flower fields, we gather the buckets of freshly-cut stems from the cooler and load up the delivery vehicles all lined up.

"You got Petals, Violet's, and Hollow Tree today, Reid?"

He slides a Lockwood Blooms van door shut. "Yep."

"Careful on those turns around Mt. Luna. Charlie knocked over half the blooms last time." I murmur under my breath. "I don't need Carla calling me again pissed because her flowers are late or damaged. We can't afford to keep replacing flowers free of charge."

Reid turns with his head canted and his eyes staring me down, as if to tell me I should know better. "I've got you covered, Loe." He walks over and kisses my cheek.

I'm still getting used to his affection. Or rather, his affection in front of the rest of the team. I've known Reid for years, but we've only been dating for a month. Things are still fresh and work romances can be complicated. Especially ones involving the boss: me.

"You better." I tap his chest with a smile as I back away toward my trusty old Chevy truck, Betty.

"I'd never dream of damaging your precious blooms."

Pointing at him, I say, "Oh, I know. You're aware of what my wrath looks like."

He laughs as he straightens the bill of his lucky baseball cap, his dusty blond hair curling over the tops of his ears. "Exactly."

After seeing off the rest of the delivery vehicles, I load up the last bucket of peonies in the bed of my truck and head into town.

USING MY HIP, I shut my truck door and wave hello to my last delivery of the morning. Alice stands on the curb at the entrance of Flower Patch with a bright smile on her face.

"Morning, Alice."

The gray-haired woman's hand lands over her heart as she peers into the bed of my truck. "Look at the size of those anemones and tulips. They are gorgeous, Chloe. Oh, and those hyacinths and daffodils." She sighs with a dreamy stare, the skin crinkling at the corners of her faded green eyes. "I should never be surprised by your blooms, but every delivery steals my breath away."

"These ones are pretty spectacular." My chest puffs with pride. "It's going to be a great season."

Her gaze softens. "Is your father still out of commission?"

A melancholy twinge tweaks my chest. "For a little while longer, yeah."

"How's your mom handling everything?"

Hands on my hips, I dig for a smile. "Like the superwoman she is. Taking care of him and still managing the finances and scheduling of Lockwood's."

"Goodness. Robyn has always been resilient and tenacious. She's a trooper, that one."

"She is indeed."

"You need a hand?"

I shake my head as I slip on some gardening gloves from the front pocket of my overalls. "No need. Just tell me where you want them."

One by one, I haul the remaining buckets of flowers inside

while Alice finishes setting up her racks and display cases. When I head out to retrieve the last bucket, someone leans against the back of beat-up Betty, twirling a pale pink tulip. I stop. It isn't just *any* someone. My heartbeats and thoughts stumble as his presence sinks in.

Standing in tan slacks and a crisp blue button-up, he doesn't look much different than the boy I grew up with. Except, somewhere in the last seven years, the boy grew into a man. The many freckles once marking his face with boyhood, distinguish the strong angles of his jawline and straight nose.

"I see nothing's changed in this town. If you want to find the prettiest girl around, you look for the most beautiful flowers."

Even after all this time, he still wreaks havoc on my stomach and heart. And not in the pitter-patter kind of way.

"Kipling Harris." While I try to keep the bite out of my tone, it slips. I'm older, more mature than when I last saw him, but the years did nothing to diminish the feud between our families and us.

"Chloe Lockwood." He continues twirling the pastel tulip between his thumb and forefinger before offering the flower to me. "I'm not surprised you still outshine all the other Lockwood blooms."

Shaking my head, I pinch my lips to hold back a snort. Smooth talker, as always, though I don't know why he's aiming it at me. "And I'm not surprised you're still laying on the excessive charm."

"It's what I do." Kip gives a crooked grin as he pushes off the truck. "You do look good, though."

Plucking the tulip from his outstretched hand, I keep a couple feet between us, not trusting his proximity for multiple reasons: both physical and emotional. My feet shuffle on the pavement as I rest my hands on my hips. I hate the racing horses in my chest.

"It's been a long time."

"Yeah, it has." Kip shoves a hand in his pocket and rakes the other through his windblown hair.

It's crazy how the years spent apart don't change my body's reaction to him, how in a matter of seconds, my teenage feelings rush back. With as much force as I can muster, I shove them deep into the once locked chest. Kip Harris won't fracture my composure this time. Or ever again.

"I was on my way to Aunt May's for breakfast when I spotted the Chevy. I can't believe you still drive this beat-up thing."

I frown at his insult. Not everyone in Seaside Pointe has a rich daddy buying them fancy vehicles. And Betty has never wronged me. She's as reliable as she is old. They don't build them like they used to.

He clears his throat when I don't reply. "So, how have you been?" he asks. "Your family doing well?"

"Yeah…Umm…" I scratch the top of my head beneath the messy bun, my eyes darting to the sidewalk. The last thing I want to get into with Kip Harris on the main street of Seaside is my dad's health. "Things are busy."

"Do you have the last bunch, hun?"

My head whips around to the floral shop. "Yes. I'm sorry, Alice." I climb into the bed and slip the tulip Kip took into the lone white bucket. "Let me get those for you."

Kip slides back a step. "Sorry, don't let me keep you from your work. I've got someone waiting on me, anyway."

Someone? His next conquest? Poor girl.

"Kip Harris. Is that you, dear?" Alice wanders closer.

His head knocks back as he lifts a hand. "Ms. Dewey, nice to see you."

"My goodness." She squeezes his biceps, an appreciative gleam brimming on her wrinkled face. "The last time I saw you you were quite a few inches shorter. You have grown into one handsome man."

"I guess life in the south agreed with me. Probably all the

good cooking. Good thing I grew up and not out." He rubs his stomach. "I should get a move on. Ms. Dewey." Kip tips his head toward Alice, a slight grin on his lips, before he looks up at me towering above from the back of the truck. The smile he bestowed on Alice is nothing like the full, face-altering, ear-to-ear grin he awards me. The early morning sun hits him in the eyes, and he cups a hand over his brows. "It was truly good running into you, Sunshine. I'll see ya."

My chest tightens at the use of his sardonic nickname. Even though I'm unsure of how I feel about us running into each other, I say, "You, too," and brush a wayward lock from my eyes, a nonchalant gesture.

How am I supposed to handle Kip being in town? How long is he here for? Not wanting to seem eager for answers, all I finish with is, "See ya."

He cuts across the street, ducking in front of a slow-passing car with a wave of thanks. It's hard to grasp his return. He's been gone for so long, and yet even with his matured features, he's probably still the same Kip Harris. Heartbreaker. Tormentor. Nemesis. Only now, I bet he's more practiced.

I return to the task at hand. I can't be distracted by that man. Kip will probably be gone soon anyway. He never comes to Seaside, and if he does, I've never cared to hear about it, or he doesn't stay for long.

After lugging the bucket to the edge of the bed, I tuck my gloves into the front pocket of my overalls. Alice takes the flowers, and I hop off the scuffed white tailgate before slamming it shut.

"I can't wait to see the poppies and anemones." She beams.

Dusting off my hands, I say, "In a week or two we'll be harvesting them. And I'll bring by our first batch of ranunculus in a few days if you'd like."

"Oh, I can't wait to see them. Those sherbet-toned ranunculus are always a hit."

I hum an agreement. "They rival some of my favorites, but just you wait for the Iceland poppies. They are something else this year. I promise you won't be disappointed."

"I have no doubt. Lockwood Blooms never lets me down. Thank you, Chloe."

"Take care, Alice. I'll see you Wednesday or Thursday."

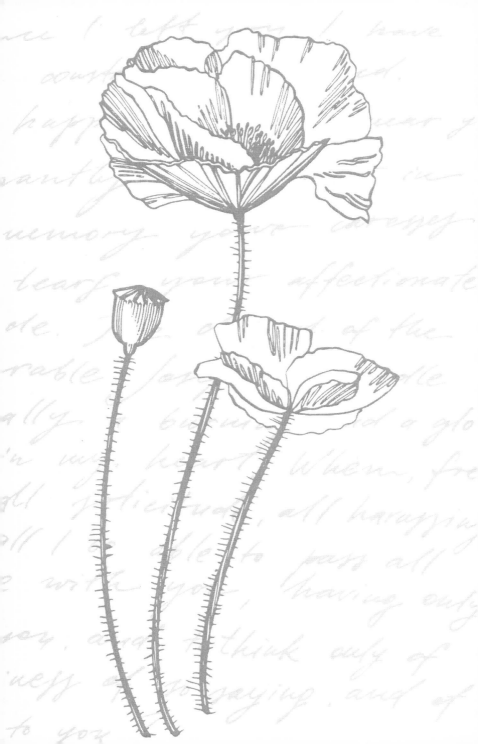

ip

I ARRIVED in Seaside Pointe less than twelve hours ago, and I've already run into Chloe Lockwood. I haven't even seen my folks yet, but for her, I go out of my way when I spot her Chevy. The timing was too perfect to pass up. I check my watch, then dare a casual glance over my shoulder from across the street. Chloe is back at work, her wild hair visible over the cab of her truck. She waves to Alice before jumping into the beat-up vehicle and taking off.

I scratch my jaw as her familiar truck fades into the distance. I'm not surprised she's making deliveries for Lockwood Blooms. No doubt her hands are wrapped around every facet of the day-to-day operations. The business is her first love, or it was growing up. Her loyalty one hundred percent to the family profession. Even as a teen, when everyone hung out and stirred trouble, Chloe refused more often than not. Always more concerned with how her reputation affected her family name than with having a good time. It was maddening. More maddening is how the woman is more beautiful today than she was then. My nemesis, if our families have anything to say about our association, has never failed to stir my blood. I'm ticked she has the same effect on me at twenty-four as she did when I was eighteen. Unlike my teen self, I won't act upon those feelings.

"KIPLING." Roger Scaritt's baritone greeting turns heads as we meet with a handshake in the entrance of Aunt May's Southern Cafe. The clatter of silverware against May's classic blue porcelain dishes pauses as diners gawk. Yep, go ahead and stare, ladies and gentlemen. Stare in wonder at the unusual occurrence of Kipling Harris returning home. Ten dollars says gossip stirrers have sent the first text. Too bad Chloe isn't here; she always loved making bets with me.

Digging deep, I muster a mask of cordiality for the onlookers while focusing on my breakfast companion. "Roger, please, call me Kip. My mom is the only person who calls me Kipling anymore." Mom, and Chloe Lockwood. A chill ran up my spine when she said my name. The same as it did so many years ago. *Focus, Kip.* I shove the past aside and clasp Roger by his beefy shoulder. "It's been a while."

His reply is cut short by May's out-of-place southern drawl. "Well, I'll be." She claps her hands, and genuine warmth fills me as I soak her in.

As the restaurant name suggests, May is 'aunt' to the Seaside Pointe community, and the woman's southern accent is as real as her platinum roots. We don't question her theatrics, though. Nope, everyone from Seattle to Vancouver is aware of May's affinity for Dolly Parton and rhinestones. As long as she keeps cooking up her southern fixings, Seaside Pointe humors her eccentricity.

"The son has returned to assume his place on the golden

throne." May's voice carries, drawing attention as she shimmies our way. I inhale through my teeth and knead my forehead as Roger chuckles beneath his breath. Count on May to cause a scene.

She takes my clean-shaven cheeks in her hands and pinches like I'm the eight-year-old she used to serve hot chocolate to every Sunday afternoon for brunch. "Gorgeous boy, welcome home. I bet your momma is happy to have you here," she says in a conspiratorial whisper, her over-made face wreathed with joy.

I ease her hands from my sore cheeks and give them a squeeze. "Hi, May. I'm happy to be home. I haven't even seen my parents. I came straight to you first."

"You always did know how to charm me. C'mon, sugar." The gold bangles climbing her thin arms jingle as she grabs two menus and waves us to follow.

No doubt there are prying eyes. They're lasers boring into my skin as we pass each table, but I remain focused on May's teased blonde hair. The attention is bizarre after seven years in Oklahoma. I forgot what being Kipling Harris, son of Denton Harris, is like. Especially in this town.

When Roger is waylaid by an elderly couple, I continue following May to a corner booth. She flips the speckled ceramic coffee mugs over and sets our menus down. "Want your usual?"

"Biscuits and gravy?" I crack the menu open, unsurprised she remembers. "As much as I've missed them, I should stick to something a little lighter today."

May reaches over and turns the menu's page with a frown. "I added a healthy section recently to appease the weekend tourists from the city. Apparently, they watch their figures."

Healthy is quite the departure for the May I grew up with. Her philosophy is food feeds the soul, and in her book, 'diet' is a dirty, four-letter word.

"Definitely a smart business decision, May. How about you let me order an egg white omelet for today?" I close the menu and flirt shamelessly. "I promise I'll come back and eat all the calories this weekend."

Huffing, she turns to Roger, who's sliding into the bench seat across from me. "I'll have my usual, May."

We settle in as a server stops by and fills our coffee mugs. Roger stirs creamer into his mug. "Denton talks about the work you're doing down in Tulsa every time I see him. He shared a peek at the project file for your mixed-use development—"

"The Omni-Plex." I shift back in my seat, my mug cupped in my hand.

Omni-Plex is a two million square foot mixed-use development in the heart of Tulsa. Built for both the booming business growth and college student population. Landing such a deal was a coup for the small development firm I went to work for after graduating from college. The project is also the reason I didn't return home. Learning Dad praised my work to others in the business comes as a surprise.

Handing out praise is as rare as a tornado in the Pacific Northwest for a man like Denton Harris. Especially when the accolades are for his only son. We butted heads often through the years, but by my sophomore year, I took to rebelling at everything he put in front of me. My junior year, when college recruiters noticed my performance on the pitching mound, Dad went into sports agent mode—making pro and con lists for each school. My answer? I quit baseball. With college athletics off the table, Dad pushed for me to attend his alma mater, Stanford. I applied everywhere but there, then accepted the University of Oklahoma in secret. At my college graduation four years ago, he gifted me Harris Development business cards with my name on them. He thought he'd secured my spot with the family business. Instead, I took a job with Weller Faison in Tulsa and enrolled in classes for my MBA. Weller Faison owns half the assets of Harris Development, but they are determined, and they don't want me on a leash.

The Omni-Plex, a project I began during my internship at the firm while still in college, earned a full spread in a national development magazine. The deal also earned Weller Faison more contracts than they can handle and me the title of Golden Boy among my managing partners.

Roger snaps his fingers. "Yes, that's right. What a deal." He lowers his voice. "Denton is determined to do something similar with the riverfront property."

Talk of development in Seaside Pointe never fails to send the locals into a frenzy. Few people like change, especially when the change comes at the expense of scenic views and peace.

I sip my black coffee. "This entire county will fight rezoning on the property. My father may be dreaming." *Of course the hope that he isn't is why I'm here.*

Inspecting the seats nearest us, Roger leans his bulging torso over the table. "We'll get the zoning through. It will require time, but it'll happen."

His certainty has me clenching my jaw. "Roger, I don't accept kickbacks or negotiate deals under tables. If the feasibility studies come back saying what we think they will, we'll apply for the land-use permits and work toward rezoning."

Roger blanches, the implication he—as a town council member—is anything but above reproach does not sit well with him. I don't apologize. I asked for this meeting with one of my father's oldest friends and closest business allies to assure one thing: if the riverfront project moves forward, I manage the deal.

And, if I agree to assume the helm at Harris Development, everyone will play by my rules. Everyone, including Denton Harris.

HARRIS DEVELOPMENT ANCHORS a horseshoe-shaped business complex of converted warehouses and industrial buildings only blocks from May's on the west side of town. It's close enough to walk, but since my homecoming is meant as a surprise, I drive. As much as I enjoyed unexpectedly bumping into Chloe Lockwood this morning, I don't have the time, or patience, for more reunions before seeing family.

I open the sunroof on my crossover and inhale. I've missed the Pacific Northwest air. The briny tang of the ocean fills my nostrils. Seven years living away from the coast is seven years too many. The water beckons me, but my cell has three missed calls from Dad's office. He's not expecting me until tonight; why does he keep calling? The coast will wait. It's time to see Dad.

My adult eyes study the building's landscaping and exterior with the eye of a realtor as I turn into the parking lot. They've done a good job renovating this complex. Dad maintained the old red bricks and metal facing of years gone by while updating the common areas, lighting, and signage to a sleek modern style.

Years ago this area was run down. The town is not a mecca for big industry and corporate offices, although things are steadily changing. Seaside is an outdoorsman's delight with outdoor sports and national forests in every direction. This part of the state is a dream vacation spot—quiet, beautiful, clean—and only an hour north of Seattle and two hours south of Vancouver. The majority of residents prefer living this way. After seven years in Tulsa and building for the future, I'm not sure I can handle small-town USA again.

"CARRIE-ANN, try Kip again. If that boy doesn't answer his phone, I swear, I'll fire him before he has the chance to start."

The words bellowed at Denton Harris's long-suffering secretary bring a sense of familiarity as the office doors click closed at my back.

"He's on the interstate, Denton. He's being safe." Carrie-Ann glances up from the chrome and glass reception desk, and I brush my index finger over my closed lips. She pops up from the seat typically occupied by the firm's receptionist Joan and rounds the desk.

"He's something else today, Kip," Carrie-Ann says in a hush as she greets me with a swift embrace. "You're here early." She swats my arm.

I was a kid when Carrie-Ann came to work as Dad's secretary. A single mom, barely an adult herself at twenty-two, she somehow found a way to endear herself to a man who barely tolerates his own flesh and blood. She's worked tirelessly for Harris Development for fifteen years. She watched my older sister and me when our parents went out of town. She put up with Denton's brusque temperament. She is also the one who called three months ago after I had another fight with Dad and begged me to reconsider joining the firm.

"How's Mia?" I ask after her teen daughter.

"She's about to graduate high school." She blows out a breath.

I'm floored. "How did that happen so fast?" It's not like I didn't know. I keep in touch, but the news has me feeling old, and I'm not quite twenty-five.

"She's excited to see you in person. Four years is too long."

My happiness dims, another person I haven't made enough time for. Carrie-Ann thumps my chest. "But, hey, you're here now, and—"

"Did my wayward son answer his…" Dad's mouth snaps shut as he steps into the reception room.

Slipping my hands into my pants pockets, I settle a look of satisfaction on my father. "Your wayward son is here."

His lips twist. "Something wrong with your phone?"

I hold my tongue. Dad doesn't fluster. He isn't an emotional man, or not with me, so his begrudging welcome is expected.

"Nope, I figured I'd arrive on your doorstep as a surprise. Glad to see you still hate surprises."

Carrie-Ann chokes at my flippancy, and Dad shoots her a

scowl. I study him as we stand across the room from one another. His hair is still cropped short and combed back neatly. Though the strands aren't as dark brown these days. The facial hair he's had my entire life is groomed evenly over his jaw and cheeks and contains more salt than I remember. Like me, Dad maintains his waistline. He's an avid runner and healthy eater. He lost his father, Winthrop Harris II, to hereditary heart disease at a young age, so he understands the importance of maintaining good health.

Since he'll never initiate the first move, I cave and go in for a hug. I love him, even if he is the most difficult man alive.

"I thought you weren't arriving until tonight?" he asks as we part.

So, why were you calling me? "I made good time yesterday and stayed in the city last night with my college buddy, Hayden."

"Your mother and sister won't be happy they couldn't welcome you properly."

"If I know Mom, she's in a frenzy, cooking all my favorite dishes for dinner tonight and would have my head if I showed up early and without warning. As for Brynn, I imagine," I pause when a flash of red streaks by the window and slams to a stop at the curb outside the building's entrance. "She'll be here in twenty seconds."

Harris Development's glass double doors fly open. "You jerk!"

Brynn hurries across the tile floor into my open arms. At five foot five, she's roughly a foot shorter than my six-three, but her sky-high heels bridge the difference.

"Boy, the Harris family could use a lesson in welcoming home long-lost loved ones," I say against Brynn's hair as our hug lengthens. "I hope Mom isn't as rusty at this as you two."

Brynn pushes at my chest. "You better hope she doesn't hear about your early return the way I did. Three texts, little brother. Three. And not one of them came from you."

As I suspected. Good to know the gossip mill is as strong as ever in my hometown.

Dad regards us with a curled lip, the only hint he finds his children amusing, as I sling my arm around Brynn's shoulders. "I had an important meeting with southern food and the city council. What can I say?"

Our father's ears perk up. "The council?"

"And a flower farmer," Brynn adds with a smirk. "Or so I heard."

Chloe Lockwood's face pops into my mind at Brynn's offhand comment, but Dad is honed in on the business aspect of my morning.

"Who did you meet with from the council?" His severe face chases Chloe's freckles and soft mouth away. Always business with him.

"Scaritt," I say. "Let's go into your office, and I'll tell you all about our conversation."

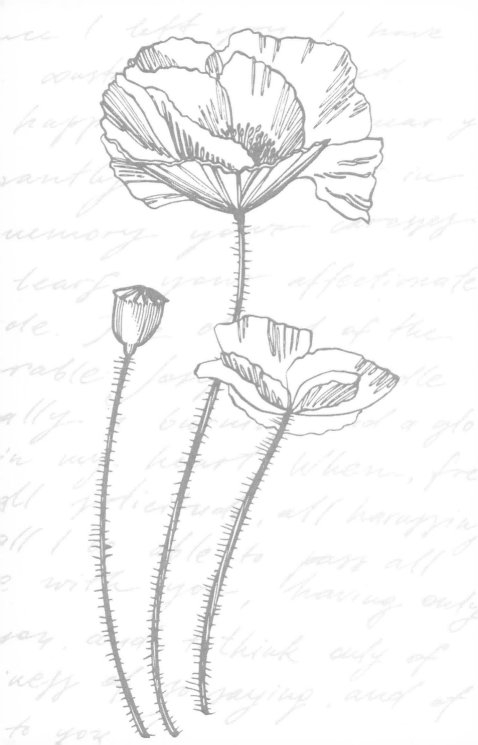

hloe

WALKING into the house on Tuesday morning to grab a water bottle after working in the ranunculus hoop house with Reid, I stumble onto Dad sitting on the bottom of the staircase, struggling to lace up his trusty boots.

"Where do you think you're going?"

He looks up, his newly graying sideburns catching the sunlight through the open curtains. "I need to go into town and speak with Denton."

"Dad, you need to be resting, not getting into an argument with Denton Harris." I bend to help him with the laces, but he swats my hand away with a grumble. "I heard what your doctor said. Just because Mom isn't home this morning doesn't mean I'm going to let you do whatever you want."

"He said I needed to exercise." Dad tries getting to his feet, boots loosely tied.

"Yes, your *rehab* exercises." I guide him to his worn recliner in the living room. "Like walking up and down the stairs or those hand exercises to regain the full function of your hands. Maybe some crossword puzzles for your mind. Not traipsing around town and arguing with Denton Harris. Your body isn't ready."

"I feel fine." With his hands raised, he refuses to sit. Stubborn man. "The best I have in weeks, fit as a fiddle. I just need—"

"What you need is to take it easy. I don't care what you say or how you feel. This family is not taking any chances of you suffering another stroke."

"But, Loe, with the increase in business since last year, if we don't purchase land soon, we won't be able to get your seed line up and running. And by the following year, we'll be behind and drowning. We'll lose all the new business we've gained."

Tilting my head, I ask, "What's this about? You've been trying to get Harris's land for years without success. What's so important you have to talk to Mr. Harris right this instant?"

"I saw the Gardiner-Middleton order was canceled."

Dang it. I hoped he'd miss that. He shouldn't have been nosing around the orders in the first place. Record keeping is Mom's job, and she would have his hide if she knew he was worrying himself with the business.

I sigh. "I tried telling them we could create a beautiful wedding with the crop we have, but they wanted more flowers than we could provide in the timeframe. We have the Booth-Davenport wedding the same week and the Carpenter family reunion, not to mention the funeral for Sandra Hilliard. Combined with all our regular scheduled deliveries, I couldn't spare any more flowers."

"I'm not blaming you, Loe, but how much more business will we have to turn down in the future if we don't get more land? Before people stop coming to us because we can't deliver?"

As to not add to Dad's stress level, I keep the Dudley account who backed out last week to myself. Hopefully, he won't find out about them, too.

He's right. We've done our fair share of searching Seaside Pointe for the right soil with enough acreage, but anything decent falls through, and nothing is as good as the neighboring acres—Harris's land. If only the property belonged to anyone else. It's the kind of soil the flowers need to flourish and continue the Lockwood legacy. We can't expand without more acreage, but I'm not going to get worked up. I can't. I have to believe the issue will work itself out.

"Dad, you put me in charge for a reason." I smile reassuringly. "I'll take care of it. Okay? You've taught me enough over the years; I think I can handle a Harris."

"But what about the harvesting today?"

"Reid and Denise are already on it. They'll get the team going. I'll be back in no time to lend a hand."

Dad eyes me wearily, and I give his shoulder a squeeze. "You can trust me, Dad."

"I know. I do. Okay." Slowly, he sits in his recliner. "But if Denton Harris is anything less than professional and courteous to you, I want to know."

"I promise full disclosure." I laugh.

As I walk to Betty, Reid emerges from the flower fields, a tool belt attached around his hips.

"Where are you headed?"

"I need to talk to Mr. Harris about his land before my dad marches into town and winds up in the hospital with a heart attack."

Reid raises his eyebrows and scratches his dark blond scruff. "Need some moral support? The crew's up and running. I've got my break coming up. I was going to grab lunch soon anyway."

While I want to do things on my own, I can't deny the relief at the thought of not going alone, even if Reid doesn't go inside with me. Though I can handle him, Denton Harris is an intimidating man.

"Yeah, maybe you can help me figure out how to approach it on the ride over."

"Mind if I drive?" he asks, and I toss him the keys.

Rounding the passenger side, I hop in.

Reid turns over the ignition, and the ancient truck rumbles to life. "The old man putting up a fight?"

"I practically had to tie him to his recliner to keep him from marching down to Harris Development."

Reid chuckles. "Is it any wonder Lockwood Blooms is what it is today? The man's got heart."

Letting out a deep breath, I nod. "And all I have to do is not drive his business into the ground. I want to make him proud. If I can just convince Denton to sign the land over to us."

"You've got this, Loe. How can someone say no to a pretty face like yours?" Reid gives me a flirty smirk, placing a hand on my leg.

While Reid is two years older, I've known him my whole life. We haven't hung out in the same crowds, but we went to school together from kindergarten until he graduated two years before me. After his senior year, he started working for Lockwood Blooms and we've been around each other almost every day since.

"I don't think flashing Mr. Harris a smile will get me my way." I laugh. "He's a little too savvy for phony flattery. I'm only hoping for a foot in the door. If I can get him to consider the idea of selling, we'll be one step in the right direction."

"If I know anything about you, Chloe Lockwood, it's that you can make anything happen you set your mind to." He squeezes my thigh before he retakes hold of the steering wheel.

"Thanks." I offer Reid an appreciative smile and turn my attention to the passing lush green landscape. "I need to hear some encouragement every now and then. Can you keep a secret?"

"Always."

"When I was a teenager, I used to let our dog, Daisy, onto

Harris's property to poop so I wouldn't have to clean up after her." I chew the corner of my bottom lip, my eyes dancing with mischief. "Mr. Harris knew, but he could never pin it on me because he never actually saw me let Daisy out or see her do the deed. He'd come to our house and point fingers, but my dad would defend Daisy and me until he was blue in the face." Reid laughs. "My dad still doesn't know I let her over there on purpose. But I'm a Lockwood, what can I say? The Harris-Lockwood feud carries on."

"Well, hopefully he's forgotten about your transgressions."

I tuck away my satisfaction. "It's doubtful, so I'll need all the good vibes I can get."

"I'm your guy if you need someone in your corner." He winks the way he always does. It's kind of his thing. Winking can be skeezy if done by the wrong guy, but when Reid does it, somehow it's winsome and heart-palpitating. "James knew what he was doing when he handed you the reins. A man like Denton Harris is nothing to stress about. You're up at the crack of dawn, head up a team of twenty people every day, and are the last one to leave the field after sunset. You're a tough girl, Loe. You'll figure it out."

"I'm going to try to anyway."

When we pull up to the industrial complex, I take a deep breath.

"Loe." When I keep my eyes on the imposing building, Reid hooks his finger under my chin, drawing me closer. "If anyone can make this sale happen, it's you." He kisses me, lingering, and kisses me again, a flutter of butterfly wings coming alive in my belly.

"I'll wait in your truck." Reid pulls away and runs a hand through his wavy sun-kissed hair before tucking the flyaways back under his ball cap. "Knock 'em dead."

With a nod, I hop from the truck and straighten my shoulders.

I've never set foot in Harris Development. I know the flower fields like the back of my hand, can close my eyes and name every flower and on what square inch they're growing. Dad has always been on the business side of things. I'm learning, but this is uncharted territory.

The inside of Harris Development is exactly as I imagined. All glass and sleek lines and little to no warmth—aside from the woman behind the reception desk. Smiling with a phone in the crook of her neck is Joan. Spunky, sixty-year-old yoga enthusiast Joan. Her russet eyes brighten when I enter.

"Yes, I will have him return your call as soon as he's available. Have a nice day." She hangs up the phone and fluffs her bleach blonde spiky hair. "Good afternoon, Chloe."

"Hi, Joan. Is Mr. Harris in?"

"Sure, let me buzz him." She cradles the phone between her shoulder and ear again. "I bought a bouquet of your tulips at Clover's Garden yesterday. Your blooms have never looked better."

My heart trips. The compliments never get old. "Thank you. We're really pleased with the season. They are thriving this year."

"You know, he's not picking up." Joan replaces the phone on the receiver. "He ran out earlier and must not be back yet. I'm sorry. I don't have you on the books. You didn't have an appointment, did you? He hasn't settled in yet, so we're still working the kinks out."

One of my eyebrows lifts in confusion. Hasn't settled in yet? "I don't have an appointment, but I was only hoping for a small amount of his time."

Through the glass wall behind Joan, Denton walks by. Glancing to his left, he pauses when he notices me. He backtracks to the opening in the glass.

"Miss Lockwood," Denton says, his tone curious. "What brings you here?"

"Hi, Mr. Harris." I lift a timid wave. "I know I don't have an appointment scheduled with you, but I was hoping I could meet with you for a minute."

Joan presses her hand to her chest. "Oh, I'm sorry, dear. I assumed you were looking for Kip."

"No, I—" Why would I be looking for Kip? And here of all places?

Denton waves a hand. "I have a minute. Come on back."

I follow Denton to the right, down a narrow hallway to a conference room. One wall is solid floor-to-ceiling glass with a view into the hallway. He offers me a seat at the end of a large oblong table and sits in the adjacent chair.

Crossing his ankle over his knee, he taps his thumb against his leg. "What can I do for you, Miss Lockwood?"

"As I'm sure you're aware, my father had a stroke last month." He nods, his lips pursing but not sympathizing. "And he's put me in charge for the meantime. Our little flower business has been doing rather well recently. So well, in fact, we have difficulty keeping up. I wanted to talk to you about your vacant acreage next to our farm."

BARELY CONTAINING MY ANGRY TEARS, I fly out of Harris Development like a woman on the hunt for blood. If I had fangs, they'd show, curling over my bottom lip. With my fists clenched and my teeth grinding, I don't make it far when I collide with Kip Harris dressed in a tailored navy suit, making his way down the sidewalk.

"Whoa. Someone's in a hurry." He grabs hold of my shoulders, steadying us both. "Two days in a row, Miss Lockwood, how'd I get so lucky?"

I shrink back, and his gaze peers past me to where Joan stands behind her desk. His hands rise in surrender. "Is everything okay?"

"All of you Harrises are the same. Stubborn, heartless little men who wouldn't know compassion if it bit you in the behind." Unable to control my expressive arms, they swing in all directions with every point I drive home, my voice rising. "That land does *nothing* but sit untouched. Has remained untouched for *years*, and yet *still*, he refuses to consider an agreement. You would think after all of these years, your father could grow up and get over this ridiculous feud!"

Without giving him an opening to respond, I storm past and around the corner of the building to Reid leaning against the passenger's side of the truck, leaving a stunned Kip Harris in my wake.

KIP

"Heartless little men?" I walk into the office with Chloe's insult on my lips.

Joan busies herself, ducking her face from my view. She saw me glance her way from outside. There is no reason to pretend she didn't witness the smackdown Chloe laid on me.

"Hey, Joan, did Miss Lockwood have a meeting with Denton?"

Her grimace propels me toward Dad's office without a second thought.

Carrie-Ann perches on the edge of the chair across from Dad's desk, a stack of files and a steno pad full of scribbled notes in her lap when I knock on the doorframe. "Got a minute?"

Rolling away from his desk, Dad reclines in his chair. "Where did you run off to? I thought we were going over some files."

"I took a drive out to the riverfront property. It's been years since I've seen the land in person."

Dad's chair creaks as he shoots forward. "Why didn't you tell me? I would have driven out with you."

"I promise you I can handle checking our assets on my own." I send Carrie-Ann a signal. "Though, I find myself wishing I'd asked, considering the trouble you caused while I was out."

Having correctly interpreted my glance as a 'give us a moment' request, Carrie-Ann exits the office, shutting the door behind her. I settle in her vacated seat.

"What in the devil are you talking about?" Dad straightens the folders scattering his desktop.

"Would you care to tell me why Chloe Lockwood ripped into me outside the office two minutes ago?"

Dad waves a hand through the air like he can brush my words away. "Oh, nothing to worry yourself with. That girl is over-emotional. Understandable, I suppose, after James's stroke."

Gripping the chair's arms, I slide to the edge of my seat. "Wait, what?"

"James had a stroke back at the end of February." Dad imparts this information like he's reading the weather forecast.

"How is he now?"

"Who, James?" He closes one manilla file and picks up another.

My knuckles blanch as my grip tightens on the armrests. "No, Mayor Pete, Dad. Yes, James Lockwood, the man we are discussing. Chloe's father."

Dad stills. His blue eyes narrow the same way they did from across the dining table when I was a teen and he was tearing into me for one thing or another. Only this time, I stare back. Denton Harris doesn't intimidate me as he once did. He needs me a hell of a lot more than I need him these days.

Willing my anger to a simmer, I sit back. "How is Chloe's father?" I ask with patience.

"From what I hear, he's recovering, and she's taken over the business."

"Dad?" I want more. Chloe's extremely close to her father, or she was. I wish I could have been here or had known. The thought is ridiculous because what could I have done? Except for a handful of moments in our twenty-plus years on this earth, we've never been cordial with one another.

Dad plucks a pen from the cup on his desk. "What do you want to know, Kip? You're aware of our history with the Lockwoods. I don't wish him ill, but we don't keep up with each other's lives."

His pen flies over the forms on his desk as my brain comes to terms with Dad's words.

"Lockwood Blooms wants to buy some of our acreage abutting theirs?" I deduced as much from Chloe's rambling tirade.

He ignores me.

My fingers go to my temple, massaging in circles. One day in the office and already with this stress. "Please don't tell me this is about the feud."

"No, Kip, this is about my land. Land that's not for sale." He flips through a stack of papers, then sets his pen down. "You know how valuable real estate is."

"Yes, and we're talking about a parcel of land you'll never develop for business purposes. Why not sell to Lockwood?"

Resting his elbows on the arms of his chair, Dad's fingers steeple, his boredom with our conversation showing in his deep frown. "Your mother doesn't want the noise so close to her house."

Noise? "My mother loves Lockwood's flower fields and has commented on numerous occasions throughout my life how much she'd love to be surrounded by them. Or has her love of flowers dimmed since I moved away?"

"Kip." There's a warning in his tone. I press anyway.

"Dad, the lot's what? Less than thirty acres? Broker a deal with them."

Shadows darken his blue eyes. "Since when do you care about Lockwood Blooms?"

"I don't." I care about the tears filling Chloe Lockwood's golden brown eyes, though. A revelation that only serves to frustrate me because I don't want to care. My need to not care has me poised to walk away from this project and Seaside Pointe so I can keep my sanity. How does one woman—who I'm supposed to hate—do this to me?

"This is ridiculous." Talking about more than this argument with Dad. With a deep sigh, I prop my ankle on my knee. "This isn't about the Lockwoods. They want the land badly enough, and you could set an above market rate. We don't need the property and they do. It's business. Supply and demand."

"I'm not interested in selling our property and doing that family any favors." He gives me a once-over before retrieving his pen and another contract. "Now, what do you think of the riverfront property? Think we have what your clients are looking for?"

Case closed. The land issue isn't between Dad and me. It's between Denton Harris and the Lockwoods, and Denton Harris won't cave. Why should I bother? Chloe insulted me at my place of business not less than fifteen minutes ago and insulted me when we were teens. I have bigger deals to close.

Removing my cell from my pants pocket, I bring up the pictures I took earlier. "The riverfront is perfect. The place has more potential than I remembered."

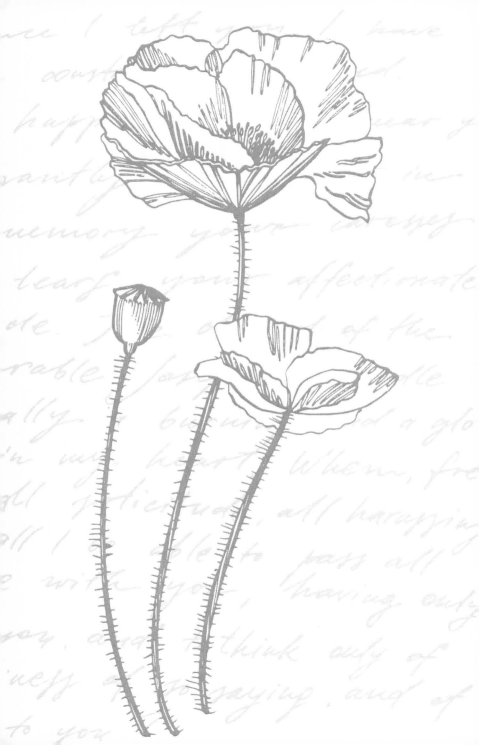

4

 hloe

"I don't know what I'm going to do, Grace." She shakes her head in solidarity as I vent. "My dad trusts me to keep everything afloat, but procuring more land is impossible. Mr. Harris will never give up the most viable property in Seaside."

Grace and I move along the ranunculus patch, harvesting the full blossoms. "Well, not to make matters worse, but Kip Harris—"

"Is in town. I know." I groan, wiping sweat from my brow with the back of my gloved hand. "Don't remind me. I laid into him earlier today after speaking with Mr. Harris."

"No," Grace says with hesitancy, "what I was going to say was Kip Harris moved back."

My shears halt mid-snip. "He's not here visiting?"

"Not based on what Gina said. Mary was going on about him at Fig yesterday. So happy her boy is home for good."

After the encounter with Kip outside of Flower Patch, my

heart experienced a slew of sensations over the last twenty-four hours. Stopping, racing, exploding, but not sinking—until Grace's words submerge my heart in dread.

"What is he doing back? I thought he was off living the life in Tulsa."

"I don't know." She shrugs. "Maybe his dad made him an offer he couldn't refuse. You know he likes making bets." Her brow arches and I groan at another reminder of my history with Kip.

"What does it matter? Are you going to be okay?" She eyes me across the vivid plants.

The thought of regularly bumping into Kip around town is enough to give me an anxiety attack. The last time we saw each other before he moved away, we didn't exactly part on normal terms. Normal Harris-Lockwood terms, that is. Kip's return can't have come at a worse possible time. It's the last thing I need when I can't afford any more speed bumps or distractions.

"I have to be," I say. "I can't think about Kip right now. What I need to do is stay focused on the business and search for another piece of property so I don't give my dad another stroke."

"You shouldn't put so much pressure on yourself." Grace bends down, placing a bunch of coral ranunculi in the bucket at her feet. "I think you've done pretty fantastic keeping everyone in line since you took over. I even overheard Reid talking to your crew about how much he loves working with you." She stands and continues cutting the stems. "He was complimenting your management skills and reassuring them he's never met anyone who knows flowers better than you do. And I don't think he said it because he's dating the boss. It was very genuine."

"He did?" My pulse quickens, grateful for Reid's support. Coming from him, it means a lot. Apart from me, he's practically my dad's right-hand man.

"And I agree," Grace says. "I know I don't officially work here, but while helping harvest through the years, I've witnessed enough. Your dad is a great boss, but you at the helm on the fields is a no-brainer. You've already found more efficient and cost-effective ways to keep the blooms lasting longer. And it's been what, a month?" Grace stops cutting as she reaches the end of the hedge of colorful blooms. "You'll find the right property when the timing is right."

Since I started working full-time in the family business after high school, my mind has overflowed with ideas for the future. The potential for growth of Lockwood Blooms is limitless if we have the resources we need. We've remained a solid source for local florists and larger events since the beginning, but I want to do more, give more desirable colors and varieties, and expand.

For now, my pet project is Lockwood seeds. The best of the best of our blooms available for growing at home. With a little bit of guidance, I want anyone to be able to have a yard full of our flowers.

Over the last couple of years, I've done everything I can to learn more about flower seed production and breeding. It's been challenging but so rewarding and has taught me so much about our blooms I wouldn't have known otherwise.

On a shelf in the flower studio—which is basically an unused garage I turned into a place for research and to take pictures of our blooms for social media—I have vases and bags of dried flowers and pods to collect seeds. So far, we have about fifty varieties, but I want to do more. If we had the land, we could do two-hundred and fifty.

I enter one of our propagation greenhouses where our seeds sprout in a temperature-controlled environment. Gotta keep the air above fifty degrees so our babies can flourish. We've been using our own seeds to replant our fields for years, but in here, I'm testing a new variety I think will be a perfect addition to the Lockwood Blooms name and grow beautifully in anyone's yard.

As I check the cell trays, sinewy arms wrap around my waist and a scruffy chin rests on my shoulder. A fresh earthy musk surrounds me. *Reid.*

"How's it going in here?" His easy, rich voice murmurs in my ear, tickling the sensitive area.

"Good, I think." I lean my back into his chest. "These peach and blush China Asters are germinating just as well as the others."

"Good, good. I stopped by the studio first searching for you. Thought I might find you with your project. How's it coming along?"

It's hard to stifle my excitement. "By January, I think we'll be ready for our full line. There are some other varieties I want to test out, but those can wait for next year. I just need to gather the rest of the seeds from the harvested blooms in the studio, and from there, we should be good to go with packaging." I refrain from clapping and jumping up and down.

Reid's stubble grazes my skin as he turns his head and plants a languid kiss on my neck. His voice is husky when he says, "You're amazing. I can't wait to see what you do with this company."

I shiver as his lips move to my jaw, and I sigh. "There will only be so much I can do if we can't get more land."

"You want me to rough up a Harris?" Reid pulls away, moving to my side, and rests his hip against the wooden table, facing me with his arms crossed. "I'll do it happily. Give me the word." The corner of his mouth curls up.

"If it were as easy as a punch to the gut, I'd have asked you a long time ago," I joke.

His mouth thins out. "I'm sorry Denton is so pigheaded. He should've at least mulled the idea over."

"It's nothing new." My shoulders rise in a shrug. "I shouldn't have gotten my hopes up. It doesn't make sense for him to cut a deal with us. It was wishful thinking on my part more than anything. The worst part was telling my dad I failed."

"You didn't fail. I think Denton's mind was made up long before you entered his office." His hand outstretched, he runs his knuckles along my bare bicep, and goosebumps pepper my skin. "Do you think there will ever be a day where the Harrises and Lockwoods aren't at each other's throats?"

"The day I stop loving flowers." I smirk, canting my head.

"I didn't know Kip Harris was back in town."

His name douses me in cold water and shoots flames through my veins.

"When I saw you reaming into him, I thought you were going to deck him. I'd have paid good money to see Harris flat on his back." Reid chuckles and grips my hips, pulling me flat against him, and I loop my arms around his neck.

"I almost did deck him." But it wouldn't have done any good. He's not the Harris who refuses to show a little mercy. This time anyway. And it feels strange talking to Reid about Kip, so I ask, "Is everyone finished up for the day?"

He nods, tightening his hold around my waist and bringing our lips closer. "You and I are the last ones."

As always. It's how we began. The last two on the farm every day. Aside from me, Reid is the most dedicated Lockwood employee. First to arrive, last to leave. A few months ago I finally caught onto how most of the time he was done with his work and was making up things to do around the farm to stay longer with me.

I've always found Reid cute and had a little schoolgirl crush on him since grade school. Who wouldn't? With his honey-blond waves and green eyes, the kind of smile to turn any girl's head, but I never knew he thought of me as more than a co-worker.

I'm the boss's daughter. I'd barely gotten my braces off when he first started working for Lockwood Blooms. I assumed I'd always be little Loe in his eyes. Then one stolen kiss in the daffodil fields after I broke down following my dad's stroke turned into another and another until we were an item. We fell into place, an easy transition.

Reid bends his head, meeting my lips with his. His tongue traces the seam of my lips, asking permission, and I grant him access. With assertive lips and a languid tongue, he explores my mouth.

Reid's kisses have never been anything to complain about. At twenty-seven, the man has had his fair share of experience, and it shows. I've kissed five guys. And as much as I revel in kissing Reid, there's only one man who's ever left me breathless and craving more.

I break away, preventing us from getting too carried away.

Giving me one last soft kiss, he asks against my mouth, "You almost done here?"

"I can be done, I think."

"Good. I'm starving." He cinches his arms around my waist, lifting me off the ground with a sly grin. "Let's go grab some dinner. I'll head home and shower, then we can meet at Los Rancheros."

"As tempting as a night out sounds, I'm drained." My lips meet his again. "I want to shower, put on comfy clothes, and stay in."

"Okay. You want me to join you? We could order a pizza."

"Would you hate me if I wanted some me time?" It's not that I don't want to spend time with Reid, I've just been nonstop for weeks, and it's taking its toll.

"I could never hate you." He kisses the tip of my nose then my lips. "You've been running yourself into the ground. Go relax for the night and I'll see you tomorrow. We can plan a date for this weekend." Setting me on my feet, Reid heads for the door. "Later, Loe."

"See you."

Before Reid walks out, he turns and says, "You really should go relax soon. Take a bubble bath or something. Don't get roped into something else."

Easier said than done, but I'm exhausted. I'm going to enjoy my evening walk through the fields because they're prettiest at sunset, then I'll head inside.

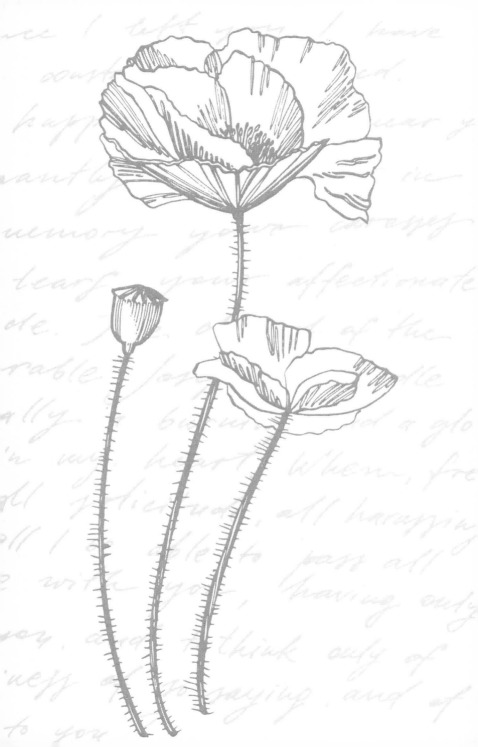

 ip

BRYNN APPEARS in my office doorway a few minutes after five. "You work too hard. C'mon, you know Mom will have made something spectacular for dinner. I think she plans on cooking all your favorites this month."

"I work too hard? What are those?" I point to the stack of folders and magazines peeking out of the bag slung over her shoulder.

Shifting, she slips the bag behind her hip. "Side business. I'm heading out. Don't stay too late."

"I'm home a few days and you're already nagging," I call after her retreating form.

TWO HOURS LATER, I close my laptop. The illusive sun made an appearance this afternoon. Damn shame I had to spend the second half of my day pouring over files and getting up to speed on our properties with Dad.

My phone buzzes and I ignore the call from home. Becoming used to parents and a sister checking in on an hourly basis will take time. The cell buzzes again.

"Fine, I'm on my way. Man, I'll need my own place and quick if I stay in Washington," I speak to my empty office as I grab the phone and respond with a text.

Response sent, I grab my things and turn off the lights.

Stepping into the brisk air, I draw a deep breath and stop. A bush covered in pink buds stands out among the greenery near the front entrance. The emerging flowers bring Chloe to mind.

"Ah, what the heck." I slip my cell from my pocket and search online for the number to Lockwood Blooms. "She probably won't even answer since it's after seven," I reason, locating the listing and hitting call.

I stroll toward my car as the call rings, then clicks over, and rings some more.

"Lockwood Blooms, this is Chloe." Her winded voice knocks me off guard.

"Chloe? Hey, it's Kip. Harris." I dig the heel of my palm into my forehead. Like she knows a bunch of Kips. I clear my throat. "Did I catch you at a bad time?"

The phone is silent. Did she hang up? Her name is on the tip of my tongue when she expels a breath.

"Yes, I mean...no. I'm just finishing up on the farm. What do you need, Kip?"

The clip of her words confirms she isn't pleased to hear my voice.

Too bad, Sunshine. "Yeah, sorry to bother you. I spoke to my father after you left the other day, and he mentioned your dad's stroke."

I pause, and she doesn't respond. Leaning against my car, I continue. "I was thinking or wondering how he is? I mean, how are you?" I drop the phone from my ear and exhale. Why is this so difficult?

Chloe remains silent on the line.

"Look, I know things with our families have been a mess since before we were born, but I know how important James is to you. I wanted you to know I'm sorry. I hope he's recovering."

"Well," she says curtly, "thank you. He's as good as he can be, all things considered." She releases a heavy sigh. "Though he'd be better if your father would let go of his pride."

Her brusque tone coaxes a choked laugh from my throat. "I'm sorry, what?"

"Twenty years that land has been underappreciated—"

I'm offering support and she's fighting me. I wish I could say I hate it. "I thought maybe we could be above all their pettiness."

"This business is not petty, it's my life, Kip. My livelihood. What's petty is your father holding a grudge, perpetuating this feud."

"Yes, because this feud is all his fault, right? Over eighty years of arguments and my father is the sole instigator?"

"He has the opportunity to end it once and for all here. The land never should've been his. It's our northern border. Your dad should've kept to the west, on your own side. Not encroach on our land like some hostile takeover."

"Never should have been his? The land adjoins our property, too, Chloe. He had every right to buy it." I mentally count to three. The line is suspiciously quiet.

"Is this about us? Is this about what happened at the tree the day before I left?" I ask before thinking better of it.

Chloe fumbles over a cluster of unfinished words and curses. "You've got to be kidding me." The line dies.

A growl rises in my throat as the words fill the screen. *Call ended.* Kicking my tire, I scrub my palm over my face. "Way to go, Kip."

The comment was stupid. I wasn't on my A-game tonight.

Granted, Chloe brings that out in me: that being my stupidity. "Stubborn woman."

IF THERE'S one thing I've never found fault with Dad over, it's how he loves Mom. The last of the evening sun paints the sky as my childhood home comes into view a full minute before the turn for our driveway. This was her dream. Renovating the over one-hundred-year-old Harris family home into something Denton Harris would find acceptable. He wanted to bulldoze the old house to build something grander, but she had a vision. The remodel was likely twice as expensive because of all the upgrades needed, but Mom convinced him the past should be preserved. She firmly believes our past shapes our future: the good, bad, and ugly.

I turn into the drive and come to a stop in the circular drive. I love this house. My business acumen comes from the Harris side of the family tree, but my eye for design? That is courtesy of Mary Klein Harris—the woman sitting on her front porch with a glass of white wine in her hand and a blanket on her lap as she awaits her youngest born.

Forcing the call with Chloe from my mind, I exit the vehicle and stop at the base of the wide stone staircase leading to the front door. Even at fifty-three, one could easily mistake my mother as an older sister. She keeps her hair freshly colored in shades of red, gold, and brown and cut to skim her trim shoulders. A style, she says, complete with eye skimming bangs, adds to her youthful appearance and brings out her hazel eyes. Brynn's resemblance to Mom is uncanny, and she often teases how she thanks her lucky stars she inherited those genes. They're beautiful women.

"I think I sort of missed this." I set my laptop bag on a step and sink to sit on the cool stone.

"Coming home to your mother awaiting your arrival?" Mom downs a generous sip of her wine.

Stretching my legs out across the step, I relax against the stone wall at my back. "Yeah. You used to sit out here when I had baseball practice."

Her head bobs. "I miss those days, too." Her gaze sweeps over me, a forlorn bend to her lips. "How did you kids grow up so fast?"

"Fast?" I tip my face and study the cloud-covered sky. "I seem to recall you and Dad suggesting more than once how you couldn't wait for us to be gone. Something about eighteen years being longer than you thought."

"And here you both are, back in my home." She releases an exaggerated sigh. "We had two whole years of freedom, Denton." She lifts her glass toward the house like she's sending Dad a toast.

With a chuckle, I give her the stink eye. "And you love it."

"And I love it." She agrees, holding my gaze.

"Brynn hasn't said much. How is she doing?"

She slides forward in her chair and pulls the blanket from her lap. "You must be hungry, sweetheart. I left you a plate in the warmer."

"Mom?"

"She doesn't talk about him, sweetheart. She works hard, smiles often, and bottles up the past. A true Harris." She drains the last of her wine as we meet at the front door. "She's happy to have you back, though. I know that much. We all are."

Taking the empty glass from her hand, I draw her into a hug. "I love you, Mom."

6

ip

STEPPING out of the baggage claim, my grip slips on my bag when Brynn's brazen copper hair catches my eye. She's standing near the exit, an oversized "Master Harris" sign clutched in her hands.

"Cute."

Brynn bows. "I live but to serve you."

I wrench the obnoxious sign from her fingers. "You know I could have driven myself to and from the airport. Nobody forced you to be my chauffeur."

"No way." She ducks and grabs for my carry-on. "I missed out on years of torturing you. I'm taking advantage now."

My fingers lock around her wrist, and I drop the bag and draw her into a bear hug. "Who's torturing who?"

Brynn returns my hug with a hum before shoving against my stomach. Swiping my bag from the ground, I throw my arm around her shoulders and steer her outside.

"Dad's torturing me."

"What's he done now?" I let her go as we cross the street to the short-term parking lot.

"I can't tell you how many times he asked if I thought you would change your mind and stay in Tulsa." Brynn points toward her car.

"Really? All I got from him was complaining." Dumping my bag in the backseat, I slide into the passenger side. "I told him I'd be a week. Plus, I worked on some things for him while I was there."

Brynn drops her sunglasses over her eyes and merges into traffic, but her head swings my way, encouraging me to continue.

"He called me over every little detail on the lease contract for Pure Foods. Like I'm some untested kid. I have a Master's in Business."

"Can you blame him, though?" Brynn asks, and I scoff.

"Hear me out." Her fingers touch my forearm before I can argue. "You left, Kip. You left with barely a warning. Then, you stayed away. For seven years."

"You know why—"

"I do, and I don't blame you, but I understand his fear. He's a stubborn, hard-headed man, but he loves you."

"Which is why he visited me twice in seven years?"

"Um, okay, hypocrite. You came home once."

"First, you didn't live here for most of those years, and second, you and Mom kept visiting me. I didn't need to come back here."

"Kip." Her tone is a little too similar to our mother's.

Dropping my head, I run my fingers through my hair. "Fine, you're right. I'm to blame, too."

"Imagine that, a Harris man who is prideful and pigheaded."

"Be careful what you say, sis. You may not have all the testosterone running through your veins, but you're a Harris through and through."

She sticks her tongue out.

Since she's poking... "Wanna talk about the wedding?"

"Want to walk home?" Brynn counters, her jaw clenching as I study her profile.

I reach over and tug her hand from the steering wheel, giving her fingers a squeeze. "I should have been here two years ago. I'm sorry."

Twisting her hand from mine, she returns it to the wheel. "You don't have to apologize, Kip. You let me stay at your place for two weeks. You were there for me."

I gave her a place. A bed so she could hide away from our parents and her friends as her life crumbled around her. Then I let her return home to deal with the fallout alone. Returning to Seaside Pointe and witnessing Brynn's life firsthand, I can't help wondering if she dealt with the past or buried it.

"I'll always be there for you. Whenever you need me. Whether I'm here or in Tulsa."

"Here or Tulsa, huh?"

"I haven't decided if I'm staying, Brynn," I say a few minutes later. "I don't know if I can be happy here." *As Denton Harris's son.*

The car remains quiet for a beat longer than necessary before she sighs. "I figured as much."

WE'RE CROSSING into town when Brynn hums. "I didn't eat lunch yet, and I assume you're hungry. Wanna stop at Saltbox before we head to the office? I could go for a crab cake salad right about now."

"Sounds good."

I'm filling Brynn in on my meetings in Tulsa when we pass a second open parking spot on Main Street. "Lord, woman, would you parallel park already?"

"Nope." We circle around and park in the nearest public lot.

"The beauty of small-town living, brother of mine, is I don't have to pretend like I know how to weave my car into a little space like some wizard."

"Parallel parking is wizardry, huh?"

"Shut your mouth."

As we walk down Main Street, I note the tenants occupying each storefront. Harris manages several buildings along the strip. Others are owned by the occupants, and others still by a larger, out-of-state developer who bought pieces of Seaside years ago when they saw the potential for growth in the tourist industry. They were smart. Projected growth is what keeps the riverfront project moving full steam ahead.

"So, you're buying, right?" Brynn's question drags me out of realtor mode when we enter Saltbox.

"Depends on how annoying you are." I elbow her as we're greeted by a waitress I don't recognize. "Two," I confirm when she asks how many.

I check her name tag: Olivia. She's cute, likely right out of college, twenty-two maybe? Blonde, petite, not my usual type, but judging how her eyes scan my body, I have an opening. If I want one.

Familiar laughter rings out and I glance around. Seated at a table for two is Chloe Lockwood with Grace Embry. And Olivia has us heading straight for the empty table next to theirs.

"Uh, can we get a booth?" I keep my voice low yet loud enough for the waitress to hear. Three weeks have passed since my disastrous phone call with Chloe. I haven't seen or spoken to her since. I'm unsure of my feelings toward her and her family, but I can't sit next to her and eat lunch. Not yet.

Brynn checks over her shoulder, her lips pursing before she nods at Olivia, who's stopped in the middle of the cafe.

And of course Grace lifts her head and our eyes connect. Grace's lips move as she holds my gaze. I can't decipher her words to Chloe, but I imagine she's giving her fair warning before acknowledging us. "Well, if it isn't the Harrises."

"Hey, Hey," Brynn sings.

Great, just great. "We'll be a moment; go ahead and leave our menus," I say to Olivia. She dips her head and flutters her lashes in a way I might respond to on any other day.

Assuming an air of nonchalance, I follow Brynn toward Chloe and Grace.

"Fancy meeting you two here." Brynn motions for Grace to remain seated before turning on Chloe. "Chloe, I swear I haven't seen you in ages. Why is that?"

I shove my hands into my pockets and maintain my blasé demeanor. Brynn is nuts. What's up with her? In this town? She certainly must encounter Chloe two or three times a week.

Chloe sits straighter while offering Brynn genuine warmth. "I guess I prefer the flower fields to the city." Her face transforms from relaxed to strained as soon as her eyes fall on me.

"Probably because they don't talk back," I say with faux politeness.

Brynn bumps into my side. "Your fields are perfection. I don't blame you. Kip seems to prefer city life. He just flew back from a week in Tulsa."

"Oh?" Grace asks. Chloe fingers the edge of the knife on the table. Contemplating plunging the blade in my chest, perhaps?

My mask drops, and I shoot daggers at my sister. "It was for business, not pleasure. I still prefer the salty sea air and Pacific coast, but I do enjoy the city."

"If only the city would keep you." Chloe cocks her head and offers an overbright curve of her soft pink lips.

"You never know"—I roll my shoulders and step back— "there's not much keeping my attention here."

I'm already walking away when Brynn excuses us, "We'll let you two eat. It was good to see you."

CHLOE

Grace mutters under her breath, "It wouldn't be a Harris and Lockwood interaction without someone taking a cheap shot."

My chest tightens as Kip walks away, looking like he stepped out of a J.Crew catalog. In his form-fitted button-down and cornflower blue sweater combo pushed up at the cuff, his tanned forearms peek out. Not to outdo his stupidly perfect tailor-made navy pants, which compliment his lean physique. And no, I did not just check out his firm butt.

It all brings out the light blue of Kip's eyes. I hate how much I appreciate the sight. One man shouldn't be allowed to look that good. Not when he's a Harris. Of course, I've been in dirt-stained overalls and my farm boots every time we've run into each other. At least today I wore my hair down and not my usual messy top knot.

"You two can't make nice for two minutes?" Grace scolds with a short laugh.

I sip my lemonade. "He started it."

"What, are we in second grade? Wait, maybe it's senior year all over again? Since that was the last time I was around you two and your jabs."

"You don't understand."

"Uh-huh. How could I possibly understand my best friend struggling with the return of her nemesis slash secret—"

I shush Grace and peer around the full restaurant. There are way too many ears in Saltbox to talk freely about our history. "You promised to take that to your grave."

"He keeps looking over here."

"He does not." I push around the fries on my plate, containing the urge to slip a glance his way.

"I think he regrets what he said."

I sit back in my chair, arms crossed. "A Harris never regrets anything. They have too much pride for remorse."

"Hmm…" Grace taps her chin. "Sounds like someone else I know. It couldn't possibly be a Lockwood."

I roll my eyes. "Don't lump us together. Lockwoods don't retaliate. We defend."

"How is there a difference? A Harris steals a family recipe, so a Lockwood steals a family tradition. A Lockwood runs over a fence, so a Harris runs over a flower patch. It's a vicious cycle. Ever think the madness could end with you two, the next Harris-Lockwood generation?"

Once upon a time, I had, but that dream faded as quickly as it formed. Kip has been in Seaside Pointe for a matter of weeks, and we're already at each other's throats.

"Grace, stop. We're not doing this. Kip is the enemy." I pop a fry in my mouth. "And he's going to stay the enemy."

My best friend sighs, pursing her lips. Disapproval is written across Grace's face, but she accepts my answer. "I just want to see you happy."

"Same goes for you, sis. When was the last time you went out on a date?"

Her full lips purse. "I am not the topic of discussion right now. Stop avoiding. Ever since Kip returned you've been different, on edge. I can't help but think—"

"Well, stop thinking. I'm with Reid. Everything else is moot." I let my eyes wander to Kip. His focus is on Brynn, so I briefly admire his profile from afar. From his styled yet somehow disheveled brown hair to every freckle on his face I'd once memorized in biology class. Before he catches me, I steer my attention back to Grace. "If I'm on edge, it's because my father had a stroke and I'm running a flower farm on my own, not because of some high school transgression who traipsed into town."

Grace stifles her laughter. "Whatever you say."

hloe

AFTER FINISHING up my Wednesday morning deliveries, I receive a call from Janet, a realtor I hired after Denton shot me down, about a piece of property that's been relisted after being on and off the market for a while. Twenty acres. I've left no stone unturned thus far, so any new land is encouraging. Though, the fact it's been for sale on and off is concerning.

Taking the short drive in the opposite direction of town, I find the farmland about ten miles from Lockwood Blooms. A fifteen-minute drive from the farm isn't horrible. Not ideal, but doable. An old wooden fence borders the roadside length of the property. After pulling Betty onto the shoulder of the road, I hop the fence and fight my way through weeds and overgrown foliage. Finding an empty stretch of land, I kick loose a clump of grass and dirt with my boot and kneel down and scoop up a handful of soil. It isn't waterlogged or rocky. It's a little sticky, but viable enough. From where I stand, there are no rotting or uninhabitable buildings on the lot we'd have to clear. It's the closest contender to the Harris property we've ever gotten. Maybe there's hope after all. I walk across the acreage, scouring for any red flags.

Pleased, I wind up at the front of the land with minimal concerns. I won't get my hopes up because there might be something I'm missing, a reason this lot hasn't been snatched up yet. With it going on and off the market, there might be issues on the seller side of things. I'll have to call Janet for more details, find out the likelihood of acquiring it for Lockwood Blooms.

I whip my right leg over the fence and lose my footing. Down, down, down I go, a lovely patch of mud cushioning my fall. With the whole right side of my body covered in brown sludge, I roll to my back and stare up at the sky, praying this isn't a bad omen.

"It's just a case of clumsiness," I murmur. "Nothing more."

A car door slams shut too close to be anywhere but near my truck. Rising onto my elbows, I look toward the street. In a matter of milliseconds, I want to sink into the mud puddle, never to be seen again. Directing my attention to the sky once more, I silently plead for his disappearance. Or mine.

"Having fun?" Kip Harris stands with his arms crossed, dressed in another one of his polished city boy outfits. Dark jeans with a heather gray vest and a faint blue button-down. I'll never catch a break.

Groaning, I hoist myself out of the mud and shake the excess muck from my worn light jeans and billowy flannel. I'd never put much thought into my clothing before. It never mattered. I need clothes that can get grass stains and dirt streaks. It comes with the territory of a flower farmer.

"Need a hand?" he asks.

"How generous of you to ask after the fact." I brush my palms against the side of my jeans, cleaning them the best I can.

"Can I ask what you're doing on Old Man Sullivan's land? You are aware you're trespassing, right? Should I call the Sheriff?"

BLOSSOMS & STEEL | 55

"Well, you are on a first-name basis with him after the stunt you pulled with the Fielding's horses, but knowing my luck, he'd haul me in anyway. Everyone *loves* Kipling Harris." I whip my head back, trying to clear the tendrils from my face without my filthy hands. "Actually, you know what? Please, go ahead. I did the flowers for his daughter's wedding last fall. Remind him he still owes me for the last-minute order of chrysanthemums on the cake."

Kip steps closer, invading my space. Using the tip of his index finger, he brushes the muddy strands out of my eyes. "Don't test me, Sunshine. Seeing you in a pair of handcuffs is mighty tempting." His voice is coated with honey, a slight Tulsa drawl making its presence known.

My breathing hitches. I pray Kip doesn't notice.

"Let me guess. You're hunting down land to expand."

"What was your first clue? Our two prior conversations or the twenty acres behind me?" I frown and place my hands on my hips.

"Or maybe I used my brilliant deduction skills."

"Unlikely. Don't tell me," I say. "Harris Development is swooping in and already made an offer the seller can't refuse. And you're planning to build a monstrosity of a strip mall."

Kip flicks a nonexistent speck of mud from the hand he touched my face with. "Actually, I represent the seller. No swooping necessary, Miss Lockwood."

My mouth opens and closes. Even worse. He has the power to sway the seller in another direction, all to spite me.

"Fantastic," I mutter. "So, what can I expect? A seller as unreasonable as its representation?"

"I'm unreasonable? Is that what you think? I'm not your enemy, Chloe. I can't force my parents to sell you land they don't want to sell, so *I'm* the bad guy?"

I take a few steady breaths. Debatable, but there's no sense rehashing—the Harris land or the feud. I fought, I lost.

"Are you insinuating the Lockwoods have a fighting chance for *this* land?"

"I'll tell you what, I'll talk to Mr. Sullivan. His kids are a bit money hungry, but I bet he'd love selling to someone who values good old-fashioned farming."

I don't want to show my cards, so I nod, hiding my appreciation. "Okay."

"Okay," he echoes.

Our eyes lock, neither backing down. I wait for the jab, for the semi-truce to crumble. The longer our stare holds, the harder it is to hold onto my pride. He's not sparring or hurling hostility. He's diplomatic, which raises my suspicion. Why? Why would he help me out? What does he get out of the deal? Because if I know anything about the Harrises, they never do anything unless it benefits them.

"I should go. I'm due at the office for a meeting." His eyes travel from my scuffed muddy boots to my matted muddy hair. I've never looked better. "I'd give you a hand, but these clothes aren't cheap and, as I'm sure you're well aware, soil is a pain to wash out."

My jaw falls open as my head slowly shakes. Kip walks backward a few steps, an overly smug smile plastered on his face, before he pivots and walks toward his car.

Before he slides behind the wheel of his Audi crossover with the salt life stickers and hood rack, he stops.

"Hey, Chloe." His words drip with poorly concealed humor. "As adorable as you are covered in mud, you really should go home and shower before you see anyone else. You stink."

And there it is. The jab I was waiting for attached to the face I hate admiring. I scoff, my tongue rolling around my mouth. *Prick.*

Hopping into Betty, I slam the door. Kip Harris is still as much trouble as he was when we were teenagers. Though now, with his unexpected civility, even with his backhanded compliment, he might be worse. Because it's enough to make me want to lower my guard, even a fraction, but I won't. Not with a Harris. And definitely not with Kip.

KIP

Try as I might, I can't deny the spark between Chloe and me. I flex my fingers—the fingers that reached out and touched her hair because they had to. Is the energy between us born of hate from years of feuding, or something more? Granted, it could be both.

I release a breath and tap the Bluetooth on my steering wheel. The connecting phone call rings through the speakers.

"This is Carrie-Ann."

"Hey, it's Kip. Would you do me a favor and pull the Sullivan file and send me his son's number? I might have the perfect buyer for the farm."

"Sure thing."

"Nothing on Riverfront yet?" I ask, eager for news.

"Nothing. I could call the planning office and get an update."

"Would you? I'm on my way in for the meeting with Tru-Alliance."

Carrie-Ann hums. "I'll call Gladys and see if she can poke around a bit for us. Oh, and call your mom; she seemed a little off."

"Off?" That's curious, if not ominous. "Will do. See you in a bit."

Ending one call, I tell the car to call home.

"Kipling Harris," Mom answers on the second ring.

"Uh oh, am I about to be grounded?" I chuckle. Ominous was right.

"When were you going to tell me you were moving out?"

I prop my elbow on the ledge of the car window and sigh. "Seaside Pointe gossip mill strikes again. How did you—"

"Norma's nephew is the young man leasing the unit out, but never mind. You've been home less than a month and you're sick of us?"

"Mom."

She continues, "Brynn told me you weren't sure if you were going to stay in town. Does this mean you're staying? Your father has said from the beginning he wouldn't bet on you sticking here for more than a year, but I thought—" She sniffs. "I had hoped—"

"Mom?" I raise my voice. "Slow down, would you? First, Brynn shouldn't have told you."

"So, you don't have plans to leave?" Her hope stabs at my heart.

I can't lie. "I don't know yet."

"If you don't know, why are you renting a condo down in Bay View?"

"Because I'm a grown man. I work with Dad all day. I work with Brynn. I need some space. Didn't we discuss this? How you and Dad couldn't wait to be empty nesters?"

She doesn't respond, and I turn to reassurance. "I promise my moving out has nothing to do with you, Mom. You can come with me if you want. I'm sure you'd like to get away from those two as much as I do."

"It's loud on the bay. All those tourists and dockside restaurants. Isn't his unit over a business in that new shopping center?"

"I don't mind loud. Tulsa was loud."

If I were standing in front of her, she'd be shaking her head. "You always did love the noisiest cartoons and toys." Her tone is resigned.

I remain quiet, allowing her time to wrap her head around the idea of my moving out again, even if I'm only twenty minutes away.

"Okay." She inhales deeply. "I'm sorry I acted like a crazy woman, sweetheart. I love you, Kipling. You know I was teasing about you and Brynn being home. I love having you under our roof again."

"I know, and you have me for another two weeks. I love you, too, but..." I hesitate, mulling over giving her a dose of reality. Brynn's accusation on the way home from the airport the other day replays in my mind. I can't do that to my family again.

"I need you to keep your head. If the riverfront deal doesn't happen, there's every chance I'll go back to Tulsa. Weller Faison has a place for me there. They want me back, but they've been cool about letting me see how this goes. I don't want you to forget this isn't a done deal. Not yet."

"I know, honey, but a mother can hope."

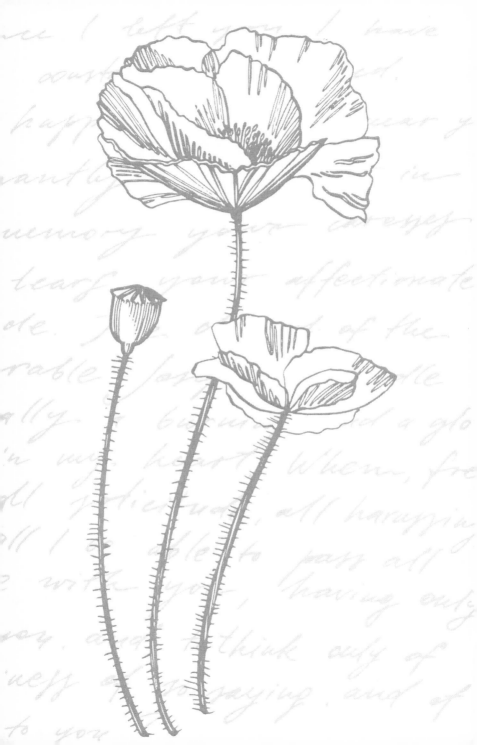

hloe

"How's James doing? I haven't seen him around the farm in a few days."

"He's making progress." I slip out of the driver's side of my truck as Reid moves to the back on the passenger's side, watching me over the rusted bed. "We're hoping by next month he'll be able to return to the fields. Nothing crazy, but to sort tubers and bulbs. Something to get him back into the swing of things and feel useful. Some exercise for his hands. Baby steps."

"If there's anything more I can do, you'd let me know, right?" Reid grips the side of the bed filled with buckets of flowers.

"Reid, are you joking? You're already doing so much. I couldn't run the farm without you. You've helped me keep my head on straight." I laugh.

"Just doing my job, Loe." Reid half-smiles and points to Hansen Hardware behind him. "Let me head in here real quick, then we can take care of the Chaucer's delivery."

With a nod, I lean my back against the truck and let my eyes wander around town. People rotate through Rise and Grind like cogs in a well-oiled machine. If I breathe in deep, the rich dark roast is strong enough to waft across the street.

It's early May and the weather hasn't warmed up much yet, so I'm wrapped in a long tan cardigan over my overalls. It might seem like it to others, but I don't wear the same pair every day. I have several. All the pockets are made for convenient use, and I don't have to constantly pull up my pants when I have to bend over or squat on the farm, which is most of the time. Today's pair of overalls are skinny, tucked into my brown work boots. They're my favorite, most trendy pair.

"Follow the flowers, find the pretty girl." Out of nowhere, Kip rounds the hood of Betty. "Second time since I've been back that's held true. I'm surprised all the guys in town haven't caught onto this trick." He produces a white poppy from behind his back.

My gaze is leery as I accept the bloom. Though I'm sure Kip doesn't realize the significance, a white poppy is a symbol of peace. What is he playing at?

"I can't decide if you giving me my own flowers is insulting or charming, considering they *are* the best in town, but they cost you nothing."

"Oh, Sunshine, giving you flowers most certainly costs me something." A hint of a broody shadow crosses his face, but he blinks, and his familiar crooked grin reappears.

"Stalking Cove Road for new girls to prey on?" I lift a taunting brow.

"Actually, I was hoping I'd run into you. I talked to Old Man Sullivan and his son the other day."

I perk up, unable to hide my hope. "And?"

"Melvin said Lockwood Blooms grew his wife's favorite flowers. Loved them so much he specifically requested them when she passed two years ago."

My hand rests over my heart. "I remember. Zinnias and dahlias. It was my first funeral."

"Well, he must've loved what you did. I think you have a good chance here. His son, Joseph, is difficult, but Sullivan likes you."

"Really?" My lips pinch to the side. "Don't toy with me, Kipling. A girl can only process so much bad news at one time."

Kip stands taller. "What's going on? What bad news?"

I shake my head. "I just meant on top of my dad's stroke and your dad shutting down our hope for your land."

"Of course you'd bring our property back up."

"You asked." I shrug.

Kip shoves his fingers through his hair, further tousling his thick windblown locks. "Look, Chloe, I promise you I'll do my best to get Sullivan's tract for Lockwood Blooms."

One of my eyebrows arches. "Why are you so willing to help us?" Though he seems genuine, it's hard not to be apprehensive. Kip's never done anything nice for me, for us.

He opens his mouth, then releases an audible huff, twisting his lips as though rethinking whatever he planned on saying. Studying me, he finally speaks, "I don't suppose you have time for lunch? We could discuss my apparent change of heart." My teeth sink into my lower lip, and he rushes on, "Or a snack? Coffee? Anything other than another one of our quick street side meet and gree—"

"Okay, Loe. We can get going." I look over my shoulder at Reid, who taps his hand on the ledge of the truck bed, the metal clank echoing.

"Right. Yeah. We don't want to be late getting this delivery out."

"Oh, hey, Kip." Reid knocks his head back in a guy greeting. "I didn't see you there. It's been a long time."

Kip steps back, a lazy smile replacing the intense look he wore moments ago as he fumbled with asking me to join him.

"Hey, man. Seems like I've only seen you from a distance since I returned to Seaside."

Reid rounds the back, coming to my side. "Lockwood keeps me busy." He smiles at me, squeezing my shoulder. It's a double meaning, but I'm not sure Kip catches the move.

I nod. "Spring and summer are our busiest seasons."

Why do I feel like I've been caught red-handed? And not by Reid but by Kip. Kip and I are nothing. We've never been anything but rivals.

Well, except for the bizarre blip our sophomore year. That truce ended as quickly as it began.

"Sure. Yeah, makes sense. I won't keep you two. Apparently, I've got prey to hunt down, and you've got deliveries to finish." He knocks his knuckles on the hood of Betty before tossing a wave. "See ya around, *Loe*."

It's the first time my nickname has sounded like a dig, and I don't know why it stings so much. Kip's attitude should roll off my back, produce an eye roll, or not cause me a second thought. Instead, his voice repeats as I slip into the driver's side. Low and snarky.

Loe.

Loe.

Was he mocking Reid…or me?

Once we're inside the cab with the doors shut, Reid says, "He wasn't giving you too hard of a time before I got out there, was he?"

I shake my head. "Kip was just telling me we have a good shot at getting Sullivan's land."

"No way."

I conjure a smile, glancing at him from the driver's side as I crank the engine.

"Loe!" Reid grips my thigh and leans across the seat. Tugging on my overall strap, he uses his other hand to cradle my cheek, landing a kiss on my lips. "See? Things have a way of working themselves out."

"I'm not going to hold my breath. There are still hurdles to jump, but it's nice to catch a little break every once in a while."

Reid slips my hand from the steering wheel. Drawing it closer to him, he kisses my knuckles. "You've got this. You're Chloe Lockwood. You deserve good things."

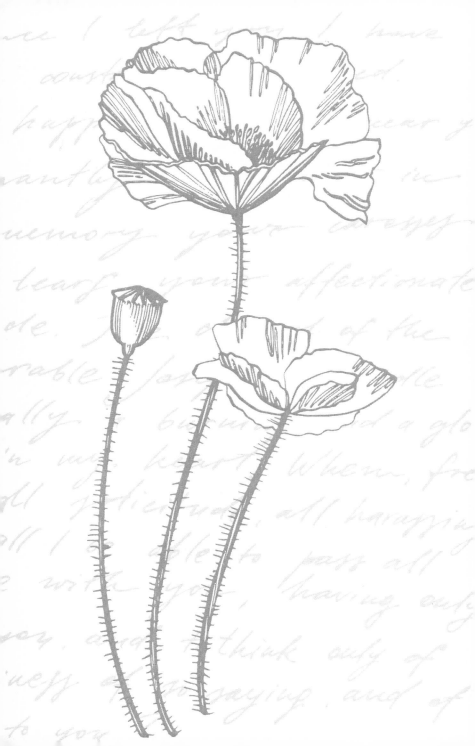

 ip

"Wow. Very impressive." Brynn enters the warehouse, grease-stained paper bags clasped in both hands. "You always were the best float captain. You put me to shame, little brother."

I drop my hammer and jump off the float we're finishing for tomorrow's Seaside Point May Day Festival, aka the spring parade, but nothing in Seaside is ever as simple as a calendar date. "Tell me you brought food and I'll let you claim all the credit."

"All the credit?" Brynn glows at the idea. She's as competitive as the next guy. I might as well be offering her a seat at the roundtable for all the glory I spy shining in her round eyes. "Burgers from Perry's," she sings, shaking the bag in her right hand.

"Bless you." I haven't had Perry's since returning home. Snatching the bag, I plop down on the edge of the grass-colored float and dig in.

"The fridge still has drinks, I hope?"

"Yep," I mumble around a full mouth of fries.

"Oh, so I ran into Grace in town. Reid smashed his hand while working on the float today."

My stomach rolls as I unwrap my burger. "Chloe's guy?" Swallowing the saliva pooling in my mouth, I sink my teeth into a large bite. *So good.* I am starving.

"Her co-worker, yeah. Don't act like we didn't go to school with him our entire lives."

"Actually, he graduated two years ahead of me, same as you. So—" I duck as a discarded Styrofoam ball flies toward my head.

"And you played on the same baseball team together, but whatever. Anyway... Apparently, the famous Lockwood Blooms May Day float is in danger of missing the parade because he was supposed to work on it and can't."

I don't muffle my snort. "Have you met Chloe Lockwood? I highly doubt she would let their float slip from the lineup. May Day is the celebration of spring, for Pete's sake."

"I don't know. Grace said Chloe changed the design at the last moment, and Reid was supposed to build the centerpiece they would cover in flowers. They kind of have nothing without his piece."

"It's not like she doesn't have other guys working for her. They'll be fine."

"Not according to Grace. The men were supposed to be done with their part. Nothing but paint and flowers left until Chloe changed the idea, so they're all tied up in other things."

Brynn leans against the side of the float, her hip resting beside my dangling legs, and reaches into the bag for her food. This conversation is mighty specific. Maybe Brynn and Grace Embry are better friends than I thought, but I suspect this is about something else.

I nudge her thigh with my foot. "Okay, give it up."

"Give what up?"

"Why are you telling me all this about Reid and Chloe's float? Why are you looking at me like that?"

"Like what?" Her voice rises two octaves. I love Brynn to death, but she's a crap actress. "You know the flower floats are my favorite. I'd hate for her not to be done in time."

Finishing off my last bite—so, so hungry—I slide off the float. A chance to see Chloe Lockwood and gloat about the situation she's in? Was there ever a doubt I'd go?

"I'll go see what I can do. You better get some help with finishing this up, though."

Brynn's victory dance skids to a halt, her panic growing as she eyes the piles and piles of glittering decorations stacked around the warehouse. Our float concept was ambitious. Glittering For Sale signs staked through equally glittering hills of landscape, with cardboard buildings representing Seaside Pointe's past, present, and hopeful future. While not a Lockwood Blooms floral design, the concept is top-notch. Plus, there are fiber optic lights hidden in the paper grass around the body of the float. *Beat that, Chloe.*

"You want me to finish this?"

"It's mostly about finishing touches at this point. Plus, there's a color-coded diagram up there." I point toward the front of the float and grab more fries.

"Of course there is." She smirks like my organizational quirks are a surprise, but we're cut from the same cloth, so she can't say a word.

"Call me if you need anything. I'm sure Chloe will kick me out the moment I arrive, so I should be back soon."

"Hey, bro," Brynn shouts. I turn, flinching as a brown paper sac flies toward my face. "She probably hasn't had time to eat."

I check the bag. My legs fail to move as I find another burger and order of fries. My eyes narrow on Brynn's smirk. "Oh, how Machiavellian of you. I'm impressed."

"Good luck, little brother."

In awe at the way Brynn suckered me into this, I make my way down the lot toward the warehouse Lockwood's float is located. The warehouses, twenty-one in all, are owned by the city of Seaside Pointe specifically for storing the hundreds of decorations they need for the various events held throughout the year. A good amount of warehouses hold the floats used for town parades. It's tradition to redesign the floats for each parade. Some businesses keep the same basic design, whether for cost-effectiveness or nostalgia and simply add minor changes based on the event. Others, like Lockwood Blooms and Harris Development, go all out, competing for best float honors. Unofficially, of course, since there isn't an actual voting system to determine a winner.

I wave at groups of people milling about eating, decorating, shooting the breeze. I've been home for over a month now, and the shock of knowing every person I come across has worn off. Seaside Pointe is home again. Even if only temporarily.

"Kip! Kip!"

I pause at the ear-splitting high octave of my name yelled by a group of girls. I swerve toward the right to the open door of the warehouse holding the float they congregate on. *Seaside High* reads the sign painted on the back of the wave-shaped float. The May Day float is a senior tradition. The last big deal event before graduating high school.

"Oh my gosh. I'm so glad I saw you. We need help, please?" Carrie-Anne's daughter, Mia, pushes her way through the bevy of girls around her and stops before me.

Carrie-Anne watched Brynn and me when we were younger, and we often returned the favor and watched Mia when she needed a break. She was twelve when I left for college. Twelve and hopelessly infatuated with me. Her little crush hasn't changed since I returned. I'm scared I'm going to hurt the poor girl. She's a month from turning eighteen and about to graduate high school. I'm a twenty-four-year-old man. I'm wary of what people might think of our friendship which has grown since I returned. She's a good kid, practically family, and I like keeping an eye out for her.

I survey the eighty-percent-completed float and the cluster of guys wearing sports jerseys sitting around on the ground, tossing a football back and forth. My shoulders shake. Things don't change.

"What's wrong?" I wipe the humor from my face.

"What isn't wrong?" a redhead whines and others join in. A chorus of high school girls are all worried about the paint not covering correctly, the glitter not being shiny enough, and how their senior year will be ruined if they don't have the perfect float.

"Can you help us?" Mia bats her dark lashes, and I swear cartoon hearts swirl around her head. "Please, we have no idea what we're doing, and our faculty sponsor flaked out on us."

"O'Connor?" Geez, things *really* don't change. Coach O'Connor's been a faculty sponsor since I was at Seaside. He never did more than stop by, sign a paper, and leave. Which is why we loved him.

Ten females confirm my suspicion, and I check my watch—quarter after seven.

"Tell you what, I need to check on another float, but I'll come back in a bit. Mia, I have my cell. If you need anything, shoot me a text. You have my number, right?"

Mia agrees, and I ignore the awed faces of her friends. I'll force Brynn to hang out as a little protection. Speaking of... Pivoting on the guys, still paying little attention to the girls or the float, I clear my throat. "In the meantime, you guys be men and help the ladies out here."

CHLOE'S MUSICAL—THOUGH somewhat tense—voice can be heard from outside the warehouse when I arrive. Curious, I lean against the door and spy.

I identify Chloe's torso on the other side of a pile of wood. She grips the roots of her hair, her eyes fixed on her partially completed float. It's a pitiful sight. Reid was obviously a crucial member of their crew.

Chloe spins around on her waiting team, rubbing her hands with encouragement. "Without Reid, we'll just have to modify, maybe go back to the original design. It's not as eye-catching, but it might work since I can't reach Charlie or Eric to give us a hand."

"But all we needed was the house. Without the centerpiece, we have a pathway of flowers leading to nothing." The brunette's body language says all I need to know. They've given up.

Chloe's head volleys between the float and her team. "It won't be a pathway of flowers leading to nothing. We have the wood, and we have the internet. We're essentially building a large dog house. How hard can this be? I'll measure. Denise, you're good with shears. Think you can run a table saw?"

Her entire crew looks at her like she's growing daisies from her ears.

"Right, because cutting stems of flowers is totally like operating a high-powered blade of death that I have no idea how to use."

"It'll be fine, you guys. We can do this. We're a team of creatives. Just because we don't have the centerpiece of our float doesn't mean we quit." Chloe's voice wavers. I'm not so sure she believes her own words. "We can use our heads and build it ourselves. How hard can it be?"

"In less than twelve hours," the brunette doubter says. *Geez, ladies, have a little faith in your leader.*

"Well, not with that attitude." Chloe claps her hands and tosses her head back. There's the Lockwood attitude she's thrown at me so many times in my lifetime. "There is no way Lockwood Blooms will not have a float in the parade, not on my watch. It'd be the first time in, I don't know, forever. We have to make this work."

Feet move and voices ring out in lukewarm agreement. I linger for a few more minutes, reluctantly impressed with Chloe's calm.

"Denise, the two-by-fours need to be cut to six and three quarters," Chloe shouts out from somewhere.

"Okay," Denise calls back as a saw roars to life.

The nervous lilt in Denise's reply is what finally moves me forward. This warehouse is surprisingly empty for the night before the parade. I glance at the other floats and immediately realize why. Lockwood Blooms keeps their float stored with the historical city floats. Those floats are rarely altered since they hold the city council and dignitaries. Only the white glittering castle designated for the festival queen and her court is newly designed. Brynn was queen her senior year. The crown sits on a shelf in her room to this day.

I round the float, ignoring the speculative gazes of both the brunette and Denise as I look for Chloe. She's ducked down, partially hidden by a giant tissue paper garden, as she surveys a partially built structure. I haven't been to a Seaside Pointe parade since leaving for college, but I can admit the Lockwood Blooms float never looked this good when I lived here. Even without whatever she's trying to add at the last minute, the float is perfect. Bright, colorful. Sunshine. *Chloe.*

The whirring of the saw dies down and Chloe stands, her back to me, as she produces a measuring tape from her apron pocket. "Do you guys think adding the house will be too much?"

"Not if you're trying to put all of the other floats to shame," I reply with sincerity.

The tape measure drops from Chloe's hands as she spins around. "What are you doing here?"

Glancing around the warehouse, I grin. "Spying on the competition?"

Chloe bends down and picks up the tape measure. "The festival isn't a competition, and you know it."

I step forward until all she has to do is sit on the float and we'll be face to face. "Huh, really? I thought everything our families did was a competition, Chloe." There's no sarcasm in my tone, no goading. I'm open and truthful—supremely difficult for me when it comes to her.

And maybe I'm mistaken, but the same regret flaring in my chest for the situation we're in flashes across her eyes. The uncertainty is gone in a moment. Replaced with resolve.

"What are you really doing here, Kip?" she asks again.

"I come bearing gifts." I dance the paper sack around from the tips of my fingers. "Dinner and two able hands with plenty of building knowledge."

Chloe eyes the brown paper bag and folds her arms. "How do I know you haven't come to sabotage the competition?"

"Like the way your gigi shared her *sugar* with mine and sabotaged the bake-off at the Christmas Jubilee?"

"Gigi did no such thing." Chloe purses her lips.

"Are you Lockwood women still sticking to that story?" I rest my hip against the edge of the float. "Please tell me how Granny ended up with a cup of salt in her famous cherry pie if not because Gigi switched the sugar and salt."

Chloe looks down on me with such superiority it's hard not to admire her. "Because your granny was too busy egging mine on to pay attention to what she was doing. All she had to do was pick the right canister."

This time I laugh. "You really *are* sticking to that story. Granny Harris doesn't make mistakes when baking her cherry pies. What an absurd explanation."

Chloe leans against the one good post to the house and crosses her arms. "Oh yes, just like she doesn't make mistakes when taking measurements."

My laughter doesn't let up. Not at the vision Chloe brings to mind.

"Don't you laugh, Kipling Harris. My flute recital dress was so tight I could barely breathe, and the hem—" Chloe huffs.

"It pooled on the ground. I know, I remember." I clutch my stomach. "It was an honest mistake; she was trying to help you."

"I don't know why my mother let her help. I knew I shouldn't have trusted a Harris with something so important."

I sober. Her words are laced with humor, but there is meaning etched below the surface. Eighty-something years of mistrust between two families. Our history is hard to erase.

Working my jaw, I study her. "There's never been a time when you've trusted me, has there?"

Chloe holds onto her words, a million responses crossing her face until she settles on, "Not a single one." Her voice is low and firm, but her eyes don't lie. Maybe, just maybe, there's one moment—a moment we've ignored for over seven years.

"Trust me now." I lift the bag with her burger. "I promise I'll double-check all my measurements so everything will be built perfectly. No sabotaging."

"If I agree, and this doesn't go off without a hitch, I will consider it an act of war, and things will not be pretty."

"Noted."

Chloe accepts the greasy bag. "It'll take more than a greasy peace offering of burgers and fries next time."

"Maybe we'll be lucky and peace offerings will be a thing of the past." I hoist myself up onto the float. "So, what are you adding here?"

"Just a simple house, like a little cottage. Four walls and a roof."

"A house?" I scratch the back of my neck. "Easy enough. If you hand me the tape measure and pen and paper, I'll take measurements and make the cuts. I'll even show you how to properly use the equipment so you're not in this predicament ever again."

Chloe removes a pencil from her pocket. "You really don't have to help. I'm sure you have your own float to finish up."

My fingers brush hers, pressing into them as I grip the pencil in her hand. "Chloe, I'm here. Let me help you."

She gives up the pencil and fidgets with her hair, tucking loose waves behind her ears. "Okay, but only because Denise probably would've cut off a finger before we could finish. Then we'd really be in a bind."

I make quick work of cutting the pieces needed to finish building the house while the brunette, Meredith, works on painting the sign hanging on the float's front. Too busy to learn how to use the saw, Chloe and Denise fill every open spot on the sprawling float with flowers, butterflies in flight, and glitter. Buckets and buckets of glitter.

"Think you can help hold the ladder steady while I finish off the roof here?" I ask.

"Oh, um, yeah." Chloe rounds the float and plants her legs on either side of the ladder, both hands gripping the base.

"What happened to Reid? He hurt his hand?"

Hammer strikes nails and Chloe waits. "Smashed it really good somehow. I'm not even sure since I wasn't here when it happened."

I hook the hammer on my jeans pocket. "Hand me that board on top there?" I hold out a hand.

Chloe eyes the ladder, like her moving will send me tumbling over, then turns and grabs the next board.

"So, are you two seeing each other?" I ask as I grab the board.

"Me and Reid?" She averts her gaze. "Yeah, kinda."

I harrumph.

"What was that sound for?"

"Kinda? You're not sure?"

Chloe's nose scrunches. "It's new. We've worked together for years. He's worked for Lockwood Bloom since he graduated high school, so we've grown close."

I secure two nails, then shift and meet Chloe's upturned face. "And he wants to be closer."

She doesn't say anything in return. The ladder teeters, and I check over my shoulder as Chloe grabs the rungs with a grimace.

"Chloe, remember when we talked about trust earlier? It goes both ways."

She bites the corner of her lip and adjusts her grip on each side of the ladder. "Sorry. I'm holding tight."

"Last board." I hold out my hand and she lifts the piece up. Finished with the roof, I climb down. My backside bumps into Chloe as she stands there staring off into space.

"Chloe." I cough. "I'm done."

"What?" She blinks and drops her arms. "Oh, sorry. So yeah, Reid and I are dating. Casually. I mean, I think it's casual. We're not dating other people, but it's not like we're super serious. It's only been a couple of months."

Her face is flushed, her eyes troubled as she chews on her bottom lip. I pop down off the ladder onto the float with enough force to shake the whole thing. Our bodies are too close in the confined space between the paper flowers and freshly framed house.

"It's not casual for him, Sunshine. He likes you. Trust me, I know the look."

I don't give her a chance to answer but shift backward before weaving my way around the artfully created flowers to the edge of the float where I jump down.

Clapping my hands, I stand like a man proud of my work. "All right, ladies. What's next?" I ask as I swing the hammer like a DIY pro and hang the claw from my belt loop with a jaunty smile.

hloe

It's after eleven o'clock, and the float is officially done. I can't believe we were able to pull it off. And I hate to admit we wouldn't have if it weren't for Kip. Not to say we needed a man, but it didn't hurt to have the muscle, and his knowledge with power saws was a plus.

Exhausted, Kip and I sit on the concrete floor, admiring our handiwork. "Not too shabby, Kipling."

After replying to a text, he says, "Nah, I built the frame; you did all the real work. I especially love the way you included the fresh flowers in the window boxes we added."

That was a nice touch. I wish it'd been my idea, but unfortunately, it was Kip's—who has checked his phone a dozen times over the last four hours. Who's so important they can't wait? Maybe it's a girl. If he's in town permanently, it makes sense he's dating. Maybe the someone he was meeting the first day I saw him outside of Flower Patch. And I shouldn't care. It doesn't bother me one bit. It isn't my place to have an opinion.

Then why does the thought cause my stomach to churn?

"The real test will be tomorrow." I lean back on my hands, my legs outstretched, matching Kip's position. "Will my house crumble in the middle of the parade?"

"Only if it's hit with a wrecking ball." He nudges my foot with his. "I stand by my craftsmanship."

Most of the crew left for the night, leaving us alone in the warehouse. I've never been prouder of my flowers. The colors are vibrant, the blooms enormous. And the structure Kip built is more impressive than I imagined. He might've done a better job than Reid, who shouldn't have insisted he could do it all. I wouldn't have had to rely on a Harris, but then again, it's difficult to say I regret accepting Kip's help. It was nice not being at war for a few hours.

It pains me to say it, but, "Thank you, Kip. I don't know why you decided to help us, but I really appreciate it. I'm sure Denise does, too. You saved her from a possible appendage loss."

Kip checks his phone once more before responding to me. "So, in actuality, helping was my civic duty. I couldn't allow an innocent bystander bodily harm all in the name of parade fun."

I bump my shoulder into his, such a strangely familiar gesture. "Of course not. That would've been cruel."

Our eyes catch, and suddenly, the warehouse doesn't seem very big with our faces less than a foot apart. Looking at Kip stirs up a forgotten memory. Not truly forgotten, only buried, and slowly making its way to the surface with each non-confrontational encounter with him.

He jumps up. "I should go."

Oh. "Right, yeah. It's late." I yawn. This morning's 5:30 wake-up call catching up to me. I don't know how I managed to stay upright this long.

"Thanks for letting me hang out and help." Kip offers his

outstretched hand. I hesitate but take it, and he pulls me from the floor. "Can I walk you out?"

"That's all right." I wave him off, removing my hand from the warmth of his. "I need to tidy up a few things before I leave. I won't be far behind you."

"Okay. Well, have a good night. I'll see ya."

Against my better judgment, I watch Kip jog out of the warehouse. He doesn't look back once.

WHILE WANDERING the parade route the next day, I stop and chat with every Lockwood Blooms customer I stumble upon, which is nearly half of Seaside Pointe. My dad always says a personal touch is the most important part of this business, so I hope I'm filling his shoes today.

When I spot Brynn Harris's fiery red hair in line at the coffee cart, I join her. "Hey, Brynn. The Harris float looks great."

"Doesn't it? It was all Kip. All I did was pick the colors." Brynn peers past me. "Hey, Karen. Joe." She tips her head before turning back to our conversation. "I can't wait to see yours. I heard it was something special."

I like that Brynn has never seemed phased by the feud. She's always friendly with me, with no pettiness or resentment between us. If only every member of the Lockwood and Harris families could be civil.

"Hopefully it lives up to expectation. Our team worked tirelessly. Especially Kip."

I'm still trying to understand Kip's abrupt departure the night before. One minute we were joking around. The next, he couldn't get out of the warehouse fast enough. Even if it was eleven o'clock, his urgency was strange. Unless it was a way not to get caught with a Lockwood after so many hours together.

"I haven't seen Kip this morning. I was going to thank him for not sabotaging our float, but the slacker hasn't shown up yet."

"Probably because he was up all night between helping you, Mia, and finishing off ours, but I guarantee he's here somewhere."

My face falls. "He, what? He was with me until after eleven."

"I know, I was at the warehouse waiting for him."

Was Brynn the one texting him all night? Or Mia Mason? "Kip wasn't done with your float when he came to help us?"

"Sweetie, he wasn't close to being done." Brynn touches my arm and moves forward in line. "Do you want a coffee?"

"Yes, please." Though I'm not keeping it for myself. My fingers tangle in my wild waves. "And he helped Mia? With the Seaside High float? He really must've been up all night," I mumble to myself.

"Sure did. He must be trying for sainthood or something. Helping a bunch of teens with a float?" Brynn shudders. "Speak of the devil." She jerks her head.

I spin around and spot Kip's ruffled hair as he works his way through the crowded sidewalk toward us. The man probably rolled out of bed ten minutes ago, and yet he still manages to make faded jeans and a T-shirt irresistible.

What the heck, Chloe? This is Kipling Harris. Stop thinking of him like that.

"Here." Brynn elbows me. "Take him a coffee. He looks like he could use the caffeine."

I planned to. "Thanks, Brynn." I smile, grateful.

Kip stops in the middle of the pedestrian traffic pattern as I walk his way. He works his jaw and shoves his hands in his pockets.

"What is this? Chloe Lockwood without her trusty overalls, apron, or mud-covered face?" His gaze flicks over my skinny jeans and cozy off-the-shoulder sweater. "You clean up nicely—for a Lockwood." He winks.

For once, I'm dressed like a person who cares about my

appearance, not for comfort. I lie to myself and say it's not for Kip.

Because it's not. It's for the parade.

"Rumor has it you left me and finished up two other floats last night."

Kip opens his mouth as the drumline marching down the parade route breaks into a cadence. His eyes roll as he touches my elbow and steers me out of the crowd and further from the street. We stand in silence for a moment as the snares and bass echo off the buildings along Main Street.

"Have you been asking around about me?"

"You wish. I ran into Brynn." I raise the cup of coffee. "Here. I'm guessing you could use this."

"Ah, bless you." His fingers wrap around the paper cup as he inhales the steam with a sigh. "This I needed. As for those pesky rumors you heard, it wasn't a big deal. Our float needed a few things, and I helped the seniors with theirs. Don't you remember decorating our senior float? Coach O'Connor hasn't changed."

"Ha. You mean, he does nothing and barely shows up?"

"Yep. Mia kind of begged me. Since she's Carrie-Anne's daughter, I couldn't say no. Thankfully, they didn't need much more than guidance."

"Something tells me you're being modest. How very un-Kip-like."

His face morphs into one of false shock. "Me? Un-modest? You must have me confused with someone else. There's not a boastful bone in my body."

"Keep telling yourself those lies. Maybe they'll come true." I cover my laughter behind my hand.

"Oh, look. I think I spy the roof of an extremely well-built house coming down the street." He shifts, stretching to his full height as he peers over heads and down the parade route. "I bet that was created by one mighty fine craftsman."

"Amateur at best," I tease, admiring Kip's proud stance. I still can't believe he bailed me out when he was bogged down with two other floats. He didn't offer an olive branch. He cut down the whole dang tree.

"Wait, Jarred Prince?" Kip calls.

The stalky ex-quarterback stops at his name and turns. His face brightens when he spots us. "Harris. Chloe." Jarred moves in and clasps hands with Kip. "Never thought I'd see the two of you together without a referee keeping the peace."

Kip chuckles. "Hey, man. I haven't seen you since graduation. I caught a few games you played for Tech, but wow, are you back in Seaside Pointe for good?"

"Nah, just visiting for the week. Though, I'm only a few hours south of here. What about you?"

I turn to Kip with interest.

"Yeah, I moved back at the first of April. I—"

"Uncle Jay! Uncle Jay!" A girl around the age of seven with wild pigtails tugs on Jarred's pants leg. "Come on," she begs.

"I better go before Charity throws a fit. Good bumping into you two. Kip, we should grab a drink." They share a fist-bump-man-shake as Kip tells him to call the office, then Jarred turns to me. "Loe, great float. I'll see around town this week, I'm sure."

"Umm, maybe." I return the smile, but it's shaky. Kip got me thinking more about my relationship with Reid. I shouldn't be going out with Jarred when he's in town anymore.

An elbow jabs my ribs. "Did you hear him? He admired the float I helped build."

"It's too bad you're not getting any recognition," I joke.

"I'll live." His eyes meet mine over the rim of his cup as he sips his coffee. "It was worth the no sleep, by the way. Helping you."

Warm tingles spread throughout my chest. I don't know how to respond. Nice Kip is new territory. I turn my attention to the parade to cover up my nerves.

"Have lunch with me today?" Kip asks out of the blue.

I chuckle, fiddling with the ends of my wild hair. "There's a festival going on here."

"Yeah? So, join me at the picnic."

I look around, suddenly aware my parents could be watching us. "You know I can't."

"You can't, or you won't?"

I swallow and face him. "It's not that simple, Kip." Plus, there's Reid. Who hasn't shown up yet. I doubt he'd be okay with me hanging out with Kip, eating lunch with him. Even platonically.

"It's the same ol' song and dance with you. I should have known." Kip blows out a frustrated breath. "You know what, I haven't spent the May Day Festival with my family in years. I think I'll go find them. Enjoy your day."

I can't conjure up a defense in time, so I watch Kip's retreating figure like I got whiplash until the crowd swallows him, hating every distancing step between us.

ip

YOU'RE AN IDIOT. Chloe Lockwood is dating Reid Pruitt. *Casually.* Inviting her to lunch, for the second time, was asking for a letdown. I swore I wouldn't lose control around her again. I swore it. How does this one woman turn me crazy every single time?

Chalking my lunacy up to lack of sleep, I search out family and friends to spend the day with. The May Day Festival opens with the parade and runs through sundown, closing with a fireworks display. There are games, food, craft booths, and live music. The festival encompasses all of Main Street, and no matter where I go, Chloe appears. An entire Saturday spent dancing around the Lockwood family. I'm exhausted and admittedly a little jealous when Reid and his heavily bandaged hand make an appearance. Jealous enough that when I bump into Olivia, the waitress from Saltbox, I offer to show her around town the following day without a second thought. Not true. I have a second thought, and it involves how attractive she is. A beautiful woman. Apparently, beauty is the barometer I'm now using for dating women.

It's the last thing I want. I don't date for looks. I rarely date at all. I prefer working long hours and hanging out with my buddies. I'm certainly not interested in playing the dating scene of Seaside Pointe. Especially since I'm not sold on staying.

Regardless, Olivia mentioned she's barely explored Seaside Pointe since moving here, and I opened my big mouth. Which is how I come to be sitting across from the beautiful blonde eating brunch at Sweet and Savory while not thinking about Chloe Lockwood. Much.

"There I was, smiling for all these cap and gown photographs with my family, an English degree in hand, and I realized I had no idea what I actually wanted to do. I was lost." Olivia pauses for her first breath in five minutes and cuts into the breakfast crepe our waiter dropped off during the middle of her life story. Her blue eyes flutter closed as a delighted moan leaves her lips.

"Good stuff, right?" I stuff a large chunk of my spinach, peppers, and goat cheese crepe in my mouth, enjoying her reaction. The girl isn't shy about enjoying her food. Understandable, considering Sweet and Savory serves the best crepes I've eaten. There are few things I can't find in Tulsa, and this is one of them. Others try, but none succeed.

I reach for my juice. "So, you went to Washington State—which is where my sister graduated from, by the way—and you grew up in Portland. How did you end up here?"

"Lockwood Blooms."

Juice burns my windpipe. "I'm sorry," I say between coughs, choking on my last sip. Olivia's fork clatters against the plate as she reaches for my forearm. "Lockwood?" I repeat, finding my breath.

She ignores my question and leans closer, hooded blue eyes scanning my face as she asks if I'm all right. I wave off her concern, clearing my throat and pushing my juice away. Even when I'm on a date with another woman, Chloe wiggles her way in.

"You said Lockwood Blooms brought you here? How's that?"

Color stains her cheeks. "It's silly, really. I saw a picture of their fields online. Rows and rows of vibrant flowers, and the valley in the background. They inspired me."

Fan-freaking-tastic. Leave it to me to find a date who is enamored with Chloe. Or Chloe's flowers. Same damn difference. Appetite gone, I pick at the last of my dish and piece together Olivia's thought process. "Inspired?"

"English major, remember? I want to be a writer." Her gaze wanders out Sweet and Savory's picture windows. "Something about the beauty in those photos, combined with the small-town feel of this place, spoke to me."

While the concept of moving somewhere based on a photograph of flowers sounds a little extreme, I admire the passion for her craft. As we finish eating, Olivia peppers me with questions about my own life choices. Questions I've asked myself lately. Like her, my passion for my career is clear. What I can't pin down is where I see myself working.

AFTER BRUNCH, we step outside into a surprisingly sunny May afternoon. Today's temperature is likely twenty degrees cooler than Tulsa's. Boy, I'm loving PNW life.

Olivia inhales deeply like she's breathing everything in. "I can't believe I've lived in Seaside three months and haven't made time to come down here."

"To the Arts District?"

"Yeah, this little village is adorable. I'm so glad you suggested coming here. Can we shop around a bit?"

I suggested Sweet and Savory because of their killer crepes. The village is a plus. Located off Main Street on the edge of town, the Arts District Village is a circle of shops and eateries catering to arts and crafts with a few boutiques thrown in. With the park and Skagit River running behind the shops, the area is packed with families picnicking and out for Sunday strolls. This is the Seaside Pointe I love. The feeling I long to replicate at the River-front property. Something for the growing population of young professionals moving out of nearby cities due to cost of living and overcrowding.

I study Olivia. Her designer clothes tell me she comes from money, but her worn converse sneakers say she's down to earth despite her money. I like her, or what I've learned of her thus far. *Why not see what happens, Kip?*

Shopping isn't exactly my favorite way to spend a Sunday afternoon, but… "Of course, lead the way."

Two hours later, I'm somewhat in awe. "I have to admit, my mother and sister have to layer on a lot of bribes to get me to shop."

Olivia laughs, her hand wrapping around my forearm like touching me is a completely natural thing as we exit Wyman's Art Studio. "It's not your favorite thing in the world?"

"Hardly." I let her weight sink against my side and focus on the feeling. She's tiny—barely above five feet. Different, but not bad. I clear my thoughts when I catch her watching me curiously.

"That's what I was about to say, I normally hate shopping, but you're making the day a little more interesting. I like your view on things."

"You mean you don't think I'm crazy for making up stories for every piece of art back there?"

She pulls a laugh from me. "No way. I especially liked the witch's tale you spun about the cabin in the forest painting. I'm gonna need you to tell me the rest sometime."

Olivia releases my arm and tucks her pin-straight hair behind her ear. "Is that your way of asking me out again?"

Taking two steps back to stand before her, I study her expertly made-up face. What an odd package she is. This girl looks like a country club regular but weaves stories for a living and works as a waitress in a small-town restaurant.

"Yeah," I say, surprising myself. "I am."

She bounces on her toes and grins. "Then I accept. Now, humor me." She grabs my hand and tugs me toward a glass door. "I've heard nothing but good things about this clothing boutique since I moved here. This can be the last one, I promise."

Women's clothes. I hold back my groan as Olivia pulls on the door handle. In bold rustic letters is the word: Fig.

Grace Embry's store. *Fantastic.*

Olivia releases my hand and rushes forward, "oohing" and "ahhing" as I eye the space hoping against hope Grace is off today. Not that my being on a date matters. Seeing Grace means my date will absolutely get back to Chloe, again, not that it matters, but there's something absurdly cringey happening in my mind at the thought of Chloe knowing I went out with someone local.

Galvanized pipe racks and industrial wooden shelves held together by more pipes line the exposed brick walls.

"Oh. I love this," Olivia exclaims.

Pulling my attention from studying the interior, I stand aside, observing as Olivia proceeds to stroke every sleeve on the rack in front of her in what I can only assume is an innate shopping gene I wasn't born with. Brynn and Mom can't shop for anything without touching everything. It's maddening.

"Well, hey." Grace stands behind a corrugated steel counter in the center of the shop. "Welcome to Fig."

Cursing my bad luck, I feign pleasure at running into her. "Grace."

"Harris." The corner of her mouth curls up in a smirk as she comes around the tall counter. Crossing her arms, she leans her hip against the metal.

"Oh, Grace." Olivia squeals from across the store. Honest to goodness squeal of a pig, along with clapping like a giddy teen.

The chic, laid-back woman I was talking with outside likes to shop. "I told you I would get in here." She turns to me before Grace can get a word in edgewise and keeps talking. "Grace wore this sweater to eat at Saltbox last week that I have to have, and she told me about this place."

We share a look, then Grace says, "I'm so glad you finally made it in. The sweater is on the back right shelf."

Grabbing Grace's arm, Olivia beams. "This place is fantastic. I wasn't sure if I'd be able to find such cute clothes away from the city." I'm pretty sure Grace forces a grin as Olivia releases her and floats away with a bounce to her step.

"Kip," she calls over her shoulder. "You might as well have a seat. I'm trying some things on."

Resigned to my fate, I face Grace. "So, you two have met?"

"And it appears you have, too." Grace's eyebrow arches, not losing her wry smirk. "Though I've been living here for three years since college graduation, and you just got into town."

"This place is yours, right?" I ask conversationally. Brynn kept me clued into things in the business world of Seaside since I left. I'm well aware of how Grace opened the shop on her own after inheriting some money from her grandmother, but if I don't ask random questions, Grace might ask her own.

She releases a quiet chuckle like she knows I'm changing the subject. "Yes, the place is mine, and no, you're not going to keep me from asking about your new friend."

"What? Are you jealous I asked her out before you?" Resting my forearm on top of a rack, I pin her with my gaze. "What do ya say, Gracie Lou Who? Me and you with a bottle of the cheap stuff down at Harper's Field?"

"In your dreams, Harris. Don't even try to use that old nickname to charm me. Besides, we both know I'm not the one you really want to ask out."

Ouch. I turn and verify Olivia is out of earshot. I could lie, but why bother. Chloe made her feelings about me clear when we were sixteen, and even if they've changed, she's still the girl who can't fathom going against her family—her father—publicly. "And we both know that ship will never leave the harbor."

She shrugs like she knows better than me, and I'm not inclined to argue.

"Hey, honestly, though, this is a great place. I dig the interior details. We do a lot of industrial designs on our projects in Tulsa. My dad hates the style. He's more about glass and steel, but he's coming around. Or I think he is."

Pride is evident on Grace's face. "Thanks. I wanted something simple, and Brynn gave me the idea. She helped me pick out a lot of the fixtures."

"Ahhh, no wonder I like the place so much. I didn't think you could pull this off on your own. I still remember the crap paper mâché earth you made when we were kids."

She slugs me hard in the arm with a sneer. "Miss Johnson gave me an A on that masterpiece, thank you very much."

"Miss Johnson was blind as a bat and gave everyone an A."

"You're such a jackass." Her amusement continues. "No wonder Chloe holds onto her grudges. You can't help yourself."

"Wow, and people wonder why I never come back and visit. With friends like you, who needs enemies." I nudge a stack of shirts at my elbow into disarray. "I can't believe I'm saying this, but I actually missed you, Grace."

"Yeah," she rolls her eyes, "Seaside isn't the same without you, either, I guess."

"As for Chloe and her grudges or mine, for that matter, it doesn't make a difference. She's with Reid."

"Reid *has* been around. Working together for so many years, I guess they were inevitable." Grace gives a non-committal shrug. "Are you planning on sticking around Seaside? Or will you go back to Tulsa?"

Is she asking out of curiosity or on behalf of her best friend?

"Since everything I tell you goes right back to Chloe, I'll say no comment."

Grace purses her lips. "And why would it matter if I told Chloe?"

Of course she calls me out on my crap.

"I don't know, maybe it wouldn't. She wouldn't hear the truth about what's going on in my head. *That* I only admit to my friends."

"Then, as your friend, tell me what's going on in your head, Kip Harris."

Rubbing my neck, I want to take the leap. Share what I haven't wanted to admit out loud. "I have two opportunities. I have a life in Tulsa. Great friends, a solid job, a name in the industry. But I miss my family, and I miss Washington. I wasn't here for Brynn when she needed me. My dad wants me to eventually take over H.D., and there's this girl." I blow out a deep breath. "This one stubborn mess of a girl, who could turn this into the easiest decision I've ever made. If only we'd get out of our own way and give what we started seven years ago a shot."

Her gray-blue eyes gape. Impressed or maybe surprised I spoke honestly?

I push off the display I lean against and shrug. "So, I dunno, Grace. You tell me, will I stick around?"

"Grace!" Olivia's muffled voice calls from where she's disappeared into a changing room.

Her mouth opens and shuts, chewing on the corner of her lip. "You know, Harris, if you were as candid with Chloe as you just were with me, you might have a reason to." Grace turns on her heel toward Olivia.

And any thoughts I have about going on a second date with Olivia die.

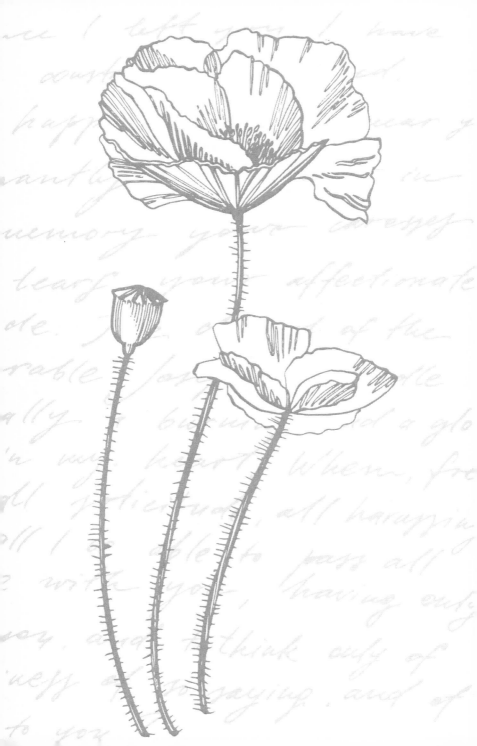

hloe

"JARRED's back in town for the week."

"Let me guess. He asked you out."

I stop by Fig while I'm in town making my Monday morning deliveries. Grace isn't Jarred's biggest fan, but it was nice to go out with an attractive guy with no strings attached. We could grab dinner, have some fun conversation, fool around at the end of the night, and he'd leave within a few days. It was just enough for me to get out and be more than the flower fields every couple of months until Reid made a move. As much as I love the farm, we need a break every once in a while.

"Yeah, but because of Reid, I kind of shot him down. I didn't specifically say no, but I think he caught the gist."

Grace laughs. "Staying in a relationship with a guy you had an infatuation with as a tween, while punishing yourself and refusing to go on a date with the man you do. Whom, by the way, you also had a thing for as a teenager."

I shouldn't have told Grace about Kip's invitation at the parade.

"I do *not* want Kip Harris."

"Sell that to someone who's buying it." Grace opens her next box of inventory and hangs the lavender blouse on the rack.

"I don't. He might be helping me with Sullivan's land, and he might've gotten us out of the bind with the float—which I'm grateful for—but he's still Kip Harris. The guy who spit bubblegum in my hair in third grade, which then required the haircut disaster of the 80s we will never speak of again." I grip the next top she unpacks from the box so she'll focus on me. "Do you remember how he'd antagonize me every time I had to give a presentation in front of any class we shared? All the stupid irrelevant questions he'd ask. Like anyone is going to know the eating habits of a newt. My project was on aquatic habitats."

Grace chuckles and takes the shirt from me.

"Everyone thought he was *so* funny, while I looked like an idiot. He humiliated me in class all the way through our senior year, by the way."

"You do know that's what boys do with crushes."

"Yeah, sure." I snort. "Which is exactly why he asked out our best friend, Chelsea, sophomore year. Who, mind you, once said she'd *never* date Kip Harris. Then, he proceeded to date every one of our other friends throughout high school, along with the other half of our female graduating class."

Grace says nothing, but there's a slight tilt to her mouth as she hides a smirk and hangs up another top.

"But none of that even matters because I like Reid. I *do*. He's fun and dedicated and supportive. He'd do anything for Lockwood Blooms. We're a good fit."

Grace nods along like she's placating me.

"Knock it off, Grace, I have no interest in being with Kip. And even if I wanted to, I couldn't. Can you imagine what my dad would do if I dated a Harris? I'd give the man another stroke."

She cocks an eyebrow. "Have you ever asked?"

A humorless chuckle passes my lips. "Yeah, I could see that going over well. *I know the Harrises are our mortal enemies, but what about Harris grandbabies? They could be cute.*"

"Well, you skipped ahead a few steps," Grace says. "Obviously, you've been thinking about the future."

"Shut up." I throw a folded T-shirt from the table next to me at her. "I have not. It was a hypothetical question. There will never be a Harris-Lockwood future. Ever."

"You get to refold that." She throws the shirt back, clocking me in the face.

"Even if I did have feelings for Kip, which I don't, it would never be simple." I tuck in the sleeves and fold it in half, putting the shirt back where I found it. "There is no dating casually to see where it goes. If a Lockwood and a Harris were going to take such a huge risk, they'd have to do it for a good enough reason."

"I can't possibly think of *any* good reasons." She glances at me from the corner of her eyes, and I almost throw the shirt at her again until she says, "You know, he came in here yesterday with the new blonde waitress from Saltbox."

New blonde waitress… "Olivia?" I think that's her name.

She leans in. "They seemed pretty chummy."

He asked me to lunch on Saturday and moved onto her the next day? Or have they been dating since he got back? Maybe Brynn wasn't who was texting him all night Friday. Maybe Olivia was.

Why am I surprised? I shouldn't be, and it shouldn't sting. Why does it sting? He gave an innocent peace offering of lunch at the parade. It probably meant nothing to Kip. Unless… Does he think asking Olivia out bothers me? Is that his goal?

It's like sophomore year all over again. A hint of a truce until he started dating Chelsea Bray, and suddenly the war was on again. Though, I still don't know why.

Whatever. I don't care. I'm with Reid. I can't stand Kip, anyway. So what if he's done a few nice things for me since he's been back in town. He's Denton's son, and he always will be. Some things never change.

"Well, good for him." My arms cross over my overalls. "Olivia's pretty." In an Elle Woods sort of way, if you're into that kind of thing.

Grace hangs up the last lavender blouse on the rack and hauls the empty box to the back of the boutique. "Yeah, she's gorgeous." Her voice carries over her shoulder. "And *really* sweet, too."

I don't care. I don't care. I don't care.

"Did you know she's an aspiring writer?" she asks. "She was telling me about it the other day when I had lunch at Saltbox. Super smart girl."

I. Don't. Care.

I meet Grace at the storage door as she collapses the cardboard box. "How cool. I'm not surprised Kip would choose someone who's the whole package." He couldn't possibly fall for someone average. What would everyone say? That might tarnish the Harris image.

"Yeah. They're an adorable couple. She's so tiny, I could fit her in my pocket. I bet Kip loves that about her."

I hold my tongue. She's goading me, and I'm not going to give in to her.

"Who knows?" she says with a shrug. "Maybe she'll be the reason Kip stays in Seaside for good this time."

"Oh my gosh. They had *one* date, Grace."

She closes the storage door with one hand while raising the other in defense. "Hey, you were the one talking about having Harris grandbabies not five minutes ago."

"I'm leaving."

Grace laughs and hollers as I walk through the clothing racks and around tables stacked with jeans to the front door. "Have fun with your flowers. Maybe they'll be able to break through your thick skull."

"Good luck finding a new best friend," I shout over my shoulder.

"Oh, I don't know. I think Olivia would be pretty great."

"Suck it, Embry."

Her laughter follows me all the way out the door.

I BEND and kiss Reid's cheek before hopping over the row of ranunculus chamallow in the hoop house.

He looks up, adjusting his navy cap over his shaggy hair. "You've been gone quite a while. Deliveries take you that long?"

"No, I stopped at Fig to talk to Grace for a bit." A twinge of guilt finagles its way into my gut. Seeing Grace isn't a problem. Our conversation, on the other hand…

I *did* shut down all of her speculations and prodding, though. That should count for something.

Pulling out my shears, I kneel by my bucket on the other side of the pink ranunculus. "How's your hand doing today?"

"It's slowing me down, but it's nothing I can't work through." He flexes it in his glove. "Luckily, it's my left hand, so I can still harvest and plant the dahlia tubers."

I nod. "We'll start on those tomorrow. We're doubling them this year."

"Speaking of." Reid stuffs the last of his row in his bucket. "My little brother's friend, Tyson, is looking for a part-time job. He's fifteen, on the Varsity baseball team with Wade. With my hand, I thought he could help out around the farm."

"Sure. An extra hand would be nice without my dad, too. We'll probably be mostly without him for another month, though he does want to help with the tubers, so we'll see how that goes. Not to mention, we're going to have to gear up for planting the perennial cutting garden next month. It'd be nice to have help with preparing the beds."

Reid stands, bucket in hand. "Do you want to interview him or anything?"

"Is he a good kid?"

"As far as I know."

I shrug. "I trust you. Whenever he can start, we'll put him on the payroll."

Reid leans over the blossoms, tugging the back of my neck to meet his mouth. "You're a gem, Loe. I'll be back with more buckets to harvest the rest."

As I watch Reid's backside in his jeans walk down the dirt path, I appreciate his lean, muscular physique. The way his biceps ripple under his short sleeve as he switches his navy cap to face forward and exits the hoop house into the sun.

And I realize…the butterflies are gone. The feelings of admiration are still there, but the spark has fizzled.

I suppose mellowing affection is what happens when relationships progress. They lose the new, exciting feel. But is that normal this early on? Two months in? Reid is the first guy I've dated more seriously since high school. And the guys I dated in high school never gave me the feelings Reid has, so that makes sense, right?

Honestly, the only person to ever get under my skin to feel passionate about is Kip Harris.

Passionate hatred, that is.

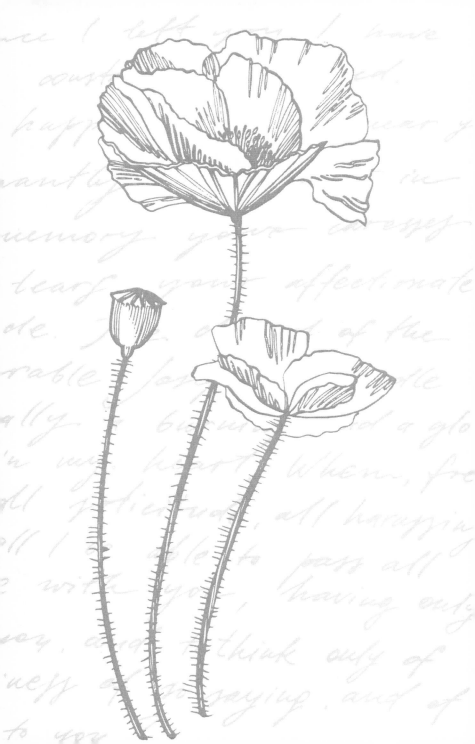

ip

"Hey, Kip?" Dad calls from somewhere down the hall as I end my call with Weller Faison. Can the man not pick up his phone or wait until he's at my door to speak with me like a normal person?

Across from my office, Brynn works behind her desk. Though her glass door is closed, she obviously hears our father because she looks up.

With glowing eyes, she mouths, "You're in trouble," pointing at me and drawing her index finger across her neck. I flash her a universally known finger and rub my temples while waiting for Dad to appear.

"Kip." His heavy palm slaps the frame to my door, startling me. "I ran into Joseph Sullivan at lunch."

"You don't say," I drawl. I've been waiting for this conversation. It's been two weeks since I reached out to Sullivan about a possible deal for Lockwood Blooms. Dad was bound to get wind of our conversation eventually.

"Prime land like Melvin's for a flower farm?" Dad swipes at his cellphone. "What were you thinking?"

Scrubbing my palms over my face, I recline in my chair. "I was thinking Chloe—" I catch my slip and clear my throat. "Lockwood Blooms is poised for amazing things if they could expand their acreage, and our client *Melvin* Sullivan has acreage to sell and is a farmer at heart."

Blue eyes narrow. Denton Harris hasn't changed a bit; he hates being challenged by anyone. It's unfathomable when that someone is me. "We're not in the business of hearts, Kip. We're about making money. They can do better."

I push to my feet, snapping the lid to my laptop closed and stacking some files I need to go over. "Is that right, Denton? Thank you for pointing out the Harris business plan, as if I haven't known the drill my entire life. Lockwood's agent and I have discussed terms. Melvin likes the idea, but he wanted to sit on the offer for a bit. We don't have other interested parties right now. I'm thinking about money, plain and simple."

His arms cross over his chest as I shove the files and my laptop in my bag. "I just hung up with Trina, and they need me in Tulsa for an urgent issue. I'll text Brynn my flight info, but you can reach me on my phone if something comes up. I need to go pack."

"Kip."

My fist hits the corner of my desk. "Geez, Dad, give it a rest, would you?"

Movement snags my attention as Brynn hurries around her desk. I close my heavy eyes and curse beneath my breath. Tiny drums tap a constant cadence at the back of my head.

"If keeping up with your projects in Tulsa has you so uptight, maybe you should consider—"

"Dad," Brynn snaps, announcing her presence behind our father's back.

"You don't want to go there." I sigh, opening my eyes and meeting his gaze. "You press me on a decision, and you won't like the one I choose."

Brynn pinches her bottom lip between her fingertips as Dad and I stand locked in a silent battle of wills. He's not a weak opponent, but neither am I. I'm not beholden to him. I won't bend; bending to his will ended in my teens.

"This conversation isn't over. Take the rest of the week to deal with what you need. I'll see you Monday." With a final frown, he exits my office.

Brynn side steps to prevent being run over, her fingers still working her lip. Slinging my bag over my shoulder, I wait for one of her sarcastic comments. She surprises me with an, "Are you okay?" instead.

"My head hasn't hurt this bad since college, and I have to fly to Tulsa to soothe over ruffled feathers." Not to mention I have to return a call to Olivia, who apparently holds out hope I'll ask her out again even after I explained I needed time. If we'd never stepped into Fig, I would have been fine. She's a cool girl. But after running my mouth to Grace, it became clear my dating Olivia would be unfair considering the unresolved feelings I nurse over Chloe. I knead the back of my neck. "What do you think?"

Her face softens, and she waves me to follow. "Dad's right, Kip. I don't think you can keep doing this back and forth thing. You've been home for a little over a month, and this will be the second time they've called you back."

I switch off my lights and cross the hall into her office. She's digging through something in her drawer as I close her door behind me. "I'm not so sure I can work for him, Brynn. I can't deal with his crap. He wants to own me and pull my strings. I'm not a Harris puppet."

She tears into a travel packet of headache medicine and hands the pills over. "You need to talk to him. Yes, he's stubborn as hell, but he genuinely wants you here. I promise."

I swallow the pills down dry and toss the packet in the trash. "Why do you think I gave him a chance? This crap he keeps pulling with Lockwood, though. I don't want to play into his feud."

"Speaking of…" The grin on her lips spells trouble.

"No." I back into her door. "I do not have the time or energy to get into that with you today. I need to pack a bag and get to the airport." My pocket buzzes, and I pull out my cell. "See, Trina with flight info."

"Fine." She stands and drags me into a hug. "You'll be back for this weekend, right?"

Returning her hug, I kiss her temple. "Shouldn't be an issue. Worst case scenario, we get to the campsite Saturday morning. Do you think I'd let you go camping with Hayden and Bodhi alone?"

"Not likely. Besides, they're your buddies, so if you don't get back in time, I won't be going."

"What? You don't want to spend the weekend with two single guys in tents? Where's your sense of adventure, sis?" I pinch her side and jump back before she can hurt me. "Love you, see you in a few days."

My PLANE from Tulsa touches down with two bumps and a skip, and I sigh a breath of relief. Twenty minutes early. Another hour and a half, and I'll be home. In five and a half hours, I'll be on a ferry to Friday Harbor and one, maybe two, beers into forgetting the past forty-eight hours.

What a week. Vendor issues, needy clients, and trouble-making zoning commissioners. All standard issues in this business, but smash them into a forty-eight hour time period with ten of those hours being in the air, and I'm toast. Add an unresolved fight with Dad, and I'm searching for the nearest exit off this crazy train.

The nearest exit, aka finding my sanity, turns out to be Chloe Lockwood. Yes, that's damn telling.

I need to update her on my conversation with Melvin Sullivan from Monday. I'd meant to call her Tuesday before Trina begged me to fly to Tulsa. I hate leaving her hanging for so long. A transaction like hers should be simple. It's the purchase of land. No major building issues or ingress/egress headaches. She wants to grow flowers. Done deal, if not for Joseph Sullivan and his siblings nosing into their father's business all in the name of greed.

I'll stop by Lockwood Blooms, tell her the news, see her face, and poke the bear for fun. Then I'll pack for the weekend's festivities and enjoy a weekend with my best friends and Brynn decompressing.

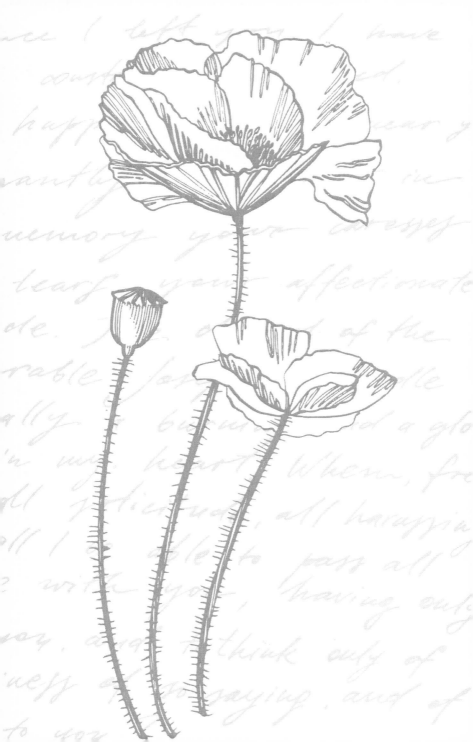

hloe

WHEN I WALK into the flower studio with a pail of daffodil pods to lay out for harvesting the seeds later, something feels off. My eyes drift over the shelves of pots and vases to the back wall, where I keep the flowers drying and waiting for seed collection. Setting the bucket of pods down on my workbench, I approach the wooden shelving the flowers are lined up on. Correction: were lined up on.

My heart plummets. Where are my seeds?

I search every shelf, shifting vases and pots. I scour counters and corners where they couldn't possibly be and burst from the studio. "Does anyone know what happened to all of the drying blooms in the studio?"

Meredith and Charlie shake their heads with frowns as they lay fabric for the dahlias. "I haven't been in there in days," she says.

I move on, asking everyone I see, peeking in hoop house after hoop house for anyone else to ease my mind. But no one knows anything. My panic rises. It's possible someone moved them. They could still be here somewhere.

I stop when I find Reid with Tyson in the supply area organizing our new shipment of T-posts and hoops.

"Hey, do either of you know what happened to the drying flowers on the shelves in the studio?"

"Yeah, Reid had me toss them yesterday when he had me clean out the studio."

"You what?" I can't suppress my shout.

"Whoa, whoa, whoa." Reid swipes out his arms. "I did no such thing. Ty, I told you to clean *up* the flower studio. Sweep, take out the trash, organize the pots and vases. I never said anything about throwing out the flowers."

Tyson's nervous gaze drifts between my rattled eyes and Reid. "They were a bunch of dead flowers on paper towels. I figured they were trash."

I grip the bib of my overalls. Oh my gosh. I'm going to puke.

"Bud, those were drying out to save the seeds." Reid grips Tyson's shoulder. "If something is ever questionable, you need to ask."

I find my voice. "Why would you have him go in the studio at all? That's my space. We need him in the fields or the greenhouses, not my studio."

Reid opens his mouth, looking lost. "I thought you could use the help. I had no idea he'd misunderstand simple directions."

The seeds. My heart sinks a little further. I didn't even think to look. "Did you clean out the refrigerator at all?"

Tyson glances at Reid, his Adam's apple bobbing. "I…I saw a bunch of envelopes in some metal canisters, and I thought it was a weird thing to have in the fridge, so I tossed those, too. I just assumed everything needed to be cleaned out."

The bile is rising. Tears gloss over my eyes. I shake my head. I'm going to pass out. "I have to go."

"Loe."

I hold up my index finger. "Stop talking, Reid." My jaw clenched, I spin on my heel. I don't want to yell at him. It's not his fault, but he'll get the brunt of my anger if he doesn't let me be.

"Chloe!"

Shaking my head, I holler over my shoulder. "Don't follow me, please."

Before he tries holding me back, I rush off, running through the fields, past the poppies and anemones and foxglove. Past the tulips and cosmos and irises. I run until I hit the end of our property line, where I'm completely alone.

When I reach the farthest fence post, I turn and lean against the wood. Sliding down to hide behind the sweet pea grove, I bury my face in my hands and let the tears flow.

My heart sinks, twisting and writhing. All of that work, gone. Months of saving and collecting. Every new variety I cultivated and harvested. Gone. What am I supposed to tell all the promised orders? This pushes us back another year, maybe more.

Full of discouragement, my shoulders shudder as tears fill my palms. I swipe the backs of my fingers across my cheeks and stare at the clouds passing over the sun. Shaking my head, I take deep breaths.

What else is life going to throw at me this year? Next thing I know, Kip is going to tell me Sullivan's land is off the table. Because, why not? Why wouldn't it be?

As though thinking of Kip conjures him up, his gentle voice startles me. "Chloe?"

I gasp and lurch to my feet, wiping excess wetness from my cheeks. With my back to him, I ask, "What are you doing out here, Kip?"

"Would you believe I was walking over to see if you were around?"

Clearing my throat, I face him.

He peers down the fence line to where a gate joins our properties a few yards down. Instead of walking there, Kip jumps the fence. "Hey, what's going on? Why are you crying?"

Blinking, I square my shoulders. "I'm not crying." Not in front of Kip Harris, of all people. He can smell weakness.

"No? I don't see any rain." His gaze raises to the sky before returning to my swollen eyes. He tips my chin. "What's the wet stuff I see on those pretty cheeks of yours?"

I should tear my face from his touch, but I turn my eyes away instead. "Never heard of a flower farmer working with an irrigation system before?"

His fingers brush over a wayward curl escaping my bun. "Huh. Funny how your hair and clothes are completely dry. And if I'm not mistaken, don't you use a drip irrigation system?"

How does he know? "Fine." I sigh. "You caught me, but I was aiming for privacy, in case that wasn't obvious."

His hands slip into his pants pockets, his tan forearms showing beneath his rolled sleeves. Kip steps back. "Then I apologize for interrupting. I was stopping by to let you know I spoke with Melvin Sullivan. He's asked for a little time to decide. He likes your plans for the lot, but he's not the type of man to make hasty decisions. If the timeline is unreasonable for you, I could try helping you find another property or—"

"No. I can wait." With the seeds gone. No need to rush now. I'll have to start over anyway.

He retreats further, then stops. "I… Look, you don't have to confide in me, Chloe, but could you ease my concern and tell me everyone's okay?"

"Physically? Sure." Though my heart has a pretty large chip in it. When I take a deep breath, it quivers. Tears rising again, I swallow them back. "Everyone is fine, but my seeds aren't."

Sucking in a breath through his teeth, Kip says, "Sounds pretty rough. Would knowing I had a crap week, too, help you feel better? Maybe I could sit here and wallow for a while with you? This seems like the perfect spot."

I rest a hand on my hip, leery but caving to his charms. "What are you playing at, Kip?"

"I'm not playing at anything. I know how much joy seeing me strikeout brings you. If I can offer levity, I'll humble myself for your benefit."

Suppressing a grin, I roll my eyes. "Well, you're not wrong." With my back to the fence, I rest my backside there and cross my arms. "Misery does love company."

"As a matter a fact…You know what?" He pauses, his forehead furrowing like he's deep in thought. "Okay, so I have an insane idea. Brynn and I are heading to San Juan Island for the weekend to camp with two of my college buddies who live down in Seattle. Come with us?"

"I'm sorry, what?"

"Camping. You, Brynn, three awesome male specimens." He taps his chest as if to point out he's one of those three specimens, in case I didn't know. I crack a smile, and so does he. "See, I enjoy that look much better than the one caused by the *irrigation system.*"

"You're out of your mind."

"Yeah, yeah. Spare me the details of how the idea of going anywhere with me repulses you. Repulsive or not, Brynn always complains you two never hang out, and I'm not exaggerating when I say I had a week from hell. By the tears on your face, I'd bet you have too."

I *cannot* go with Kip Harris on a weekend getaway. Platonically or not. Where is this even coming from? We've never spent time together for fun, only when forced. Even when we hung out in the same crowds in high school, we were either plotting against one another or avoiding each other.

Getting away doesn't sound horrible right about now. And he did say Brynn would be there, as well as two other guys, so it's not a couples thing. Wait. Olivia won't be there, will she? He didn't say her name, and I do *not* want to ask. Then he'll know Grace told me they were at Fig together, like I care. Which I don't.

But so what if she is? It'd be a weekend for friends. Nothing more. That's perfectly acceptable. Except, no. If Olivia were there I'd be miserable. There are a lot of things I don't want to admit to myself, but I'm not a glutton for punishment after losing my seeds.

As if he knows my mind, Kip says, "Five people, no more. You and Brynn. Me and my two best friends. Nothing crazy."

Am I contemplating this?

Kip dips his head and reels in my wavering gaze. "C'mon, Sunshine. When was the last time you took a moment for you?"

Let me count… Umm… Never? My moments consist of walking in the flower fields at dawn or sunset. There's been no time to go anywhere.

"You can bunk with Brynn. We'll explore the island, sit around the fire. How long has it been since you've been out there?"

One of my shoulders shrugs. "Probably middle school."

"Exactly." A spark ignites in his blue eyes. "What do you say?

Screw it. It's one weekend away. I deserve that much. Even if Kip will be there. San Juan Island is beautiful. I'd be an idiot to turn this down, and getting away from Reid is a good idea. He didn't mean for Tyson to ruin all our hard work, but the disappointment is too fresh. If I stay here, I might pounce in a not-so-good way. "Sure. Why not?"

"Really?" Kips moves swiftly, his arms rising up and toward me like…is he going to hug me? I lean back to avoid an embrace that doesn't come. His hands seemingly stop midway between our bodies and rub together instead.

"We've got a spot booked on the six o'clock ferry. The Harris cab leaves here at four-thirty. All you have to do is grab some clothes and toiletries. Everything else is taken care of. Probably cutting it close, but think you can handle it?"

Four-thirty? Only two hours. I'm not nearly done on the farm yet. The seed fiasco threw me.

Kips glances at the silver watch on his wrist and frowns. "There's a seven-fifty ferry that might have a vehicle reservation spot left. It would get us there around nine. I'm sure Brynn will have no problem waiting if you need more time."

I don't want Brynn waiting around for me. It's not her fault I'm being invited last minute and there's still work to be done. Reid can finish up. After allowing Tyson in my studio and tossing out a year's worth of work, he can do this for me. "No, it's fine. I'll make it work." Even if he puts up a stink.

"Great. Do you want us to swing by the house to pick you up, or would you prefer to meet us at my parents? Considering."

"Oh. I'll come to you guys." I can only imagine the fury on my dad's face if Kip and Brynn Harris showed up on our doorstep, waiting to steal me away for the weekend.

A classic Kipling smirk follows. "Thought so. Okay then, we'll see you in a couple of hours. Be sure to pack warmer stuff for the night and comfortable clothes for a lot of walking in case we want to hike or something and…" he cuts off. "Who am I kidding. You're Chloe Lockwood. I don't have to tell you how to dress."

Whether he meant it as a jab or compliment, I can't tell, but I purse my lips all the same. "I think I'll manage."

Using the fence post as leverage, Kip hops back to his side of the fence effortlessly. "Don't be late, Lockwood."

"I think you have us confused with Harrises. A Lockwood is *never* late."

"Never, huh? I'll hold you to that." He walks backward, watching me for too long. I turn my back and start for the office.

"Oh, and Chloe?" I look over my shoulder. "You won't be sorry you said yes. We'll have a good time, and I promise not to antagonize you beyond reason."

Wanna bet that isn't true?

And why does a thrill surge through me instead of dread?

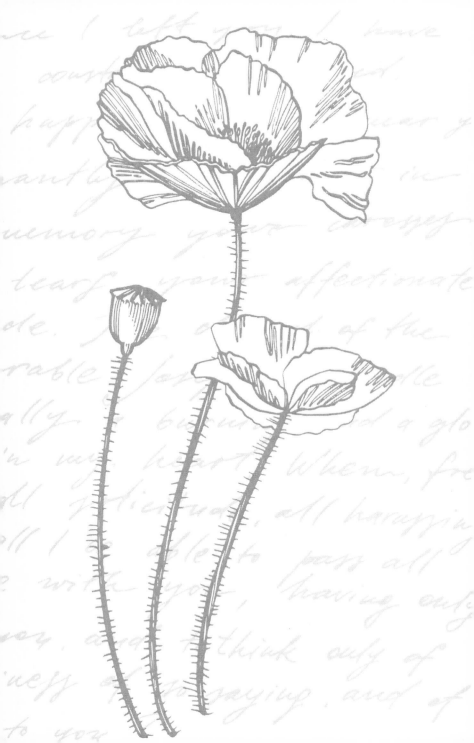

ip

As a kid, I hid on our acreage as a way of dodging my chores. As a teen, I used the land as an escape from Dad. I've always reveled in the freedom of being out here. When Great Grandfather Winthrop Harris Sr., moved to Seaside Pointe in the early 1940s as a newlywed, he bought a version of the house Mom and Dad live in today along with ten acres for farming. Through the years, he purchased more of the surrounding property. As did Grand-daddy Harris. The Harris way of farming and raising livestock as a living was gone around the time Dad was born. Land development and management came next, and more land. The Harris family owns so much of Seaside Pointe I'm astonished Dad's never run for Mayor.

Standing on the back veranda, I can make out the edge of Lockwood Blooms farm. Rows and rows of colorful flowers and the knowledge Chloe Lockwood is likely lost amongst them lures me outside more than I'll admit. Looking over at her land is something I did growing up and something I've done since coming home. Daily. Which is how I wound up standing out back after returning home from the airport. One peek, as is my habit. But today, my sneaking one peek pulled me off the veranda and sent me wandering through our backyard much like I did as a kid. Looking to get lost in the land, even while I was supposed to be packing for a trip for that very purpose. This land is part of my very makeup, like my bones. The more I walk, the more centered I become. It makes sense to wander over to Lockwood's in person. Yes, I could've called, but the prospect of seeing her is too tempting to pass up.

Never would I have considered I'd come across her sitting along the fence, crying her eyes out. And asking her camping? I'd have laughed anyone out of town who would suggest such a thing. Not true. My asking Chloe Lockwood to go away with me isn't a surprise. Chloe's saying yes is what likely has Grandpa Lockwood and Granddaddy Harris rolling in their graves.

BY THE TIME Brynn arrives at the house, I'm as nervous as a teen embarking on his first date. What did I do? Chloe and me, on an island, for forty-something hours?

"Hey there, traveling man," Brynn says when she enters the kitchen. "I packed last night, so let me change and grab my stuff, and we can hit the road."

She knocks into my backside, typical Brynn, and continues by, her heels clicking across the floor. "Kip?"

"Yeah?"

"You're staring out the back window. Everything okay?"

Debatable. "Yeah. My brain is fried, and I'm jet-lagged, but I'm great." Then, in direct opposition to my cheerful statement, I add, "Um, I did something."

Toeing off her heels, Brynn sighs. "Okay. I saw Dad at the

office before I left, so I know you didn't murder him." Her purse hits the counter with a heavy thunk. "Unless there's a hitman."

My sister, the comedian, everyone.

Her breath catches. "You hired a hitman, didn't you? I knew I should have gone to law school. Please tell me he was an expensive one and not one of those 1-800-whack-a—"

"You're not right, sis." I press my tongue against the back of my teeth, holding back a laugh.

"Okay, I'll assume your answer means we're not killing anyone. Good. So, grand theft auto? Embezzlement? Oh, Lord, is someone pregnant?"

"Holy hell, would you shut up?" I snatch a folded dish towel from the counter and toss it at her head. It falls miserably short of my target. Turning from the window, I roll my shoulders and admit, "I invited someone along for the weekend." I fully expect her to assume I'm speaking of Olivia since she's aware of our date.

Cocking her head, she flips her fiery red hair from her face. "You invited someone along?" I grimace as she says each word with purpose. "A female, someone? Because that's not fair, Kip. You can't leave me with Hayden and Bodhi while you…" She trails off, her frown flipping to a gaping grin.

"No, you didn't." Brynn's attention sweeps to the window and back as she hurries to my side. "You asked Chloe?"

Either she took one lucky guess, or…

Through the back window, Chloe traipses across the manicured field toward our house. Holding the straps of her backpack, she peers around almost like she doesn't want to get caught. She traded her overalls for slim jeans and a sweatshirt, her booted feet marching through the grass with purpose. Casual and practical. The way she always is.

Brynn exudes giddiness. "You invited Chloe Lockwood on a weekend away, and she said yes?"

"I did." So help me. "I think I caught her at a weak moment.

She's probably going to get one glimpse at us and turn around, screaming." That is if she makes it far enough to spot us.

Pushing through the back doors, I stand on the veranda as Chloe enters what Mom refers to as her garden. She glances around, stopping once and running her fingers over the soft foliage of a bush I can't name, but I imagine she can. As if she senses my stare, she lifts her head.

"You didn't change your mind." I point out the obvious.

"Oh, I changed my mind lots of times. I just left my house before I could change it again."

Brynn appears at my side. "Well, don't worry, if you come to your senses later, Kip will slow down enough for you to jump out of the car." She hurries down the stone steps.

"I'll be sure to tuck and roll." The corner of Chloe's mouth curves up.

I remain on the upper veranda, following Brynn's movements as she gives Chloe a quick hug and whispers something I wish I could hear. The scene isn't one I ever thought I'd witness. Brynn and Chloe should have been the best of friends growing up. Girls two years apart, living on neighboring properties, attending the same schools. How different would things be if our great-grand-parents' feud never happened?

Brynn leads Chloe through the garden and onto the stone patio, exclaiming how happy she is to have another female joining us. Chloe slows when they reach the stone steps leading where I wait.

"I'll change, and we can get this show on the road," Brynn says, jogging up the steps and jabbing my side as she passes and enters the house.

With what I swear is a deep sigh, Chloe climbs the steps and stops when I block her path to the house. "Hey, again." I search her face for a trace of the tears I saw earlier. "You good?" I reach for her bag.

She waves me off. Either she doesn't trust me or doesn't

understand I'm aiming to be a gentleman. Or both. "I will be. A distraction will help, I think."

"I think you're right. After you." I step aside and watch as she enters my childhood home for the first time ever.

THE DRIVE to Anacortes Ferry Terminal is a little more than thirty minutes to the west. Brynn, who insisted Chloe sit up front, peppers her with questions about the farm and flowers most of the way. I'm grateful. I'm still torn between wondering if this is the smartest move I've ever made or the stupidest. I guess we'll find out in two days.

"Oh, Kip." Brynn smacks the back of my seat. "This is the exit to your new place, right?"

Honing in on our exact whereabouts, I nod.

"Your new place?" Chloe asks.

I open my mouth, but Brynn beats me to the punch. "The jerk found himself a condo to rent so he can get out of our parents' home."

"The jerk"—I find her smug reflection in the rearview mirror —"offered you the second bedroom anytime you need to get away."

Brynn mutters beneath her breath, and I spare a glance at Chloe before returning my focus to the road. "After years on my own, it's difficult adjusting to living under Denton and Mary Harris's roof again. The place is ready now, but I'll probably wait for next weekend to move in."

Chloe messes with the cuffs of her sweatshirt. "I can't say I blame you. I only live with my parents because it's convenient staying so close to the farm. My five-thirty wake-up call comes early. And on delivery days, I should skip sleep altogether."

"Well, this is nothing but a small place over in Bay View. It's only twenty minutes from home and the office, and it'll keep me by the waterfront. The ocean is what I truly missed about living in Oklahoma."

"Besides your favorite sister, of course."

"Of course." I steal another glance at Chloe. She's wearing an amused expression as she peers out the windshield but says nothing. I'm sure as an only child she finds Brynn and my relationship entertaining.

I CONTEMPLATE ENGAGING Chloe in conversation once we're finally on the ferry to San Juan Island. The ride is an hour and would be a good time to set the tone for the weekend. Showing my sincerity toward finding some balance in our relationship would be nice. We don't have to follow in our parents', and their parents', footsteps. We could be friends. Or, at the very least, co-exist without the constant animosity. Working together on the May Day Festival float proved a truce is possible. However, the moment we're settled and on our way, Chloe excuses herself to find the restroom on the boat, and I field two work calls I can't ignore.

By the time I silence my phone and go in search of Chloe, she's made her way to the top deck. I pause near the staircase and watch her as she lifts her face to the sky, shaking her head. Her wild curling hair flies about her face in the wind, and her eyes close as she pulls her feet onto the seat and wraps her arms about her legs.

I can't interrupt her. She's too serene. Too... in the moment. Lost in her thoughts. Or that's how she appears. I comb my fingers through my windblown hair and blend into the crowd, finding a seat where she can't see me keeping an eye on her. A bit creepy, yes, but she's up here alone, and I'm responsible for her this weekend. Though we both know she would deny it.

When we're ten minutes from docking, I head back to the car. What did she tell Reid about this weekend? Is he aware she's with me? Does he care? There's no way in hell I'd want my girl going off on a weekend camping trip with three single guys. Reid likely thinks I'm not a threat. That's the only answer. He knows Chloe has no interest in ever dating me, a Harris, so he isn't concerned about this getaway. He's either confident in their relationship, or she lied about what she was doing. Since I've never known Chloe Lockwood to be a liar, the former must be true.

Chloe and Brynn find their way to the vehicle as we're docking in Friday Harbor. In twenty minutes, I'll be sitting around a campfire with my best friends, drinking a beer and letting go of all the stress eating away at me these days. The riverfront project, Tulsa, Old Man Sullivan, Dad, even my confusing entanglements with Chloe Lockwood. Nothing matters for the rest of the weekend but having a good time.

"Hey." I greet Chloe when she slips in the front seat less than a minute after Brynn climbs into the back. "I sent the guys a text. Hayden has dinner ready and waiting," I focus on Brynn as I speak. I'm resolved to give Chloe space. It's a new resolution. Only about two minutes old, but I need to keep this one.

"Ohh, good. I'm starving." Brynn digs into her bag and pulls out a brush. "Turn on the heater? I'm frozen."

"Your wish is my command, Your Highness." I turn the temperature setting lower and flick on the seat warmers. They won't help Brynn, but Chloe and I should be nice and toasty soon.

"I'm glad I trained you so well when we were little."

"Be nice, sis. It'll be three against one this weekend. You know my guys won't hesitate to help me bury a body."

Chloe's face scrunches up. "So, tell me about these guys. They're friends from college?"

"Oh, yeah. I guess that would be nice to know, huh?" I pull off the ferry and turn left toward the campgrounds.

Brynn chuckles in the back seat. "Chloe Lockwood, are you telling me you agreed to accompany my brother on a weekend away without the barest of details about who's coming and what we'll be doing?"

"I was in distress."

"I'm honestly shocked you didn't leap off the ferry when it all sunk in. I kept watch, just in case." I curse the moment I say the words. *Teasing her isn't giving her space, Kip. And telling her you watched her wasn't part of the plan, either.*

"I thought about it, but the water's too cold." There's a trace of a smirk on her face as she deadpans, "I weighed my options very carefully. The farther we went, the less appealing bailing sounded. It's a long swim back."

Brynn forms a heart with her fingers in the mirror, and I choke. Chloe looks back in time to see my meddling sister brushing her hair like an innocent angel. I might kill her before the night is through.

"Thank you for staying put. I'm not any more fond of swimming in cold water than you are. If you jumped, I'd have been forced to go in after you. Talk about a way to ruin the weekend."

Chloe eyes me, and I get the feeling she's uncomfortable. I'm not flirting. Am I? A protectiveness overtakes me when she's around. Something kicks in when I'm considering the well-being of a girl I've known my entire life. Feud or not. Before leaving Seaside, I'm not sure if I ever went more than three days max without seeing her. Holidays and vacations don't count.

Mentally shaking my head, I answer her earlier question. "So, Hayden and Bodhi. Yes, we went to school at Oklahoma. Roomed together, actually. Hayden's twenty-eight, so he was ahead of us, but Bodhi is the same year we are. I promise they're not maniacs or whatever else Brynn might say later when I'm not around to defend them."

"Ha. Ha." Brynn mocks. "I can't speak for Hayden because we only met once, and there was drinking, and football, and some brunette biker chick involved. Bodhi, though, so cute, Chloe. And super funny."

Chloe taps her chin. "Are you interested in either of them?"

"Nah, there was this one time in college. It was a phase." I wink.

Chloe chokes on a laugh, swatting my shoulder, and I almost miss turning into our campground.

"They're too good for him," Brynn chimes in. "And no, I'm not interested in either of them. I'm not interested in a relationship with anything other than chocolate and my television. I'm still pathetically licking my wounds from the last man."

My fingers strangle the steering wheel at the mention of douchebag Preston.

"It's his loss," Chloe says.

"Damn right," I mutter too low for Brynn's ears, but I catch Chloe's side-eye. If she only knew Brynn's whole story. No one, other than our family and the d-bag himself, does. No one deserves a break as much as Brynn.

Driving through winding roads shaded with towering trees, we turn off the road and pull up to a relatively secluded camping spot beside Bodhi's black SUV. My breath hitches at the sight of two canvas cabins illuminated by the last of the setting sun sitting at the water's edge. Like the flick of a switch, I'm lighter. Smelling the musk of a campfire before my door opens, I waggle my brows at Chloe and Brynn and hop out—more than ready for this weekend to officially start.

Leaving our bags in the car, we skirt between the cabins toward the smoke wafting into the tree limbs overhead.

"Hayden's the one covered in ink. Bodhi's the one playing with the fire." I point out before the guys spot us. "They'll probably want to get you drunk and be a nuisance, so buckle up, buttercup."

"I honestly wouldn't hate drinking into oblivion right about now." Chloe laughs.

Oh, how I'd love for Chloe Lockwood to let loose and not

care about anyone else's opinion for once. "That can be arranged, Sunshine. You help yourself."

"I just might."

Shouts from the firepit keep me from saying more. Eager to greet Hayden and Bodhi, I head their way as Brynn throws her arm around Chloe's shoulders. "Don't worry, I've got your back."

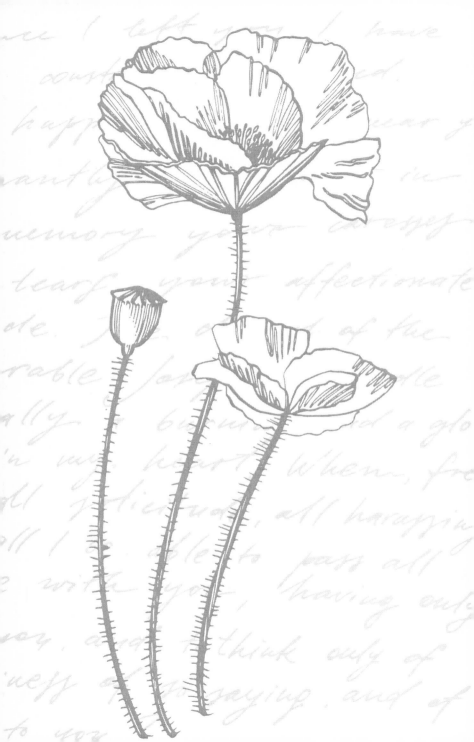

hloe

GLAMPING. I was not expecting that, but it's something I can get on board with. Rather than tents, there are two large canvas cabins side-by-side with long wooden steps leading up to them. The flaps are tied back, and inside I spot actual beds. I'd planned on my sleeping bag, but I guess I'll be sharing a bed with Brynn tonight. It will definitely up our familiarity with one another.

Brynn and I follow behind Kip over the gravel to the campfire as he greets his buddies with pushing and slaps on the back. Try as I might, I can't keep my eyes from roaming over him in his faded jeans and fitted thermal. Glamping or not, the outdoors is meant for grungy clothes and unkempt hair. Kip didn't get the memo, but I can't say I'm mad about it. He's still in sensible attire, but the man knows how to dress. When you come from money, I guess having a fashion sense comes with the territory.

The guys howl with laughter as Brynn and I enter the circle made by the chairs around the firepit. Kip shoves his friends away, directing a curse at them before he turns toward us. "Hayden, Bodhi, you know Brynn, but this tagalong is Chloe."

"As in Lockwood?" The one not covered in tattoos arches a brow over eyes that look an icy gray in the firelight. Bodhi.

It's impossible to stifle my exasperated sigh. "Our notorious feud has spread. Lovely. Hi." I wave, offering my most polite smile, hoping to squash whatever preconceived notions they have of me. "It's nice to meet you."

If Reid saw these guys, he wouldn't only be losing his mind over Kip, he'd be pissed I was camping with all three of them. Bodhi and Hayden can't even be classified as attractive or decent-looking. They're built and *gorgeous*. Men that could easily snatch women's attention and hearts in seconds.

Not mine, of course, but some other girls.

Though, honestly, right now, I don't care what Reid thinks. I couldn't bring myself to care when his jaw clenched and his eyes narrowed after I told him what I was doing this weekend. He's not the type to expect me to ask permission, but he definitely wanted a say-so. I understood, I did, but he shut up real quick when angry tears welled in my eyes. This isn't about retaliation or making Reid feel bad for his mistake. This is about me taking my mind off a disheartening blow. A weekend away from the farm, from him, from everything, is what I need to clear my head and return refreshed with a new game plan.

Intricate tattoos peek out of the neckline of Hayden's dark gray shirt, and while his arms are covered in an army green utility jacket, I assume from the black ink also creeping onto the tops of his hands and fingers, his arms are covered as well. But his light eyes and the smooth features of his face soften the contrast of the black ink.

Bodhi might not have tattoos, but he's no less intimidating. With his bright white smile and broad shoulders, it's possible he's a giant teddy bear, but there's enough mischief in his eyes to tell me these two can be a lot of trouble.

Compared to Kip's friends in high school, some of which I dated, these two don't strike me as guys he'd normally hang out with. He had a lot of jock and pretty boy friends back in the day. These guys don't fit those molds. Which begs the question, what is Tulsa Kip like?

"Well, aren't you a ray of sunshine." Hayden winks, his words laced with a thick and not unbecoming rasp.

I'm feeling a little bit less like sunshine and more like a dark rain cloud at the moment, but sure. I keep my smile and tuck my hands in my back jean pockets.

"It's good to finally meet you, Chloe." Bodhi's grin stretches like he has a secret.

Finally? How long have these guys known about me? I'm sure they know all about the Harris side of the story, but right now, I don't have the strength to stand up for the Lockwood side.

Brynn abandons me, walking toward the guys as Hayden leaves the firepit. She throws herself at Bodhi, his arms reeling her in tight as he presses his mouth to her ear and whispers words only meant for her. Curious what that's about, I sneak a glance at Kip to gauge his reaction. He's standing to the side, rubbing the back of his neck, his jaw tense. Like he senses someone watching, Kip turns and waves me over to the waiting wooden chairs around the fire pit.

Hayden reappears and tosses Kip a beer before handing one to Brynn once Bodhi's done with her. Thanking him, she tucks her red hair behind her ear and kicks at the ground with the toe of her sneaker, and now I'm interested in the dynamics of these guys and Kip's sister. Sneaking a second peek at Brynn, Hayden sidles up and offers me one too, and while I hate the taste of beer, I'm not much of a drinker, I accept. Anything to mask my sorrows.

Kip pulls up an extra chair from around an unused fire pit since they weren't expecting me and offers me the seat. I murmur thanks and sit. While my guard is still up, I could get used to this well-mannered Kip.

I half-expect him to plop down in the seat next to me, but instead, he moves to the opposite side of the fire and lowers beside Hayden. Bodhi takes the empty chair on one side of me while Brynn settles into the other.

We eat the hotdogs the guys roasted and had ready for us. While they tell stories and laugh, joking about the good ole days, I quietly observe. Kip is still the self-assured guy from our youth, but he's matured into a laid-back man. His cocky, smug attitude has turned into cool confidence. And as the fire licks the darkness, I can't keep my eyes off him.

The combination of his five o'clock shadow over his freckles along his sculpted jaw and the perfected-disheveled waves of his hair—Kip Harris is irritatingly more handsome than he was in high school.

"So," Bodhi leans back in his chair, resting his ankle on his knee, "The infamous Chloe Lockwood."

I release a breath and roll my eyes. "I can only imagine what Kip has told you, but there are two sides to every story."

Kip's head turns our way, proving he's been monitoring me. His words further confirm my suspicion. "In our case, I think there are more like ten sides, but I'm all ears, Lockwood, share your side."

Brynn sinks into her chair with a groan.

"Where would you like me to start?" My arm crosses my chest, holding up my elbow with my bottle of beer, and I smirk. "With your great uncle who released a fox in our hen house. Or your grandpa who stole my grandad's prom date. We could go all night, Kipling."

"How about we start with the basic history for these two. They know nothing."

I cock an eyebrow. *Nothing, huh?* And yet, *I'm* infamous.

Kip ignores me. "Chloe's great-grandpa lived in Seaside

Pointe first. Owned the same land her family owns today. My great grandparents bought our house and around ten acres a year or two later. By all accounts, they were friendly."

"At first," I say.

Kip grunts. "Yes, at first. Because in typical Harris fashion, Great Grandpa started buying the land around him."

"You mean, he started hogging the land around him? Did they even live there for more than a few years before he tripled his property?"

Kip eyes me across the flames with a smirk. "Seeing as how he had the money, and buying land isn't illegal, I don't understand the issue."

"Other than buying the land just to buy it. Tell me, please. Does your family still use your property to provide for their family? Or do they just let the land sit untended?"

"Well, it does get great use as a dog park. Or don't you remember?" Kip brings his drink to his mouth.

Even if I wanted to, "Couldn't always control Daisy." I shrug. "She was just using land she thinks should've been hers."

Brynn's forehead ruffles as she looks between the two of us.

"So help me, Chloe, if I ever walk outside to find you marking our yard…" He shakes his head, nearly spilling his beer.

Taking a swig of my drink, I say, "How do you know I haven't already?" My teeth sink into my bottom lip to stifle a laugh.

"Oh my word, you two. Get back to the story before I tell it, and you know I don't have the details right," Brynn says.

"Do either of them?" Hayden asks with a deep chuckle.

At the same time, Kip and I answer, "Yes!"

Our gazes hold, challenging, and I almost crack a smile, but I suppress the urge. Kip continues, "Fast forward fifteen years or so. Our grandfathers were actually friends, in spite of the animosity between their dads. So, here's the story." He leans forward. "Winthrop Jr., my grandpa, and Eugene Lockwood came back from swimming in the river one day. This everyone agrees on."

As much as I hate to, I nod.

"They jumped the fence on our property and walked to the Lockwood's, going through the gate connecting our two properties, but they left it open. The same gate is there today, by the way. The boys went inside for some reason. I think that part is up for debate," he says offhandedly. "This is where the fun started. While the boys were inside, a trip of my great grandpa's goats made their way into Lockwood's farm, trampling and eating their flowers."

"Which my great-grandpa had planted the previous year to establish the beginning of Lockwood Blooms," I interject.

"Whatever, Sunshine." Kip dismisses me with a wave of his hand. He's lucky I'm not beside him because he would've been awarded a sore shoulder or smashed toe. "Anyway, Eugene's mom ran outside yelling for the boys, and they spent hours wrangling the goats. By the time they fixed the mess, they'd missed the fact that Lockwood's bull had snuck onto our property and was having himself a grand old time with the ladies."

"Not our fault Winthrop Jr. didn't close the gate. Maybe if he had, Lockwood Blooms wouldn't have lost out on years of progress, and our bull wouldn't have impregnated your cattle."

"It's cute how you Lockwoods still blame Winthrop for not closing *your* gate."

"Well, the last person through the gate is typically the one who does it, don't you think?"

"Hold up," Hayden sits forward. "Your bull knocked up one of Harris's cows?"

"Two of our cows." Kip holds his fingers, and Hayden and Bodhi burst into laughter.

"I'm sorry, Chloe, you know I think this feud stuff is ridiculous, but how do you know who went through the gate last?" Kips asks, the firelight flicking across his face.

"My dad told me, as his dad told him." And as I say it out loud, I'm embarrassed. The feud began over something so ridiculous.

Kip stretches his legs in front of him and sits deeper in his chair. "Did he also tell you about how they tried to get my great grandparents to pay for their breeding services?"

Bodhi grunts. "Now, that's something you never hear about. The ladies paying the men for being a baby daddy."

"Shut up," Brynn says.

After swallowing the last of my beer, I say, "I'm not saying my family is without faults but wasn't your great-grandpa the one who retaliated first?"

Kip looks at me as the others continue making absurd jokes about calf daddies. Our eyes meet over the fire, and there's a moment where we stare. One second, two. Then he grins. And dang it, I can't stop myself from grinning back.

"It's pretty ridiculous, isn't it?" he asks, and the others seem to disappear. "A gate left open by two friends escalated a sixty-year feud with ruined pies, and bragging rights, and grudges."

I shake my head. "One retaliation needing to outdo the last, and here we are." My hand presents the forest.

"Two Harrises and a Lockwood camping together."

A short, low chuckle leaves Hayden. "Damn, Brynn, make sure you don't forget to close the tent tonight. We don't want Kip looking for breeding retaliation."

Out of the corner of my eye, I catch Brynn fake-puking while Kip sucker punches his best friend in the bicep.

"She wishes she could be so lucky," Kip says.

He's lucky my aim is terrible, or my empty bottle would wind up clocking him in the head. Instead, I set it on the ground and say, "Maybe you need to make sure your tent is closed. The woods are perfect for burying a body."

"I'm not touching that with a ten-foot pole." Kip stands. "Anyone need another drink?"

The boys wave empty bottles. I shouldn't, so I'm not going to. Being a lightweight, I have a good enough buzz, and I'd rather not wake up with a hangover in the morning.

Brynn stands and stretches. "I think I'm turning in. You boys are going to revert to college antics at any moment, and I'm not sure I can handle the chaos tonight." The guys grumble about her being a party pooper, and she flips them off. "You coming, Chloe, or are you taking your chances with these degenerates."

"I think I've had enough fun for the night. This early riser is ready for bed."

"Hold up, we left our bags in the car." Kips hands a beer off to Hayden and Bodhi before heading for the car.

"Oh good, grab ours, would you, baby brother?" Brynn sings from the porch of our cabin.

"It's okay." I follow Kip, not wanting him to do me any favors. "I'll get mine, so I can get yours, too."

We walk through the dark to the car without a word. Kip pops the back hatch and swings the strap of his bag over his shoulder before grabbing Brynn's.

"I can take it to her." I reach for Brynn's bag, but he keeps hold of it.

The car's dome light illuminates his face enough to distinguish his tight features. "About what Hayden said." He toys with the strap of his bag. "I...I don't know if I should apologize to you or what. They like to give me a hard time. I respect that you're with Reid."

Hayden's comment isn't the one that bothered me, which is telling, but I'm not going to dissect those feelings while I'm buzzed and tired and in the middle of a mini-crisis.

I swat the air. "He saw an opening for a perfectly timed joke and took it. It's fine."

"I'll get him back eventually." Mischief makes his face younger. Just as fast, the expression disappears. "Look, retelling the feud story got me thinking. We don't have to relive our family history, you know? We could put the feud behind us."

"Lofty goal, don't you think?" My head cants.

Kip shrugs. "I'm up for the challenge. We could bet on it, for old times' sake."

"A bet, huh?" How would we determine the winner? First one to sling mud loses?

"I don't want to keep fighting with you, Chloe." There's an earnestness about him.

"So, you want to be friends?" Kip and I have been at odds for so long, it's hard to believe we could get along. I want to, but could peace be that easy?

"You've got to know I could never dislike you simply because our grandparents couldn't settle an argument about a damn gate being left open."

A chuckle falls from my lips. "It was never about the gate but a culmination of things. Loyalty to family, all the retaliations, you know." I shrug.

"We've done a lot of crap to each other through the years, but I think we're both too busy to keep carrying their issues on our backs. I dunno. I'd like to be cordial. Maybe we can use this weekend as a fresh beginning. Plus, Brynn could use a friend."

"So really, this is all about Brynn?" I can't help but poke.

"Absolutely."

After everything we've done to each other, do I want to be cordial with Kip? And is he being earnest in his desire to put everything behind us, or is he looking for a way to turn the tables on me in true Harris style?

And gain what by being nice? A friend? All right. Amicable with another Harris. I can do that. I hold out my hand. "Friends?"

He drops Brynn's bag in my hand instead but softens the blow, bumping into my side. "Friends."

We walk back to the campsite with only the glow of the fire

to guide us. Bodhi and Hayden lean into each other, chuckling as they say things too low for me to hear.

"Goodnight, guys."

At the same time, Bodhi says, "Goodnight, Chloe," Hayden calls, "Night, Sunshine." And his ray of sunshine comment becomes a little clearer. Did he know Kip's nickname for me before tonight?

With my first step up to the canvas cabin, I check over my shoulder. Kip's eyes are on me, his bag still over his shoulder as he pauses at the base of my tent cabin, and my heart jumps. It shouldn't, but it does all the same.

I offer a meek smile and another goodnight.

He says, "Night," with a wink. And I hate myself a little more for the flutters wreaking havoc on my stomach.

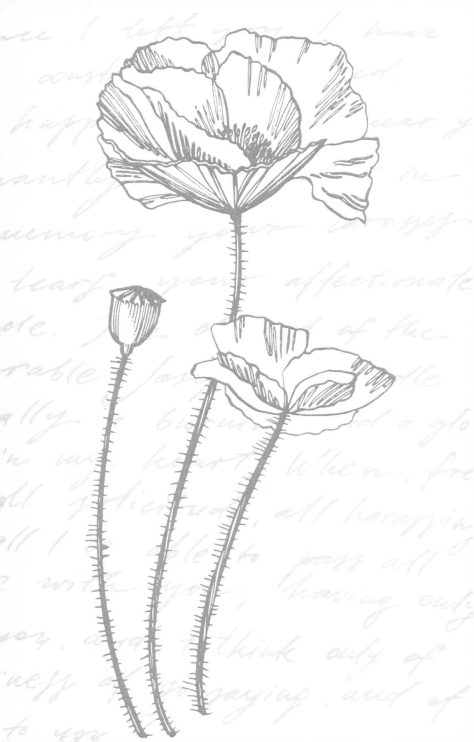

 ip

I'M STOKING the embers from last night's fire, getting the little heat stirred to a flame when the crunch of gravel announces I'm not alone. I didn't expect anyone else this early, considering how late we stayed up.

"Morning," I call out without looking.

"Morning."

Chloe.

I lift my coffee mug, buying time. Time to peek over the rim and admire her messy bun and fresh face. Time to settle the acceleration of my pulse. Something shifted between us last night. The change manifested in her final smile before she disappeared into the cabin with Brynn. From foes to friends. I grin as her hands slip inside the sleeves of her hoodie, and she wraps her arms around her waist.

"Nice sweatshirt."

"Just a little flower humor." She releases a small chuckle.

"I wish I could order karma like flowers and have it delivered," I read the script written across her chest out loud. "Should I be worried?"

"Around a Lockwood?" Chloe smirks. "Always."

"Not even eight hours and the truce crumbles."

Her head falls back with a soft laugh. "Anyone else up?"

"This early, not in a million years." Brynn would sleep half the day if we let her, and after the drinks we downed last night while hanging out, I expect Hayden or Bodhi won't be up any time soon.

"And yet, you managed to come out unscathed this morning, waking up before everyone?"

"I guess we know who the real man is."

"Yeah, that's it." She humors me and points to the mug in my hands. "I don't suppose you know where I can get one of those."

"Sure do. I'll pour you a cup." I move toward the picnic table, and she follows. After digging out a tin mug from the plastic bin we store our campfire supplies in, I slide the bin toward her. "I drink mine black, but Brynn's a coffee snob. We've got some flavored creamers and sugar in there if you prefer." I explain, pouring her coffee from the fresh pot I made when I woke.

After adding sugar, Chloe pours in the hazelnut creamer and asks, "So, what's the plan for the day?"

"We didn't devise any major plans for this weekend. We booked a whale watching trip, but that's not until five o'clock. I called yesterday and added you to our party."

"Whale watching?"

Topping my coffee, I chuckle. It's a given the three men in our party do not seem the type. "It was Brynn's one requirement, but don't let Bodhi fool you. He was all in. He's a true ocean lover, as is Hayden. Really, we're all partial to the water."

With a smirk, she lifts her coffee and inhales. Her brown eyes close as she enjoys her first sip, and the temptation to move closer has me stepping back. There isn't much difference between the Chloe standing before me and the Lockwood Blooms Chloe I run into in Seaside. Same wild hair, same beautiful face with the light freckles scattered over the bridge of her nose and peppering her cheeks. Same girl I've known my entire life, but the backdrop is different. There's no audience. No one to gossip about a Harris and Lockwood making nice, and that… damn, that awareness makes the forbidden tempting as hell.

I return to the fire instead. *She's with Reid. Period.* Dropping a new log on top of the low-burning flame, I stare out over the water.

Chloe joins me by the fire. "So, a lazy day? Sounds refreshing."

"You don't get many of them, do you?" I turn and toe the leg of the nearest chair closer. "Have a seat."

Chloe sits, and while Reid's name marches through my mind, I drag a second chair closer to hers.

"I don't let myself. There's a lot to be done for the business. My parents don't take breaks, so why should I?" She blows on her coffee before taking another sip. "And truthfully, I don't mind most of the time. Being out in those fields is my favorite thing to do."

Telling people how much she loves her life isn't necessary. Happiness radiates from within when she discusses Lockwood Blooms. A vision of a little girl running between rows of flowers, the sunlight bouncing off her wild hair, assaults me. *Sunshine.*

"You stuck your tongue out at me." I laugh into my mug at the unexpected memory.

"I what?"

"When we were kids. I was riding my bike through the mud on our property after a rainstorm. You know, being generally cool like I always was." She rewards my wink with a hard roll of her eyes. "I spotted you on the edge of your fields. You skidded to a halt when you saw me watching. I swear you must have thought I was a rabid beast the way you stared with your eyes bulging. Then you cocked your head, shoved your hair from your face, and stuck your tongue out at me."

A full grin stretches across her face as she hides a chuckle behind the rim of her mug. "I remember, actually. I wanted to think of something intimidating to say, but you made me so nervous, I stuck out my tongue instead."

"Then you took off running like you were afraid I'd chase after you."

"You were a boy on a bike, and I was a girl surrounded by flowers. My defenses were minimal."

I can't stifle my laughter. Her parents must have warned her from Brynn and me the same way our dad did her. It took until our teens for us to be civil. We screwed that up, too.

"I don't know, Sunshine. I think you scared that boy pretty good back in the day." She terrifies the man well enough.

Our muted laughter gives way to the nature surrounding us. The gurgle of the water running by, a hawk circling overhead. Sinking deeper in my seat, I stretch my legs and relax. I could sit here all day, with this peace and her company. I covertly watch Chloe. She's studying the flames growing taller in the pit. Her long fingers, free of nail polish, unlike Brynn's, are wrapped around her mug as it rests on the knee she's drawn into her chest. She seems lost in thought, so I let her be until I can't.

"Have you ever stopped and wondered, how in the hell did I end up like my parents?" Her brows furrow, and I rush on. "I don't mean my question as a knock to your family. I'm speaking about my life, too. As much as I wanted not to be Denton Harris, here I am."

The corner of her mouth pinches as she turns her head, staring out at the lake. "You're nothing like Denton." Her voice is soft. "I don't know. There are some things I wish I'd done differently, but since my father's stroke, as horrible as it was, it's helped me come into my own. To implement things in the business I might not have yet." Drifting her attention back to me, she says, "Sure, I haven't left Seaside, and I probably never will, but this is a good, honest life, and I'm happy."

"It's a great life, and from what I've seen you've got the business running better than ever. I'm not surprised, but I am curious." I pause, unsure if I should open a possible can of worms when we're both enjoying this moment. "If you're so happy, what made you so upset yesterday you were willing to come here with us?"

"I guess I could ask you the same thing. If you think Seaside is so great, why did you leave?"

"Ha. Touché, Miss Lockwood." I hold my coffee mug out between us and wait. Smiling when no more than a second passes before she reciprocates—our tin cups clinking in cheers. "What do you say we start breakfast for the lazy people?" An understanding passes between us.

"Change of subject. Great idea."

I grab the bin of cooking utensils Hayden brought from home off our cabin's porch and set up a kitchen space on the picnic table.

"Funny, I always thought camping was cast iron skillets over a fire and all that rustic stuff." Chloe points out when I plug our griddle into an extension cord.

"I'll have you know we've made many trips without electricity and beds. Primitive camping is an experience, but I'm not ashamed to admit I prefer this glamping life more. And"—I dig into the bin of supplies—"we do have a skillet. You do the bacon, and I do pancakes?"

We prepare breakfast side by side, taking turns egging each other on playfully.

"You shouldn't flip them until there are more bubbles forming," she informs me when batter splatters off my spatula as I turn the first pancake.

"Hey, mind your bacon. I know how to cook pancakes. This is the tester." I point at the sizzling pan. "Don't forget to pour the grease out, so you don't get burned."

"I think I can fry bacon without your help, Mr. Know It All."

When she yelps five minutes later, jerking her hand into her stomach, I can't help looking down my nose at her. "Told you to empty the grease."

"Give me another I told you so, Kipling. I dare you." She winces.

"Let me see." I pry her hand from her chest.

"Don't touch it." She sucks in a breath when my thumb smooths over the red welt on the web of skin between her thumb index finger. At my touch, she flinches and attempts wrestling away.

"Oh, sorry." I keep my grip and dig into the supply box for the burn medicine. "This isn't my first bacon grease injury." I pop off the top of a spray can.

"I can do it."

"You can." I tug on her arm, drawing her away from the food. "But I want to," I say before giving her hand two shots of the numbing spray.

Chloe releases a squeak. The spray is cold and stings. I've had reason to use it many times on others and myself, so I raise her hand to my lips and blow.

Her breath catches. I wouldn't have noticed if I weren't so clued in to everything she does. Chloe's fingers curl into a fist, and I keep my eyes on the welt, too much a coward to check her face for her reaction.

I release her hand and meet her gaze. "After breakfast would you be up for a trip with me? I have something I want to show you."

She pauses, staring at me. "Just you and me?"

"You two what?" Chloe and I jump at Brynn's voice.

"Damn, do you have stealth-mode on or what?" I glare at Brynn and bend down to pick up the spatula I dropped while Chloe puts a step between us.

"When have you ever known me to be stealthy? Don't blame me for the two of you being all lost in whatever was going on here." She waves her hand between Chloe and me.

"I burnt myself." Color blooms up Chloe's neck.

"Ignore her. She's a witch before her coffee." I swat at Brynn, who flips me off. "What's going on here is we *were* cooking you lazy asses breakfast. I'm not so sure you deserve any."

"You'd deny me bacon?" Brynn's eyes go round. I send her a silent warning. *Lay off the Kip and Chloe kissing in a tree act.*

"Fine." She huffs, procuring a mug from the bin. "I'm on my best behavior, I promise."

"Chloe and I were talking about what to do this morning and afternoon. She hasn't been out here since middle school."

Brynn snags a slice of bacon from the stack Chloe made on a plate. "I'm up for whatever."

Hayden and Bodhi's deep voices travel across our site, alerting us they're awake, much earlier than I expected.

"Hey, what kind of trouble are you three cooking up over there?" Bodhi's voice draws Brynn's attention as she stirs creamer into her coffee.

Witnessing the drop of her jaw, I turn back to the cabin in time to see Hayden tug a shirt over his head. *Really dude? You had to come out like Tarzan?* Thankfully, Chloe is distracted with the job of flipping the last of the bacon, so she can't be dazzled by the colorful artwork covering my best friend's abs.

"Pick your tongue up off the ground, sis."

Sending me a sneer and sparing Chloe a smile when she looks between the guys and us with confusion on her face, Brynn spins toward the cabins and answers Bodhi's question. "I think we're going on an island field trip."

In typical Hayden fashion, he shrugs, though I don't miss the way his gaze touches on Brynn before sliding my way.

"I'm up for anything." Bodhi hops off the cabin's deck and makes a beeline for us. "As long as you give me coffee first."

Stacking the last of the pancakes on a plate, I turn to Chloe. "I guess it'll be all of us."

Chloe nods, a flicker of something disappearing from her eyes before I can pinpoint the emotion. "I'm just along for the ride."

IT'S NEARING lunch by the time we eat, clean up, and head out. Our destination isn't far, and Brynn keeps us engaged with her story about seeing a snake slithering under their cabin earlier.

"One of you guys is inspecting our room before I step foot in there again. What's the saying? How to tell if a snake is poisonous?" No one answers. "Oh, come on, you know it, Kip. The colors. Red with…" Brynn snaps her fingers, her face flushed as the others chuckle.

"Red touches yellow, kills a fellow. Red touches black—"

"Friend to Jack," Brynn finishes in tandem with Hayden's thicker voice. "Yes, that's it. Thank you."

Checking the rearview mirror, I spy the hint of amusement shining in his eyes as he looks at Brynn. "There are no poisonous snakes here, but I'll check for you when we get back. Relax, okay."

"I know I sound like a raving lunatic, but I'm terrified of snakes."

"We're all scared of something, right, Bodhi?"

Bodhi curses and Hayden's deep laughter echoes through my Audi.

Chloe's been twisted in her seat talking with the others the entire ride, but as Brynn pits my best friends against each other and attempts coercing them into revealing their fears, Chloe twists back in her seat and faces forward.

"So, what are you scared of, Kip Harris?"

Verifying we aren't the focus of the occupants stuffed in the back seat, I shift sideways in my seat and lean my elbow on the middle console. Chloe edges toward me as I lower my head, keeping my eyes on the road at all times. "Ask me when we're alone sometime." My request is soft, so only her ears pick up on it. Straightening, I dare one glance her way. "Okay?"

Her teeth grab her bottom lip, tugging it into her mouth. Her reply is breathless, "Okay."

Less than three minutes later, I'm tapping my thumbs against the steering wheel, anticipation eating away at me, when the first flash of purple comes into view in the distance.

Chloe perks up in the seat beside me. "Are we going to the lavender fields?"

Of course she's heard of this place. "Yep. This morning I remembered seeing it when I researched the area for things to do."

She tilts her head. "I thought there were no plans for the weekend?"

Brynn snorts and sticks her head into the space between our seats. "Never let my brother's relaxed demeanor fool you, Chloe. The man has lists for his lists."

"You've got that right. He used to make grocery lists when we roomed together." Hayden chimes in, and Chloe laughs.

I grit my teeth. "That's a normal human thing to do, jackass."

"Dude, remember the time he was headed out the door to grab dinner stuff, and I asked him to get cookies—"

"And he didn't buy them because it wasn't on the list?" Brynn finishes for Bodhi, her voice deep like she's imitating mine. "I've had the same experience."

Driving this vehicle into the water to our left sounds like a plan; if only I weren't worried about Chloe and myself.

"When we were lab partners our sophomore year, he made detailed spreadsheets for me with all of my responsibilities. I thought he was just particular about his grade, but listening to you all…"

My head snaps to Chloe, who bites back her laughter. "Seriously? You're hitching your wagon to those degenerates?" Shaking my head, I give her a side-eye. "Your betrayal is a sharp knife in my back, Chloe Lockwood."

I hit the volume on the radio until music drowns out their laughter.

AFTER PARKING, Brynn and Chloe walk toward the farm side by side as I give my best friends a hard time.

"Fair warning, a day will come when you two want to make a good impression on someone, and I am not holding back. This game goes both ways."

Bodhi wags his brows. "So, you admit you're making a move?"

I admire Chloe and Brynn ahead of us. Their heads are so close, Chloe's golden brown waves meld into Brynn's smooth red tresses as Chloe points something out in the distance. "I told you she's seeing someone."

"She fits you," Hayden says with sincerity. Bodhi agrees.

I don't disagree, but say, "A few hours around the two of us does not give you an accurate picture of what things are typically like between us."

"I think we've seen all we need to," Bodhi says. "Plus, you know what they say, making up is the best part."

"Hell yeah." Hayden looks ahead, then punches my arm and tips his head to where Chloe stands in awe as she peers out at the fields. Flashing me an encouraging grin, his long legs eat the distance between the girls and us, and he snags Brynn's hand, pulling her toward the right.

Bodhi slaps me on the back. "No worries, I'll be sure he behaves himself." He hurries after them.

I stop beside Chloe and follow her gaze to where acres upon acres of bright green foliage and purple blanket the landscape framed by a lake and Mount Olympic in the background. I didn't expect them to be so in bloom this early in the spring, but a mild winter must have helped.

Chloe takes a deep breath, inhaling the floral scent in the air. "I've been meaning to come out here for years, but it just never happened."

"When I remembered it, I realized I couldn't skip the chance to take the flower girl to the flowers."

It's hard to tear my eyes off the serene set of her features. "You pegged me right, but I suppose that's not hard to do."

"You wanna explore?" Her face glows with eagerness. "Come on." I snatch her hand and lead her left. Yeah, we're going in the opposite direction of the others. They'll be fine without us.

"So, where do your parents think you are this weekend?"

Chloe lets out a humorless laugh. "They know I'm camping. They think I'm camping alone."

The warmth of her palm in mine is a reminder of who I should ask about. Drawing a breath, I risk upsetting this moment. "And Reid? What does he think?"

"To say he wasn't happy is an understatement." She releases a heavy sigh. "He knows I'm here with you and Brynn, but after our afternoon, he sort of had to accept it."

I release her hand and stop. That wasn't a 'we broke up' and I shouldn't be holding her hand. It was a reflex to reach for her in the first place, and she didn't seem to mind, but still.

"Chloe."

She touches my forearm, stopping me. "How about we don't

talk about Reid or the farm or Seaside right now? Let's enjoy the rest of the day, yeah?"

"Yeah, of course. You know I saw online they do demonstrations somewhere around here to show the diversity with lavender, and they have an on-site oil distillery."

"Now you're speaking my language, Kipling."

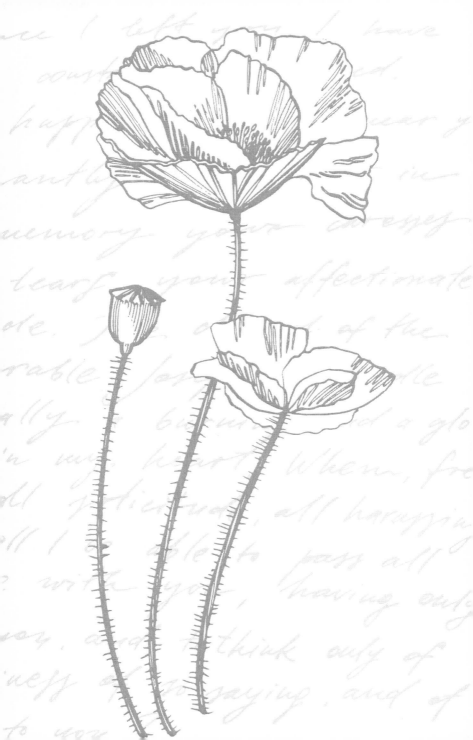

hloe

As we meander through the lavender fields, an irrational part of me wants Kip's hand back. He was right to let go of mine. I should've been the one to remove it first. I don't know what I was thinking.

Actually, yes, I do. There was something right about how my hand fit in his. In a way it's never felt in Reid's grasp. Which is crazy; this is Kip Harris I'm talking about. Maybe we've had a moment or two in the past, but nothing that could be lasting. Nothing that wouldn't be trampled by the feud—truce or not.

And he was only holding my hand to tug me into the fields, so I don't know why I'm even having this conversation with myself.

It didn't mean anything. It didn't.

While we might not hold hands, Kip and I still walk side-by-side, taking in the landscape. Our fingers occasionally graze, but with Reid in the forefront of my mind, I try not to think of the tingles Kip's unintentional touch sends through my veins.

Because lavender isn't high in demand for our local florists, we don't grow it, but oh how much I love it: the fragrance, the color, the texture. Maybe we'll have to grow a row for the heck of it. We might have a few interested shops if we offered them. Though that's an endeavor for the Sullivan land if the sale pulls through.

While I said we shouldn't talk about Seaside, I can't stop my big, dumb mouth. "So, you and the new waitress at Saltbox. Olivia, right?"

"Mmm-hmmm."

"She seems great. I ate there the other day, and she was very sweet." What am I doing? Why am I bringing her up? And it's a total lie. I haven't eaten at Saltbox in weeks. He's going to know Grace talked.

"Yeah, she is great. Actually, she told me Lockwood Blooms is the reason she ended up in Seaside."

I stifle my surprise. If she were to have served me and realized I was a Lockwood, she'd have said something, right? Except I didn't talk to the woman, and Kip will know instantly if I try to play off a fake conversation.

"Really? She didn't mention that. Though I didn't give her my last name or anything. I know we're pretty amazing, but what an interesting reason to land in Seaside."

Kip scratches at his jaw. "Let me guess, Grace told you Olivia and I came into the store together?"

I open my mouth to deny it, but what's the use? "She might've mentioned it in passing. Couldn't miss the opportunity to rag on you for already dating someone in town."

Touching my elbow, he stops walking. "Chloe, it was one date. I showed her around the Art District, and we ate lunch, nothing more. Not even a kiss at the end." Kip stuffs his hands into his pockets and resumes our stroll. "In case you were wondering," he says over his shoulder.

Why does that make me feel better? It shouldn't matter. Nothing about Kip should matter. And yet, the weight on my chest lifts and my heart beats normally once again.

And I wasn't wondering. *Liar.* "You don't owe me an explanation, Kipling."

"Maybe not, but I wanted to offer you one."

"You know," I say, "there was a time when this truce could've held a long time ago."

My mention in the car of us being lab partners in biology got me thinking about that year. When we were paired at the beginning of the year, I thought my life was over, that it would be the year from hell, but within a month, we'd formed a sort of friendship. I haven't admitted it to myself since then, but it wasn't long before I had a thought-consuming Kip crush. And it didn't take but another month before my crush was extinguished when archnemesis Harris reappeared, and the year from hell commenced.

"Biology." He reads my mind. "If we're honest, though, we both know it wouldn't have kept. We were under our father's thumbs."

He's not wrong. Some might say I'm still under my father's thumb, considering he has no idea who I'm with this weekend. I can lie and say it's to protect him in his weakened state, but if my dad hadn't recently suffered a stroke, would I have told him? To avoid a fight, probably not. Would my dad care if it were just Brynn and me? To him, a Harris is a Harris is a Harris. But Brynn isn't *Kip*.

"Maybe. Brynn and I have been able to do it so far, but that's a little different now, isn't it?"

We stop in the farm store and browse the handcrafted soaps and oils and lotions. While it might be sixty degrees out, when I see a lavender ice cream sandwich advertised on a wooden sign, I can't stop myself from getting one.

"Lavender ice cream, huh?" His mouth twists like he's unsure.

I hold out the treat peeking out of the silver wrapper. "You want to try?"

Kip contemplates.

"Do you like mint ice cream? It's a little like that."

Leaning in, he takes a bite, his head tilting in pleasant surprise. "You know, I'm not big on sweets, but this is tasty." He grabs my hand and drags the ice cream back for a second bite. "Not overly sweet like all the chocolate things Brynn always insists on ordering."

At Kip's ease of eating from my hand, a zoo of butterflies takes up residence in my stomach. I'm not even mad at him for almost eating half. I like his intimate touch too much.

And I shouldn't be having these thoughts. I shake my head, chastising myself. Boyfriend or not, Kip Harris is still on the wrong side of our history. Even if our history is a little ridiculous.

Before we leave the store, I ask, "We can cut our own bouquet in one of the fields, right?"

"As if I'm going to tell you no. Let's find you some shears, flower girl."

Even though July is the peak time for lavender, they still have beautiful varieties to harvest in the cutting field. Some white, some pink mingle with the purple. I kneel down beside a few plants with the shears and snip myself a bouquet of different colors.

Kip runs his hand up a stem and sniffs his palm. "Name another flower that smells this fragrant by brushing its stem. Are there any? There can't be."

"If there is, I don't know of it." I suppress my chuckle at Kip's appreciation for the lavender.

Closing my eyes, I bring the spray to my nose and breathe, an instant balm for the soul, back to the basics. This is why I stay in the family business: the beauty and this smell of life right here, this rejuvenation and euphoria.

When I open my eyes with a sated sigh, Kip watches me with intensity, sending a wave of goosebumps over my skin. He blinks and clears his throat. "Do I need to give you two a minute?"

I almost smack him in the chest with my bouquet, but I think better of it and use my free hand to shove him instead, cradling the lavender in my arm.

"Of course we'd finally find you guys picking flowers and fighting." Brynn appears with giant shopping bags in both hands.

I'm so relaxed, I bump my shoulder into his arm. "He started it."

"She was trying to incite my jealousy with the plants. Can you blame a guy, really?"

Jealousy? Jealous I was smelling my bouquet?

Tilting my head, I lift my gaze to Kip with a contemplative smirk. "I guess Mr. Sensitive over here can't handle a girl paying more attention to the flowers than him."

"Hate to burst your bubble, Sunshine, but I was talking about you busting into my moment with these stems here."

I roll my eyes: Kip and his weird obsession with lavender. I turn my attention to Brynn. "Looks like you found yourself some lavender products."

"Eh, I bought one candle. These are for those manly men over there." She tips her head toward Hayden and Bodhi. They're stretched out on the grass, eating ice cream sandwiches and drinking purple-tinted lemonade. They look like they're shooting a pictorial for Southern Living.

A giggle trickles out of me. "I guess not even the manliest of men can resist lavender."

"All right. Chloe's seen flowers, Brynn you get whales later. It's Hayden's and my turn."

"And what do your hearts desire?"

"There's a reason I said wear your comfy shoes. We're going to head over to Lime Kiln Pointe State Park and do a little hiking through the forest and along the cliffs."

WHEN WE RETURN to the campsite that night, the five of us put together our own foil dinners and set them over the coals in the pit by the guys' canvas cabin. Wrapped in a blanket, I tuck my knees into my chest on a chair between Bodhi and Brynn around the fire in front of ours.

This weekend has been a pleasant surprise. I always knew I liked Brynn, but after spending so much time together, talking and sharing a bed, I can see us being good friends. I want to hang out with her more often. Hayden and Bodhi aren't half bad either. I'd be lying if I said I wasn't worried about having to endure a weekend with a couple of guys I didn't know, on top of spending it with the Harris siblings. It had disaster written all over it.

But Kip. He might be the biggest surprise of all. Before we left the lavender fields, he went back to the farm store with me, and I chatted with them about their process. And what do you know? Kip stood by patiently as I asked question after question. Even though I guarantee he was ready to head out for some hiking, he didn't razz me or rush me along.

It might only be a little more than twenty-four hours since the seed disaster, but I already feel better about the future of the line launch. Maybe it happened for a reason, and we'll be able to offer better varieties when the time comes.

After we eat, Hayden passes out more drinks as we take up the same seats as the night before. Without my permission, my eyes chance glances at Kip. And each time, I'm caught. Either because he's already looking at me, or he feels my eyes on him and shifts his gaze across the fire, sending my insides on a roller coaster ride. We're eye-flirting, and as much as I know I should stop, I can't. The curbed smiles we exchange only make it harder to control the urge.

"So. Bodhi. I can't say I've ever met anyone with that name."

I twist my head to him to block out thoughts of Kip. "How'd your parents come up with it?"

"My dad went through a phase of spiritual, um…uncertainty, I guess you could call it. He was in the military and was visiting all these different places. When I came along, he was apparently stuck on Buddhism, so I got the name Bodhi. Its translation is 'awakening,' which I guess is what I was to him. He wasn't married to my mother."

"Have him tell you his full name," Hayden's green eyes gleam with mischief as Brynn drags him toward the cabins in search of the snake she insists is hiding on our site.

Oh, this is exciting. I wait, rapt.

Bodhi throws daggers at Hayden's back before turning to me. "My mom was an islander Dad met after too many drinks at some bar the sailors frequented. She was of Samoan descent, so while she let him give me the first name, she picked the middle —Tupuolevasa."

She *was* of Samoan descent. My gaze slides to Kip, who discreetly shakes his head. Taking his cue to mean the topic is off-limits, I swallow and ask his full name again.

I try repeating him but fumble and butcher the pronunciation, laughing at myself. "I'm sorry. That was horrible, but it's a really beautiful name. What does it mean?"

"Ruler or King of the sea. In all honesty, it turned out rather prophetic."

It all makes sense. "Kip mentioned you were an ocean lover. Do you surf?"

"Surf, fish, boat, ski. I definitely find my peace on the water."

Not his connection to the ocean, but with his easy-going demeanor, something tells me… "You know, I think you should meet my best friend Grace. I could see the two of you getting along really well."

Kip, whose amused attention hasn't left Brynn and Hayden as

they circle around the cabins with flashlights, chuckles. "Now, that would be something. Grace couldn't handle him."

"You don't give Grace enough credit."

"I'm not saying Grace isn't a firecracker, but I think you've fallen under the spell of Bodhi's pretty face. He's not as nice as he seems, Sunshine."

I look at Bodhi, and he shrugs like Kip isn't wrong.

"And with that," he says, "I think I'll go make sure Hayden and Brynn aren't finding any snakes that'll end up with him sporting a black eye in the morning."

"Ah, hell." Kip cringes. "I appreciate you running interference."

"Anything for my boys." Bodhi tips his chin before tapping my leg and meeting my eyes. "Chloe, you have a good night, and if Grace is the firecracker Mr. Know it All over there says she is, then I'd love to meet her someday." With a smile that would burn through my best friend's panties, he leaves.

Kip and I stare across the fire as Bodhi walks away. My mind plays a million conversations. Is he having the same problem? As if he knows, Kip's lips curve into a warm smile.

"So." He stands, stretching his arms toward the star-filled sky. "Is that seat taken?" The fire's glow flickers across his skin as his gaze volleys between Bodhi's vacated chair and my face.

He's already moving my way before I reply, "It's yours now."

As he settles in, I say, "She's a grown woman, you know? If Brynn wanted Hayden, would you stop her?"

"Stop her? Hell no, I'd walk those two right toward a preacher if they wanted. They're two of the best people I know, but her ex did a number on her. I don't want her doing something she'd regret. You know?"

I glance at the cabin. "Sometimes we have to make mistakes to know what we really want."

Kip's chest rises with a deep inhale. "Speaking of mistakes... are you glad you came?"

"Surprisingly, yeah." I laugh. "It was a really good day. Beautiful flower fields, beautiful hike. Whale watching was fun and relaxing. And you seemed to enjoy yourself, too. I can't say I've ever seen a peaceful Kipling Harris."

"It was a good day. I needed this. As much as there is to love about Tulsa, there's something about the air here. I feel like I can breathe." He rolls his head against the back of his chair and holds my gaze. "In case I haven't made it clear, I'm glad you came, too."

Calm the heck down, heartbeats. "Don't be offended, but I questioned my sanity from the moment I said yes all the way to your back deck. And now, all I can think is how I had nothing to worry about. It's been good to get away and get my head on straight." Or maybe my head is more skewed than ever but in a completely different way. At least my plans for Lockwood Blooms' future aren't ambiguous.

"No offense taken. I had a moment of terror myself when I realized what I'd done. Granted, I was more concerned we'd kill each other than anything else."

"I *am* surprised I didn't have to dig any graves. What do you know?" The corner of my mouth quirks up. "Miracles do happen."

"Amazing, huh?" Pushing the cuff of his hoodie up, Kip checks the watch at his wrist. "And would you check that out? Our truce has held for an entire twenty-four hours."

I remove my hand tucked in my sleeve and hold out my fist for a bump, which he obliges. "We deserve a gold star or something."

"Maybe we should save the gold stars until we see if this one lasts?"

"Oh, the tenth grade truce." A chuckle tumbles from my lips. "Didn't last very long, now did it? What was it, a month before you declared war again?"

Kip jerks like I punched him. "*I* declared war?"

I nod. "All I remember is one day we were friendly lab partners going over your color-coded spreadsheets, and the next I was your mortal enemy again."

Something dark flashes across his face. "I wouldn't exactly say mortal enemy. We were cool before the holidays, then I started dating Chelsea and suddenly you hated me."

"I never *hated* you." A short laugh leaves me. Even if he did make high school miserable at times and date every one of my friends except Grace. And what do you know? She's the only one I'm still friends with. "You started dating Chelsea and suddenly gave me the cold shoulder."

Apprehension lines his face. "Do you honestly want to do this right now, Chloe? Hash out our past because I don't know if this truce will hold up once we open the door."

My brows knit together. "What are you even talking about?"

Resting his forearms on his thighs, he concentrates on the fire. "You know that day I mentioned when I saw you in the field and you stuck your tongue out?" I nod. "That was the day I started calling you Sunshine in my mind."

Of course it was. I scoff inside—a snarky little nickname for my bratty reaction to him.

"It stuck for years, that picture of you, but the image slowly eroded thanks to my father's animosity. Every mention of a Lockwood brought another story of how they wronged a Harris. Eventually, I bought into the feud. I stopped seeing the beautiful, happy girl with a sunshine halo and began seeing my competition."

Wait. Sunshine wasn't an ironic nickname?

"Until Mr. Dumas decided to make us lab partners thinking it would be hilarious," he says.

Maybe Mr. Dumas thought we'd learn to put aside our differences, or maybe he was trying to end the generations' long feud. Either way, his decision backfired.

"I don't know how it happened, but the longer we worked together, the more the ice thawed. I was fifteen, and you smelled like flowers every day. Maybe it was the hormones, or maybe it was just me, but damn, I wanted to ask you out so badly."

Pitter-pat goes the beats of my heart. "You did?" I lean into him on the armrest of my chair between us. "Why didn't you?"

"Because you made it clear you'd never date a Harris."

"When did I say that to you?"

"You didn't." The space between us widens. "I overheard you and your friends."

My shoulders slouch. "Overheard?"

"Right before Christmas break, Chloe. I was rounding the corner, and I came upon you, Grace, Chelsea, and some other girls. You were talking about guys, and I'm not proud of myself, but I stopped and listened." He lifts his head. "What I heard insinuated what was between us was one-sided."

"So, you judged my feelings about you based on one over-heard gossip session with my friends?"

"You girls were brutal. I don't know who brought up my name, and I wish I could recall who all said what. I mean, it was super nice hearing I was such a catch because I'm rich. And how nice my backside was in my baseball uniform. Anyone who says girls don't talk about boys the same way we talk about girls is deaf.

"The point is, I finally worked up the courage to tell my dad to screw himself and ask you on a date, knowing his wrath wouldn't be pretty, and there you were telling a group of our classmates how I'd never get out from under my *daddy's* thumb, and you'd never go out with me."

"Kip." I can't believe he was so hurt by my flippant comment.

My mind races to remember the conversation he's referring to. Before he started dating Chelsea. It might've been ten years ago, but their relationship was a turning point in high school for me. It was my first real heartbreak.

Oh gosh. *That* conversation? Considering jabs at Harrises by Lockwoods aren't uncommon, I might've never recalled saying those things, but that was the day Chelsea said she'd never go out with Kip.

"It's not a good excuse, but we were a bunch of immature girls pretending like we didn't care the most popular and gorgeous boy in school never looked our way. It was dumb girl talk."

I might've said those things, but with our open feud, it was expected of me. It didn't mean I didn't want to date him. It was a comment said among friends, something to keep up the façade, a knee-jerk reaction. Truthfully, I was talking about myself. I couldn't go against my dad, my family. Even if I'd wanted to.

Had I been honest with those girls, I'd have confided in them how mortified I was for crushing on a guy who would never like me back, crushing on someone who belongs to a family that's hurt mine for so many generations. I was the quiet flower girl still figuring out who I was. Heck, I still had braces then—a sure way to boost a teenage girl's confidence.

He shrugs. "I liked you."

"And I felt the same, but instead of asking me out, you went out with Chelsea Bray. For months. You don't know how much that hurt."

"Likely about as much as hearing half the girls in school thought I was some Harris puppet. Like I'd amount to nothing on my own. Like I had no worth beyond my name and money."

"So, rather than talk to me about it, you decided to go out of your way to hurt me. It wasn't a Harris versus Lockwood war. It was personal."

"Hell yeah, it was personal. I shouldn't have been surprised by the comment. Up until then, we'd made enough bets, played enough pranks on each other to have our stories added to the Harris-Lockwood Feud history books. I wanted to move past our family disputes. My interest was in dating the sunshine girl, and she shot me down publicly. On purpose or not, it was a blow to my pride and very, very personal."

"Did you not hear the part where Chelsea said she'd never date you?"

"Yeah, I heard her. Why do you think she was the first girl I asked?" He's truly indifferent. "Like I said, it was a pride issue. And I know you're well aware of how unbending the Harrises are. We have prides made of steel."

"How's that pride issue coming along now, huh? Ten years and something a self-conscious sixteen-year-old girl said still bothers you."

Surging to his feet, he grabs the fire poker from where Hayden left it. "She wasn't *some* sixteen-year-old girl. She was you. And believe me, I'm pissed as hell to find it still bothers me after all this time."

"Kip—"

He attacks the fire, stoking the flame and sending sparks floating into the air. "We can't go back, Chloe. What happened and what was said doesn't matter now. Bygones and whatever, but I figured you should know I overheard you. You were right, I did come back from winter break with Chelsea on my arm and a chip on my shoulder toward you. Now you know why."

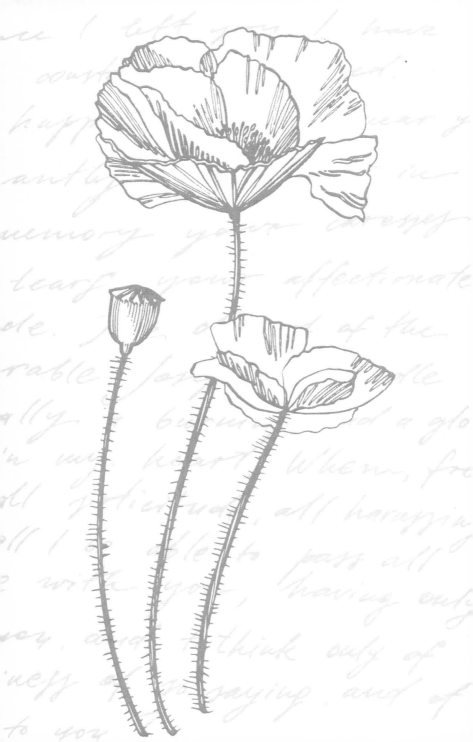

ip

THE FOG SETTLING over the island Sunday morning is as thick as the tension. The difference is the fog drifts away.

I might have claimed bygones as I walked away from Chloe last night, but bringing up the memory feels like a picked-over scab. We were healing. Things were fine, then we scratched at the rough edges until a drop of blood appeared.

In a true act of cowardice, when Brynn brings up her desire to visit the nearby alpaca farm after breakfast, I bow out and tell her to drive my car. Chloe joins her, leaving the guys to hang back with me.

I go for a long run to avoid Hayden and Bodhi, and by the time I return and shower, we're packing up and on the road to meet Brynn and Chloe for lunch before our ferry home.

A few hours later, after a short goodbye where my best friends overwhelmed Chloe with their bear hugs, we park in the circular drive of my parents' house. Chloe and Brynn climb out and grab their things while I remain glued to my seat, staring out into the distance.

What the hell happened?

I yank my keys from the vehicle. No, we're not doing this again. This feud. This act of indifference. I slam my door closed.

In the midst of a hug, the girls' heads jerk my way. "I'll walk you back," I offer.

Chloe's lips part, but instead of refusing, she nods her acceptance. I head toward the gate on the side of our house. There's not a chance in hell I'm walking her through the house where Mom and Dad are likely sitting by the television. Behind me, Brynn gushes about how happy she is they were able to spend time together. Chloe agrees, her soft laughter a song in the air.

A song in the air? I pinch the bridge of my nose. It took one month back in Seaside for me to crumble to the lure of Chloe Lockwood. I'm not too proud to admit that. She's the girl who got away in some aspects. I'm furious I admitted how much her words from the past affected me, but I'm not mad she knows I was interested. She wanted me, too.

"I'm ready," she says, inching by me and leading the way home.

We walk toward where this weekend started without a word. The same place where our families' feud began. She smells of lavender, the bouquet poking out of the top of her backpack, and the scent brings forth an image of her at her happiest moment from this weekend—a sunshine flower girl surrounded by blooms. I snuck a few shots on my phone's camera when she wasn't paying attention because I couldn't help myself, and I figured she'd like them. I'll share the pictures with her someday.

"I don't know where this weekend leaves us." I break the silence when we near the gate between our properties.

"Me either."

"Last night." I angle in front of her, and she stops walking. "I don't want what was said to end our truce. I don't want to fall into a pattern of bickering again."

Her eyes read my face, searching. "Then let's not. We're adults. We can have an argument and remain friends, right?"

Friends. Right, because she has Reid, and if we are anything to each other, we're friends.

Removing my body as a roadblock, I continue toward the fence. "A Harris and Lockwood who fight and make-up? Such a tall order." Though my chest is heavy, I keep my tone as light as possible.

"Why don't we try defying history for once, Kipling Harris?"

"I like being defiant." And I especially like the way she uses my full name.

Unlatching the hook, I step back and open the gate between her world and mine enough for Chloe to slip through. Her shoulder brushes my chest. She pauses and looks up at me.

"I'll see you around?" There's so much uncertainty between us. Then the sun peeks through the clouds, and a single ray illuminates Chloe's profile like a damn sign.

"Yeah," I reply low, bending down and pressing my lips against her smooth cheek.

It's subtle and quiet, but she sucks in a breath at my touch, and I long to read her thoughts when my mouth whispers over skin as I add, "We should talk in a few days. I'll call you."

Chloe nods, and I withdraw because the other option has my mouth moving two inches to the left, and while it's something I want, it's not something I should do.

Closing the gate, I verify the latch is secure and lean against the top, my gaze following her as she heads home.

"Hey, Chloe?" I call before she's too far for my voice to carry. "I'm sorry about whatever had you so upset Friday when I found you here, but I'm not sorry it led to you going on the trip."

She turns fully, an unknown revelation softening her features. "In the end, it turns out, it wasn't as important as this weekend."

MONDAY OPENS with an eight o'clock Central Standard Time conference call because some clients are too important to turn down. This client, Alleycat—a high-end eat, play, event space concept company—is one such client. They anchor the Omni-Plex in Tulsa and are a huge key for securing the Riverfront Center's success.

The call goes well; they like the preliminary specs I sent outlining the proposed property, anticipated tenants, and break-down of the demographics for Seaside and the neighboring communities. They'll bring the idea of opening this location to their board. Peter, the head of Alleycat's Real Estate Development team, reminds me they were not in the market to expand this far west any time soon, but I'm confident we've reeled in our first big tenant. Now to ensure nothing prevents us from moving forward with the development.

Easier said than done. Carrie-Anne meets me at the office door, a pile of emergencies in hand. An action committee was formed to oppose the development of our property citing crime, traffic, and noise concerns. Not an unexpected move, but another headache to contend with.

It's after seven p.m. before I leave the office, and while the temptation to call Chloe is strong, I hold out. Her words from yesterday refused to be stifled: *It wasn't as important as this week-end.* What did she mean? Was she talking about her needing the downtime? Was she referencing our truce? The argument we had? Either way, I need to respect her relationship with Reid enough to allow it to run its course. She can't do that if I'm shoving my way into her life every day.

Tuesday afternoon and two showings and a meeting with Dad later, I've changed my tune.

"Chloe, hey. It's Kip," I say to her voicemail like she doesn't know my voice. "Just thinking about you and wanted to say hi. Nothing new with Sullivan. Give me a call when you have time to chat."

Wednesday goes the same. I work on some lease agreements and think of Chloe. I have a working lunch with Roger Scaritt at City Hall and think of Chloe. I deal with lingering issues in Tulsa and continue thinking of Chloe.

The woman won't stop entering my mind, especially after a second and third call goes unanswered. To be fair, I called the farm the first time and didn't leave a message when they said she was out. I tried her cell the second time. "It's Kip. Call me." Short and to the point.

I'm a stalker.

Then Thursday arrives, and hell breaks loose in the form of Denton Harris.

The note stuck to my office door is my warning. *"See me."*

Son of a— one would think I'm a teen again as I drop my bag on my desk and head for Dad's office. He's kept a low profile since our argument about the Sullivan land last week. Even at home, he's been on his best behavior, keeping talk of business out of the house. I do wonder if that's not Mom's mandate rather than his choice.

"When were you going to tell me about meeting with Jenkins?"

"Our HVAC contractor?" I blink, taken aback. "I didn't know I was supposed to."

A vein pops in his forehead. "You don't meet with our largest vendors without having me sit in on it."

My lip curls as I stare down at him sitting behind his desk. "I'm sorry, did you not beg me to return to Seaside?"

"Don't take that tone with me, son. You're young and untested."

"Don't you dare patronize me." I step further into his office, slamming the door behind me. "I may be young, but I am not untested."

While the tips of his ears are red, his tone tempers. "Jenkins likes to play hardball. He requires a certain finesse to handle."

Finesse? Like extra bonuses, and use of our family's mountain house, and other perks I'd rather not be aware of?

I snort. "Jenkins merely needed a reminder when it comes to maintaining our units, they aren't the only air conditioning repair company around."

"Jenkins has the best crews in the area."

"Which must be why his bills to us are increasing exponentially, and his repair times have doubled." Dad's jaw clenches. Oh, it feels so damn good to be right when it comes to him. "We could hire and train our own HVAC team for what we pay Jenkins. That is why I put him on notice. He's taking advantage because you let him."

"I've worked with the man for over twenty years, Kip."

"Exactly. You're lining the pockets of your friend at the expense of our clients and *our* bottom line."

His chest puffs up, the lines around his mouth deepening. "Are you insulting the way I do business, son?"

"You're the great Denton Harris; how could I possibly insult you?" I grasp the door handle at my hip and twist. "I'm simply letting you know I won't always make the same choices you have. If you don't like it, tell me to pack my bags."

I'm walking out when I spot a file on his desk. "Why do you have the Sullivan file?" I cross the space to his desk and pick up the file before he stops me.

He shrugs. "I was double-checking the property lines."

"I repeat, why?"

Tapping his pen on the desk, he sighs. "Because I'm not

convinced that's the right space for Lockwood Blooms to expand."

Swallowing my ire, I rest my palms on his desk and lean in. "You don't have to be convinced. Chloe Lockwood wants the land, and Melvin Sullivan has agreed with her offer."

A shadow crosses Dad's face. "He agreed? Do you have a signed contract?"

"Not yet, but I will. Leave it alone." I step back. If I'm not careful, my feelings will spill out across his desk, and *that* will cause a bigger mess than him nosing around in this deal.

"Kip, Joseph Sullivan doesn't like the idea of selling their land to a Lockwood. You'd do best to turn her down now."

"Like hell, I will." My fuse lights. "Joseph doesn't own the land, he has no say, and if he doesn't want Lockwood to own it, it's because of you. Twice you've insulted me in less than ten minutes. I'm doing the job you wanted me here to do. As I said a minute ago, if you don't like it, tell me to pack my bags. Otherwise, stay the hell out of my way."

I yank the door open. "Oh, and don't call me *son* at work again. You want me here? You'll treat me like your peer in the business." I can't say employee because while he runs H.D., Brynn and I have ownership, too.

I'm grabbing my bag and walking out the door before I've taken a breath. Of all the pompous, arrogant— Why did I come back? The man thinks I'm a child. I have a featured property in a trade magazine, and still, I'm not good enough. I can't with him. I need out, I can't...

Tap, tap, tap.

I open my eyes and find Brynn standing outside my car window. Preparing myself, I roll the window down.

She leans her forearms on the door ledge and cocks her head. "What did he do?"

I hate pitting Brynn against Dad. While he's a monumental

prick when it comes to me, he's supported her in a way only a father who loves his little girl could since Preston.

"It's nothing." I shoo at her, but she doesn't budge. "Fine. He proved to me exactly what it'll be like if I stay here. He doesn't want a partner, Brynn. He wants to control what I do."

"That's not…" She frowns and sighs. "He's been the face of H.D. for so long. Can you blame him for having trouble letting go?"

"No, sis, I don't blame him. This is his life." I pat her hand and start the vehicle. "I blame him for loving it more. I blame him for his inability to show me I'm important enough."

"Kip."

I shift into *Drive,* and Brynn steps away. "If we're not going to kill each other, I need space. I'm going to move into the condo today instead of waiting for this weekend. Maybe separating home from work will help."

"Hey, Sunshine. I would say it's not like you not to return your calls, but then again, I don't know if that's true. I've called you more this week than I have in our entire lives. I've called you, and you haven't called me back. I'm sure you're busy. Taking the weekend probably set you way back. Then again, maybe you're working on those seeds you were so worried about. I hope that's the case. A good busy."

I toss back the shot of whiskey I said I wouldn't drink because I don't drink during the day, and I don't drink when I'm overly stressed. That's not my style. Today I'm making an exception. Just as I'm making an exception with my words.

"I'm going to be honest for once. I'm calling because I wanted to hear your voice. My dad and I had it out, and I'm moving into the condo tonight and, truthfully Chlo, I don't know how much longer I'm going to be here, and…"

Heavy kicks hit the bottom of my door, and I end the call like I've been caught red-handed.

Flipping the lock, I open the door to a flustered Brynn. "Hey."

"A pre-furnished condo with a waterfront view, shopping and food beneath your feet, and no Mom and Dad? Sign me up." She squeezes by and drops into the nearest chair, the grocery bags in her hands hitting the floor unceremoniously. "How long did Justin say he would be out of the country?"

"Nine months guaranteed. Possibly longer if he signs on for more work." I glance around my new, *temporary* home. "I lucked out."

"Yeah, you did, but you do realize you can't see Lockwood's from here, right?"

"Don't be a pain in my ass."

"Then tell me what's going on with you two. It's Thursday night, and you haven't seen her since Sunday." Brynn digs into the bags at her feet, stacking the refrigerated stuff in her lap. "And don't say nothing, Kip Harris. I'm not an imbecile."

"What do you want me to say?" I swipe the milk jug from her fist and head to the kitchen. "Our fathers hate each other, I'm not sure I'm moving back, and she's dating another man. What can happen?"

"What can happen?" she asks at my back, her arms laden with food. "You can tell our fathers to get over themselves, make the damn decision to stay, and steal the girl."

"Steal the girl?" I cross my arms and lean against the counter as she dumps my food into the refrigerator. "I'll have to organize everything later. "Isn't there some sort of code between women when it comes to stealing men from other women?"

Brynn swings the door closed and mimics my position, leaning back. "One, you're a man, and everyone knows men don't live by the whole honor other bro's girls code. Two, you have

182 | MINDY MICHELE

wanted Chloe since you hit puberty. And three, she wants you back. Therefore all rules don't apply anyway."

"You're insane."

"And you're in denial."

She grabs my arm when I go to leave. "You want to know why you haven't done anything? You think if you come home, Dad wins."

My heart rate ticks up at her nugget of truth.

"He doesn't win, Kip. You didn't do what he expected. You did your thing. You got your degree where you wanted. You got your MBA. You made a name for yourself without his help, and you're not even twenty-five." Brynn flattens her palm to my chest. "He knows what an asset you are. That's why he wants you here. We're talking about Denton Harris; you know he'd never hand his legacy over to just anyone. He could give it to me if that were the case—"

"And he'd be lucky to have you at the helm." Brynn is the oldest, and she deserves the family business. Not me.

Brynn's features open up as awareness hits. "You think I want it? Don't you? That's why you're so set against taking over?"

"No, that's not…" Shaking her off, I pace the living room in need of space.

"Kip. He asked me a long time ago if I wanted larger owner-ship." My pacing halts. "He asked me again…after Preston ended things. If you're refusing him because of me, your chivalry is in the wrong place, little brother."

She's mistaken. True, I didn't think it fair he wanted me taking over a company where she's worked longer, but there's more. There's Denton and Kip, and we're like water and oil.

Walking across the room, Brynn stops before me and takes my hands in hers. "You and Dad need to declare peace eventually. I'm selfish, and I want my best friend here, but if you can't stomach him, go back to Tulsa. You've made an amazing life there, and I'll be happy you're happy."

I drag her into my chest and kiss the top of her head. "You're a sap, but I love you."

"I love you, too," she murmurs into my chest before shoving back an inch and craning her neck and holding my stare. "But, I still remember how Chloe hurt you when you wanted to ask her out. Rejection doesn't hurt so badly if feelings aren't real, Kip." I suck in a deep breath. "And if they're real, and you don't try, you'll regret walking away."

hloe

WHEN I WAKE with my alarm clock bright and early Monday morning, after the way things were left with Kip on Sunday, I'm not nearly as eager to get out in the fields with Reid as I should be. I should want to see my boyfriend. When I got home yesterday, he should've been the first person I wanted to see. I should've wanted to race to his place, tackle, and kiss him. Instead, I laid awake in bed last night thinking about how I wished Kip kissed my lips and not my cheek.

That's not okay. On so many levels.

I'm in the cooler handing Meredith buckets of harvested blooms for delivery when Reid appears over her shoulder. His smile is meek like he's waiting for proof I'm over my anger. We didn't text or talk all weekend. Or I should say, I didn't respond when he texted me. I wasn't trying to avoid him, I just didn't want that to be my focus, couldn't face it. I wanted a complete shut-off from Lockwood Blooms, which included Reid.

"Meredith, will you get started carting these to the vans? I'll be right behind you."

She nods, and I step out of the fridge, sliding it shut behind me.

"Good morning." Reid steps into me, switching his ball cap around so the bill doesn't knock me in the head as he kisses me.

"Morning." I offer a gentle smile in return.

"Am I forgiven yet?"

I shake my head. "You didn't need to be forgiven. It wasn't you I was mad at, or Tyson, for that matter. Just the situation as a whole, you know? I lost my temper, and I shouldn't have. It was just so disheartening to have so much work gone."

"I know, and I'm so sorry." Reid grips my hands, bending his head to be eye level with me. "I'll do everything I can to help you make up for the varieties we lost. As soon as we can, I'll head up a team to prepare land and hoop houses for as many blooms as you want. You just tell me what and where."

It's a sweet gesture, but we need more land to do what I want, and with Sullivan's property still on hold, there's no telling when I'll be able to replenish the seeds that were lost.

"It's okay, Reid. Honestly. We'll just launch the seeds with a smaller line to test the waters for interest next year. It's probably what I should've done in the first place. If they do well, we'll try for more the following year."

He slips his arms around my waist, drawing me against his chest. "No matter what you do, Loe, it'll be a hit. I know it. You've got the golden touch."

"Reid—"

Meredith's footsteps interrupt. "Are you two coming or what?"

"Yeah, sorry, Mere." I step out of his hold and pick up a bucket of peonies. "I didn't mean to leave you hanging." Turning to Reid, I say, "We'll talk more after the deliveries, okay?"

His smile is uncertain as I leave. I suppose it matches mine.

TALKING to Reid after the morning deliveries turns into cleaning up messes and taking care of things I'd missed because I left early on Friday. I've been nonstop, barely taking a break to grab something in the house for lunch.

The sun is making its descent by the time Reid finds me in the poppy breeding patch observing their progress. We've created some new varieties I'm excited to add to the Lockwood Bloom family next year, but they don't have names yet.

"I figured I'd find you here. The flowers at sunset are your favorite."

Well, dahlias at sunset, if we're getting specific, but those will have to wait until mid-summer.

I tip my head up from my crouched position, taking pictures with my phone. "They're just so dreamy at this time of day. The light hits them just right." The ethereal glow, like each individual blossom wears a halo. And at the perfect angle, depending on the color of the sky and the shade of the bloom, they become one with the sky.

Reid flashes his handsome, easy-going grin. "Their owner doesn't look too shabby, either."

I stand with a bashful smile. His compliment should warm my insides but instead fill me with guilt.

Tucking his hands in his front pants pockets, Reid takes a deep breath. "So, how was the weekend?"

The weekend. I hardly slept last night, going over every moment on San Juan Island. I'm not sure I'm ready for this conversation. Not in the flower fields, my happy place.

I pocket my phone. "It was enlightening, relaxing."

"Enlightening, huh?"

"Yeah. We visited the lavender farm, and it helped center me. I learned a lot, got some great ideas to implement here." But who am I kidding? It's so much more than the lavender fields. My feet move, and he follows down the dirt path. "Reid—"

"You don't have to explain." His voice is low. "The moment you said yes to Harris, I knew."

I stop, turning to face him. "Knew what?"

His mouth pitches at the corner as he shrugs. "That we were done. It's why I didn't want you to go. It wasn't just jealousy, and it wasn't because I didn't trust you. I hoped I'd be able to change your mind if I kept you close, proved to you I can treat you better."

My heart trembles, my shoulders sagging. "How could you know if I didn't?"

Reid turns away, the bill of his hat casting a shadow across his sharp, stubbled jawline. "The fact that you were so desperate to leave, you agreed to go with the son of the man your father hates the most—a guy you've claimed is the bane of your existence for years—was telling enough. I'm not really sure how I didn't see it when he first got back to town."

"See what?"

"That you have feelings for Harris."

"I…" I didn't. At least, I didn't think I still did, but maybe I was in denial. There was a shift this weekend, a lot of revelations made. "It's complicated."

A short laugh passes his lips, but it's not one of amusement. "Isn't that original."

I don't snap at him because his heart is broken, and I don't get to be angry with him for having hurt feelings, but it doesn't mean his comment doesn't sting. "I'm sorry, Reid. I really am."

He nods but doesn't meet my eyes as his stoic stare shifts around the land. "Some things just aren't meant to be."

"Nothing happened, just so you know. The five of us went everywhere together. It really was a bunch of friends camping out. I slept in a bed with Brynn." Though I didn't physically cheat, enough inappropriate thoughts crossed my mind—

thoughts a girl shouldn't have about a man who's not her boyfriend.

"Friends, huh?"

I hadn't even realized I'd said the word so freely. "Yeah, I guess the feud is going to end with us. At least we're going to try."

Reid's lips crook. He might believe me, he might not.

I step toward him. "I don't want this to ruin the friendship we have. I still want to be able to work together without it being awkward. You're a good man, Reid, and I respect you. I appreciate and respect all you do for this farm."

He shakes his head. "It's going to take time, Loe. My feelings are not a switch I can just shut off."

"I know." I was dumb to start a relationship with someone I work with, with Reid of all people. He's not a help-out-for-the-season kind of employee. He's here for the long haul—a Lockwood Blooms staple. If we didn't work out, it was bound to make an uncomfortable environment, and I don't want that kind of drama here. I should've been smarter about this. It would've saved us both the heartache.

"I'll give you space. Time off. Whatever you want. I can set you up to work the northern delivery routes, so you can spend less time on the farm."

"Don't do me any favors, Loe. I don't want pity."

"I don't pity you." My hand moves to reach out to him, but I clutch my fingers into a fist at my side. "I just…this didn't end the way I thought, and I want to make it easier for you. I really do like you, Reid."

His mouth spreads in a close-lipped straight line, the corners of his eyes downturned. "Just not the same way you like Harris."

I don't react. I don't reply. And maybe that's answer enough because Reid walks away, leaving me standing alone in the poppy patch.

WHEN I ENTER Fig Wednesday morning, Grace looks up from the counter in the center of the rustic boutique. "The Flower Queen has finally decided to grace me with her presence. No pun intended."

I snort, walking toward her. "I'm sorry. It's been a rough few days."

"Yeah, I'll say. You ghost me all weekend, just to shoot me a text Monday night that you ended things with Reid. And you've left me hanging since. What the crap?"

My fingers massage my temples. "Everything. Everything is crap."

"What happened?"

After explaining the seed catastrophe and Kip finding me during my pity party at the property line, I bow my head. My running off the way I did wasn't right. It was unprofessional and unfair to Reid on a personal level, and yet…

"You left for the weekend with Kip Harris, and you didn't think that was important enough to tell me? What kind of a best friend are you?"

"I know. I know." My head falls back with a groan. "It was *the* most uncharacteristic move I've ever made. It was also one of the best."

Grace blinks, mouth agape. "So, what happened? What did you do? Where did you go? Did anything happen between you two?"

Leaning my weight on the counter, I tell Grace everything, from the moment I walked up to the back of the Harrises house to Kip walking me home and kissing my cheek.

"And then you proceeded to break up with Reid the very next day."

"Not for Kip," I say. "Just…we started dating right after my dad's stroke. He was dependable and attractive and comforting. I think I liked the stability he provided in a time when everything fell apart. But after this weekend, I realized he doesn't make me feel the way he should, you know?"

"And Kip makes you feel that way."

"Yes. Maybe. I don't know." I grip the roots of my braided mane. "Kip's called me a couple of times, but I haven't called him back."

"Why? I think the man would like to hear you broke up with your boyfriend. Reid probably threw a wrench in Kip's illicit weekend plans with you."

"There was nothing *illicit* about our weekend. It wasn't even just the two of us, remember?"

"It doesn't matter. Something obviously changed if you and Kip wound up home alive after three days together. As *friends.* So, why haven't you returned his calls?"

"Because I don't know what to say. We left things so weird at the fence. Like pleasant enough, but I don't know."

"You say, hey, Kip. I broke up with Reid. Let's get jiggy."

"Never say jiggy again." I pinch the bridge of my nose. "And how horrible would it make me to break Reid's heart just to turn around and hook up with Kip? What a jerk move."

"Is that all he would be? A hookup?"

I pause, thinking about Kip leaving me at the firepit Saturday night after our quarrel and Hayden joining me. "He told his friends about me."

"The college buddies on the camping trip?"

"Yes. Which, by the way, Bodhi would be perfect for you." My eyebrows rise with my grin.

"As much as I want to dig into that whole chestnut, what did Kip tell his friends?"

I let out an exhale. "Hayden didn't give specifics. Just apparently, Kip didn't date much in college, and it was casual when he did. The only girl they ever knew by name was me. And not because of our family's history. They knew he called me Sunshine and why."

Grace leans her weight on her elbow resting on the desk, her head cocking to the side. "You're telling me Kip Harris has carried a torch for you for all these years?"

I haven't thought of it like that. "Maybe? No, that would be insane. It doesn't make any sense."

"Chloe Mae Lockwood. You call that man right now."

"We don't know anything. Hayden was talking about college days. He didn't say how Kip feels now."

"Right. Because it's totally normal for a man to ask a woman to get away for the weekend with him, completely platonically."

I nibble on my bottom lip. "I'll call him after work on Friday. My week is hectic enough without adding another emotional complication. Reid deserves more than two days before I pursue another man."

"As much as you want to deny it, this isn't just *any* man, Loe, and you know it."

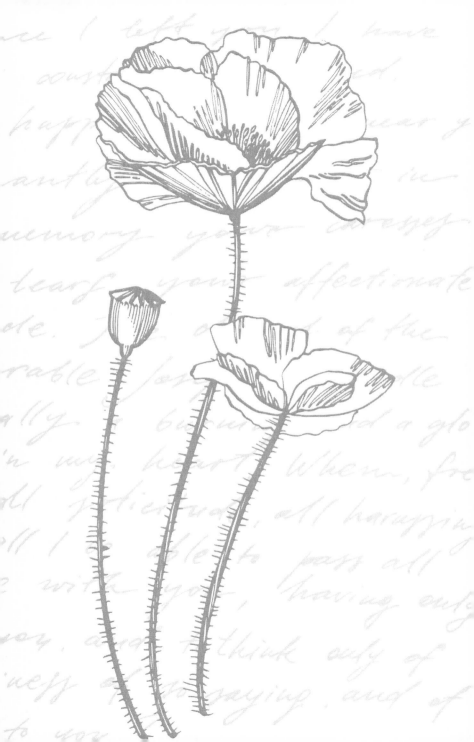

ip

BEFORE I HIT the Lockwood's driveway, I turn left down the gravel road toward the flower farm. Circling the property, I park next to an old barn at the edge of the fields. Speckled around the land are workers bent over beds or hauling around buckets of flowers, but I don't spot Chloe.

I walk past rows and rows of different flowers, acknowledging anyone who notices me. None are close enough to ask where she might be until I reach the first greenhouse on the outskirts. Peering inside, I find Reid shifting around black fabric on the dirt, like he's trying to lay it flat.

"Hey." I clear my throat. "Is Chloe around?"

His head turns at the sound of my voice. With one forearm on his knee, he straightens his hat with the other, eyeing me. "She's not." Dismissing me with his silence, Reid scoots along the ground.

All right then. Seeing how I invited his girlfriend away for the weekend, I'll let his cold shoulder slide. I turn for the exit, figuring I can find someone else to help me locate her.

"How long are you sticking around here, Harris?"

Pausing, I spare him a glance. "Excuse me?"

"You think anyone believes you're here long term? How long do you actually plan on staying in Seaside? Another month? Two?"

"I'm sorry." I retrace my steps and stop before him. "Is there a problem here?"

Reid rises to his feet and clicks his tongue as he wipes his hands on his soil-stained jeans. "You take my girlfriend away for a weekend and ask me if there's a problem? You Harrises really think you can have whatever you want, don't you?"

It's petty, but his jealousy tugs at the corners of my mouth. "Your girlfriend was visibly upset. I invited her for a weekend with friends. Nothing more. Don't blame me because she found the idea appealing."

"Your cocky rich boy smile doesn't work on me." Reid ambles a couple steps toward me. "We both know you took advantage of Loe's low point. She never would've said yes otherwise."

"My cocky rich boy smile?" Is that supposed to piss me off? "Wow, someone's still upset I beat him for the ace pitching spot on varsity."

His head shakes with a dry laugh, and he moves another step toward me until we're toe-to-toe. "Some things never change. You're still the same smug prick you were in high school."

"And yet, Chloe chose to spend the weekend with me instead of you."

My head whips sideways as Reid's fist connects with my jaw. "Son of a—"

"What in the world is going on in here?"

Working my jaw, I peer over my shoulder and spot Chloe in

form-fitting overalls and a long sweater with her hands on her hips.

"I came here looking for you, and your boyfriend thinks he's Holyfield."

Chloe's gaze darts from Reid to me and back.

Touching my cheek, I find a smear of blood on my thumb. "You're lucky she showed up, Pruitt. You wouldn't have landed a second shot."

"Kip," she chastises.

"Oh, yeah, of course. I'm sure this is my fault. I'm a Harris, right?" I raise my hands in surrender and move backward. If I don't walk out of here now, I may say something I'll regret.

"Kip, wait." Her soft gaze pleads for me to stay.

"Why don't you deal with him and come find me when you want to talk." I exit the building and pause. I'm so pissed. I turn left and keep going until Chloe and Reid's raised voices fade out. Heading home isn't an option. After all the unanswered calls and voicemails I left Chloe, no way. I'm speaking with her before this day is over.

It's been years since I wandered this field, but eventually, I'm staring down a familiar tree on the opposite side of the fence.

I head for the gate, leaving it ajar, and walk toward the tree. It's the only full-grown oak this close to the Lockwood's property line. Dad keeps most of our acreage on this half of the land neatly manicured and mowed. Whether he likes it or not, Mom loves admiring Lockwood's blooms from the back veranda. The square lot to the east of our house—the land Chloe wants to buy— grows wild grasses, attracting local wildlife in abundance come dusk. The property boundary to the west is all brush and mature trees until you hit Marvin Road, and elaborate garden beds pepper the remainder of our property back to where a significantly narrowed Skagit River runs through the land.

Chloe calls my name, her voice faint. She must have finished with Reid and spotted my car parked out front. I move to retrace my steps back to her and stop.

Nope.

If Chloe wants to find me, she'll end up here. This is our tree. Or, in my mind it's ours. We shared a moment here once, but it was *the* moment. The moment that kept one sunshine flower girl on my mind for the last seven years. Even when I tried my best to forget her.

THE SKY GROWS DARKER, sure sign a storm is coming, as I walk around the yard for the last time. Tomorrow I'm on a plane headed for Oklahoma. It's crazy to think I'm leaving here. College, two thousand miles away.

Thunder rolls in the distance, becoming louder, followed by the airy jangle of a dog tag. Daisy. *I pause as the Lockwood's Collie jumps through the brush and runs straight for me.*

"Hey, girl. That thunder scare you?" I can't help but laugh at how Chloe has allowed her beloved dog into our backyard. Again.

Picking up Daisy, I carry her to the suspiciously left open gate.

"Daisy!" Chloe shouts, the clap of her hands echo through their fields.

I meet Daisy's black gaze. "Well, this is perfect. Come on, girl." Chuckling, I sit at the base of our large oak tree and wait. Daisy, the people lover she is, happily settles in my lap.

"Daisy, here girl."

Daisy's tail wags, and she wiggles to get free, but a few scratches at her ears and a belly rub keep her happy.

A flash of yellow amongst the rows of flowers catches my eye, followed by Chloe's voice, closer this time.

"Have you lost something?" I call out.

The yellow halts, and oh, how I wish I could see her face right now. After a moment, she steps out of the cover of climbing flowers and foliage and moves toward the open gate. Her head swivels around. She doesn't notice me under the tree. Daisy's cheerful yelp at the sight of her owner remedies that.

"Looking for this?" I ask when her eyes meet mine.

Chloe's eyes go round, caught red-handed, before narrowing as she plants her hands on her hips. "Daisy." She slaps her thigh. Daisy doesn't budge.

"It's funny. My dad has accused you of letting her out over here for years. I guess now we have proof."

In truth, I've known. It began when Daisy was a puppy. Chloe used to run with her around their yard, and one day Daisy slipped through a space in the fencing. I was building a fort in the trees nestled in the back corner along the stream cutting through our lot, and Daisy made a beeline for me until something better caught her attention. The puppy's nose hit the ground, and before I knew it, Daisy was doing her business, and Chloe appeared. She didn't notice me hiding in the brush, and before Daisy could give me away, Chloe scooped the puppy into her arms, looked around, and hightailed it back to her yard. It was years ago, but I've never forgotten the mischievous smile playing on her lips when she praised her new dog for "giving the Harrises what they deserve."

Chloe huffs. "So, the gate unlatched and Daisy got out. Doesn't mean anything."

"Right, funny how that happens." Standing, I keep a constant scratch at Daisy's ears and head to keep her at my side. The little beggar won't move as long as she's shown some loving. "You know, if you wanted to say goodbye so badly, you could have picked up the phone, Sunshine."

"Don't flatter yourself. Seeing your taillights out of Seaside will be the highlight of my life."

I harrumphed. "It's sad what that little comment says about your life, huh?"

Her irritated mouth purses. "What's sad is you have to go all the way to Oklahoma to find girls you haven't already dated."

"Yeah? I'll be sure to shed a tear for you while you're dating the same ten losers for the next four years." I step closer, my tone cruel. "Oh wait, forget what I said. You can't find dates these days, can you?"

Chloe's jaw clenches. "Better to go to prom stag with good friends than wind up with some cliché horror story about my date puking on my shoes."

"Everyone knows going solo to prom isn't really a choice. Sure, you hid it well with all the hashtag squad goals posts, but come on, the only reason you did was because Fletcher dumped you in favor of K.C." Sadly enough, he did end up puking on K.C.'s shoes. Idiot.

Her face twists with a different anger, one tinged with hurt. "That's low, even for you, Kipling."

She averts her gaze, her hair curtaining her face, and a pang of conscience stirs in my gut. Forgetting Daisy, I round on Chloe, grabbing her wrist to keep her from leaving as the first raindrop falls. "Aw, come on, I'm giving you a hard time. Fletcher's a moron and—"

She punches me in the ribs and twists away from my grasp, backing into the tree. "Oh, shut up, Kip. Don't act like Fletcher breaking up with me surrounded by the whole baseball team wasn't the karma you prayed for. You'd have paid for a front-row seat."

I'm on her in a flash, invading her space. She's taller than most of her friends, my exes, but at six-foot-three, I still tower over her. Which is why her fierceness is so impressive. Though I'd never admit that to her.

"Is that how you want to play this?" I rub the spot where her fist connected with my side. "Why don't you admit the real reason you send your dog to our yard every day?"

Shaking her head to clear the stray curls from her eyes, she says, "I still have no idea what you're talking about."

"Ah, sweetheart, if you're going to open the gate so she can come through, you should really keep an eye on her. You don't think she's found her way toward the back patio of the house a time or two? My bedroom window faces the back. So, try again."

"Don't call me sweetheart. And just because she's wandered into your yard a few times doesn't mean I let her." Chloe arches a challenging eyebrow. "Daisy's pretty smart. She probably opens the gate on her own."

She'll never admit she willingly allows Daisy on our property. Dad ripped into Mr. Lockwood once years ago about stepping in a pile. If James Lockwood knew his daughter opened the gate out of spite, he…well, hell, he'd probably give her a high-five, considering.

I shake my head. "Keep lying to yourself, Sunshine."

Her tiny hand halfheartedly shoves at my stomach. "Stop calling me that."

The ground vibrates with another round of thunder, and Daisy hauls tail through the gate. Rain hits our bodies, even with the shelter the tree provides, but neither of us moves to leave.

"You think I haven't seen your brown eyes staring at me during lunch?" My chest presses her further into the tree at her back.

"If I stare it's because I'm still trying to figure out why so many girls are willing to go out with you."

How can she be so freaking beautiful and infuriating at the same time? Lowering my head until we're nose-to-nose, I wag my brows. "Wouldn't you like to know?"

Her chin tips up, putting us closer. "Not even for all the flowers in the world. I'd rather plot your demise. It'd be a thing of beauty."

"Yeah, I bet you would." Dang, her and her smart mouth. I swallow back the laughter itching to spill from my lips. "It's curious how you go out with all of my friends."

"I could say the same thing."

"Just admit it." I lean in, whispering in her ear. "Admit you wish it were me walking you to your door at the end of the night."

Her bare leg grazes mine, and my fingertips dig into the tree's bark to keep from grabbing hold of her. When I draw back enough to see her face, her cheeks are pink, her brown eyes clear and wide.

"With how much you seem to pay attention to me, maybe you're the one wishing you were walking me to my door."

"If I were, it would only be because I have a misguided desire to see what that sassy mouth of yours tastes like."

Then Chloe's mouth is on mine. She isn't touching me anywhere else, not a hand, not her chest brushing mine. Just my mouth and hers. Chloe Lockwood is kissing me. Then I'm kissing her back.

She inches away, her eyes on my mouth before they lift to mine. Breathless, she says, "This changes nothing."

"Why would it?" I scoff, my mouth already seeking round two.

Chloe's lips part under my assault, or maybe mine yield to hers, because the girl is all in. Wrapping her arms around my neck, one hand holding the back of my head, Chloe kisses me like she's wanted this as much as I always have.

THE FAMILIAR CREAK of a gate has me circling in place to find Chloe, her chest rising and falling with labored breaths, standing part-way between the tree from our past and the fence which has always divided us.

"I still hate you." The heat in her eyes could ignite fires.

I run my tongue over my bottom lip. "Good, I wouldn't want it any other way."

Her hands fell from my neck, and I stepped away from the tree. Those were the last words spoken before taking off to our corners of the world. I left for Oklahoma and didn't return for two years. Then it was five.

I'm done with the division.

My stride consumes the space between us in ten steps. Skimming my palms along her cheeks, I'm drawing her face up and swallowing my name before she has a chance to speak it. My head slants, my lips crush, and my tongue grazes. Over her mouth, across her teeth, and finally, against the warmth of hers.

"You don't like him, Chlo. You know you don't," I say against her lips, afraid if I pull away, we'll never be here again.

Her exhale washes across my mouth. "And what makes you so sure?"

"Because I know how you look when you want someone." The memory of our first and only kiss fresh in my mind. "I *remember* how it feels when you kiss someone you want."

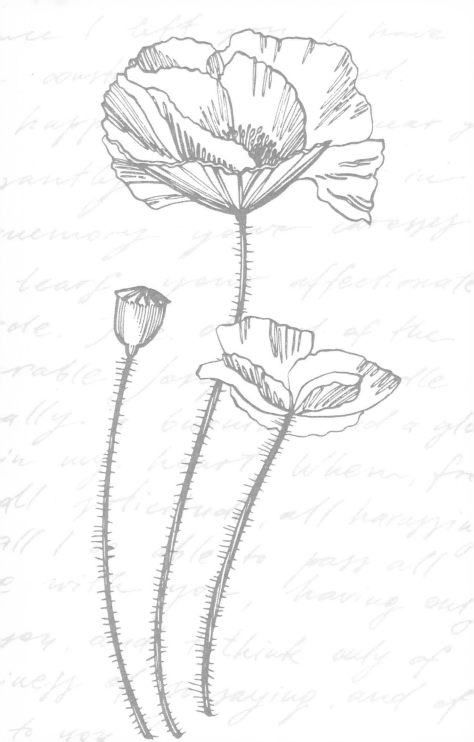

2 2

hloe

My hands fist the collar of his dress shirt. "Don't pretend to know me." Though he does, somehow, even with all the discord, he does. Kip lowers his mouth back to mine.

Years later, and here we are again, but this time the kiss isn't fueled by mutual animosity or a challenge, or even the curiosity of what it would feel like. It's years of built-up involuntary longing and regret. The fingers of my right hand trail up his chest and brush his clean-shaven jaw as he slips a hand beneath my cardigan, at the curve of my waist, melding me to his firm body.

Holy roses, Kip can kiss. The same thought crossed my mind when we were teens, but as a man... His eagerness has become a raw passion, his adolescent skills—smooth precision. My brain abandons me, my mouth and hands in full control. Or maybe control doesn't exist because kissing Kip relinquishes my power in the best way possible.

His hold on my cheek is tender and possessive. The kind of

touch I never want to lose. Except, he's kissing me, and he has no idea I broke up with Reid.

Coming back to myself, I push away and smack his chest. "What is wrong with you?"

"Me? Your boyfriend punches me, and somehow it's my fault?"

Even though our bodies aren't flush with one another, Kip keeps his hold on my waist.

"So, what? Kissing me is a way for you to get back at him?"

His shout of laughter vibrates through his chest to my hand pressing against him. "Oh, Chlo, if you think I'd kiss you for any reason other than my own pleasure, you don't know me at all."

"I see." My mouth pinches, my jaw clenching as I stiffen. "Typical Kipling Harris. You want something, you take it. No matter who stands in your way."

"I work damn hard for my accomplishments, the same as you. If I took what I wanted, I would have kissed you the moment I saw you on Sullivan's property covered in mud. Maybe sooner." The air in my lungs suspends as remorse flits across his blue eyes. "I never would have stepped on Reid's toes, but he lost my courtesy the moment he punched me today."

I shove his chest again, but not hard enough for Kip to budge. "He lost the girl, and from the sound of it, you egged him on. I might've punched you, too."

"Wait." His hand presses harder at the base of my spine, drawing me closer. "He lost the girl? When in the hell did he lose the girl?" Shaking his head, he clarifies, "Lose you?"

I straighten my shoulders, staring him square in the eyes. "I broke up with him after we got home from San Juan, you idiot."

"Run that by me again."

"You heard me the first time." I swallow, my eyes darting over his shoulder, unable to hold his confused stare. "On Monday, after work. I ended things. It was never going to last. And deep down, I knew that, but everything became clearer after being away from Seaside for a few days."

"Why?" His shallow breath brushes across my cheek as his fingers on my spine fidget with the back of my overalls. "Why did you break up with him?"

I swivel my head back, pinning him with a brazen stare. "Well, you seem to have all the answers already. Why don't you tell me?"

His infuriatingly handsome smirk appears. I want to smack it off as much as I want to kiss it again. "Nice try. Why did you break up with him, Sunshine?"

Freeing a heavy sigh, I give in, "Because I don't want him. I want you. Happy, Kipling?"

"Happy?" He inhales through his nose. "What would have made me happy was you telling me this Monday."

"I'm sorry I didn't cater to your schedule. Things have been a little hectic this week."

"What happened to *I'd never go out with a Harris*?"

My eye roll can be seen from the moon. "You can hold that over my head all you want, but it was never true."

"Damn straight, I'll hold it over your head, Chloe Lockwood. I've been processing that burn for a decade."

"Processing, right?" I scoff, shaking my head. "By dating all of my friends one-by-one. I think you coped just fine, Kipling."

"Jealous, flower girl?"

"Not in the slightest." Of course I was, but he didn't deserve the satisfaction of the confirmation.

"Liar." He narrows his eyes before relenting. "Fine, I'll go first. I was jealous. I hated every one of the guys you dated. You and Caleb. Why do you think you two didn't last long?"

The shortstop from his baseball team. "You didn't…"

"Guilty." He shrugs without a hint of remorse. "You know what else I did? I told Fletcher to dump you before prom. Then I set him up with K.C."

My eyes widen, shoving away from him, but he doesn't let go. "You wanted to get back at me so badly, you left me without a prom date?"

His hand wraps around the side of my neck, anchoring my attempt at looking away. "The dude came into the locker room bragging about how he was going to deflower the flower farmer's daughter. I was protecting you. I told him if he wanted a sure bet, he'd ask K.C. because you were a daddy's girl who would never go past second base, let alone sleep with him at some prom afterparty."

Kip might've been right. I never would've slept with Fletcher or any of the other guys I dated in high school, but what he did wasn't okay. "I didn't ask for your protection."

"And I didn't ask to fall for my pain in the ass neighbor, but go figure."

"Oh, wow. I'm sorry. How hard that must be for you to like a decent person."

"Be mad at me all you want, Sunshine. I'm not going to apologize for saving you from a prom nightmare." His thumb strokes my jawline, and I hate how easily the touch softens me. "I do apologize if you were hurt, though." His voice is low and soft, flirtatious, and it revs my anger back up.

"I couldn't care less about going to prom with Fletcher."

"Then why are you mad?" He flashes his teeth. I could stab him with my pruners.

"You had no right talking about how far I'd go on a date, especially in a locker room full of who knows how many guys."

"Wait. Are you telling me you weren't the sweet girl I assumed you were?"

My hands plant on my hips. I can't touch him when I'm mad. It fogs my brain. "That's beside the point."

"Is it, though? Now I'm curious, Miss Lockwood. You know guys talk. Most of them said nice things. There were a few, though. Do you want to settle the rumors once and for all?"

"Oh, shove it, Kipling." I maneuver out of his hold, putting distance between us.

"Actually, I don't want to know. I had a vision of ripping Reid's arm off at the May Day Festival when I saw him holding your hand. I hate to admit I don't have a lot of self-restraint when thinking of you with other men."

"Then just shut up about them." I throw my arms in the air. "They don't matter anyway."

We quiet, and I exhale my frustration. What are we doing? Why do we continue letting the past haunt us? No matter the strides we make as friends, there's this. This *thing* between us that can't be ignored. We don't control who we want, and yet so much stands in our way.

Kip shoves his hands in his pockets and cocks his head as he studies me.

"Chloe?" His gaze flicks to Gigi's necklace I wear around my neck. Stepping close again, he lifts his hand and slides his thumb along the chain. His smirk deepens when goosebumps pepper my skin. "Let me take you out."

My head whips up. "Are you serious?"

"Do I look like I'm kidding?"

"Kip, we've called a truce, kissed, and we still can't stop fighting. No matter how we feel, it can't be a good idea."

"Like hell it can't be. Our fighting is exactly why we're a good idea. You're a Lockwood, and I'm a Harris. There'll never be a dull moment. The kissing part is new, but I'm gonna go out on a limb and say it went pretty damn well. If anything, we should continue working on it." He continues tracing a path along my clavicle with his fingertip, and my breathing shudders. "Get as good at that as we are at driving each other crazy."

Tilting my head, I bite the corner of my curving mouth, hindering a smile. "Before I even consider saying yes, we have a few things we should discuss, don't you think? You and I can't exactly walk around this town hand-in-hand. Not yet."

"Sunshine, you're already considering saying yes, but fair enough. Have dinner with me tonight, at my place. We can call it a date, or we can call it dinner. It doesn't matter to me. Let's figure this out."

I must be the most insane woman on the planet because I can't stop myself. "Okay."

"Okay." His gaze drops to my lips. "I'm going to kiss you again now, you know, for practice. We're way behind."

Kip cups my face, locking our mouths in a crushing kiss. An embarrassing mewl slips between my lips, his tongue taking advantage and tangling with mine. His hands in my hair tighten like he's restraining himself. Abandoning my lips, he runs his nose along my jaw. "You know, the last time we kissed here, you said our kissing changed nothing."

"And?" I chuckle.

"And." He nuzzles the space between my jaw and ear, then pulls back. "You said you hated me."

With a coy shrug, I say, "Maybe I lied."

"Good, because to quote my eighteen-year-old self, *I wouldn't want it any other way.*"

I cover his lips with mine.

ip

As Brynn pointed out last night, living in a condo situated above an upscale shopping complex is a plus. I gamble on dinner and order several tapas dishes from the Spanish restaurant across from my place. Concerned a platter with various exotic dishes might come off as pretentious, I add a salad as a backup. Then, in a panic, I call back and throw in a request for Spanish chicken soup. Complete overkill, but this is Chloe.

Chloe, who is worried about us going out in public. I understand where she's coming from, especially with her situation with Reid. He's worked at the farm for years, and she relies on him. The thought of his name has me inhaling through my nose and releasing the air slowly. I'll forgive him for today's sucker punch because I would have done the same if I were in his shoes. Had I known she broke up with him, I wouldn't have goaded him. We showed our caveman behavior today. Hopefully, Chloe can see past the churlish behavior in my case.

214 | MINDY MICHELE

I'm unsure what I expect out of tonight. Maybe we have honest conversations about our lives and chalk up the chemistry between us as leftover emotions from childhood. Or maybe our complicated Capulet versus Montague-style family feud will prove to be our downfall.

Then the doorbell rings. My mouth goes dry with having her standing at my front door, and all my doubts fade when I kiss her cheek and she offers a shy smile as she steps inside.

This is right. All I have to do is prove it to her.

Closing the door, my gaze tracks Chloe as she steps further into the condo's entrance and glances around. The place is nice. High-end, open concept, but not my style.

"Fancy place you've got here."

"Hey, no judgment about the cliché hip, young, and wealthy bachelor decor. The place came fully furnished. The only stuff belonging to me is in the bedroom." I step close behind her, inhaling her fragrance. "Want to see?"

Chloe looks over her shoulder. "Slow your roll, Kipling." Her flirty chastising smirk could be the end of me.

Twisting her around, I draw her to my chest and lower my face to hers. "You know, Kipling from your mouth is a whole lot sexier than when my mom says it." Did I... A shudder runs through me. "And now I don't think I can kiss you like I wanted to."

She lets out a soft chuckle. "I can't decide if I want to call you Kipling more or less."

"Which is why I like you, Chloe Lockwood. You enjoy antagonizing me to the point of craving more. I'm a glutton for punishment." My lips brush over hers, the touch quick and light. "I'm glad you're here."

She inhales like she's thinking it through. "Me, too."

Taking her hand, I lead her to the dining table. "So, lesson one about adult Kip, I don't cook," I wave toward the food on the table.

"A man who can't cook? Unheard of."

"Of course not. I'll expect my barefoot wife to handle everything while popping out my babies," I say drolly. Chloe's face twists with annoyance. "I can cook, smartass. I just don't. I'm single and busy and have a lot of friends in Tulsa. We liked to eat out."

"Oh, you have a lot of friends in Tulsa?" She rests her cheek on her fist like she's ready for a full-length discussion. "Tell me more, Mr. Popularity."

"I imagine this is a foreign concept to you, but while your flowers are pretty company, most of us like having friends who talk back." I pump her hand in mine. "Speaking of friends, I ordered take-out from Muy Caliente. Carrie-Ann raved about the place when she found out I was moving in here. Have you been there?"

"Not yet. I've wanted to, but I don't drive to this side of town often since my flower friends prefer staying in." She cocks her head with an impish smile. "It smells delicious, though."

I wouldn't know. From the moment she walked in, her scent surrounded me. I'm in sophomore bio all over again. "I have to admit, I snagged a bite of the melon while waiting on you. I couldn't help myself." She scans the table while I pull a chair out for her. "Have a seat. Can I get you a drink? Wine, beer?"

"Umm...wine. White, if you have some."

"I do." Rounding the island separating the kitchen and dining area, I remove a bottle from the ice bucket. Chloe mumbles as I open the wine, and I glance up to see her chewing.

"Oh my gosh." She covers her mouth with her fingertips, pointing at the platter of food. "The melon. So good. Chili powder and lime? Who knew?"

"Surprising, right?" Pouring her glass, then popping the stopper from an already opened red and pouring mine, I pick them up in one hand and the bottle of chardonnay in the other and carry them toward the table. Then I stop. Chloe leans forward in her chair, her fingers dancing over the food platter like she can't decide what to taste next. This girl once covered my entire car with thousands of pink sticky notes, and here she is. With me.

My frozen state of hovering on the edge of the kitchen must draw her attention because her head lifts, and she sits back without nabbing food off the plate.

"What?" Chloe self-consciously runs a finger beneath her eyes. "Did I smear my makeup?"

"No. No, you're perfect. Sorry. I'm just amazed you're here." After all this time.

Setting the wine glass before her, I sit to her right. "We're really doing this, huh?"

Chloe fiddles with the stem before taking a sip. "At least a solid attempt." Her tender reply cuts through my reflective musings.

"Then to solid attempts," I toast, raising my glass to hers. "That's all we can ask for, right?"

My mind wavers, going back and forth between keeping this light and digging in deep. We're not on a normal first date. If that's what we're calling tonight. We've seen each other at our worst, hello, middle school, and we could fill notebooks with stories of our antics through the years. Still, with all our history, this is new. We're older than the kids who kissed under a tree all those years ago. Older, and fingers crossed, wiser.

Angling my chair to face her, I dare the first step. "Okay, let's dig in"—I lay my napkin across my thigh and draw the tapas platter closer between us—"and have this out."

Chloe mirrors my action, drawing her napkin into her lap before reaching for a slice of chorizo. "I think we need ground rules."

Rules. "I don't have any paper or colored pencils at the table. Do you think we can do this without charts?"

A quiet laugh slips out of her. "Maybe you should ask yourself."

"I'm all about sacrifice if it means we get a chance. Hit me with your rules."

The edge of her mouth twitches. "Aside from the obvious," she says, helping herself to a chicken-skewer. "I can't flaunt something like this around town so close to breaking things off with Reid. He deserves more respect than that."

"A clandestine affair? I suppose I can get into the forbidden aspect." I push the salad bowl her way.

I get the sense she'd like to call me Kipling, and not in a sexy way, with the way her mouth purses. I flash an apologetic grin.

"In all seriousness, I never set out to steal you away from Reid. I go after what I want, but I wouldn't steal another man's girl. Not on purpose. I shouldn't have kissed you this afternoon knowing, or well, thinking you were still with him." I swivel in my seat and tap her foot with mine under the table. "It's just… you make me crazy."

Chloe closes her eyes and opens them on an exhale. "We make each other crazy. And if I'm honest, since you dropped me off last Sunday, I haven't been able to stop wishing you'd kissed more than my cheek."

"Come here," I say, crooking my finger.

We come together over the corner of the table, our lips meeting in a light connection. A simple touch. One that has us smiling when we part.

"Better?" I ask while considering the prospect of kissing more than her cheek…or lips.

She gives me a cheeky grin. "It'll do for now."

"I'm surprised to hear you say you wanted more," I admit.

She had Reid, and she wanted me. Playing this game of making rules and acting like we're not going to happen is pointless. Then again, she ignored me all week. Why? "Especially since my calls this week went unreturned. And my voicemail last night…I figured I'd scared you off."

She shakes her head. "I'm sorry I didn't call you back. I was going to after work today. At first, it was out of respect for Reid and just needing to get my head on straight. But the voicemail you left yesterday… I lost my phone on the farm Thursday morning and it died, so I didn't hear it until today. Otherwise, I would've called you right back."

I wave her explanation away. She doesn't owe me anything. "It's fine. I shouldn't have said those things, considering your relationship. Chloe, from the moment I ran into you my first day back, I've fought a losing battle to stay away. The passing of seven years doesn't matter. I have this insane curiosity to finish what we couldn't back then."

"This could blow up in our faces," she says. "My parents, your parents, Reid, your job in Tulsa. That's a lot of adversity."

There's so much truth in her statement. "You're right. It could. However, something you don't know about this Kip is he likes adversity, and he loves winning."

"Well, *that* Kip I do know." I can't help admiring her sass.

"I feel like you're referencing something specifically?"

"Ohh, you know, just a few hundred bets made over the years." She taps the tines of her fork on her plate.

"I can't help it if I rarely made a bet I couldn't win."

Her lips pucker, calling me out. "You mean a bet you couldn't cheat your way to winning?"

"I have no idea what you're talking about. Using my brain is not cheating."

"Being underhanded *is* cheating. You enlisted so many people to help you beat me every time; it's not even funny."

God, I was such a prick as a teen. So much steel pride when it came to her. "It's a little bit funny."

"One of these days Kipling Harris, I'm going to knock you off your high horse."

"So, back to ground rules then." I resume eating.

Chloe kicks at my shin. "Mmm-hmmm, way to ignore the past, Kipling."

"Since we're as likely to kill each other as kiss," I say with meaning, and she chuckles. "It's probably smart we move slow."

"Slow is good." She nods, but I note the skepticism in her wrinkled brow. Is she unsure about us or about taking things slow? "There's so much we don't know about each other anymore. Seven years is a long time. We're different people. And what about the lives affected if this gets out…"

"Chloe." I reach between us and cover her hand resting on the table beside her wine glass. "Let's do this. Maybe we could start by talking about the past?"

She chews on the corner of her bottom lip, the skeptical glint in her eyes remaining.

"Our past," I clarify. "Not our father's feud, us. High school. It's probably fair to say we wronged each other more than either of us knows."

"Understatement." She takes a sip of her wine and licks her lips. "Though, elementary school is where it *really* began."

"Sad, but true. I guess now's the time to admit to stealing your pencil sharpener from your desk in second grade?"

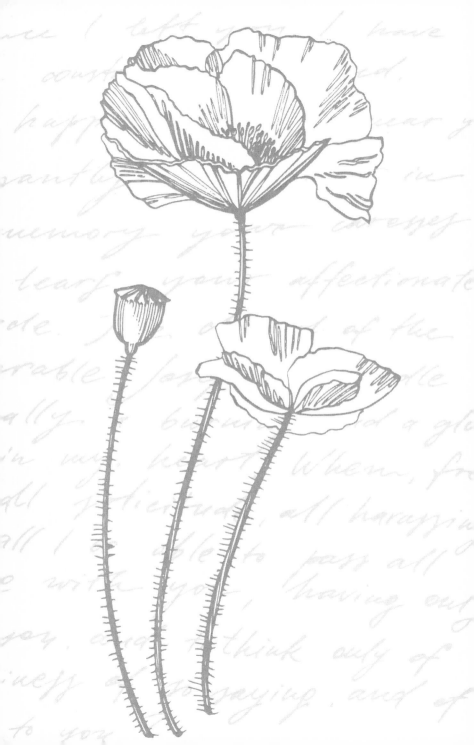

ip

"Okay, Miss Lockwood." I lead Chloe to the couch once we're too full for another bite. We've walked through our complicated past, and I'm not sure if I've ever laughed as much. Certainly not on a first date. Who knew confessing our childhood foolishness would produce such enjoyable dinner conversations? "Explain what it is you want to do with Sullivan's land. Why is expansion so important to Lockwood Blooms?"

Shifting, I give her my full attention while maintaining personal space. Space is imperative because she's ridiculously tempting tonight in her skintight jeans and pink cardigan, the shade of which perfectly matches her flushed cheeks. The lace-trimmed tank she wears beneath her sweater is what's doing me in. Lace, Chloe's smooth skin, and the memory of our kiss this afternoon? I move another inch toward the couch's armrest for her protection.

"Oh, so many things." She lights up. "I'd love to plant a field where people could come and cut their own blooms. Bouquets, by the bucket, whatever they want. Though if it became too successful, I'd probably have to limit it. And there are so many new varieties to be discovered for our selection if I had the land for it."

"Hmmm, isn't this where we started a month ago?" I tap my temple.

Chloe sets her empty wine glass on the coffee table. "Remember that little pity party you found me in at the fence?" How could I forget? "My pet project is the Lockwood Blooms seed line. I've been collecting data on seeds for the last few years." She holds up her palm with a light chuckle. "Don't let your eyes glaze over just yet. The concept is a lot more challenging than it sounds, but it would be a dream to provide others the opportunity to grow our flowers. I'd had about fifty varieties ready to be packaged for a few local nurseries and florists this month. A new employee mistook the collection and tossed it out. So, we've been set back about a year, maybe more. I'll have to wait until we get more land to start over." She frowns, her eyes downcast. "And all the new varieties I'd grown and harvested are gone. I can't recreate them."

"And your current fields have no room for these things due to demand for flowers?"

"We only have so much land. And recently, we've had to turn away customers. We hate disappointing potential and loyal patrons."

She needs Sullivan's land. She needs the land Dad won't sell her, but he refuses to budge. The crap he's pulling with Sullivan's assures me of that. "Too many customers is a great problem to have, Chloe. You should be proud of yourself and your family for the success Lockwood Blooms has achieved."

"I'm trying, but I could do so much more."

Of course she could. I drink my wine and nod. In the space of one conversation, Chloe's happiness, her livelihood, seems to have fallen on my shoulders. The Harris family owns, represents, or manages a sizable portion of land in this town and beyond city limits. What if I can't give her what she needs? What Lockwood Blooms needs? Mixing business and pleasure is never smart. Reid Pruitt is living proof.

"What about you? There's gossip all over town, but what truly brought you back to Seaside?"

"That explanation might take a while, and more wine." I swirl the last sip of my red wine and down it.

She leans back and rests her arm along the back of the couch. "I think I have some time."

I check the hour and contemplate her empty glass. "I hate you had to drive yourself here. I should've picked you up. I can drive you home when you're ready—"

"It's okay. I'm a big girl, and I'm done drinking." She tucks a leg beneath her and gets comfortable. "Plus, it's Friday night. I don't have to be in the fields at the crack of dawn."

Verifying once more she's comfortable driving later, I move to grab the bottle cabernet from the kitchen where I left it, explaining the Omni-Plex as I go.

"My dad approached me months ago about developing the same type of project here," I say, returning to the couch. "In truth, I think he knew it would require something big to lure me back. Allowing me free rein with the riverfront land was something I couldn't pass up. At the same time, my firm in Tulsa doesn't want to lose me, so they essentially loaned me to Harris Development. It's a headache, in all honesty. Dad wants me to move home, but he and I…"

"Have a difficult time getting along."

I reach across the back of the couch and lace my fingers with hers. "That's a nice way of saying it."

The sympathetic tilt of her head pushes me to continue.

"I know your relationship with James is different than the one I have with my dad, but I imagine you understand the feeling of wanting to be who you want to be. Leave your own mark. I'm not willing to sit around for another fifteen years waiting on Denton Harris to retire so I can run things the way I see fit."

"For sure. It's why I've been brainstorming ways to take Lockwood Blooms to the next level."

"Exactly. So, if that means I establish myself in Tulsa or elsewhere, then so be it."

Chloe's gaze drops to her lap, her teeth capturing her lower lip. I recognize her disappointment, likely because I feel the same.

Squeezing her fingers, I add, "I do miss Seaside. I hate how I haven't been here for Brynn since the whole Preston fiasco. I miss my mom. And the water and mountains. There are a lot of reasons for me to be here." I dip low and meet her eyes. "And this budding attraction with a pretty little flower girl I know is one of them. Pun intended."

Chloe shakes her head with a light laugh. "Oh, Kipling. Ever the charmer."

Drawing her hand into my lap, I slide closer. "Chloe, there's a lot of history between us personally, and a lot of crap…" I frown. How do I say this? Can we set aside business and our families and give us a chance? Are those things irrevocably tied?

"Hey." She tugs my shirt, wrenching me from the negative road my thoughts veer onto. "We should do this, Kip Harris. Of course I have my reservations, and it won't be easy, but I want to. Now, I know more than ever, I want you."

Leaning in, I kiss the edge of her mouth. "I want you, too." My hand tangles in her waves. She wears her hair up for work most of the time, but I love this wild look. The look she wore when we were younger. The waves are soft in my palm. Soft like her skin, and her cheek, and her lips. "Did I tell you how gorgeous you look tonight?"

I draw back, and her sexed-up eyes with their heavy shadow

and liner flutter open. "I don't know. Maybe. I can't remember that far back." Her voice is breathy as she reaches for me.

"That far back, huh?" I'm smiling at the way her hands tug on my shirt until I'm twisted and hovering over her body.

"Mmm-hmmm." She licks her lips, and my brain stops operating. "Anything before you kissed me is gone."

I intend on replying, but Chloe has other ideas. Her strawberry-tinged lips mold to mine, matching every move. I want to touch her, to wrap her in my arms, but our position—twisted and side-by-side—isn't helping. Reaching for her hip, I pull at her body with undefined intentions. I want her closer. Chloe seems to agree. As my palm grips her thigh, she stretches her leg over my lap and pushes me into the back of the black leather couch, straddling me. I groan inwardly, sinking further into the cushions and taking hold of her hips, adjusting her on my lap until we're flush. A perfect match.

Our mouths never part as my hands slip beneath her cardigan and up her spine until I'm running my fingertips over the bare skin along the top hem of her tank. She hisses in my mouth when my index finger wraps around her strap, toying up and down. Her body radiates heat. Her skin is on fire beneath my knuckle. When my hand skates around the curve of her backside, I summon the strength to tear myself away.

"We should stop," I murmur against her lips, gripping a belt loop on her jeans and deepening our kiss again.

Chloe hums in agreement, but it's more of a moan as she sinks her fingers into the hair at the back of my head, showing no signs of slowing down. Her hips rock forward as her tongue taunts me, tracing the inside of my bottom lip.

"Chlo, stop." I trap her bottom lip in my teeth, then release. "We need…" My thumbs push her tank up along her sides. The quiver of her stomach at my touch stills me once more. "Slow," I rasp. Snatching my hands from her skin, I lift them in surrender. My body throbs for her touch, but this is not the time.

"You're right." Her breathing is shallow as her hooded eyes drift between my eyes and mouth and back. "Slow." She repeats like she's trying to convince herself. "Yeah, probably smart." With a bashful smile, Chloe climbs off my lap.

Running my hands through my hair, I release a deep breath. My jeans are uncomfortably tight. I sit forward on the couch, discreetly adjusting my position, and a fluttery giggle floats through the condo.

Taking in the temptress beside me, I grin. "You're proud of yourself, aren't you?" Her already flushed face flushes deeper. "Gloat all you want, Sunshine, because you look thoroughly kissed and salacious yourself."

I tuck her mussed hair behind her ear, only for it to fall forward again. "See?"

She shrugs, her flustered smile turning brazen. "I'm not ashamed about what you do to me, Kipling."

"Yeah?" My finger traces over the lace edge of her top, and her breathing trembles. She's so beautifully tempting I find myself gravitating toward her again. My hands lock on her hips as my head dips, and before our mouths connect, I flip her onto her back on the buttery leather cushion and throw my body on top of hers.

"Do you like what I do to you?" I nip at her neck and pinch her sides, loving her peal of laughter as she squeals my name.

"Stop! Kip!" She giggles, her hands fighting to block my playful assault. "Please, stop!"

My smiling mouth covers her ear. "Are you ticklish, Miss Lockwood?" Her shirt bunches around her ribs as I poke at her sides. "I'm learning something new every hour."

"No, noooo. I swear—" Her words become indecipherable as she begs between gasps of air. "What do I have to say?"

"Say you'll go out with me."

"I'll go out with you!"

"Actually, say I'm the most handsome guy around, and you can't believe you ever considered refusing my—"

"Shut up!" She laughs, her body wiggling beneath my weight.

Stealing a kiss, I roll to my feet. "Good enough."

"You monster." A smile downplays her words.

I offer my hand, yanking her against my chest when I heave her to her feet with more muscle than necessary. "Sorry, I needed to cool down, or I was never going to let you leave." My gaze scans her disheveled clothing. Her cardigan is off one shoulder, her top is twisted. She's a tousled mess, and my ardor did not cool down.

She steps back and rights her sweater, tugging down her tank top with her eyebrow arched. "Don't think I'd have been able to resist you, huh?"

She's cute. "Wanna put your willpower to the test?"

She's quiet for a beat, and I can't say I don't hope she's considering it, but then she gives a small smile. "If you do, in fact, want to slow things down, better not."

"Want and need are two very different things, aren't they?" Pinching the hem of her shirt, I tug twice, wordlessly asking her to come closer. "We should get you home."

With a nod, she gives me a peck.

My mood deflates as we exit my building and cross the parking lot to where she parked. She wraps her hand around my arm and leans her head against my shoulder, and I want to savor the moment.

"Thank you for dinner," she says when we stop at her beat-up truck.

Betty doesn't offer much of a cover if we're doing secret rendezvous, but thankfully the complex is home to multiple restaurants and a bookstore that remain open late. She could technically be here visiting any of those places.

"Thank you for coming over," I reply as she leans against the door, and I step closer. *No further, Kip.* "Next time, and let me remind you, you did agree to a next time earlier on the couch, I'm picking you up. I'll park down the road or something. Call me old-fashioned if you want."

"Okay. You're old-fashioned, but I accept. I'll climb out my bedroom window and run through the fields to meet you at the dirt road." She smirks, teasing. "But, really, I will have to sneak away somehow if I don't drive. It's silly, I know."

"Hey, I agreed to the ground rules." *Reluctantly.* I tip her chin and kiss her goodnight. "I think you could be worth the hassle, Miss Lockwood."

She sucks in her bottom lip, blushing before climbing into the driver's side.

"Drive safe, and call me when you're safe and sound inside?"

hloe

WHEN I GET HOME and climb into bed, I call Kip to let him know I survived and arrived undetected. Even though I'm a grown adult and my parents don't normally keep track of my whereabouts anymore, it's rare for me to stay out so late. Knowing my parents, they went to bed hours ago, so I didn't have to sneak in.

Kip and I reminisce about moments of us growing up and the truth about what we thought about one another. Mostly how much we hated how attracted we were to each other and wanted to forget the other existed. We fill each other in on where our classmates are now and the regrets of who we dated. Before I know it, the sun casts a hazy glow through the blinds of my childhood bedroom window. As a teenager, I never talked all night with a boy, but this feels like that. Sneaking a late-night phone call when I should be asleep.

When I pry my eyes open the next morning and check the

clock on my nightstand, it's after twelve. I haven't slept this late in, well, ever. And I could sleep longer. I almost roll back over, but I check my phone first and find a couple texts from Kip.

> **Kipling: Hey, gorgeous, if I made a gratuitous visit to my parents' house today, would you have time to sneak over to our tree for a...um, conversation?**

> **Kipling: I know it's only been ten hours since I saw your face and four since I heard your voice, but we're making up for lost time, right?**

He only slept until ten? Well, I'm a slacker. All the hours I could've spent in the fields this morning. I even missed first light in the flower fields for him.

> **Me: I might be able to sneak away. Tell me when.**

> **Kipling: I'm already here, sleepyhead. Doing lunch and helping Brynn. Text me when you can break away, and I'll be there.**

When I finally make it downstairs after showering and dressing, I text Kip when I head out to check on our breeding patches and tell him I'll meet him in twenty minutes. Mom asks me if I'm feeling well as she does the dishes. *Chloe not making it downstairs until almost one?* Unheard of. I invent an excuse about having an upset stomach and needing a few more hours, which she buys, because why wouldn't she? Her daughter never lies to her. Thankfully, Dad is napping on the couch, so I don't have to lie to him, too.

I've made up white lies over the years. What child hasn't? But it's the first time guilt festers deep like I'm betraying her.

My phone pings from my jeans pocket, but I don't check the

screen until I'm out the door. Anticipation dances in my stomach when I read Kip is on his way.

I pass through the rose patch and around the zinnias. Our taller blossoms line the property butting against the Harrises, so I can't see if he's there yet. When I reach the edge of the towering sweet peas, Kip is waiting under the oak tree, one jean-clad leg draped over the other with his arms crossed. His head turns as if sensing my approach and his freckled face brightens.

How did I let so many years of conflict keep me from being on the receiving end of that look? There's no other smile like it. Warm and infectious and irresistible. Not to mention, every time he lifts that crooked smile, all I want to do is kiss it. My self-control throughout the years has been impeccable.

Passing through the gate, I latch it behind me and peek back at the path to verify no one saw me. Even though I'm normally the only one in the fields on Saturday, this secret rendezvous has me a little paranoid, but all is quiet on the flower front.

As I approach Kip, he pushes himself from the trunk and meets me halfway. Bending down, he kisses me hello without a word. Before he can pull away, I wrap my arms around his neck and kiss him fully. I don't know what's gotten into me. If it's all the time we wasted or the build-up of years of passionate banter, or if it's simply because this is Kip, but I can't get enough of his mouth.

He sucks in a breath and groans as his arms tighten around my waist, lifting me on my tiptoes. I'm weightless in his arms, every worry vanishing. I sigh into him as he sets me back down, kissing me lightly once.

"Hi," I say against his lips.

"Hi." He returns my kiss and looks over his shoulder in the direction of his parents' house. "Come with me." Grabbing my hand, Kip tugs me into a crouching jog. I can't stop my giggle.

We run to the Harris property line along the water's edge, where a thicker brush and tree line grow. As we slow, the outline of a teepee made of logs and branches comes into view. Hiding us away in an old fort? I laugh a little more.

Once he tugs me inside, Kip draws me into his arms and swings me around. I'm not much of a runner, so I'm out of breath as his lips crush against mine. His kiss doesn't help as I pant into his mouth, reveling in his ardent affection.

Kip presses his forehead to mine. "Sorry, Brynn was tenacious as hell about my leaving the house. She claims to have a gift at reading my lies. Apparently, she decoded so many growing up, I can't hide them anymore."

My breathless chuckle is embarrassing. "Think she'd keep our secret?"

"Are you kidding? I mean, yeah, she would. One hundred percent, but…" Puffing his cheeks, he releases a deep breath. "She would be a nightmare. She'd be asking you for wedding colors and preferred baby names before the end of the day."

"What are big sisters for if not to harass you?"

"Talk to me again when you're the one she's harassing," he says, locking me in his embrace.

While I might not be ready for all of those things, Brynn is amusing. Though, I can't tell if the ideas of the future scare Kip or annoy him. Maybe it's neither. Maybe it's both. I'd understand if they did. It's been less than a day since we started seeing each other. Those things are leaps and bounds ahead of us.

Last night Kip did say he was curious about us. Curious. The word doesn't exactly scream commitment. And I mean, his casual approach shouldn't bother me. He still hasn't decided whether he's staying in Seaside. After he's finished with his riverfront deal, he'll probably wind up back in Tulsa. With an overbearing dad like his, I would, too.

After listening to his last voicemail, I'm leaning to believe he isn't staying. Which is fine. Really. How would I tell my parents I'm dating Denton's son? I'm not sure my dad would ever approve. The hurt runs too deep. He wouldn't disown me, but I can't say his disappointment would be easy to endure.

This works the way it is. It does. We can have our fun in private until he leaves. Fun. I can do fun, especially with Kip. *Right?* Sunlight peeks through the crevices between the wood, casting a ray on the left side of Kip's face. "Oh, your cheek." I carefully cradle his jaw, his skin shaded bluish-purple. "Does it hurt?"

"I'll survive."

"I'd say I'm sorry, but you kind of deserved it." I gnaw on the corner of my lip, scrunching the bridge of my nose.

"There's no reason for me to argue your point since I won in the end."

Gently, I kiss his jawline before lifting my gaze. I take in the inside of the makeshift teepee. "Nice fort. Is this where you lured all the ladies? Charming them with your prepubescent boy skilled craftsmanship."

"Well, there it is, proof Chloe Lockwood doesn't know boys at all." His arms fall to his sides, his fingers twining with mine. "Girls are not allowed in forts, Sunshine." I can almost hear the sneer of a bratty eight-year-old Kip.

"Oh, so we're breaking all the rules now, huh." My eyes light with mischief.

He sinks to the ground and draws me across his lap. "Hell yeah, we are." His lips crash into mine, mouth open and devouring. My front arches into him, begging, wanton. It's so unlike me. When it comes to intimacy, my default setting is to let the man lead most of the time, but Kip flips a switch inside me, and rational thought sails away. All that's left are the lustful desires of a deprived woman who can't get enough of him. Reverting to an impulsive teenage libido, maybe? Or maybe Kip just makes me feel like I can be who I am, be more than the obedient people pleaser I've been my whole life. He allows me to let loose without question like he knew this woman was in me all along.

"How busy are you today?" Kip breaks the kiss while keeping his arms loosely around me. "Do you want to get together tonight? Maybe a movie?" His nose nudges mine. "What can we do around here where no one will see us?"

"Around here? Nothing." I chuckle. With our last names, Kip and I are too recognizable to be seen anywhere in public. "But I'm sure we could think of something outside of Seaside."

"So, my place it is." He frowns falsely.

Kip's hands slip beneath the hem of my sweatshirt, gripping the edge of my jeans at my hip. He lowers his mouth to mine, tucking my bottom lip between his, and sucks. Putty. I'm putty in his hands. Shape me into a peony or a dahlia. I'll be a bed of weeds. I don't care. I'll be whatever he wants.

A sated sigh passes between us as his tongue traces my lower lip. I sink into Kip, savoring every touch and stroke. His fingertips skim my lower back, dipping under my shirt.

With a low growl, he breaks our kiss. "If I'd known having a girl in here was this much fun, I would have invited one in a long time ago." Desire burns behind his blue eyes before he buries his face against my neck. "To, uh, practice my skills."

My head falls back. "Just some girl, huh?"

At the swipe of his tongue across my sensitive skin, I fist his hair, holding him close. He found my weak spot. Any request could pass his lips at this point, and I'd say yes.

"Just you."

"We'd have been so much trouble," I whisper. "Much to our parents' dismay, probably would've wound up with the first generation of Harris-Lockwood in high school." A breathless chuckle trickles from my lips.

His hand curves around my thigh, his fingers stroking the underside of my knee. Even with the denim separating his touch from my skin, a shiver runs down my spine. "Well, well, this fits right into my barefoot and pregnant plan. I guess now we have the answer to whether or not you can resist me."

My fist tightens at the roots of his hair, pulling his head away to meet my lips. "Don't pretend like it wouldn't have gone both ways."

"Oh, don't worry your pretty little head, Miss Lockwood. I'm aware you're my weakness." He shifts under my weight on his lap. "If we're not careful, we could still give our parents a Harris-Lockwood surprise. Wonder if they'd take it better now since we're self-sufficient adults?"

I stiffen, breaking the Kip fog. *So* sure of himself. "You wonder how *they'd* take it? You might want to ask how *I'd* take it. Like I'm gonna roll over and let you have your way with me?"

"How much you wanna bet you would?" His smirk sets me over the edge.

I scramble off his lap and knock my head on the logs of the teepee. *Ouch.* "That's not a bet you're gonna win, Kipling." We are not about to have our first time in Kip's childhood fort.

Laughing, Kip stands and nabs a fistful of my sweatshirt, pulling me into his chest. "Chloe, we haven't had an officially official date. I'm not contemplating knocking you up." His forehead gently touches mine. "Granted, if you want to practice, I promise to be safe."

I swat his chest and slip out of his hold, stumbling out of the teepee on wobbly legs. "You're impossible."

"So, I'll pick you up at six?" he yells after me. I wave my middle finger in the air. His laughter bellows, following me as I march away.

After a minute, quickened footsteps come up behind me through the tall grass, and Kip's arms swoop me up, kissing beneath my jaw. *He knows.* I melt against him.

"I'm teasing. Please know I would never push you for sex, and any talk of a future with kids is obviously a long way away."

A future with kids? Is he actually thinking about a future with us? It wasn't just a euphemism for getting in my pants? "Careful, Kipling. One might confuse you with a gentleman." And while I appreciate a gentleman, his lack of asking permission isn't unappealing.

"We wouldn't want that now, would we?" As if to prove his point, his teeth clamp down on the curve of my neck, with a bite equal parts pleasure and pain.

"How's Reid doing?" Mom folds one of Dad's T-shirts and moves to the next.

Sighing, I plop down on the couch beside her, all dreamy thoughts of the last hour with Kip trampled. "Ignoring me for the most part."

"The boy is heartbroken; can you blame him?"

"No, but it'd be nice to not have tension affecting the whole Lockwood Blooms family. It seems like everyone is taking a side."

"You don't think you two will be able to work it out?" Dad asks from his recliner. "He's a good man. I'd be proud to have him as a son-in-law."

"*Dad.*"

He raises his hands. "I'm not saying you have to marry the guy. I just don't understand why it didn't work out. You seemed so happy with him."

"Because she doesn't love him, James." Mom sighs, picking up a pair of Dad's pants.

"Well, it'd only been a couple of months. They didn't give it enough time. It might've happened eventually."

"It wasn't going to happen," I say. Not even without Kip.

I just might send the man to an early grave if he finds out I ended things with Reid because of Kip Harris. Well, not because of, but it wasn't not because of him, either.

"Just give it time, Loe." Mom stacks the folded clothes in the laundry basket. "Before you know it, he'll find someone new, and you'll be back to working well together as you always have."

"Maybe I should get out in the fields more again. My presence might dissipate unnecessary drama."

"I don't need my dad to save me from awkward breakup tension. It's my fault. Planting the dahlia tubers was too much for you as it was. I've got this, Dad."

Thankfully, he accepts my answer. "Any word on the Sullivan land?"

"His son, Joseph, is still stalling, but we should hear something soon."

Heaving a heavy exhale, he says, "I wouldn't put it past a Harris to sabotage the deal. Like father, like son."

"Kip is doing what he can." It requires everything I have not to sound too defensive. "He wouldn't sabotage a deal that would make the Harrises money. Feud or not."

Dad scoffs, crossing his arms. "Don't let his pretty-boy smile fool you, Loe." I tense at his insult. "We can't give Harris Jr. too much credit. A Harris will do anything to destroy a Lockwood, even if it means hurting themselves in the process."

I'm a grown twenty-five-year-old woman, and yet, when Kip texts me that he's waiting on Wicker Road around the corner, I tell my parents Grace is here to pick me up to go out for the night. I never even told them these kinds of lies in high school, pretending to sleepover at a friend's when instead I was going to a party or sneaking off with a boy.

My parents sit on the couch in the living room watching TV and holler they love me as I walk out the front door. I shove down the guilt rising inside me and breathe in the thrill of seeing Kip.

His Audi is running, the brake lights on as I come up behind him. Before I reach for the handle, the slink of the locks sound, and I slide inside.

"Hey, gorgeous," he says, producing a rose. "Standard grocery store variety, but only because I was afraid of being caught in your garden."

With a light chuckle, I lean across the console and kiss him. And can I just say how strange and natural it feels all at the same time? I'm kissing Kip like we've been doing it for years, like this is what we should've been doing this whole time. His signature smirk is in full swing when I sink against my seat like he's reading my thoughts.

Get out of my head. You're not that *great.*

Not that great. Right. And yet here I am, lying to my parents about sneaking around with the enemy because I can't stay away. I don't want to.

We pick up two pepperoni pizzas on the way to his condo, because he likes pan crust and I prefer thin, and the smell of it alone has my mouth watering as I hold the warm boxes on my lap. Settling onto the leather couch in his living room, Kip scrolls through movies available online until we agree on one. A little action flick with comedy and a dash of suspense.

When we've made a dent in the pizzas and our bellies are full, I curl into his side, my hand crawling across his chest. With a mind of their own, my fingers stroke his hard pecs. He wraps his arm around my shoulder and tugs my legs across his lap, cradling the underside of my knee. Puzzle pieces fitting together seamlessly. His mouth presses a kiss to the top of my head before resting his cheek there.

Before our trip to San Juan Island, I wouldn't have believed it if someone told me I'd be snuggled up to Kip Harris in his condo watching a movie, and nothing about it felt weird or wrong. Dare I say, it feels right.

What is this world coming to?

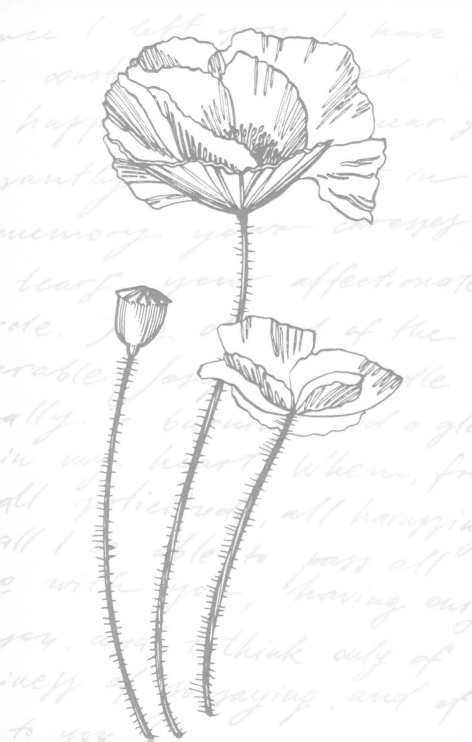

 ip

SECRETLY DATING in a gossip-thriving town like Seaside Pointe is challenging. Secretly dating Chloe Lockwood in Seaside Pointe is challenging but proving well worth the ten year—if I count back to sophomore biology—wait. I can't get enough of her. Her 'no going public' ground rules don't phase me. I mean, I hate keeping us a secret, but I can deal with the lies when the alternative is losing this time with her. Whether it's dinner Friday, staying up and talking on the phone, stolen kisses in my child-hood fort, or pizza and a movie on my couch, I'm discovering she's the type of woman I always assumed she'd be.

This is why I drive twenty minutes to Fidalgo Island and spend Memorial Day hiking trailheads alone. Chloe had to work, the flower business doesn't take a holiday, and my head needs clearing. When I agreed to come home it was understood that if the riverfront did not pass zoning changes, I would return to Tulsa. Dad began the rezoning process months ago. He was confident the development project would tempt me. And while it took an effort by Carrie-Ann to convince me once and for all, he wasn't wrong. Denton Harris lured me to Seaside with a lofty project, but there's nothing saying he can keep me. We should have an answer by June. Local politics have stalled our going before the zoning commission, but Roger is confident we'll be on the schedule in the next two to three weeks.

Where does that leave me? I spend hours at Rosario Head Monday working through my options. I can oversee the development from Tulsa while traveling back and forth. Not ideal, but I trust Dad to run things smoothly if I'm not local. He wants this complex as much as I do. Or I can stay in Seaside during construction, manage it and keep my hand in every decision made by contractors every step of the way, and return to Tulsa once completed.

It's easy enough to hand over management responsibilities. Most owners do. They sign over their land, shopping centers, or office complexes to Harris as a managing partner and sit back and rake in the money, minus a management fee. That is why Harris Development exists. This is my deal. Can I find a way to work with Dad? Step after step, as I spend the day hiking, I ask myself these things.

Then there's Chloe. Can two people who grew up conditioned to loathe one another find love? Even if we do, would Chloe let us happen? She's a people pleaser. Especially when that person is James. Could she find the courage and take a leap with me, even if he disapproves? Would he disapprove? She's his only child, and this damn feud has gone on long enough.

FOR THE FIRST time in years, going to work Tuesday morning is a chore. I have something, someone, else I want to spend my time on. For the last seven years, I've worked tirelessly, in college, in grad school, in internships, in my career. I've focused my energy on proving Kipling Harris is good enough. He doesn't need his daddy's money and name to be someone. Two months back in Seaside, and I find I care little about what anyone thinks of me. Anyone, except Chloe Lockwood.

"Good morning." Joan's contagious joy greets me when I enter Harris Development's lobby. "Did you have a good long weekend?"

My mind automatically goes to Chloe, and our morning texting conversation:

Chloe: Freshman year, you glitter bombed my locker, allowing me to discover glitter in places I didn't know existed for weeks. True or false?

Me: First, you wake up way too early! Second, good morning. Third, I have no idea what you're talking about, but I'd like to hear more about these places harboring glitter. Show and Tell?

Chloe: Don't you dare deflect, Kipling. I know it was you.

There's no hiding my good mood today. "It was excellent. You?" I ask Joan.

"I can't complain. The weather was lovely and right on time for the start of our Saturday yoga on the lawn classes." She passes me a stack of mail I didn't pick up Friday before I snuck out early to find Chloe.

I flip through the envelopes and chuckle. "I tried yoga at the student center a few times when I was in school. I don't know how people keep up. Every time I mastered one pose, we were moving to the next."

"Once you learn the names for the moves, it becomes easier," she says, adjusting her headset.

"In all honesty, it was a way to meet girls," I confide, leaning over her desk. "Let's keep that between us, okay?"

Shaking her blonde head, Joan zips her lips with a grin. I head down the hallway to my office.

The day is long and busy, as is Wednesday.

I call Melvin Sullivan to discuss his property and end up leaving a message. I entertain calling his son for all of one minute before putting the phone down. I'll give Melvin time to return my call before bothering with Joseph. The Sullivan children are pushy heirs to their parent's money. In truth, Lockwood Blooms is the perfect buyer. If I can convince him before Dad gets in his head more than he already is.

I haven't told Chloe about Dad's interference with her deal. I can't. Maybe my silence is dishonest, but I'm hoping the issue resolves itself.

DAD HIJACKS my Wednesday afternoon in the name of business. We spend the day stopping by our properties, driving north to survey land for sale, and meeting with a contractor to go over plans for the full remodel of one of our strip centers. In the midst of all my busyness, Chloe once again brightens my day.

Chloe: In Mrs. Ansell's class, fourth grade. I walked around all day with tape on my butt because someone placed a strip on my chair without my knowledge. This wasn't you. True or false?

Me: True. It wasn't me. Bucky put the tape there. I only told him to. Ha. I can still visualize it. It was that crazy duct tape all the girls were using to make wallets and bracelets with. White, black, and hot pink zebra. It was great.

Chloe: Everyone called me sticky butt for like a month. I don't think my retaliations were nearly harsh enough.

Smiling at my screen, I pocket my phone when Dad's curious stare lingers too long. He'd love to hear about the girl whose existence may affect my future choices. What he doesn't want to hear is her name. So I stick to the plan. Secret dating, for now. I have no doubt I'll tell Mom and Dad about Chloe one day, but today is not that day.

By the time we're finished with work, Dad ropes me into an early dinner at May's, where he is unaccountably agreeable.

"How are you liking living in Bay View?" he asks once May finishes bending our ears over the common area maintenance bill she's received for the restaurant. Thankfully, we don't manage this section of buildings on Main Street.

"It's a good complex. The restaurants are nice, the boutiques and other retail stores are high-end, so it's not as loud as you would expect living upstairs from them."

"A lot of younger professionals live there? Singles, I would guess."

"I've been there a week, I haven't had much time to meet people, but I would say so." A normal person would wonder why he's interested. I already know. In our business, familiarity with the demographics of residents is important. "The guy in the unit beside me actually works outside Seattle. He said he prefers the commute from here over living in the city."

"That's what we're banking on, isn't it?" Dad points out, and I tip my drink in agreement. When you develop and manage real estate, that is exactly what you want.

Dinner with him is not the worst thing imaginable, but our day out of the office, combined with an earlier call from Tulsa, means I'm behind on two leases and an eviction notice for lack of rents paid.

I'm busy playing catch up, sitting on my couch with a

Mariners game on in the background, when there's a knock on my door. Muting the television, I comb my fingers through my hair and adjust my sweatpants. When I swing the door wide, I find the best surprise package a man can receive: a beautiful Chloe Lockwood, her shapely legs encased in skinny jeans, and her body swallowed by a thick, cozy sweater.

"I hope you don't mind me dropping by. I was out running errands and thought I'd come see you."

"Mind?" Snaking my arm around her waist, I draw her inside and kick the door closed. "You're a sight for sore eyes, gorgeous."

Chloe lifts to her toes with a grin and covers my mouth in a way too abbreviated kiss. "I don't know about you, but this week has been draining."

"Tell me about it." I motion to the stack of files and open laptop on the coffee table.

"That looks terrible. See, this is why I work with flowers. They don't come home with me. And if they do, it's to make my house pretty and smell good."

I can't argue there. "Can you stay for a bit? You didn't stop by as a tease, did you?"

"Tease you? Always. But yeah, if you don't mind me hanging around for a bit. You're not too busy, are you?"

"Nah. You don't even have to ask." Taking her hand in mine, I kiss her knuckles and draw her over to the couch. "So, tell me what's going on with your flower friends to make this week so painful."

Chloe plops down, unlacing and toeing off her boots as she talks. "It's just awkward with Reid. He's trying to be professional, but the ease of our working relationship is gone. His tone is short, and he avoids eye contact most of the time. Some of the employees are distant. It'll all work itself out, but in the meantime, it sucks."

Settling beside her, I reach my arm around her shoulders and press her against my side. "I'm sorry, Chlo."

She props her chin against my bicep. "You don't have to be sorry. I shouldn't have dated him in the first place. Even without this," she gestures between us, "it was going to end eventually. It just happened to be earlier than later."

"Enough about Reid." My fingers glide over her neck, kneading her tight muscles. "I'm glad you're here, actually. I was going to call you later. I have a meeting in Tulsa Friday morning that I was going to do by conference call, but they called today and asked me to fly down." Her lips twist as I continue. "Since I have to be there, I figured I'd stay the night. See friends, check on my place. I'll come home late Saturday."

"Oh." Disappointment shadows her eyes. "Okay. That stinks."

"Worst possible timing, right?" This thing we've got going on is new. It's not like my being gone three days will ruin what's brewing between us, but with having to sneak around and with Chloe living at home, we have limited time together as it is.

She shrugs, attempting nonchalance. "Yeah, but what's a few days?"

I tug on her still damp hair. No wonder she smells extra delicious; she showered before coming over. *Running errands, my ass.* "Think we can plan something for Sunday?"

Wincing, she flashes an uncomfortable smile. "I already told Grace I'd help her out at Fig. She has to do inventory, and Gina is out."

Well damn. "Sunday night then? Come over afterward for dinner?"

She touches my knee. "I think I can make that work."

"Good." I kiss her forehead and scooch deeper into the couch while stretching my legs up on the coffee table. With a heavy sigh, Chloe installs herself against my side, her head on my chest and legs curled beneath her.

"Today has been exhausting," she says with a yawn, one arm wrapping across my hips.

My hand runs the length of her arm, eager to touch her. "Tell me more about work. Anyone I know getting married?"

"Oh." She lifts her head, and I balk.

"Don't move." I press her head to my chest. "I'm comfortable."

"Are you now?" Her legs and hips shift like she's finding a better position, forming us close together.

"Yes, Chloe, I like your body pressed against mine." My thumb strokes over her cheekbone. "Now, keep talking before I get ideas."

Her shoulders shake. "Why do I get the impression you already have ideas, Kip Harris?" I jerk when a sharp jab pokes my ribs.

"Don't you dare start something you can't handle," I warn, trapping her hand and lifting it to my mouth. "Who's getting married?" I kiss her palm, then proceed to tease each fingertip across my lips.

Chloe's voice wavers. "I can't believe I didn't mention it. You remember Sarah Rinaldi? She's marrying Scott Ketcham. Their flower choices are interesting."

I kiss her index finger. "There are interesting flowers?"

"Yes. Well, for weddings there are. In my opinion, wedding flowers should be timeless, or at least go well together…" she trails off.

I kiss her middle finger. "Okay, so what type of flowers would you want?" I'm glad she doesn't twist in my lap and gape at me. Because, yes, I asked her what type of wedding flowers she dreams of.

She doesn't pause before answering. "Hmm… Tough to narrow down, but probably dahlias. Or maybe peonies and ranunculus. Or all of the above." She laughs.

"I bet you could get away with a little of everything." I suck the tip of her ring finger into my mouth, and she inhales sharply. "Somehow, I picture you getting married right in those flower fields, anyway. Sunset, a thousand flowers, and a couple hundred bumblebees."

"The dahlia patch," she says breathlessly. Maybe it's the image she has of her wedding. Maybe it's my tongue caressing her finger.

I release her hand, and she leans away from me.

"The dahlia patch at sunset." She shrugs and rubs her thighs together. "It's my favorite." Pink flames color her cheeks. Desire or embarrassment? "Not that I've imagined it or anything." Embarrassment, then.

"Flowers and wedding planning have surrounded you your entire life. If you hadn't daydreamed about your wedding, I'd be worried." I touch the crease between her brows, smoothing it. "Don't worry, wedding talk doesn't incite my panic reflex unless you tell me you've already penciled in your groom."

I'm sunk into the couch enough that Chloe hovers over me as she straightens taller, her jaw-dropping. "I'll need a groom?"

"Well, you are an independent woman. I guess you could go without." I concede. "It makes procreating rather interesting, but you do you, Sunshine."

"Hey. Adoption is always an option." She smirks. "Concerned about who will be my groom, Kipling? Never thought I'd see the day."

"Not concerned." I walk my hand up her chest and tug on the collar of her sweater. "Call me a man with an invested interest."

She frowns at my arm and rolls her eyes but allows me to draw her closer. "Invested, huh?"

Moving from her neckline, I wind my hand around her neck and cup the back of her head. Very seriously and very quietly, I offer Chloe a truth and a vulnerability rarely shown. "Yes, I'm invested. Don't write me off."

Her eyes study me. My breaths halt, waiting for a beat, a pause. "Maybe I'll pencil you in instead."

With her promise of a chance, I tip my chin, and she meets my mouth, and we sink into a languid kiss. Where Friday was invade and conquer, tonight is taste and exploration. I draw away slowly, carefully, pressing kiss after kiss to her swollen lips as I force myself back. She causes me to lose my senses with the slightest touch. *Slow.* We agreed. Hard as it is, and *it* is hard, I have to be strong enough for both of us.

With a sigh, Chloe settles in again, head on my chest. Her fingers skate over the waistband to my joggers, sneaking under the plain tee I wear until my stomach quivers from her teasing. The glutton for punishment that I am, I let her be.

"Tell me more about what you do? Explain all the properties you manage," Chloe says.

Using her request as a distraction, I launch into my job. A business my grandfather, Winthrop II began as a young man. She asks question after question, and I answer as much as I can. Real estate isn't exactly a sexy topic. Eventually, she stops responding. Dead asleep.

I rest my cheek on the silky top of her head. In a handful of dates this woman has burrowed further into my heart than any other. The notion is too much, too soon, but we've known each other forever. The years count for something, right? I know almost everything about Chloe Lockwood, and what I don't know doesn't matter. Marinating on these crazy thoughts, I enjoy her presence while letting her nap. After an hour, I reluctantly wake her. She needs to be in the fields by dawn, and if I don't let her go now, I may keep her here indefinitely.

hloe

I MIGHT'VE SEEN Kip last night, but knowing he's on a plane to Tulsa right now makes me miss him. I mean, I missed him the days we didn't get to see one another earlier on in the week, but this is a different ache, knowing I *can't* see him. We had three days apart before I dropped by his condo last night, and we're going to have three more. Does he go to Tulsa often? Is this what being a couple would entail? Sporadic days together between several apart until he picks up and moves back to Tulsa for good? That's what our end looks like, isn't it? Because this will end.

Won't it?

Last night he asked me not to write him off, but what exactly was he implying? Is he considering staying here? Does Kip want something serious? Something real? An actual future. Can I honestly picture Denton Harris as my father-in-law?

Slow it down there, Chloe. What is going on with me? It's bad enough I showed up on his doorstep unannounced. I didn't have a single errand I was running, but after so many days apart and with how tense things have been on the farm, I wanted to lay eyes on him and ease my heart. Nothing about it makes sense. After so many years of trying to make each other's lives miserable, all I want to do is be around Kip. How is my former rival the only one who calms me?

It's a dangerous line of thought, especially for a man who might not stick around. For a man who could cause a severe divide between my parents and me—the only family I have.

As I kneel in the zinnia hoop house, harvesting blooms, my phone chimes from my tool belt on my right hip.

Kipling: I hit a baseball over the fence into your fields back in seventh grade, and when Caleb and I snuck over to find it, we found you, but no ball. You had nothing to do with its disappearance. True or false?

A laugh tumbles from my mouth. Someone landed in Tulsa.

My mind rewinds back to that day. I'd been spying on them from the flowers, and when their baseball came crashing onto the tulips, I picked it up and hid it in the daffodils. At the time I did it out of spite. It destroyed some beautiful flowers, but I never put much thought into why I kept it until today.

I liked that it reminded me of Kip, even if it was for something as juvenile as stealing his favorite toy.

Before texting him back, I snip the last of the bloomed blush zinnias and load the bucket into the bed of my truck. I pull up outside my floral studio and walk to the shelving in the back left corner. Tucked between a few pots sits the scuffed-up baseball.

I slip my phone from the leather pocket of my tool belt and snap a picture. Attaching it to a text, I type…

Me: This ball?

Kipling: Oh, you little thief! Since we're confessing, I should tell you I used to sneak into the fields and cut some blooms for my mom's birthday every year.

Kipling: I also know she would leave cash in an envelope in your mail to cover their cost, so I guess I wasn't truly stealing. Grabbing a ride to the office. Talk soon!

Should I reply or just let it be? And with what? I miss you? No. I'm going to let it be.

No more than an hour later, while I'm stacking landscape fabric in the supply bay, my phone pings with another text.

Kipling: If I had a boat, you would go fishing with me. True or False.

Me: Is this one a deal-breaker? I'll go out on the water with you. I'll even put worms on hooks for you—this soil lover isn't afraid of a little ol' worm—but for the love of dandelions, please don't make me touch a fish!

Kipling: I haven't come up with a deal-breaker where you're concerned yet, but no worries, fishing won't be it.

With our history, you'd think we'd be able to come up with a million deal-breakers—our last names being at the top of the list.

Me: Then you have yourself a fishing buddy.

On Friday, Denise shows up in the studio's doorway with an arranged bouquet of our peonies as I sift through dried daffodil pods. I'd know our blooms anywhere.

"Flowers came for you."

I tilt my head. "Like from a florist? You didn't pick these?"

She shakes her head and sets the white vase full of Peony 'Copper Honey'—a variety only we grow in town—on the center studio bench.

When I pluck the mini envelope from the bouquet and open the note, there's no name, but there's an inscription.

BEAUTIFUL FLOWERS *for my beautiful flower girl.*

KIP. That dork. Of course he'd send me my own flowers. My own *peonies.* A flutter affects my heartbeats. How many places did he have to call to know which shop carried them in Seaside?

"That's quite the grin there, Loe."

My head whips up. Denise. She's still here, propped against the door jam with a raised eyebrow. "Who are they from?" she asks.

"Grace." I shake my head with a forced chuckle. "Just playing a dumb joke on me."

Her forehead creases like she doesn't quite believe me, or maybe she doesn't get why it would be funny to have someone send me my own blooms.

And now I have to tell Grace she sent me flowers.

Me: I got the most beautiful flowers from a secret admirer today. You wouldn't happen to have any idea about them, would you?

Kipling: I hear they're great for weddings. And I'm glad you like them. I'd hate to have to give the grower crap if you were unhappy. Is it Sunday night yet?

This might be the longest three days to exist in the history of ever.

"So, you guys have been like, hanging out."

"You could say that." I can't keep the smile from spreading across my face.

Grace's latest shipment is stacked around us in the backroom of Fig. Sundays are her slower shopping days, so we leave the front unattended while she shows me how to tally her inventory.

"Chloe Mae, you little minx. You haven't slept with him, have you?"

"Grace, it's been like a week! Give me some credit."

"Well. You made a face like you were doing more than hanging out. Is he a good kisser?" Her eyes gleam, conspiring.

Heat pools in my belly, flowing through my veins at the memory of Kip's mouth. "Good doesn't even touch the surface."

"I knew it."

I shove her. "You are not allowed to imagine what it's like to kiss him."

"Well, I won't anymore. Not while you two are sneaking around like an illicit affair."

A quiet bell chimes out, alerting us to new customers walking through the front door.

"I'll be back," she says. "Once you're done with that box. Come and get me."

"Roger that."

I've only opened the box, ready to pull out the dresses, when Grace comes back, peeking her head in the door. "I need you up front."

I fluff my sloppy bun. "What? Why?" In jeans with holes in the knees and an oversized sweatshirt, I might not be in my farm clothes, but I didn't exactly dress to greet customers.

"You've got visitors."

Me? No one even knows I'm here today.

Kip.

I can't stop squeaking. "Kip?"

Grace zips her lips before leaving me. He's here. Taking a breath, I stand and grab my phone from the shelf beside me. I flip the camera to face me and check my appearance. Curly mess of hair? Check. Minimal makeup? Check. Slouchy, cozy sweatshirt? Check.

This is me. And he knows it. If only I'd have been more prepared.

I roll my neck, loosening my shoulders, and step out the door Grace left open a crack.

Brynn leans her elbow on the center counter, chatting with Grace, but my eyes hone in on Kip standing beside his sister. He watches them, but his eyes are distracted like he's not truly listening. Of course the man would walk in here like a damn model with his hair perfectly coiffed and his T-shirt forming to his fit torso while I look like I rolled out of bed. *Thanks, universe.*

When I step further into the shop, past a rack of bohemian shirts, Brynn's attention shifts to me, her mouth dropping.

"Shopping my butt, Kip Harris." She shoves his shoulder. "You lured me down here so you could see Chloe."

He slides his hands into the front pockets of his gray chinos and rocks back on his heels. "What are you talking about?" His blue eyes steal a glance my way, and I bite my cheek to keep from smiling. "I'm grabbing lunch and hanging out with you."

Brynn looks between Grace and me and back to Kip. "Liar." She wags her finger.

A soft scoff passes my lips. "Like I'd hook up with that ugly mug." It's the weakest lie I've ever told, and Kip's lips begin to break.

"And you"—Brynn points at me— "I thought you had better sense than to let this guy sweet talk you into whatever this is."

Grace, who's been biting her tongue, bursts out laughing. "You two are awful secret lovers."

I send a glare her way and hiss, "And you're an awful secret keeper."

Her amusement continues, unfazed by my annoyance. "You screwed up all on your own."

"You knew?" Brynn asks Grace before glaring at Kip, "She knew? You're a crap brother."

Kip throws up his hands. "I didn't know she knew. Someone said we had to be a secret." He gives me a pointed look.

"If I could've kept it from Grace, I would have, but she's not stupid. She knew how I felt before I knew."

Everyone's attention moves to Grace.

"My best friend went away for the weekend with her child-hood rival and came back to break up with her boyfriend. Of course I knew something was going to come of it." Grace rolls her eyes like our little secret affair was inevitable.

"Fine, whatever. Gracie Lou, you're a regular Sherlock Holmes. Brynn, you're a clueless big sister. Now, if you two will excuse us, I need to borrow Miss Lockwood." Kip rounds the counter and takes my hand, leading us toward the dressing rooms at the back of Fig.

Grace hollers, "You can't go in there without merchandise, Harris."

Kip pauses, his frustrated inhale echoing through the store. "Merchandise, huh?" he asks with a bite.

The girls roar with laughter. Brynn crosses her arms over her chest and shouts, "And Chloe doesn't count!"

Kip winks at me and grabs a billowy cream blouse hanging on the nearest rack. "Happy?" He shakes the hanger at Grace and swats my backside into the small space.

"This cut would be lovely on you." I run my fingers down the long sleeve.

His black shirt stretches across his broad shoulders as he

draws the curtain closed and hangs the blouse on a hook. "Something in this dressing room would be lovely on me, but I don't believe it's the shirt, Sunshine."

Kip spins around, his body stalking me until I'm flat against the tall dressing room mirror affixed to the wall. He's a man on a mission. Need darkening his eyes as his pelvis presses against mine, and my hands grasp at his hips, reveling in the pressure of his body while his legs scissor mine and his arms brace on either side of my head. I'm a mouse trapped by a ravenous cat, and it took him all of fifteen seconds to ensnare me.

"I missed the hell out of you," he says, low. His gruff tone is a testament to the control he's exerting.

"I could play the blasé card, but you'd see right through me. I missed you more than I care to admit." I brush my nose against his.

"It wasn't supposed to happen like this, Chlo. We're supposed to be chill and cool. Play this slow. I'm not supposed to want you this badly. You aren't allowed to turn me into a crazed man after so little time."

I might be a little crazed myself, but it runs a lot deeper than a physical need. Is that all this is for him? "I'd apologize, but maybe you need to feel a little out of control every once in a while."

I barely draw a breath before he seizes my lips, his body crushing mine. My mind can't respond quick enough to the speed at which he works. Before I know it, his hands are beneath my thighs, and I'm leaping up, hooking my ankles around his back. Kip rocks into me as his fingers dig into my backside, securing me against him.

I vetoed christening his little childhood teepee, but I might make an exception for Grace's shop. If there was more to shield us than a piece of fabric, I'd be eating crow after what I said to Grace in the stock room.

Kip sucks on my tongue, gently holding it hostage between his teeth, before he whispers against my lips, "Hi, by the way."

He's expecting verbal communication right now? With what brain exactly? "Hi." The two-letter word is about all my mind can conjure up before my tongue dives into his mouth and my fingers thread through his hair.

We're like hormone-crazed teenagers, wild and moving too fast. Logic and rationality flew out the front door of Fig the moment Kip stepped through. His mouth is hot as he kisses the corner of my lips, across my cheek, along my jaw, down my neck. I shiver, and he tugs the neckline of my sweatshirt aside. It's just loose enough to give him access to my collarbone, and his tongue traces the sensitive crevice back and forth. When his mouth clamps over it, my thighs quiver and clench around his waist. Our grip on one another is so tight, so fierce, even if Kip were to pull away from the mirror, I wouldn't fall.

A splintering sound crackles behind me, but I ignore it. The only thing that matters is the tension detonating between us. Kip chases the same path back to my mouth, crushing our lips together.

"You guys about done in there, or should I close up the store and leave you alone?" Grace's laughing shout is followed by Brynn's. "We should really discuss a wedding before the babies arrive, you two."

Kip groans. "Shut up and buy something, sis." He huffs with exasperation. "What did I tell you? She's known for less than ten minutes, and she's moved to weddings and kids."

I chuckle. "I managed to survive your aggravating antics my whole life. I think I can handle Brynn's big sister ribbing."

Kip squeezes my butt. "You're way more accommodating than I ever gave you credit for. I appreciate your indulgence." His mouth touches mine, his tongue teasing the seam before pulling back with haste. "We should probably exit this dressing room before they riot and come in after us."

Reluctantly, I untangle my legs from around him, and he gently sets me down. "I should actually take care of the inventory I came here to do, anyway." I turn and look at myself in the mirror. "Kip," I hiss. "We broke it."

"Are you really all that surprised at us breaking things when we're together?" His mouth curves into a self-satisfied smirk as he studies us in the full-length mirror.

This will be fun to explain to Grace. Staring at my reflection with a long crack down the center, I redo my messy bun that's now more of a chaotic ponytail.

Kip clears his throat. "If you want to head out there, go on. I'm going to need a minute."

I turn and face him. "You expect me to deal with them alone?"

His hand hooks into my stretched-out neckline and draws me in. His whisper tickles the shell of my ear. "Then wait here with me, but stop looking so damn kissable." He slips his arms around me and hugs me tight.

I settle into him with a sigh. You never know how much you need a hug until those arms hold you close, hearts beating against each other.

My hand massages his neck as I ask, "So, tonight? Are we still on for dinner?" And I can make myself the presentable, irresistible woman I wanted Kip to come home to.

Releasing me, he fixes the mess I made of his hair. "Of course we are."

"Your place?" He agrees, and I ask, "What time?"

"I'm yours any time you're available. Come over when you're ready."

"You're going to let me drive myself this time?"

"I am, but only because you're not staying late since you have to work in the morning."

For the first time, I have zero desire to get up and be with my flowers. All I want is to ask Kip to play hooky with me, but even if I ask, I can't. It would raise too much suspicion.

"Thank you, warden," I tease.

Kip tweaks my side, and a squeal slips out. "How do you feel about breakfast?"

"Breakfast? Like, in the morning?" Is he asking me to stay over? I... Could I?

"For dinner. I don't cook much, but I can whip up killer veggie omelets." He chucks my chin like I'm adorable. "But table the other thought running through your mind for discussion later, okay?"

Heat fills my cheeks. "Well, since I don't normally eat breakfast, breakfast for dinner is the best kind."

Kip shoves aside the thick curtain, and we walk out hand-in-hand. Grace is wrapping Brynn's purchases in tissue paper, both their heads swiveling our way. Eyes assessing.

"If you two want to remain in the know, you will make zero comments," I say as we stop by the counter.

Grace's hands lift as she bites her lips together. "I didn't say anything."

Taking her shopping bag from Grace, Brynn swings around. "Grace, thank you. I promise to come back more often. Chloe, we need to have coffee or lunch soon so we can chat." Brynn gives me a loose hug.

Chat. I laugh. Yeah. About wedding dates and all the nieces and nephews she wants me to give her, I'm sure. She'll have to interrogate her baby brother. Her hopes might be set a little high.

"And you." She shoves at Kip's solid frame. "We need to let those two get back to work, and you promised me lunch."

Pressing a chaste kiss to my forehead, he shuffles backward. "Brotherly duty calls."

"I'll text you when I'm done here." I wave.

Kip's one foot out the door when he stops in his tracks.

Retracing his steps, he returns to stand before Grace and me with an irrepressible grin. "By the way, Gracie Lou, you can bill me for the mirror." Sweeping his gaze over my body, he says, "See you tonight, gorgeous," before he exits out the door to where Brynn is waiting.

"The mirror?" Grace looks at me.

My mouth curves up uncomfortably apologetic. "We may have cracked it." One of my shoulders lifts.

"You two could never do anything halfway. You better spill every detail of that hot little encounter, or I'm not letting you leave this shop to meet up with him later."

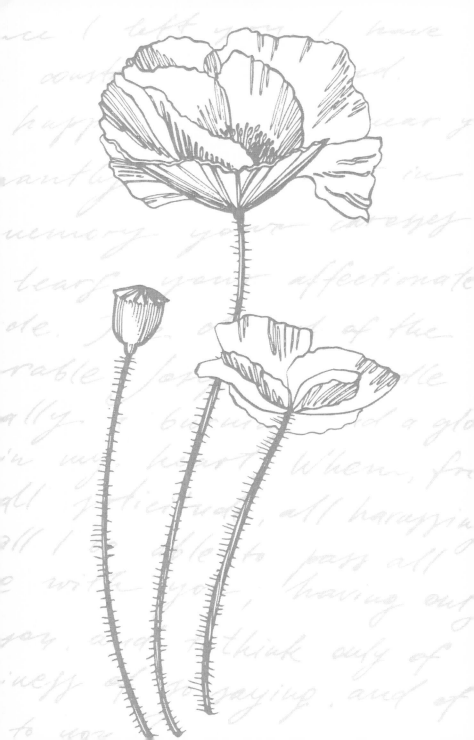

hloe

WHEN I ARRIVE at Kip's condo, his kitchen counter is covered in chopped fruits, vegetables, spices, and eggs. He tells me to sit at the bar, and I watch as he stands at the stove sautéing vegetables. While he cooks, he fills me in on his friends in Tulsa and what they did Friday night. I'm not jealous he went out for drinks. Nope, not at all. I bet there weren't even any beautiful women there.

"I'm glad you had a good time with your friends." It's not a total lie. Kip wouldn't have been checking out other women with them, would he? It's not like we've made this official, but I'd hope the exclusive part was implied because I don't want to ask.

"Speaking of friends." While I carry a bowl of fruit, Kip carries our plates to the table. "I talked to Hayden earlier today. Bodhi will be home this weekend, and Hayden scored tickets to a Mariners game. Wanna come?"

As we sit, I ask, "Did you tell Hayden and Bodhi about us?"

"Well…" He pops a chunk of pineapple in his mouth like he wants to make me forget my question by the time he's done chewing. I tap my finger on the table, waiting for him to finish. "Fine. I know I threw you under the bus about Grace today, but only because she's Grace. She's here. Hayd and Bodhi are harmless, and trust me when I say they can keep a secret."

"Oh, no, no. You don't get to shame me for telling my best friend when you told yours." My lips purse, reprimanding. "Look, I don't care about them knowing. It's not like they're going to go to our parents. I just want to know what I'd be saying yes to."

He spears a melon cube and tries to feed me. "You'd be saying yes to spending a weekend with me in Seattle. Remember when I said table that breakfast discussion for later?"

I pause before opening my mouth and accepting the fruit.

"It's later."

I chew, staring at the darker flecks of blue in his eyes. A weekend away with Kip is a lot different now than the weekend away with friends before our truce. It'd be more of a romantic getaway. With expectations. Not to say it scares me. But what are his expectations? A weekend getaway doesn't exactly follow our taking things slow plan.

It's so unlike me to plan vacations on my own. Rarely did we take them as a family growing up, always too busy with the farm for much of a break. And I just lied to my parents about camping alone three weeks ago; how will I get away with this so close?

His brows dip deeper the longer I remain silent. "Hey, you don't have to say yes."

"So, wait." I lift a forkful of omelet to my lips. "Do you want me to go? Or are you looking for a way to tell me you want to go hang out with your buddies, and you're inviting me out of pity?"

Kip's mouth presses into a straight line, eyeing me like I should know the answer. "No, I'm looking for a way to tell you my buddies invited me, and since I was gone this weekend, I…"

He rubs his jaw. "I know we don't owe each other anything at this point, but—"

"Are you worried I'd be mad at you for going out of town?"

He chuffs. "Not mad, per se, but I care about what you want. We're trying to see how this works, and… Damn, I'm doing this all wrong. Let me try again." He moves to the edge of his chair and settles his hand on my knee beneath the table. "Chloe, I really want to take you to Seattle this weekend. I know baseball isn't exactly romantic, but the guys want to see you, and fine, the truth is I don't want to spend two weekends in a row away from you. I could not go, but I think we'd have fun."

Oh. "Yeah, it'd be fun to see your friends again. And I don't want to spend the weekend apart either. I just need to figure out logistics."

I'd have to come up with another lie. Say I'm going to Seattle, but with Grace. She would cover for me. Knowing her and being in the corner of Team Kip, she'd probably pack my bag for me. But it also means she'd have to lay low for the weekend. She wouldn't be able to work at her shop. I hope that's feasible.

Giving my knee a squeeze, Kip shifts back and returns to his food. "At some point we're going to have to reconsider these ground rules. You're aware of this, right?"

Maybe, but there isn't a point unless… "We can reconsider them if you decide to stay in Seaside."

Kip stills, his fork hovering in the air over his plate. "So, if I don't stay." He stabs his eggs. "We end? Just like that?"

My brows knit together. "Do you want a long-distance relationship?" Why is he murdering his omelet? "That seems really complicated. And we already have complicated, Kip."

"Right. Because a secret relationship under everyone's noses is easier than doing long-distance? Life is complicated. I can figure out complicated just fine, Chloe."

"Why are you getting so mad? You agreed to this, were all over the idea of a *clandestine affair,* as I believe you called it.

What's the point of long-distance if you have no desire to live here? This is home for me, and it always will be, but if I'm not reason enough to stay, this conversation seems pointless."

"You won't even tell your parents about me." He pushes his plate away. "You'll only risk their wrath if I commit to being here? Seriously? How do I commit to being here if I'm not worth the time for a long-distance relationship?"

I sit back. "Why would I rain hell down on us for something that's not going to last? For someone who doesn't care enough to stay?"

"And you'd be willing to go public if I stayed?"

"Maybe not right away, but eventually, if this were more. It's a delicate situation. Don't pretend like it's not."

His light laugh is sardonic. "How can we know what we have if we can't actually be together in public? You're twenty-five and sneaking out of your house for dates."

"I thought this was a fling for you. Why does it matter what I say or don't say to my parents? That's my business."

Kip jerks like I've shot him. "Are you kidding me right now? Chloe, why do you think I'm still here? I don't have to be here."

"Because you have your riverfront deal. Your *baby*. It's the whole reason you came back to Seaside."

His palms dig against his eyes. "You're right, and you could be the reason I stay, but I don't know if I can commit to staying. Especially for a woman who thinks I'm only worth the *complications* on her terms."

This is ridiculous. Of course he'd put this on me. This is Kip's way out, and he doesn't have to own the blame because *I'm* the bad guy, and I'll always be the bad guy.

I shove away from the table, the force flipping my chair back, but I don't stop to pick it up as I gather my things. "We were kidding ourselves to think this could be something," I mutter, slipping my arms through my jacket and snatching my keys from the table by the front door.

"Chlo?" My name is a plea. Kip curses; the scrape of chair legs across wood flooring spurs me to move faster.

"This isn't going to work, Kip." With my stomach in knots, I turn the knob, cracking the door open.

His body blankets me from behind as his palm against the door prevents me from leaving. "Chloe, babe, c'mon. You can't leave." His other hand circles my waist and flattens against my stomach. "I'm sorry. I shouldn't have blown up. I…"

A shuddering breath leaves me as I fight tears. "What are we doing, Kipling?" I whisper, my gaze on the floor, my head hanging. "How did this get so tangled so quickly?"

His hand flexes at my belly as his mouth lowers to my ear, and he whispers back, "Because this is real, Sunshine."

I crack, and he twists me around. Dipping down, his hands cradle my face as the tip of his thumb swipes across my cheekbone, spreading the moisture leaking from my eyes.

I nod into his hand, my eyes shut. Oh my gosh, is it ever real, and it hurts. The thought of Kip going back to Tulsa, even if we remained in a relationship, is nearly unbearable. I want him here. I want him in Seaside forever.

"If you've had even one moment where you thought you weren't reason enough for me to stay here, then I've screwed this up." His voice is thick with emotion as his forehead drops to mine. "Do you know why we're fighting right now?"

I don't think he expects my answer, so I wait.

"We're upset because we're scared. This is moving fast. We're… Chloe, I'm falling fast."

My eyes shoot open, and I lift my gaze. Blinking, I replay his words. Did I hear him right? But Kip doesn't shy away, and he doesn't repeat himself.

"Do I need to say it again? I'm falling in love with you, Chloe Lockwood. The same as I did when I sat next to you in bio and made you memorize my color-coded spreadsheets because that meant I had more time with you. Don't you see? This isn't something new."

I bring my hands to the sides of his face and rise on my tiptoes, our noses inches apart.

"I told you I'm invested. I asked you not to write me off." The muscle in his taut jaw ticks, and he swallows. "It felt like you just did."

I seal my mouth to his, once, twice, before pulling back. "I'm not. I'm sorry. I shouldn't have said that. I've been trying so hard to hold back, reminding myself this is probably temporary, but it's not for me. I'm pretty sure I started to fall again when you saw me crying at the fence and gave me a way out."

"Started to fall again?" He asks the question so simply, but I spy the hope in his eyes.

A little smile curves my lips. "Yeah, dummy. This isn't one-sided."

"Wow. Dummy, huh? You really know my love language there, babe." Divesting me of my keys and purse, his strong hand curls around mine as he draws me to the couch.

"Would you prefer something more affectionate? Like pooky? Or cupcake? Or I know, snapdragon."

Pushing me into the corner of the couch, Kip moves on top of me. "You can call me whatever you want, as long as you never walk away like that again." His lips swipe over mine. "This isn't going to be easy, and we're going to fight, but I want this to work, Chlo."

"That's all you had to say. I can handle a little work. It's kind of in my blood."

Running his hand down my thigh, firm fingers cup behind my knee, and pull me closer. His face hovers inches from mine as he grins. "I came here with my future up in the air, but I swear from the moment I ran into you outside the Flower Patch my first day in town, I knew I was in trouble. I swore I wouldn't let myself get crazy over you again. What the hell do I know?"

"The first day you gave me my own flower?" I chuckle, out of breath. "It's starting to become a habit with you."

"This isn't a fling. It never was. Come to Seattle with me. Let's go somewhere where we can act like a real couple. Where I can stop in the middle of a sidewalk and kiss you. I'll sleep on the couch, or we can get a hotel. Whatever you want, no pressure." His lips suck my neck's responsive skin, and my heartbeats falter. "All I want is to spend my time with you, Chloe Lockwood."

"You wanna kiss me on a sidewalk in Seattle?" My breathing hitches, a quiver running through me. "Very romantic."

"I do. You know what else I want to do?" His tone deepens, and I hum a response. His hand slips beneath my sweater, his splayed palm gliding up the side of my ribcage while his mouth continues its siege across my neck and jaw. "I want to eat hotdogs and drink beer with you while shouting curses at the umps. And I'll smugly show you off to my jealous best friends while they try to convince you to dump me. Then later, if you're lucky, I might even share my ice cream."

"Mmm, ice cream." My fists tighten in his hair, gripping him like this is what will keep me anchored, not gravity. "I don't suppose they have lavender ice cream at the stadium."

"You'll probably have to stick with plain old vanilla or chocolate." Nip, lick, kiss.

A breathy moan slips out of me. "Let's go. Take me to Seattle…" And my brain cycles through a thousand things I can't say aloud, all euphemisms about balls and bases that would come out wrong. Or right, depending on who you ask.

"You've got goosebumps, Miss Lockwood." Kip grins, his brow arching like he knows exactly where my mind has landed.

Sighing heavily, he pushes himself into a sitting position and drags me with him. "Maybe it's best we make a decision about the weekend now then. We're not sleeping together."

Oh, he's gonna make that decision for us? How does he even know where my mind was going?

"Before you pout at me, let me explain. I could happily devour you right here, right now, okay? Do not misconstrue my words as a lack of interest. I don't want to rush you, Chlo. I don't want to make a mistake that could hurt us."

"So, sleeping with me would be a mistake." My eyebrow juts up.

He chews on the inside of his cheek, contemplating. "Is this a trick question? Can I plead the fifth?"

"No, but I suggest you choose your words carefully."

"Choose my words carefully?" He taps his finger against his lip, lazily sinking back against the sofa. "Okay. My bedroom is right back there. Shall I show you the way, Sunshine?"

I almost tell him to lead the way, to call him out, but he might call my bluff, and my words are bolder than my intentions. "So, you think *I'd* end up regretting it."

"I can guarantee you won't regret it." His handsome face is obnoxiously sure.

Cocky bugger. "How about we let things progress naturally, rather than trying to set more limits? Especially since you don't seem to like those very much."

His nose wrinkles with distaste. "Eh, I don't know if slow works for me anymore. I say we do it and move on? The suspense is killing me."

"Then show me to your bedroom." I shrug. "I'm waiting."

I knock him off guard for all of two seconds. Two glorious seconds of pure lust burning behind his eyes before his head falls back. "Did I not say I won't sleep with you less than thirty seconds ago?" He leans my way and bops my nose. *I want to break that damn finger off.* "I know it's hard, but you're going to have to try controlling yourself around me."

I nail him in the shoulder. "Ah, the return of Gentleman Kipling."

"Always at your service," he says with a wink.

I can't help. I lean down and give him a quick kiss.

"I don't know about you, but I'm still hungry," he says. "Want to warm up our dinner, then make-out?"

"I thought you'd never ask. I'm starving."

LATER, after dinner and making out and getting a tour of his bedroom—though he stood in the doorway to *protect his innocence*—Kip pins me to the side of my truck. My arms are above my head, our fingers laced, as every inch of his body connects with mine. He's kissing below my ear and inhales my scent as he likes to do when his breathing wavers, and he says my name.

"I'm sorry, Chlo." He squeezes my hands like a vise. "About earlier. Fighting with you…"

"Don't." Wanting to touch him, comfort the man whose voice trembles, I exert pressure to move. He doesn't budge. "We're fine, Kipling. We were acting crazy. That's what caring about someone does, right?"

Letting my hands go, he holds either side of my face in his palms and looks at me—just stares. I open my mouth to speak, but he kisses me. I try again, and I receive another kiss.

"I'm asking you to forgive me when I'm an idiot because I've never done this. I've never cared about a girl like this. I'm bound to screw it up a few times."

"And when you do, I'll be here to call you out."

"That's all I want." Kip's mouth connects with mine again. "Call me when you get home?"

"If you're lucky." I slip out of his hold with a giggle, kiss his cheek, and hop in my truck.

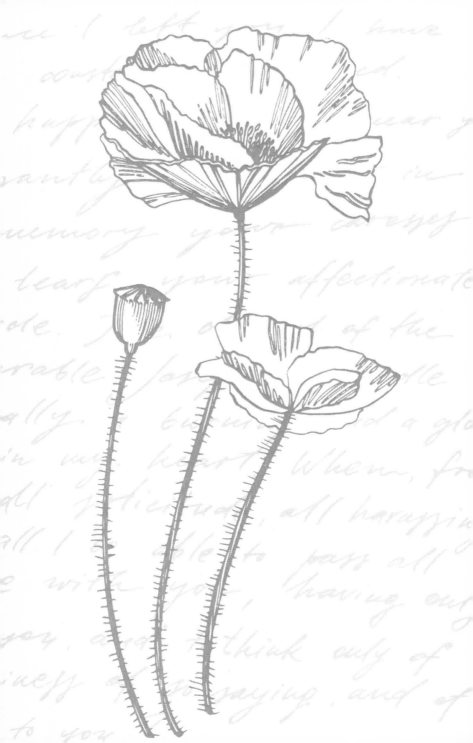

29

Kip

STROLLING into Brynn's office Tuesday afternoon, I prop my hip on the edge of her desk. Unlike my neat stacks of folders and perfectly placed notebooks, Brynn's space is organized chaos. Files, notes, and color swatches are artfully scattered over her desk. She might seem a mess, and her personal life is, but she can recall names and facts about our clients and properties and their history quicker than anyone. Funny enough, as good as she is at the business, she doesn't love this job. She's here because I left.

Her hazel scowl spares me one second before she returns to scanning the spreadsheet open on her monitor. "I have two chairs, you know."

I pick up the paint deck from her desk and fan the color swatches into a fan. "I set a deadline with Weller Faison."

Now I have her attention. "A deadline? You mean for whether you stay or go?" She leans back in her chair.

"Yep."

Indecision lines her forehead. Brushing her bangs from her eyes, she pushes her hair behind her ear. "When?"

What she wants to know is how long she has. The unease is plain to see. She just got her little brother back, and now she worries I'll leave again. "The first of July."

"The first? That's…" She presses her lips closed and inhales through her nose. "I thought you had six months to decide? Why set a deadline now? You've been here for two."

Standing, I wander to the board hanging on her office wall. A design sample board; her true love. Brynn maintains the files and finalizes all decisions for our color schemes. She often provides consulting for new tenants who don't already have interior designers. Sometimes I wonder if that's the real reason she wants me to return to Seaside Pointe. If I'm here, working for Dad, she can focus more on design. Turning, I sweep her office door closed.

"It's why I flew to Tulsa," I admit. Ignoring the palm she slaps over her mouth, I pull up a seat and rest my ankle on top of my knee. Since she's aware of my relationship with Chloe, I can share. "I don't want to be stretched between here and Tulsa anymore, Brynn. Dad's unbearable every time I put him off for something there. I'm tired of working non-stop, and…" I shrug.

"And Chloe," she finishes.

I scrub my palm over my face, reminded of our fight Sunday night. I'd already given Weller Faison my self-imposed deadline, and still, I fought with Chloe over the possibility of not moving here. It was childish. It was my pride. The same pride that wrote her off because of one overheard conversation she had with her friends when we were teenagers.

"Stupid, right?" I ask after a beat. Brynn's grin grows. "I shouldn't make a life decision based on a woman I've dated for two weeks."

"Oh, please, Kip. You and Chloe have known each other your entire lives. It's not like you picked her up at a bar."

"Yeah, I know." I prop my elbow on the chair's armrest. "We're going to Seattle this weekend."

Brynn bites her lip, her breath catching. "To see the guys?"

"Yeah, we're staying with Hayd. I figure it gives us time to discuss the important things—"

"Like who tells their parents about you two first?" She looks like the cat who swallowed the canary.

"You're enjoying this too much."

"Enjoying seeing my baby brother happy? Yeah, I am." She scoots her chair forward and leans her arms on her desk. "Kip, Dad rode you hard. Especially after I left for college. I know what people in this town think about him, what they say about the Harrises.

"We don't apologize for our family name, and we don't apologize for our success. Grandpa, Dad, me, you…we've earned these things. We've worked our tails off. Yeah, we had the advantage of money to pave our way at school, but we earned the grades. We build relationships that make us good at what we do. You can stop trying to prove yourself."

"Damn, I might have a tear." I mockingly swipe under my eye as a pen ricochets off my chest. "Thank you, sis. You're right, of course."

Flicking her hair, she preens. "Of course."

Brynn *is* right. I work so hard to prove I'm good enough. It's why Chloe's words hurt the other night. I wanted her to say she didn't care if I was here or in Tulsa. I wanted her to fight for us.

I swipe the pen Brynn threw from the floor and toss it back as I stand.

"Wait. Where are you going? I need more details. If Chloe is part of your decision, does that mean you'll stay regardless of whether Riverfront falls through?"

Twisting the doorknob, I open her door. "I guess we'll know more after this weekend."

"Not an answer, little brother."

I'm not ready to share everything about Chloe and my relationship with Brynn. Not yet.

"If she's in this, I'm in it." I walk across the hall accompanied by Brynn's whines. Sitting at my desk, I meet her glare through the small glass panels by our doors. "Put it this way, sis. There's no way in hell that woman will leave her flower fields. So, where do you think I'm going to be?"

"Our momma raised you right, Kip."

THURSDAY AFTERNOON I pick Mia up from school for a little one on one time. Carrie-Ann moved to Seaside Pointe and began working with H.D. when Mia was barely three. Through the years Mia was like a younger sister. We helped raise her. Carrie-Ann has no family, and Mia's father isn't in the picture. This is why guilt is my constant companion where Mia's concerned. I left for Oklahoma and became less available to her during the years she needed a big brother the most. I did my best at making time for phone calls and video chats, but I packed college and grad school into five years. I was busy.

Since returning home, I've made her a priority, though. Treating her to a weekly dinner date and being someone she can confide in. Mia's talking my ear off about graduation tomorrow as we walk up Main Street toward Aunt May's for an early dinner.

"We've had all these rehearsals. As if it's so difficult to form straight lines and walk across a stage."

Remembering taking part in those mindless hours-long rehearsals, I can't fault her disgusted tone. We're sharing a laugh when, up ahead, Reid Pruitt exits May's. He turns our way and stops, a wave of tension turning his posture rigid.

Walking by would be preferable, but I take Chloe into consideration and tip my head in a cordial greeting. "Reid."

"You move on quick, Harris," he mutters. "*And* you're

robbing the cradle. What, have you already gone through all the women in town, so now you have to move onto the teenagers?"

Chloe. Chloe. Chloe. I chant, my pride be damned. Mia glances at me, her lips curled in confusion, and the urge to laugh hits. Unlike many of her constantly made-up friends, Mia appears younger. Especially today with her dark brown hair in double braids and make-up-free face. The oversized T-shirt she wears over black leggings hides the curves keeping Carrie-Ann in a constant state of worry.

I sling an arm around her shoulders and tug her into my side. "She'll be eighteen in a few weeks." Scratching my jaw, I ask, "Are you still in the cradle, Mia?"

The little actress pops her hip and creates a big production of answering me with enough sass to make Chloe proud. "Nope." She pops her 'p' like a pro and slides her gaze toward Reid. "I actually graduated to the toddler bed last month. It was a huge deal," Mia says with faux excitement.

I'd bet Chloe a date night movie choice Reid is mentally strangling me right now. As much as I hate introducing them, the last thing I need is a baseless rumor circulating around Seaside about how I'm scamming on underage girls.

"Reid Pruitt, this is Mia Mason. My secretary's daughter," I say pointedly. "Mia, Reid works for Lockwood Blooms."

"Hey." Her Bambi eyes scan him like he's a bug beneath her shoe. Pure loyalty. Mia knows it's not in my nature to treat people unkindly. Obviously, picking up on our tense vibes, she removes herself from the scene. "I'll go get us a table."

"I'll be right there." I give her a nod of thanks.

When she's out of hearing range, I turn on Reid. "Seriously, Pruitt?"

Reid shrugs, crossing his arms over his chest with a huff. "Well, you weren't above moving in on another man's girlfriend. How am I supposed to know what lines you're not willing to cross?"

My fist connecting with his face would feel extraordinary. It would also cause a world of harm between Chloe and me. "I hate to break it to you, but I didn't move in on Chloe. Not really." I held her hand and kissed her cheek, and yes, I flirted a lot harder than I should have. Fine… "I'm not going to say I'm completely innocent here, but it was never my intention to start something with her—that just happened."

Reid's face doesn't soften. His hand adjusts its hold on the take-out bag he carries. Maybe he's mulling over my words, or maybe he wants to try his luck at punching me again.

"Look, we've known each other since high school, Reid. We don't have to be friends, but…" How do I smooth things over with him without making it seem like it's all for Chloe's sake.

"Whatever, man." Resignation takes over his features. "It is what it is. She's a grown woman who makes her own decisions."

"Right. I should get inside then." I inch toward May's. "See ya around."

Reid tosses an offhanded wave and turns down the sidewalk, heading in the opposite direction.

As I'm stepping inside May's, I realize my mistake. I play the confrontation back, unable to recall my exact words, but I'm sure I alluded to Chloe and I having something going on. I curse, my mind working double-time as I cross the restaurant and join Mia. Maybe he didn't notice. Hopefully, he thinks the extent of our association was fooling around one weekend. He didn't call me out. Surely, he would have said something if he connected the dots and assumed we were in a relationship.

Allowing Reid Pruitt to slip from my mind, I focus on Mia.

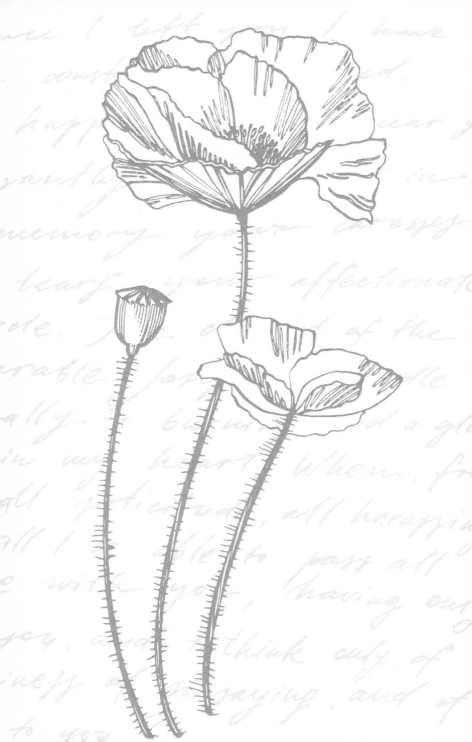

hloe

"You're going to need to take a picture with these hot guys, so I can see them. Find out myself if you're telling the truth."

I shift the duffle bag on my lap in the front seat of Grace's Honda. "Are you joking? I can't have proof I was with Kip this weekend."

She shakes her head with a sigh. "Harris must really like you if he's willing to be kept a secret."

"Yeah, I don't think he's as fine with it as he lets on. Every time it's brought up, he grumbles a bit."

"Can you blame him?" Keeping her hands on the steering wheel, she gives me a look. "Are you ready?"

"Ready for what?"

"Waxed, lingerie, protection."

"Grace Elizabeth!"

"What?" She chuckles, turning left toward Kip's place. "You're going on a weekend getaway with him. What do you think is going to happen? I just want to make sure my best friend is prepared."

"We're not setting any expectations. Kip actually shot me down, so."

"He did not."

"He did!" A small indignant laugh flies from my lips. "Even when I toured his bedroom, he stayed in the doorway so I couldn't lure him to his bed."

She muses her icy blonde hair with a smug grin. "He is so in *love* with you."

"Shut up." I roll my eyes.

"He *is*. A man shoots a woman down for two reasons. He's not interested, or he wants it to mean something more when it happens. And we both know Kip is *interested*."

I shrug, aiming for nonchalance, and peer out the passenger side window. "He might have already mentioned he's falling for me."

Her gasp draws my eyes. "Oh, sister. You are so getting laid this weekend."

"We're done talking about this."

Grace can't stop laughing as we drive into the parking lot of Kip's complex. I'm nervous enough as it is without Grace's help. Even if Kip doesn't plan on anything happening this weekend, it's still just the two of us. No buffer of Brynn. Hayden and Bodhi are nothing but reinforcements for Kip.

When Grace shifts her car into *Park*, she says, "Don't get knocked up this weekend."

I shove her before hopping out of the car. "Don't tell me what to do." I fling the door shut, but the whir of the window rolls down behind me.

Kip is already waiting, his white sneakers crossed at the ankle as he leans against his freshly washed crossover.

Lifting his gray thermal-covered arm, he waves at Grace.

"Don't worry, Gracie Lou. I'll take good care of our girl this weekend."

"I'm sure you will." Her suggestive brows rise with her knowing grin.

My eyes are daggers as I put my bag in the backseat of his Audi, but Grace's amusement only continues as she pulls away.

"Driver controls radio," Kip says when we get in, and he starts the engine.

"Oh, really? You've obviously never been on a road trip with me." I fiddle with the knobs, searching for something decent.

He grimaces when I stop at a country station and turns it down. "You are such an only child."

"Not my fault my parents didn't want to mess with perfection."

"I can't argue there." His sexy hum of agreement flips my stomach as his gaze scans me.

I prefer comfort while traveling, so I paired a white tank top and mustard cardigan with my favorite black leggings.

Twisting in his seat, Kip leans over the console and hooks his hand around my neck. "Hi, gorgeous," he says with a petal-soft kiss.

"Hey yourself," I sigh into him. "How was the graduation this morning?"

"Good, it brought back memories. I hadn't heard our alma mater since we graduated." He motions to the sack by my feet. "What's in the bag?"

"Road trip snacks." *Duh.*

Returning behind the wheel, his face scrunches. "For a seventy-minute drive?"

"Again, you've obviously never been on a road trip with me. Don't you get the munchies?"

Kip scoffs. "You've never been on a trip with Denton Harris. There was no eating in his vehicles."

I blink and blink again. "What kind of a torturous childhood did you have?"

"Well, you see how I turned out. What do you think?"

Flipping my fingers out one-by-one, I count as we hit the road. "OCD, perfectionist, anal…" Come to think of it, his condo is spotless, too. "You're a neat freak, aren't you?"

His eyes squint as his lips pinch to the side. "Define freak."

"I didn't see a single spec of dust in your condo. Not a single article of clothing tossed haphazardly. There wasn't even an empty water glass by the sink." I swipe a finger over his shiny console. "And your car sparkles like it just came off the lot."

Kip chuckles. "Wow, when you list it out, you make me sound like an alien. I'm afraid to ask about your habits. Judging by your assortment of provocative overalls, tempting boots, and sexy buns, and how I see you covered in mud more often than not, I have a feeling we'll need a maid."

I almost snap back at him in our usual banter until what he said registers. My heartbeats trip, and my lungs seize. Swallowing, I cover the effect his words have on me. "I'm an artist, Kipling. I see beauty in the chaos and mess." I laugh when his eyes widen, though he's trying to cover his horror. "Don't have a heart attack. I might not be the perfect housekeeper, but I'm not a slob. When you work in the dirt all day, you learn how to keep it where it belongs real quick."

"You're an absolute mess on a good day, Sunshine. It's part of why I adore you."

"You could use a little mess to offset your order."

"I haven't had a whole lot of order since the day I returned to Seaside Pointe." He stretches his hand across the console and grabs my fingers, intertwining us in my lap. "Though, I'm not complaining."

"You're welcome."

"Oh, I forgot. Look in the backseat. There's a package for

you." Next to my duffle on the leather seat is a FedEx envelope. I stick my hand inside the open sleeve and pull out a white shirt. Holding it up, I read the script across the chest.

Roses are red. That part is true. But violets are purple. Not freaking blue.

My head falls back with a loud laugh. I think I peed myself a little. "This might be the most perfect shirt I own." With my elbow on the console, I press a kiss to his cheek. "Everyone at the farm is going to love it."

"I couldn't resist. Perfect shirt for my favorite flower girl."

"Thank you." I hold it up again. It even looks like he picked the right size. "You know, I'm gonna put it on right now."

Shrugging my cardigan off my shoulders, leaving me in spaghetti straps, Kip's head whips my way a few times. "As much as I appreciate the view, could you refrain from removing your clothes until we arrive? I'm in danger of wrecking this car."

I swat his sinewy arm before slipping the shirt over my head. Not too big, not too small. "Perfect fit."

He smiles, pleased. It shouldn't surprise me he'd get my sizing right. The man knows clothes. Though Brynn could've helped him, too, something tells me it was all Kip.

For the rest of the drive, we sing, and Kip humors my inability to carry a tune. We talk about everything and anything not involving our families, things we've never known about each other, or rather, never tried to learn.

One surprising thing, Kip loves power ballads. Can't say I ever pictured him as a singer, but he belts the lyrics like he's on stage in a sold-out stadium.

"Are you going to break out in some Bon Jovi later? Maybe a little Celine?" I'm torn between swooning and collapsing because my stomach aches so bad. "Please let it be Celine."

"I sense your sarcasm, you know. How can you not appreciate a good power ballad? Over the top sentiments and dramatic instrumental solos." I press my fingers to my lips to hold back my amusement, but Kip continues, "And when the music and lyrics crescendo into the soaring finale? Pure gold."

I'm dying.

"Laugh all you want, Sunshine. I'll stand by my choice."

"Is this going to be a bromance fest I'm crashing?" I tuck my curls behind my ear as the elevator carries us to the tenth floor. "Am I going to be the fourth wheel?"

Kip adjusts our bags on his shoulder. "With these two? No way, I'm pretty sure the words *she can come alone* passed through Hayden's lips more than once when I told him I wanted to invite you."

"Oh. Tempting." I laugh. "We should've brought Brynn. Oh, and Grace. I wish I'd thought of that. I stand by my opinion they should meet."

"You're determined to kill me by setting up my best guys with my sister and your best friend, aren't you?" He blows out a deep sigh, ushering me out of the elevator when the doors open. "So many things could go wrong with those scenarios."

"As if nothing could go wrong between us." I give him a challenging smirk.

When we get to a door at the end of the hall, Kip knocks twice and walks in without waiting for a response. "Hey, a-holes," he shouts before I'm through the threshold.

"Hey, Sunshine." Bodhi shoves past Kip and bear-hugs me. "I can't believe you let this overprivileged d-bag talk you into going out with him."

He sets me on my feet, keeping his muscular arm around my shoulders as we face Kip.

"As opposed to what? You?" Kip walks further into the living room and sets our bags by the couch, his gaze never leaving our embrace. "Too bad she's got taste, man."

"If I'm honest, I only gave Kip a chance because of you guys. I figured if he had friends as decent as you two, he might not be too bad after all." I smile at Kip, teasing him with a wink.

Hayden's deep voice greets us as he walks out of the hall. "Oh, baby girl, we've got you fooled." He tugs me from Bodhi's side, engulfing me in his thick tattooed arms, my face buried in his broad chest.

"For the love of… Get your own girl. This one is mine."

"What's the matter, bro? You jealous?" I peek out of Hayden's chest in time to witness Bodhi yanking Kip into a hug. "You want some love?"

Hayden lets me go and reaches for a leather jacket draped over the back of the couch with a baritone laugh. "Let's go get something to eat."

Shoving Bodhi away, Kip turns to me. "Do you want to change?"

"Yeah. Real quick, if that's okay." I look from one guy to the next. Leggings are perfectly acceptable pants, but if we're going to some bar, I'd rather I put on something for a night out.

"I'd wait forever for you, Sunshine." Hayden grins as he slips his arms into his jacket.

"Your forever won't be very long if you keep it up," Kip warns his best friend, and I chuckle. Hayden wags his brows my way. Their friendship reminds me so much of Grace and me.

Scooping up my bag, Kip knocks his head toward the hallway between the kitchen and the living room. "C'mon, I'll show you the guest bedroom."

He stops at the second door on the right and flips on the light, dropping our bags on the queen bed. "So, yeah, um, I guess we didn't decide on sleeping arrangements. You can have the bed, and I'll get the couch."

The real question boils down to, am I supposed to be the subdued female who accepts his manners, or do I own what I want?

"You don't need to be chivalrous on my behalf. I think as grown adults, we can manage sharing a bed without breaking any *rules*. We can sleep with pillows between us to protect your virtue." I try, but my smirk can't be stifled.

He grabs me by the hips and jerks my body against his. "You're going to continue throwing that in my face, aren't you?"

Wrapping my arms around his neck, I peck his lips. "It's what I do best when it comes to you. Giving you a hard time is what I live for."

"I'm telling you right now, if we share a bed, there will be no pillows between us." His fingers press deeper into my skin. "What happens next is up to you."

Heat blooms in my cheeks. "Sounds about right. Leaving the hard work up to the farm girl."

"Chlo, babe, you're making it way too easy for me to make a whole lot of inappropriate comments." With a pat on my butt, he walks backward. "I'm going back out there so you can change, and we can head out before I say screw them and lock this door."

"Well, then get out of here already."

Kip stops at the door and turns over his shoulder. "I know it'll be hard, but could you try not being too sexy? Those two are going to give me hell."

My brows knit together, a little laugh seeping out. "I only brought so many things to wear. Would you like me to keep on my new *violets are purple* shirt?"

His gaze skims over my chest. "I would, actually."

"Kipling," I say, chuckling. "Let a woman dress up every once in a while, would you? You see me in overalls enough as it is."

"By all means, dress up, but don't get mad when I can't concentrate."

"All right." My mouth upturns as I shoo him out. "I don't think sexy is in my repertoire of clothing, so you should be fine."

I slip on a black lace bralette beneath a slouchy gray long-sleeved sweater and shimmy into some frayed jeans with holes down each leg. Cute and casual. Add my little black ankle boots, and I feel dressed up just enough for a night out without going all out.

I stop at the bathroom before heading out to the guys and check my appearance in the mirror. With my curls on the verge of feral, I work them up into an updo, slipping some locks out to frame my face and brush a swipe of nude gloss on my lips.

Hayden is perched on the couch armrest while Bodhi leans against the kitchen table when I walk out.

"What's everybody waiting for? Gosh," I tease. "Let's get out of here already."

Kip stands between them with his hands tucked in his front pockets and turns at my voice. As if he can't wait, he closes the distance between us and presses his lips to my ear, whispering, "You are the sexiest woman I know, Chloe Lockwood."

I flush. "Wow. That's saying a lot, considering the number of women you know."

He tweaks my side, and I giggle as the four of us exit.

We don't go far, maybe three blocks down the street from Hayden's place to a bar he frequents. Upstairs is a taco joint, while downstairs is an eclectic tiki bar. He had me at tacos. We slip into a booth, Kip beside me, as Bodhi and Hayden scoot into the other side. Hayden names off a few of his favorites as the server takes our drink orders. I want everything. When he comes back with our drinks, we thank him and order dinner.

"I couldn't help but notice your shirt when you first arrived at my apartment," Hayden says, tipping back his bottle of beer. "Violets aren't freaking blue, huh?"

"They are *not*." I laugh. "Kip got it for me. I'm a sucker for floral humor."

"You should ask Hayden about his T-shirt collection," Kip says.

"Oh?"

Hayden points the mouth of his bottle at Kip. "Your boy's a sucker for a good pun, so every one of them is a history pun."

My face must give way to my curiosity because he says, "I'm a high school history teacher."

"*Oh?*" Of all the occupations, history teacher wasn't even in my top one-hundred possibilities for Hayden. Personal trainer, marine, fireman maybe. *Way to stereotype, Chloe.*

"Dude owns a shirt with Thomas Paine's face on it that says *T. Paine, before it was cool.*" Bodhi smirks as he scratches at the label on his beer bottle. "I don't know where in the hell Kip finds them all. I have one with, *Let minnow if you enjoy the ocean as much as I do* across the chest."

Kip's cheeks redden. "I like buying my favorite people gifts, sue me."

Laughter bubbles out of me as I give Kip's leg a squeeze beneath the table. "That's amazing. I need to see this collection. How did we spend the weekend at San Juan Island and never talk about what you guys do for a living?"

"We were a little busy playing interference between you two." Hayden smirks.

"A lot of good you did." Kip takes a swig of his beer.

I turn my sights on Bodhi, who drapes his arm along the back of the booth, wedging himself against the wall. "What do you do?"

"I'd tell you, but then I'd have to kill you." His face is wiped clean of emotion, and I'm leaning toward believing him until laughter breaks his character and the server arrives with our food. Every other thought floats away because the tacos smell mouth-watering.

After finishing off my tacos, my margarita has gone straight through me. Kip stands to let me out as I excuse myself. When

I return no more than five minutes later, I lose sight of our table. I thought it was the one near the far right corner currently surrounded by three women. Then Hayden's head falls back with booming laughter. My limbs tense. Beautiful. They're all beautiful, and they're charming the pants off Bodhi and Hayden, but I can't spot Kip around the leggy blonde on our side of the booth.

Jealousy stronger than any I experienced while Kip dated my friends in high school fills my veins. Did these women pounce as soon as I left? Or just happened upon the most attractive booth of men in the place? Though Hayden and Bodhi are free for all, a bit of possession takes hold of me for my new buds, too.

The leggy blonde leans forward, drawing closer to the booth, and Kip's bored face comes into view. As if my stare is searing enough to reach him, his head swivels in my direction. Without waiting a single beat, he gently shoves out and walks my way. Behind him, the blonde's eyes bug, her mouth hanging open at his retreating figure.

That's right. This one is mine.

Before I say anything, Kip bends his head down and lays a kiss on my mouth. "Whatever you're thinking, don't," he says against my lips.

I swallow, trying to calm my jealousy. It's an ugly trait to possess, and part of me doesn't want to give Kip the satisfaction. "I wasn't thinking anything."

"No? Those eyes of yours don't lie, Sunshine. I felt the heat from twenty feet away." His knuckle brushes my jaw. "Not one of those women hold a candle to you."

"Wise choice of words, Kipling."

"They're more than words, Chlo. They're a promise. I don't see anyone but you. Okay?"

His confirmation settles something in my heart I hadn't realized was bothering me. Exclusivity. It was implied but never stated.

298 | MINDY MICHELE

I give him a light kiss. "How quickly we've changed to reassurances over barbs."

"If you miss the barbs, we could talk about your singing." I glare and give him a shove, and he catches my hand at his chest. "Want to go downstairs to the bar and dance?"

I look at the table to see the girls still talking with Bodhi and Hayden. "Show me your suave moves, Kipling."

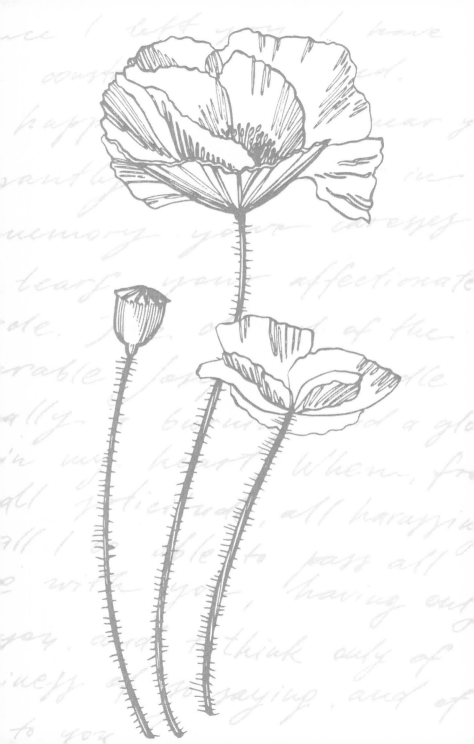

ip

BODHI HEADS HOME when we get back to Hayden's. With Chloe snuggled into my side, the three of us stay up talking. Mostly Hayden and I talk about work. I share my plans for Riverfront, and he tells amusing stories about his students. He's teaching US History at Seattle Prep. It's a well-paid position at an exclusive prep school, which he was lucky to fall into thanks to a family connection.

"I hate to break up this party, but I was up with the sun this morning." Chloe sits up, stretching. "If I'm going to be my chipper self for our big day tomorrow, I should get some sleep."

Kissing my cheek, she tells me to stay and talk. "I'm coming," I counter. She's crazy if she thinks I'm missing one moment of sleeping by her side.

Hayden smirks when Chloe disappears down the hall. "Should I wear earplugs?"

Shoving him, I follow after my girl. "Have fun in bed alone, prick."

After using Hayden's bathroom to wash up, I'm in bed—wearing a tee and knit basketball shorts instead of my usual boxers only—when Chloe finishes with her nighttime routine. She steps into the bedroom and closes the door behind her. Her back faces me for longer than necessary, her body folded in like she's nervous.

"Chlo?" I prop up to my elbow and admire the view.

She's not in sexy lingerie. No, that wouldn't be her style. She's in a little pajama short-set similar to what Brynn wears at my parents'. It's no more revealing than a T-shirt and shorts. Possibly less so, but those long, bare legs stir my lust. I haven't seen her legs clad in anything but jeans since we were teens. Not touching her tonight will be a chore.

"Chlo?" I repeat.

She turns, her fingers playing with the buttons on her top. The bedside lamp reveals her pink cheeks. "I don't know why I am so incredibly nervous right now." Her sheepish expression is charming. "It's not like I've never done this before."

"Well, I sure hope you've slept before." I don't want to delve into an awkward sexual history conversation. I fold back the blanket and pat her side of the bed. "We're sleeping. Nothing else."

Chewing on her lip, she crosses the room and climbs into bed beside me. "Just sleeping, huh?"

"And cuddling." I sink down and hook her waist, sliding her into the middle of the bed beside me.

Hiding her face in my neck, she kisses my Adam's apple. "I could get used to this."

Kissing the top of her head, I hum my agreement.

"So, THE ONE WHO GOT AWAY?" Hayden hands me an empty mug when I wander into the kitchen the following morning.

"Don't start in on me before I've had caffeine." Especially when I was awake half the night in a state of unfulfilled desire. I nudge in next to him at the counter and drop a pod into his fancy machine. "And, technically, she never got away."

He moves across the kitchen and leans against the counter. "I like her."

The faint hum of the shower echoes through the apartment making Chloe a safe topic of discussion. "I love her, man."

Hayden knows me too well to ask for reassurances. I don't share my feelings lightly. "What about the whole feud thing?"

"I couldn't care less, though, Chloe's not as nonchalant about it."

"If you don't face the past, having a future might be difficult." A shadow darkens his face.

"And how are you doing with that lesson?"

"Did I show you my new tat?" He lifts the edge of his shirt.

In the silence between us, we hold a wordless conversation. There isn't much we don't know about each other. We've shared many of our secrets while at our lowest points through the years. I'd go to bat for him in a heartbeat, and he'd do the same for me. Bodhi's no different.

A tattoo is his answer to my question. How is he dealing with his personal demons? Not great.

I HAVEN'T BEEN to a home Mariners game since high school—another thing I missed by living in Oklahoma. I convinced the guys to road trip to Arlington when they played the Rangers, but it wasn't the same. While Bodhi and Hayden are new Seattle fans, I grew up watching them. This is like reliving my childhood, but now I have Chloe by my side.

Chloe who grins down at her phone, tapping away like we aren't at a Mariners game.

I nudge her knee. "Is there a flower emergency?"

She shakes her head, her smile still in place. "It's Grace checking in."

I kiss her temple because baseball is not on her list of things to do on a Saturday, but she's here for me. "Tell her I said hi."

"Oh, Bodhi." Her finger swipes over the screen before she holds out her phone to him. "This is my best friend, Grace."

Leaning back for her arm, I peek at the picture on her home screen. It's the two of them sitting among a patch of multicolored flowers, their arms up in the air. The plants are so tall you can barely see anything but their faces.

Bodhi squints at the screen.

"Okay, not the best one." She pulls her phone back, swiping, swiping. "We're a little covered, but this one…" It's a selfie, their faces pressed close together as they grin.

"You're determined, aren't you?" I nip at her bicep, trapping her sleeve with my teeth.

She giggles, swatting me and tucking her phone into her chest. "What's wrong with planting the seed?" She winks. *Damn, I adore her.* "If we were strangers, I'd want someone to show me a picture of you and set us up."

Bodhi shoves my chest with his elbow and reaches across me. "Let me see it, Sunshine."

"You can stop using my nickname now if you don't mind." I scowl, shoving him back as Chloe hands over her cell.

"I dunno. I think the guys should be allowed to use it." Her eyes light with teasing. "You let them in on the meaning behind it before me. I think you'll be able to come up with something more suited for us now."

Does she not realize how personal her nickname is to me?

"Put your scowl away." Chloe cradles my cheek and captures

my mouth. "It'll always mean more coming from you," she says against my lips.

Hayden groans from where he sits in the aisle seat. "This is what women do to us. Geez, Bodh, hand Sunshine the phone back, and don't look at her hot friend again."

Chloe leans across me, resting her elbow on my armrest. "I feel like there's a story there I want to know more about."

Bodhi returns her phone and chuckles low. "Definitely a story for another day."

Pressing my lips to Chloe's ear before she sits up, I whisper, "What if I call you my supreme goddess?"

Her head swivels, an eyebrow arched.

"Not acceptable? Princess? Queen? Empress?" Her lips purse tighter and tighter with each ridiculous title, unimpressed. "Fine. How about I call you *mine*?"

With my hand on her waist, her shiver travels through my fingers, and she kisses me again. "I accept."

The crack of a bat against ball steals my focus as the crowd goes wild for a Mariners home run.

Chloe sinks into her chair, a winsome pout on her pink lips. "I've never competed with baseball."

Still standing with the crowd around us, I hover over her and press a kiss to her windblown hair. "And I've never competed with flowers, so I guess we're even."

"So, Miss Lockwood?" Bodhi asks midway through the sixth inning. "You seem to have our best friend on a leash. What are your intentions with Kip?" He leans his elbow on the armrest between us, much like Chloe did earlier, his face rapt with attention.

"My intentions?" Her forehead ruffles and the corner of her mouth curves up. "Do they seem less than honorable?"

Hayden laughs, his face visible because of Bodhi's position.

"Did we mention how little he dated back in school?" he asks, and Bodhi bobs his head in agreement. "Very soft-hearted."

"You imbeciles act like I'm a fragile flower. Shut it." I prod Bodhi's elbow from the armrest.

"Hey, there's nothing wrong with fragile flowers." Chloe angles away from me. "Don't forget who your audience is."

I tug on her hair like a schoolboy. "Don't pay attention to them, Chlo. They're so scared of commitment, they run from their own shadows." Ignoring the muttered insults my best friends toss my way, I tug Chloe's hair again. "Also, I like the thought of you having less than honorable intentions. You'll have to explain those to me in detail sometime."

"You couldn't handle them." Though she's angled away, I spy the edge of lips twitching.

"I couldn't?" I run my hand up her jean-clad thigh. "Try me."

Plucking my hand from her leg, she drops it over my lap and meets my gaze. "Maybe once we're alone. We'll see."

Find time to be alone. Check.

Returning my focus to the game, the guys and I talk stats and players, randomly heckling opposing batters and generally acting like twelve-year-olds. Chloe shakes her head, occasionally joining in on our antics but mostly watching in wide-eyed wonder. My sex appeal is likely going down.

Three batters into the eighth inning, I notice Chloe from the corner of my eye with her phone angled toward Bodhi and her head tilted like she's sneaking a picture. Then, she's tap, tap, tapping away on her phone again, sending the picture to Grace, I'm sure.

"Give it up, flower girl."

"What?" She chuckles, tucking her phone away.

I slap my palm over her eyes. "Quick, which team is up to bat?"

"No fair." Her amusement continues. "We've been talking the whole time. How was I supposed to be paying attention?"

"You multitask."

"You stuff me with pretzels and nachos and conversation, and I'm supposed to watch sports, too?"

"You're gonna have to figure this out for us to work." I wink. "It's a dealbreaker."

"After everything. This. *This* is your stake on a dealbreaker?"

"Hell no, but it's fun to see you sweat at the idea of a lifetime of sports."

Her eyes rove my face, blinking. A smile cracks through her stunned expression. "Sports can exist. Just don't expect me to know anything about them."

Throwing my arm around her shoulder and dragging her into my side, I kiss the top of her head. "As long as you're sitting beside me, I'll forgive your ignorance."

Her elbow jabs my side, but she doesn't move away.

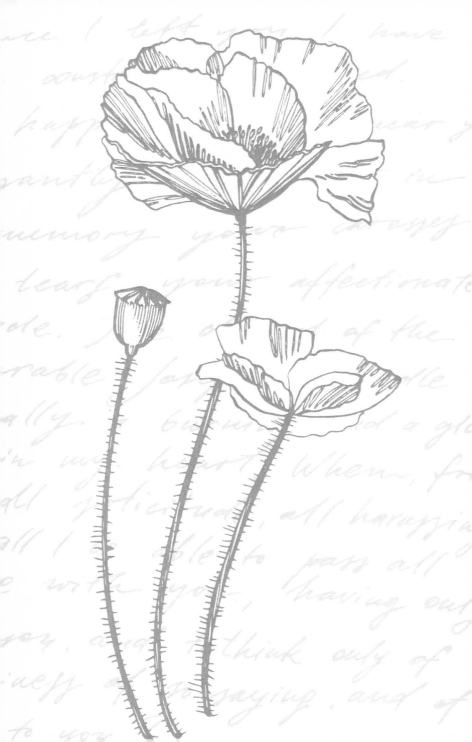

32

Kip

As we're entering the lobby of Hayden's building from the parking garage, I spy the glow of the sign for the bakery across the street. "Hey, Chlo and I are going across the street for a bit. Cool?" I shoot Bodhi and Hayden *the look.*

They flash perceptive smiles. "We're gonna head down to Bottlehouse," Hayden says. "We'll be out for the rest of the night. You've got a key."

"I know we talked about lunch, but give me a hug, Sunshine, in case I don't see you two tomorrow." Bodhi tugs Chloe into his arms.

"I'm thrilled I got to see you again," she says into his chest. "Sorry if I got a little carried away with the whole Grace thing. I'll zip my lips from now on."

"No worries, she's not hard to look at. Hit me up in a few months. You never know."

"Don't say that unless you mean it because I will." She grins, patting his shoulder.

I grit my teeth but keep my mouth shut. My relationship with Chloe has enough complications. Her matchmaking Grace and Bodhi? Heaven help us. Taking Chloe's hand, I kick at my best friend. "Give me my girl and get out of here. We're still on for lunch, idiot."

They wave as we cross the street.

"This place has the best French pastries. I figured we could chat." I should have asked first, but I didn't think she'd turn it down.

"This girl always has room for pastries."

"Which is why you're my girl." Wrapping my arms around her from behind, I steer her toward the counter.

After ordering, I carry our tray and follow Chloe until she finds a bistro table in the far back corner away from the cafe's noisier center. She looks around at the eclectic decor as we settle into our seats, her approval clear.

"This place is cute. We need a good bakery like this in Seaside."

"Not a bad idea." My inner realtor kicks into action. We have donut shops, ice cream, bakeries for special occasions. What we don't have is a cafe like this—a place serving light meals, drinks, and desserts. I jot a mental note to get a business card on our way out.

"Your head is already spinning plans, isn't it?" She scoops some of the tart she ordered onto her fork.

"I'm easy to read, huh?"

She shrugs. "I like to think just for me."

Cracking the caramelized crust on my crème brûlée, I find myself speaking my thoughts out loud. "What do you want with life?"

Chloe chuckles. "Breaking out the big guns. Where do I even start?"

Smooth, Kip. "Sorry, that was random."

"No, it's fine, and a valid question. You know what my plans for Lockwood Blooms are. Obviously, I plan on fully taking the business over once my dad retires."

Which may be sooner rather than later since he doesn't seem to be recovering from his stroke as well as they thought he would.

I nod. There was never a doubt in my mind she wouldn't give up the farm.

"The rest, though? I want a family. Kids." She shrugs. "The usual dreams."

"Kids. Plural?"

"As an only child, yes. I want more than one. My parents couldn't help not being able to have more after me, but if I can, I want my kids to be able to have siblings. What about you?"

"Ten."

She presses a hand to her chest, choking on her drink. "I meant what are your dreams, but good luck finding a woman willing to push out ten kids."

"How about four then? Reasonable enough?" I'm an idiot for asking. For planning a life with a Lockwood. We've only begun this relationship, but if I'm going to give up my place with Weller Faison, my life in Tulsa, I should know if her future plans line up with mine.

Chloe catches the edge of her mouth between her teeth and holds my gaze. "Four would be a handful, but…nice."

Sliding my hand across the table, I toy with her fingers. "I want a big family. I want to build an enormous modern farm-house by my parents' place. That's what the lot you keep asking to buy is for, you know. My dad always dreamed Brynn and I would both build and settle on Harris land."

The lines between her brows soften, but she doesn't say anything in return.

"I want to make Seaside Pointe an amazing town to live in. Advance tourism while keeping the charm. Those are my dreams.

Taking my kids fishing and hiking, coming here for baseball and football games. Going skiing in the winter and traveling the world with my wife."

After a moment, with a shaky voice, she asks, "What about Tulsa?"

"My plan was to stay in Tulsa for maybe six more years. I always knew I'd end up back near or in Seaside, though. This corner of the world is too much a part of my Harris blood. Like you and the Lockwood soil."

Chloe stills, her fork paused above her plate.

Releasing her hand, I lean back and continue. "The Riverfront Center. If the property is well managed, that place could finance not only my offspring but Harrises for generations. The potential it has, the plans I have. It's like the Omni-Plex deal I told you about. A family-centered place with entertainment, food, retail and office space, and waterfront views and green space any member of Seaside Pointe—and our neighboring communities—will love. It's a dream project." I confide a truth only four people, and a family lawyer, know. "Brynn and I own the property. One hundred percent."

"The riverfront." Her light brown eyes stare. "Just the two of you?"

"Granny and Dad bought it under an LLC when I was maybe six or seven and named Brynn and me as minority owners. Over the years they transferred small percentages of ownership to us. We never knew about it. Dad started work on getting the rezoning on the property months ago because he knew he wanted to develop it, but he didn't tell us it was ours until I came home."

"He made you a deal you couldn't refuse," she says under her breath. "That's what Grace suggested when I first asked why you were back. I'd heard so little of your life in Tulsa, but I knew you were doing big things."

Figures. "I couldn't escape the gossip mill even from two thousand miles away."

"More like I couldn't escape hearing about the great Kipling Harris no matter how far removed you were."

"How difficult for you."

"It was the *worst*." Chloe half-smiles. "So, you own the land and develop it into this complex. Then what? What does that mean for you?"

"Well, I have options. Our owning the property changes nothing other than the money we make as owners. I can go back to Tulsa and let Brynn manage it, or my dad or one of our other property managers could. I trust them to do what's best."

Nodding, she scratches the back of her neck, looking down at her plate, shifting around the tart.

"But, management's my job. I spent five years in school obtaining my business degree, and master's, and realtor license to do this. I'm the one courting the tenants. I've designed the plans with my architect, and I'm working with my contractors. You were right last week, this is *my* baby. Walking away isn't something I want to do. I want to be here every step of the way."

Her eyes snap up, her foot bouncing. "Kip, what are you saying?"

Bumping our plates to the side, I claim her hand in mine. "I'm telling you I've decided on staying in Seaside."

With a slow-moving grin she tries to bite back, Chloe says, "For the riverfront deal, of course."

I steal a chunk of her lemon-raspberry tart to swipe the cheeky grin from her face. "I mean, why else would I stay?" I pop the bite in my mouth.

Her lips purse as she feigns ignorance and swipes a forkful of my dish, but we both know the real reason I want to stick around.

"You know, I've had the chance to talk with Melvin Sullivan a few times since you came along trying to buy his land. He and his wife never lived extravagantly. He was a farmer by trade. The Sullivan's held onto the property because it wasn't close enough to their farm to benefit their livelihood, and it was never a prime parcel of real estate for development. The sale to you should have been quick and easy."

"So, why has it taken so long?"

There are two answers to her question. One—which involves Dad and the greedy Sullivan siblings—I won't give her today. I'm still banking on it never mattering. The other tells the truth of the man Melvin Sullivan is and reveals my heart.

"The land you want is acreage Marcie's family owned. Land she inherited. Melvin asked for time to come to terms with parting with this final piece of her."

Gnawing on her bottom lip, her eyes water. "So very sweet. It makes perfect sense."

"I want the same thing, Chlo. I want to be a man who shows such love and devotion to his partner. For all his faults, my dad is wholly dedicated to my mother. It was his greatest lesson to me." The tears shining in Chloe's eyes have me sliding my chair around the edge of the bistro table until our knees touch. "I love you, Chloe Lockwood. I'm *in* love with you, and yes, our romantic relationship is new, but our knowledge of one another is anything but. I don't doubt we could be perfect together. I didn't want to return to Seaside tomorrow without making *my* intentions abundantly clear to you."

With her chest heaving, Chloe stands, holding her hand out. "Let's go back to Hayden's."

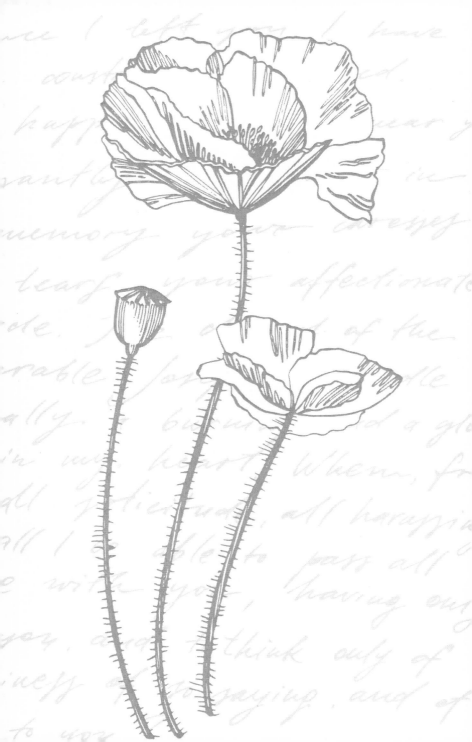

hloe

SLIPPING my hand into Kip's, we walk across the street to Hayden's apartment. When Kip opens the door, I tug him down the hallway, my heart thumping in my chest. The apartment is dark and quiet, only the two of us here.

He says nothing as I close the guest bedroom door and lock it. Turning to face him, our eyes cling. And in an instant, the room is charged.

Kip sucks in a ragged breath but stays where he is, waiting for my first move. There's a foot between us. Too far for me. One step closes the gap. My eyes descend over his lips, down his throat —his Adam's apple bobbing—across his broad chest. Pressing my hands there, my fingertips trail along the bold white Mariners lettering, over his racing heart and rapid lungs. They match mine. Down my fingers migrate, tracing the ridges of his abs until they meet the hem of his navy baseball jersey.

"Arms up," I whisper, and Kip lifts them, our eyes locked.

Slowly, I raise the form-fitted jersey, inching it over his head, and he helps the rest of the way, tossing it to the ground. I suck in a quiet breath at the sight of his tan, bare skin. I haven't seen Kip shirtless since junior year when a bunch of us went swimming at Kelly Andersen's house for her birthday. Yeah, I remember because it was a thing made of dreams. Dreams I didn't want to have of him at the time.

Sorry to break it to you, teenage Kip, but you don't bat near the same league as grown-up Kip.

My palms flatten against his lean torso, fingers dipping along the contours as I drift up. His muscles tremble under my touch, and I bite back a smile that I, *me*, Chloe Lockwood, have such an effect on Kipling Harris.

All my senses are a live wire. The sound of his heavy breathing; the smell of his sandalwood with a hint of vanilla cologne; the sight of his sinewy build; the feel of his raging heartbeats beneath his warm skin. The only thing left is a taste.

Dipping my head, my lips press to his firm pec, my tongue slipping out, sucking his skin into my mouth. The patience Kip has been exerting breaks as his hands grip my hips, his fingers digging in, releasing a pent-up groan.

I plant another open-mouthed kiss to his skin and another before my lips wander up his neck, following his pulse, rising on my tiptoes to reach him. "Kipling Harris not in control for once. How does that feel?"

My hands meander around him, one forming to his taut back muscles, the other sinking into the short hair at his nape. As I mold myself to his body, my lips graze his cheek and brush the corner of his mouth.

"It feels like a long time coming," he says, raspy. "I'm all yours, gorgeous."

Kip's hands find their way under my shirt, his fingers kneading and restrained. It makes me feel powerful, even if it's false power; he's letting me lead. I skip his mouth and press a kiss to the other corner of his lips, ascending to his earlobe, and tuck it between my teeth. His hands tense, clutching my back as he sucks in a loud breath, rolling his hips into mine.

Purposely, I keep my mouth from his because once we connect, it's all over, and something about teasing Kip in this way fills me with a heady thrill.

My fingers drift down, appreciating the toned lines of his torso, cascading over the coveted V until they find the rim of his jeans. I swallow, my gaze aimed on my hands at his waist.

The instant I took his hand in mine at the cafe and tugged him across the street, there was no turning back. But this moment, with my fingers waiting, is where my intentions will solidify. With one swipe, the button flicks open, and I peer up beneath my lashes: all the certainty and love my heart possesses, gleaming for him to see.

Moving up my bare skin, Kip draws my thin sweater over my head. My first instinct is to cover myself, but I refrain. He loves *me*. And this is me in my most vulnerable form.

Lowering his head, he presses his lips to the top of my shoulder, his mouth and tongue gliding from my bra strap to the crook of my neck, inhaling. Kip's fingers slip under the straps, sliding them down, but he doesn't move for my clasp. Instead, his fingers sink into the hair at my nape, tugging my head up as he kisses the hollows of my collarbone. A shiver courses through me, heat pooling in my belly.

The wet graze of his tongue and lips traces a path along the column of my neck to my jaw. One side. *Kiss.* Then the other. *Kiss.* Before his mouth hovers over mine. Inches are all that separate me from this man. Hungry eyes touch every feature until they find my gaze and hold. Kip wants *me*. No words necessary, everything he desires is shared in one long stare.

When our mouths collide, all at once, clothes disappear, and my back is cradled in softness as Kip hovers above me on the bed. With a wicked little smirk, he finally assumes control. I gasp at his tenderness. The reverence on his face as he drinks me in. His fingers trace over the shapely silhouette of my body, teasing my skin. His mouth explores, branding me until I'm writhing with want. A want that has my fingers steering his lips back to mine and his weight covering me.

I assumed I'd shared my one and only kiss with Kip Harris under his tree in the rain as a teen. The knowledge was more unsettling than I ever would have thought.

Two months ago, the idea of seeing him again had all but slipped my mind. He was like a myth, our long-ago kiss more of a foggy dream than reality.

Tonight, with his mouth fused to mine and our bodies entwined, I can't fathom a moment without him.

I free my lips from his as he draws my thigh higher. "I love you, Kipling Harris." With one last connection of our bodies, everything vanishes but him.

WE LAY BENEATH THE COVERS, wrapped around each other, sated and blissfully drained. With our heads laying inches apart, Kip draws lazy circles on my waist as my hand presses to his chest, our legs tangled.

"On our way to the lavender fields, you wouldn't tell me what you were scared of, said to ask you when we were alone. So, divulge your fears…" My nails wander along his hard pecs, drifting up his throat.

"Of course you remembered." His chin dips, and he captures my fingertip, sucking it knuckles deep into his mouth. His tongue loving the underside until my breath hitches.

"Are you trying to distract me? Because it's working." My teeth sink into my lower lip.

He inches closer. "There's a good chance your assessment is accurate. Or it could be that I find you irresistible, and I'm having a difficult time stopping myself from devouring you."

Nipping at his lips, my nose brushes his. "There's nothing saying you can't...after you answer the question."

"You want to know what scares me?" Kip pauses. Lowering his voice, he murmurs, "You do, Chloe Mae Lockwood. You terrify me." His arm slides to the small of my back, pressing me closer to his heat. "On San Juan, I kept asking myself what I was doing. You weren't mine to fall for, but it didn't stop me. I couldn't believe how strong a pull you held over me without doing a thing."

I bring my hand around the back of his neck, swirling the short strands around my index finger and hitch my leg over his hip. "Do you think that's maybe part of the reason we declared war on one another? Too terrified of what falling in love would mean? We fight the things we're scared of most."

"It's possible." He tucks his hand in the crook of my knee, his fingertips digging into my thigh. "I've watched you from afar for as long as I can remember. When I see you, whether it's the vague outline of your body walking through the fields in the evenings or your ugly beat-up Chevy sitting out on Main Street—"

I lightly pinch the curve of his shoulder. "Watch what you say about Betty. She's delicate."

"Right, sorry, Betty. You're lovely."

"Thank you," I murmur, kissing the tip of his nose.

"As I was saying, when I see you, I'm transfixed. You hold that power over me." He peers deep into my eyes while confessing my power, but he must see. I'm *his* hostage. "I hate it," he finishes on a shallow breath.

"I'd say I'm sorry, but I'm not." Inching my face closer, my lips glide across his, not quite kissing him.

"It's all about pride, Chloe. There were things my dad used to say, comments he made. Honestly, I never felt like I could live up to him. He expected a lot out of us, but especially his son." I tense. "He wasn't a horrible father. Please don't take it that way.

We simply butt heads all the time. I'm sure my being a bit stubborn will come as a surprise to you."

I shake my head, mouthing, "No, never."

"It's the reason I went so far out of my mind the day I overhead what you and the others said about me. It was a slap in the face. Another *Kip isn't good enough* moment. It was stupid and not at all your fault, but between that and Dad's ribbing, I decided I was going to do whatever I had to do to prove myself on my terms. And it's why I say I hate the way you make me feel."

Holding my breath, waiting, Kip flips me onto my back, hovering above.

"All the time I spent making my plans and proving myself, and all it took was one run-in with you for me to know those things meant nothing. You changed everything."

Lifting my head from the pillow, I catch his lips. "Such is the power of a Lockwood."

Kip dives in, attacking my ear and sucking the lobe between his teeth. A giggle bursts from me and quickly dies when his hand dips below my waist.

hloe

WHEN I SKIP down the stairs Monday morning, ready to greet the flowers, I hum Queen's *Somebody to Love.* Thanks to Kip, who blasted the song more than once on the car ride home yesterday, singing to every word. I'd say it got old, but it didn't. Not even close.

Stopping in the kitchen, I kiss my dad's cheek as he sits at the table in the nook reading the newspaper.

"Morning, Dad. Mom up?"

"She's out feeding the chicken." He adjusts his new reading glasses, peering at me above them perched on the end of his nose. Since his stroke, his vision hasn't been the same. "How was Seattle with Grace?"

If I imagine he asked about Kip instead of Grace, the lie flies more freely. "It was fun." I pour my coffee and lean against the counter, facing him. "We had a good time."

My dad grunts. "Did you happen to run into Kip Harris while you were there?"

I still, my mug inches from my lips. "Why would I see Kip in Seattle?"

He shifts, glancing back down at the newspaper, giving me his profile. "I had an interesting conversation with Reid Saturday morning when he came to pick up his paycheck."

Reid? *Thump, thump, thump.* The beat of my heart picks up.

"He was confused as to why we didn't know you'd been dating Denton Jr."

My stomach twists in knots. How did Reid know about Kip and me? We'd been so careful. Hadn't we?

"Why would Reid think I'm dating Kip?"

Shifting sideways, he says, "So, you're not?" It's not a question, not really. It's the tone a father uses to call out avoidance, to catch the lie.

With a shrug, I reply, "I was going to tell you guys eventually." I take a sip of my coffee, hoping to play this off.

"You shouldn't be dating that man in the first place."

In less than three seconds, I revert to my five-year-old self getting caught picking flowers I wasn't supposed to.

"I know it goes against the family motto to make nice with a Harris, but it's not a big deal."

"Not a big deal?" His mouth thins into a straight line. "Then you won't have any problems ending it."

No. I might live under his roof, but I'm a grown woman. I stand straighter. "I'm twenty-five years old, Dad. I don't need your permission to make decisions about my life."

"No, of course not, but I expect better from you. A *Harris*? You had Reid Pruitt. Hardworking, loyal, honest Reid. Of every decent man in Seaside, you chose Denton's son? Then lie about it? For how long?"

"You act like I had a choice other than lying."

"There's always a choice above lying, Chloe Mae."

"Oh yeah? So, if I hadn't lied to you and Mom about it, would you have welcomed Kip into our house with open arms?"

"You lied about it, which tells me you know how wrong it is. Otherwise, you wouldn't have felt the need."

"I felt the need because I knew how much it would hurt you, how disappointed you'd be in me, and disappointing you is the last thing I want to do, but that doesn't make my feelings for Kip wrong. It doesn't make them any less real."

Creases form at the corners of his fuming eyes, the newspaper wrinkling at the edge where his hand clutches it. "You know how badly the Harrises have treated our family for decades. *Unforgivable* things have transpired, and you don't even know the half of it."

"I know, Dad." I set my mug on the counter beside me. The taste too bitter, no amount of cream and sugar would fix it.

"No, you don't," he snaps and I flinch. "If you did, you'd *never* have let a Harris sink his hooks into you. You'd have kept a far distance the way you were supposed to do. You'd have put our family first."

My chest tightens, my fists clenching at my sides. Tears build in my eyes. "Putting this family first is all I've *ever* done, but this is important, too. Kip is important to me."

Discarding the paper, he leans back and folds his arms. "How do you know this relationship isn't just some other way for the Harrises to get back at us? That Kip isn't going to turn on you? Or play you for a fool? Make you believe he loves you just to break your heart and gloat. The Harris family has never done anything with character."

"I know because Kip's a good guy. Everything he does is with character." I step up to the chair adjacent to him, gripping the back of it, willing my tears away. "He's *nothing* like Denton. He'd never hurt me. He'd never hurt *us*, our family. We don't carry on the feud like you guys do."

"No? What about when he and his buddies thought it would

be funny to over-fertilize our rose beds and nearly killed our entire yield? Or every time you'd come home from school complaining how Kip Harris did this, and Kip Harris did that?" His eyes narrow, the wrinkles at the edges deepening his eyes to slits. "The feud seemed to be alive and well not seven years ago."

"Those were harmless pranks and bets; none of it actually affected our lives. And I participated in my fair share of revenge, but we've grown up, Dad. We've worked past it, apologized. Maybe you and Denton should consider doing the same."

"Never." The harsh finality in his tone keeps me from pressing the issue.

"Dad," I swallow, unable to keep my voice from trembling. "I…I love Kip. I know it doesn't make sense, but it happened, and he's sticking around. I think we have something big, something *real*. I'm not going to throw it away because of this family feud. He could be my family someday."

Releasing an outraged grunt, he says, "Even if that's true, if this progresses to something more, I will never accept a Harris as family." He shakes his head with a stern frown, standing. "I can't, and I never will. So, end it."

Dad walks out of the kitchen without another word, leaving me with tears spilling down my cheeks.

I dump my coffee and march out to the fields.

I'm on a mission, a mission to hunt down Reid Pruitt. It takes ten minutes, but I finally find him kneeling beside Charlie over the perennial garden, laying down thick straw on the freshly prepared beds we're gearing up to plant.

"Reid, can I talk to you for a minute."

He peers up beneath the brim of his hat. When our eyes meet, he knows. Reid looks down at the soil before getting to his feet, dusting his gloved-palms off on the sides of his jeans.

I don't wait for him to come to me before I walk away to a more private area of the fields. Once I'm far enough from listening ears, I turn with my hands on my hips.

Reid approaches me with caution, rubbing the rim of his faded cap from one side to the other.

"Are you really that pissed at me?" I ask. "I thought we were on the mend, working toward finding a rhythm again."

"We are." He sighs.

"Yeah? Because I can't think of why else you'd go to my dad about Kip, other than to screw me over."

"It was an honest mistake, Loe." He shoves his hands in his jean pockets, reprimanded.

"Really? Because to me, it seems either you're stirring up unnecessary drama to get back at me, or you're really clueless."

Reid raises his hands with a scowl. "Look, had I known you didn't tell your parents about Kip, I never would've said anything. I'm not petty, Loe. I might've been a little heartbroken, but I'm not an immature teenager."

"How did you even know about us? Did Grace tell you?"

His eyebrows pinch together. "No, Kip did." One shoulder shrugs. "Not that I was surprised."

Whiplash. My head throws back so quickly, my neck jerks. "What? When?"

"We bumped into each other in town last week, shared a few words. Some not of my finer moments, but he mentioned it so casually I figured it was common knowledge. I mean, who keeps a relationship secret?"

"We do! Are you kidding me? You know how our families are. We needed to figure out where it was going before we told them, needed to know if it was worth the backlash we're sure to receive."

"Then why would he tell me?"

Excellent question. Throwing the winning card in Reid's face? It doesn't line up with the man I've fallen in love with these last few weeks. But he'll sure be who I ream into next.

"I don't know, but it's not common knowledge, and he shouldn't have said a word."

330 | MINDY MICHELE

"I'm sorry. I really am. I'd never want to cause a rift between you and your parents. That wasn't my intention."

"Then what was your intention? Why were you talking to my dad about my dating life in the first place?" I almost say it's no longer his concern, but that's a little too below the belt.

Scratching the back of his neck, Reid says, "James asked me how I was doing, tried convincing me to win you back. I figured it was because he didn't want you dating Harris, so I said I'm not the kind of man to wreck another relationship, especially for my own gain." His teeth run over his lower lip. "When he asked what I was talking about, I mentioned Kip. The shock on his face gave it away pretty quick. I'm sorry. I should've texted you or something to give you a heads up."

I shake my head. "Advance notice would've been nice, yes, but it wouldn't have made the conversation go over any smoother."

Did my dad mean what he said? Would he ever be able to accept us? And if he couldn't, would I be able to live with the wedge for the rest of my life? For Kip?

"For what it's worth, Loe. I don't think Kip's a bad guy. Do I like him? No," he chuckles, "but I don't think he meant to tell me about you two. So, give the guy the benefit of the doubt before you lay into him. Though, if you do lay into him, can I get a front-row seat?"

I punch Reid in the shoulder with a light scowl. "Go finish helping Charlie with mulching."

As he walks away with a smirk, my phone pings, and I pull it out of the pocket on my leather tool belt and find a text.

Kipling: Missing my girl this morning. When can we have another slumber party?

Dang you, fluttering butterflies.

I tuck my cell back without responding. Kip can wait. He has some explaining to do after work, but with this morning, I'd rather it be in person.

AFTER SPENDING a couple hours in the fields to calm my frayed nerves, I wander to the flower studio for some floral arranging therapy. Having ignored my phone, I slip it out of my tool belt and listen to the voicemails I've missed since Friday.

The first is a local grower who wants to team up for some workshops, which I'm so down for. I make a mental note to call her back and skip to the next message.

Grace's voice flows through the speaker. "I would like to know where I can sign my name on the dotted line for the hunk of man meat you sent me. Why don't we grow them like that in Seaside? Also, I want to remind you I'm too young to be an aunt, so be smart. Love you!"

I laugh, saving her message for later, and move onto the one from an hour ago.

"Miss Lockwood, it's Joan with Harris Development. I'm calling to let you know the property you were interested in is no longer for sale as the Sullivans have accepted another offer. We appreciate your interest. Have a nice day."

My heart plummets into my stomach, and I grab the edge of the workbench. What? I'm going to be sick. Sullivan's land is gone? How? After everything? The talk of Mr. Sullivan's devotion to his wife and needing time to say goodbye. I bought it. I believed everything Kip said this weekend.

Was this all a ruse? A way for Kip to distract me from further pursuing the Sullivan land? Does he love me, or was this his final blow to win our feud before hightailing it back to Tulsa?

I don't want to believe it's possible he could be so cruel, especially not after the weekend we shared, but my whole life has been nothing but warnings away from the Harrises, and I didn't listen. The last thing I want is for Dad to be right.

Is he right about Kip?

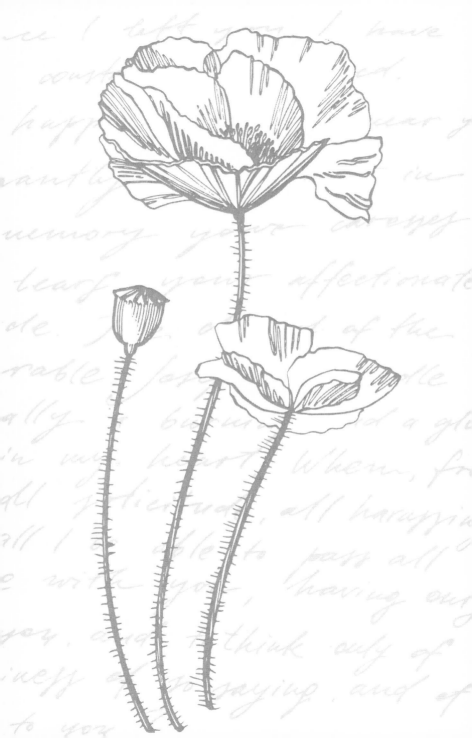

ip

BUTTONING MY DRESS SHIRT, I stand at my bedroom window and peer out over the parking lot, where the bay's dark water sparkles in the distance. Not exactly waterfront property, but I'm close. Close, but today I'm missing the view from my bedroom at Mom and Dad's. My glimpse of Lockwood's flowers beyond the backyard. Correction, what I'm missing is the view from Hayden's guest room. Waking up to the sight of Chloe's exposed back as she sleeps peacefully on her stomach. The dimples at the base of her spine, her wild halo of hair spread over the pillow. I'm missing my girl.

She's likely making deliveries or busy in some other way, so I curb my need for her voice and shoot a text instead, letting her know I miss her.

"You are so whipped, Kip Harris." The fact doesn't dim my mood as I grab my things and head out.

.   .   .

DUE TO A LEASE extension meeting and my usual drive-bys, it's ten before I pull into my parking spot at Harris Development. Carrie-Ann talks with Joan as I enter the office.

"Well, if it isn't the ladies I need," I say in lieu of an official greeting.

"Oh boy, here come the additions to our to-do lists." Joan's mumble carries to my ears, and Carrie-Ann nods. "Like father, like son."

So, yeah, apparently, my business habits came from Dad. Before moving back to Seaside, I'd never worked with the man, but somehow he rubbed off on me. The daily drive-bys to check on various properties? Something he used to discuss over family meals. The best way to reel in a client on the fence? Also, a lesson taught at the dinner table. I'm not exactly thrilled to learn how similar we go about business. Then again, those lessons serve me well.

"Carrie-Ann, Mooney agreed to a five-year extension on their space, with the terms we sent. Though, we did discuss upgrading the exterior lighting, which needs doing anyway. If you could work up a new lease, then schedule a time for us to have it signed."

"On it, Mr. Harris," she sasses with a salute.

"Joan, remind me to take a second look at Carrie-Ann's performance review, would you?"

Laughing, Joan pushes from her desk and grabs the items from my inbox behind her.

Carrie-Ann scoffs. "You wouldn't dare, Kip Harris."

"Call me Mr. Harris again and I might." I tease, accepting a file and messages from Joan. "Joan, can you have the landscapers look at the beds at Ambassador Plaza? They still haven't done the spring plantings."

"Yeah, I'll call them. They were supposed to be out there two weeks ago." Joan jots a note on a sticky pad. "There's good news in your hand, though."

In my hand? The first slip is a message from someone interested in a vacant space in the strip center on Hazel Street. The second slip is a message from Roger Scaritt. My heart rate triples as I read: *Riverfront is on the docket for Wednesday. Committee is in agreement to approve your request.*

Lifting my gaze, I meet Carrie-Ann and Joan's faces. They're beaming, and after a beat, I am too.

Phew. I feel a fist pump coming on. Barring some crazy good opposition from the community, Riverfront Center can move forward. The excitement stirring in my gut is outmatched only by the amount of stress rolling off my back. If I hadn't already made the decision on remaining in Seaside, this weekend with Chloe certainly sealed the deal. I'm sticking around no matter what, but having this development will keep me busy and help me acclimate to working with Dad. Plus, this is how I leave my mark on my hometown. I'm stoked.

"Roger said he left you a message, but he called me, too. He wanted to be sure he didn't miss you. Congratulations."

"Fantastic. Thanks." My hand smooths over the back of my hair, at a loss for words. "This can be huge for all of us. For Seaside." The office line rings, and I give Joan a nod as she answers before heading toward the door leading to the back.

Carrie-Ann follows. "You seem happy. Maybe I need a weekend in Seattle."

"I highly suggest it." I shove down the visuals of Saturday night.

Her eyes narrow on my smirk. "Mmm-hmmm. I don't want to know what you and your buddies did. You'll never stop being little Kip to me."

"Ha. I'm older now than you were when we met."

"Don't remind me, boss." With a groan, Carrie-Ann shoves my shoulder and turns toward her office. "By the way, thanks for picking Mia up and feeding her Thursday. Everything was so crazy with graduation Friday. I didn't get to say something before you left."

"Anytime, I love hanging out with her." The memory of Mia's sass when we ran into Reid pulls my lips into a half-smile. "She's a good kid."

"She is, and she's a little lost on what she wants to do with herself, so I appreciate you speaking into her life the way you do."

"Don't thank me—"

"Oh, Kip," Joan interrupts from the lobby. I poke my head through the open doorway. "I meant to tell you I didn't reach Miss Lockwood personally this morning, but I left her a message."

An unknown weight sinks my stomach. "I'm sorry?"

"About the Sullivan deal? Denton asked me to call and let her know it was off."

Dread pulses through my veins. "Off? What are you talking about?" My head swivels from Joan's rapidly paling face to Carrie-Ann, who's standing by my side in the hallway. "What did he do?"

Carrie-Ann's eyes grow round. "I don't— What's going on, Kip?"

They don't know why I'm upset. Of course they don't. "Chloe Lockwood wanted that land. Why is the deal off? What did he do?"

"I don't know. He didn't say anything to me." Her hands raise as if in self-defense. I look back to Joan.

"All I know is what he relayed by voicemail. He said call and tell Miss Lockwood Sullivan accepted another buyer's offer."

"What the—" Slamming my palm against the doorframe, I stalk toward my office, pulling my cell from my pocket on the way. He isn't in this morning; his car wasn't outside.

"You've reached Denton Harris. I'm…" Dammit. I end the call.

Dropping my bag in my office chair, I yank at my hair as I

dial Chloe, then hit end before it connects. I need to understand what happened first. I need to...a file on my desk grabs my eye.

Sullivan 151.

The sticker notes on the side tab. I move my bag to the floor and sit, opening the file.

"Kip?" Carrie-Ann steps inside my doorway, and I hold up a finger.

There lay the details for the purchase of twenty acres along Highway 151, also known as Sullivan's land, in black and white. Seething, I read the purchase agreement. *He didn't.* I note the price, the buyers, the signatures, the notary. *There aren't enough words in the English language to adequately describe my feelings.*

I can't tell Chloe this. I can't.

Carrie-Ann jerks when my fist slams the desk and my cursing fills the office. "Your father's ignored Chloe Lockwood for nearly her entire life," she says, sinking into the chair across from my desk.

Cradling my head in my hands, I lift my gaze enough to her soft expression.

"The moment you came home he began asking questions. He became interested in Sullivan's. A property he likely forgot we represented until you showed interest on Chloe's behalf. What did he do, Kip?"

My dry mouth refuses the explanation, so I push the file across the desk. Her eyes scan the agreement, cursing my father to perdition with each flip of the page.

"You're seeing her?" She closes the file with a heavy sigh. I don't answer. "Mia mentioned running into Reid Pruitt with you Thursday."

My jaw clenches. I never wanted us to be a secret. I've done this for Chloe. Chloe who... Growling like an animal, I throw my body back in my seat. My eyes clench tight as I see red.

Carrie-Ann inhales sharply. "It's more. You've fallen for her, haven't you?"

My head falls. "Do you think he knows?"

"What, because of this?" The file lands on my desk with a *thwack*. "Nah, this agreement isn't about you, Kip. That's about Denton and James."

I jump to my feet. Livid. "And why in the hell is it so damn hard for two families to let the past go? It was a mistake made by two boys, Carrie-Ann. Two kids who left a damn gate open, and now we're all doomed to hate one another because of a disagreement had by men who are no longer alive."

"No, I said between *Denton* and *James*." Her voice is so calm. So soft. I pause my furious pacing. "Something happened between them, Kip. Something bigger than all the little pranks and bets and bragging rights your two families have partaken in for years."

I press my palm to my chest as a knot twists. The burn peppers sweat across my brow. "Do you know what it was?" I ask, and she shakes her head, but I'm not so sure she's telling the truth.

"I need to find him. I need answers. Chloe's going to need answers." I grab my bag from the floor. "Do you know where he is?"

"Friday he said he might not be in at all today. He had things to do."

Right, like hiding from the son he knew would rip into him the moment I saw the purchase agreement. "Call me on my cell if you need me."

I ALTERNATE between calling Chloe and calling Dad the moment I start my car. With him, I leave three voicemails, and each time my anger escalates a degree above the last. With Chloe, I beg. "Chlo, love. We need to talk. Please call me back."

Neither return my calls, and while I could search all over this town—and I do drive a loop around Main Street—looking for him would be a waste of time. If Denton Harris doesn't want to be found, he'll stay hidden. I need to speak to Chloe. What is she thinking right now? Why hasn't she called and laid into me?

Because she's hurt, Kip.

Slamming my breaks, I turn into a parking lot and swing my car around. I need to talk to her, with or without answers. She needs to know I had nothing to do with this. I make one final ditch effort to call her, and once again, I go to voicemail.

"Have it your way, Sunshine. I'm on my way to you, and I don't care if your parents see me sitting on their front porch. I'm not leaving until we talk."

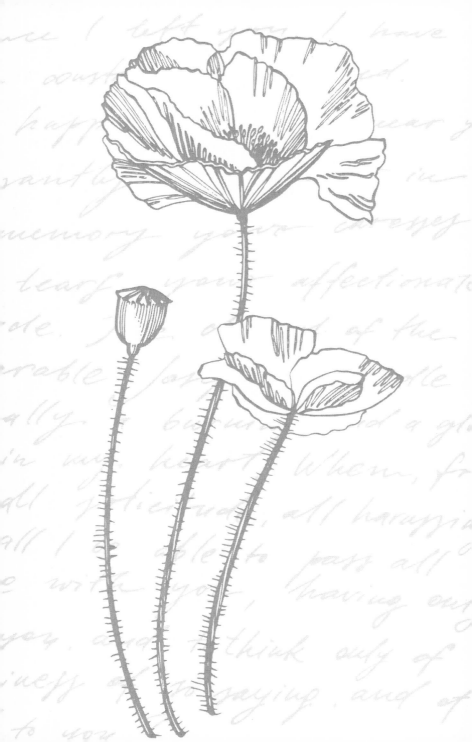

hloe

WHILE I WOULD RATHER BE WALLOWING in bed, drowning in my lost dreams, I keep myself busy instead, helping Denise and Reid unload new supplies from Betty. I can't think about Sullivan's land because the more I do, the more I cry.

A familiar engine roars down the back gravel road, but I'm not used to the sound of it headed toward the farm. I turn at the sound, holding my hand up to shield the sun. And sure enough, a silver crossover comes into view. Kip. If I'd eaten lunch, the contents of my stomach would churn.

Reid comes to my side, a stack of brand new buckets perched on his shoulder. "Do you want me to get rid of him?"

Yeah, that would go over well with Kip.

"No, I can handle him myself." I tug off my gloves and tuck them into my leather tool belt. "Can you two finish this without me?"

With an accommodating nod, he backs away. "Whatever you need."

Kip steps out of his vehicle and stops in the open door, his arm on top of the frame. Finding me, his head cants, and even twenty feet away, worry is evident in his knitted brow.

Clenching my jaw, I seal off my tear ducts. I won't let them beat me. Not in front of Kip. Just the sight of him makes my heart throb. When he opens his mouth, or his hands find me, I'll break.

I roll up my sleeves as I walk across the gravel to him, more for my jittery hands to stay busy than anything else. Shutting the driver's side door, he slips his hands into his slacks and matches me step for step.

"Chlo?" His voice is low, desperate.

"Did you know? Was it you?"

His face contorts, baffled. "Was what me?" His jaw ticks. "Chlo, you can't think…what?"

"The Sullivan land." I keep my voice even. It wants to break so badly. "Did you make a deal with another buyer and steal it out from under me?"

He falters back a step. His gaze moves beyond me to where Reid and Denise are working. "Can we?" Indecision flickers before he sniffs and steps forward, taking my elbow. "Come with me."

Kip leads me past the truck, ignoring their stares as we round the old yellow garden shed. Now that we're alone, he discards his composed anger. His eyes light with fury, mouth pinched in frustration. "Was that a serious question? You weren't playing? You actually believe I would steal Sullivan's land away from you?"

I throw my hands in the air. "I don't know anything anymore. First thing this morning I was ambushed by my dad who knows about us, by the way, because *someone* told Reid." My eyes tighten, and Kip winces. "And not three hours later, I get a voicemail telling me my dream land, my only hope for expanding

Lockwood Blooms in the near future, is gone. You tell me how I'm supposed to be feeling right now."

Pressing the heels of his palms against his temples, Kip digs his fingers into his scalp. "I would hope you'd trust the man you made love to Saturday isn't the kind who would backstab you less than forty-eight hours later. Tell me you don't think I was acting. That I didn't lay my dreams—my love—at your feet so you could call me a liar."

"I want to believe you. I do." I can't hold them back anymore. My wrecked emotions rise and blur my vision. "But we have this unending problem. After talking to Reid, I wanted to give you the benefit of the doubt until this nagging pit in my stomach reminded me of this damn history hanging over us, making me second guess everything. You told Reid about us. Why? Why would you tell him if you weren't trying to sabotage us?"

"Chloe, look at me." His fingers circle my wrists, holding them between us. "I ran into Reid while I was with Mia the other afternoon. Reid insinuated I liked them young. I was pissed, and when he accused me of going after a taken woman, I blurted how you and I just happened."

Talk about a less than finer moment, Reid.

"Why didn't you tell me? We could've gotten ahead of this. Before my dad lost his ever-loving mind."

Releasing my arms, Kip works his jaw back and forth. "I can't keep up with you here. I can't defend myself on three fronts. I honestly thought Reid didn't notice my slip. He didn't say anything. We made tentative amends—that are now shot, by the way. I was so excited to have a weekend away with you. That little blip-in-time moment with him never crossed my mind." His fists work at his sides, like he's battling his need to touch me or hit something. "Let's hold off on your dad because, excuse me for saying it, but I couldn't care less what he thinks about us. I want to go back to Sullivan's. You said you were ambushed this morning. Want to know my morning?"

It can't possibly be worse than mine.

"I walked into the office, and after Joan informed me she'd called you and left a message on behalf of my dad, I found Sullivan's file on my desk. That is how I found out, same as you. Only my dad left his deceit waiting for me in my office."

"You honestly didn't know?" The truth was there in my gut, but hearing it confirmed eases the pressure.

Why am I not surprised? My head shakes, the tears trickling down my cheeks one-by-one. "Of course your dad would do this. It has Denton Harris written all over it. Who did he sell it to? Another farmer? Local grower? Do I know them? Maybe we could negotiate with them. Buy the land from them. It's possible I could get the bank to loan us more."

"I haven't spoken to him. I don't know why he did what he did. I swear, Chlo, Melvin was set on selling to you. I...I guess his kids convinced him the money was too good to pass up."

My chest heaves. "The offer was that much more than mine?"

"Significantly." Anguish fills Kip's face, twisting and writhing. "They didn't sell to another farmer or grower, Chlo." He releases a heavy sigh. "My dad bought it."

Every last drop of air expels from my lungs. He didn't. He couldn't.

Too far... Such a cruel, conniving, heartless man.

"Why?" My voice is barely above a whisper. "Why does he hate us so much? He's so bitter, so spiteful. He needed to outbid us just to keep us from getting the land. Just to keep us from giving our livelihood the ability to flourish. Kip—"

Like dead weight, my heart drops. Denton is never going to change. My dad is never going to change. Even if Kip and I could work through this. Even if we said to hell with it and ran off into the sunset together, I never want to be tied to a man like him, to subject myself and my children to a man like that. What an exhausting, hurtful life I'd have.

Kip sighs, a helpless, heated glint in his eyes.

"You might not care what my dad thinks, but he's my *dad*, Kip. Think about the future for a moment. Let's not pretend like we haven't both imagined it." I take his hand in mine, interlacing our fingers, holding it over my heart. "Do you honestly want such divided families? Grandparents hating each other and fighting over their grandchildren constantly, like divorced parents. Families who can't agree on simple things like who gets us when for weekly dinners or vacations, because heaven forbid someone give up their pride.

"They live next door to each other, for goodness' sake. If they liked each other, there'd never have to be split holidays or birth-days or dinners." My hand tightens around his. "Or, what if they never accept the spouse as part of the family? What kind of a future is that, Kipling?"

"My mother would never do that, she would…" he trails off.

"If your dad doesn't accept me and mine doesn't accept you, are we just supposed to cut ourselves off from them? Lose our parents? Cause our moms to be stuck in the middle, to choose sides? And Brynn? I love you, but tearing our families apart is asking too much. And I'd never ask that of you."

Kip's shoulders sag, his head dropping to his chest as he presses his free hand to his stomach. "I love you, but I would never ask you to choose me over your family. I could never." Watery blue eyes lift. "So, this was hopeless from the beginning? Circling back to high school when you said you'd never date me because I was Denton Harris's son. I guess I should have listened."

I choke on a cry. "That's not fair. This is different."

"Is it?" He lets go of my hand and grasps my face between both of his, wiping away my tears to no avail. "Nothing I do will change who I am or who our families are." Leaning in, Kip brushes my lips with his. All I taste is salt. "I'm sorry. I'm sorry about Reid, and I'm sorry your father found out because of me. And, everyone knows, I'm so, so sorry Denton Harris is the man he is. You're not the one he hates, Chlo. Whatever is between our fathers isn't our fault, but of course, we're the ones paying the heavy price."

His hands fall, and he steps back. "I better go. I…" Bowing his head, he walks away.

"Kipling." I reach out. Why? I don't know. Nothing I say will change this outcome. But watching his retreating figure severs something within me, like we share a ventricle, and now my heart struggles to beat without all its parts.

Kip doesn't look back as he turns the corner.

It's more than a ventricle. It's two, three. Maybe all four. This is heartbreak.

My hand presses to my chest, rubbing like the motion will alleviate the ache, but it throbs, squeezing out more tears than I knew my body could create. I stumble back into the metal wall of the shed and slide down to the ground.

I don't know how long I sit there with my face pressed against my knees, sobbing, when a voice calls, "Loe?"

I can't look up. I don't want anyone to see me like this. This is my heartache, my agony to bear alone. Keeping my face buried in my hands, I say nothing, unable to control my emotions, hoping I won't be found.

"Oh, hell. What happened?" He must kneel down in front of me because his voice is closer, at my level.

I don't answer. Nothing coherent would come out anyway.

"Where's your phone?"

He's asking like I know. Like I care. My main focus is my heart, laying in pieces scattered on the dirt, waiting for me to pick them up and put myself together. I don't picture that happening any time soon.

At some point he must find it because he says, "Grace, hey. It's Reid. Loe needs you."

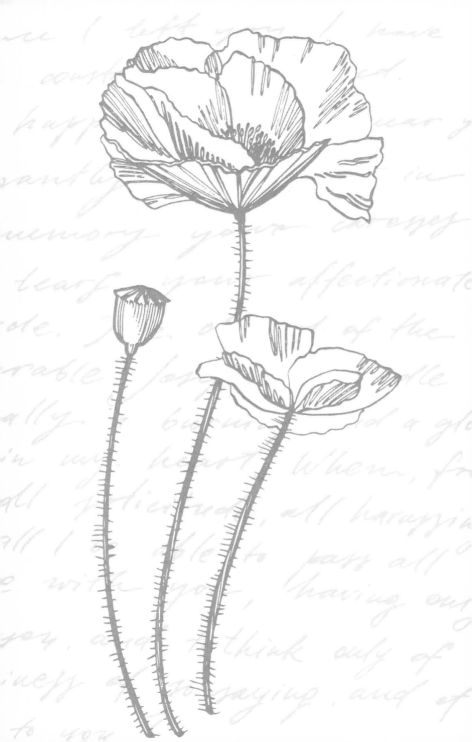

37

Kip

MISSED calls and unread texts light up my phone when I climb into my car, but I ignore them. I'm dazed. Shocked. I buckle my seatbelt and sit helplessly as Reid Pruitt hurries around the building where I left a crying Chloe. *Yeah, go comfort her, prick.* I'm one second from running after him. My fingers wrap around the door handle, my leg twitches, then the burn in my chest returns. The heavy pressure choking what little joy pummeling Reid's face into the soil would bring.

What would be the point? I gasp for a breath. *Reid is a bystander.* My vision blurs. *Denton Harris, though?* I settle my forehead on the steering wheel and inhale long and slow.

Denton is the founder of our misery.

THE CONSTRAINTS in my chest ease when I park in front of the house. The two-minute drive from Chloe's to here is a blur. I was on auto-pilot. Numb, angry, hurt. Once again, my head falls against the steering wheel. My fingers choke the leather as I yell curses into the void. How did we land here this afternoon when last night I was convincing her she had to go home to her own bed instead of sleeping in mine?

With a war raging between my head and heart, I rest my chin on the wheel and find Mom sitting in her customary spot on the front veranda. As if this day needed more piling on, her witnessing my meltdown is the cherry on top.

"Hi, sweetheart, meeting with your father?" She calls before I've fully exited the Audi. Her tender voice confirms she's clueless to the storm shredding through my happiness.

Slapping on a smile she can most certainly see through, I hurry up the stairs and steer right for the front door. "He's in his office?"

Recognition dawns, and her expression falls, but she nods without a word.

I shove my way into Dad's home office without the courtesy of a knock. "Give me one reason," I snap.

He's behind his large mahogany desk, sitting in his leather chair, with his privileged rich guy awards, first edition books, and framed photos with local celebrities as a backdrop. I've never loathed him more.

He pays me little heed as he says, "Because I can."

"You smug son of a—" I lunge, my pain and heartache manifesting into hatred for the man who caused it. Only his desk, and his wife, save him.

"Kipling!" Mom grabs me by the shirt collar and heaves me back. She breathes quickly like she chased after me the moment she realized I wasn't here for a social call. "What in the world is going on between you two?"

"Ask your husband."

Her hazel eyes double in size. I've never used that tone with her. "He is your father."

Ha. "Nah. I don't think so." Crossing my arms over my chest, I hold a wide stance and give Denton Harris my full attention. The attention he doesn't deserve. "I think I'm about done claiming you."

He gives me nothing. Not a bat of the eyes, a frown, a flinch. His only son speaks of disowning him, and he comes off like he's relaxing at his damn cigar club. While beside me, Mom hisses my name.

My teeth grind with anger. "Do I have to repeat myself? Or do you not care?"

"It was a piece of land, Kip. Don't be so damn dramatic." He rolls his chair back from his desk.

Unflappable. Growing up I wanted to be like him. Insult me? I don't care. I lose? It rolls off my back. Tough, iron hide, unbreakable. He's good at it, so good I've come to hate him for it. Being the rubber band things bounce off of is helpful in the business world. Being so thick even your family can't chisel their way into your heart? That's just putting a wall between you and them. That ruins everything. When did he become this way? I was maybe twelve or thirteen, I guess.

"Why don't we let Mom be the judge?" I challenge, and Denton's lips sink. Without using Chloe's name, I explain the issue. How my client wanted some property, and how Denton Harris came along and swooped it up from under us.

"Denton, is that true? Why would you—"

"That lot is off Highway 151." He shrugs, seemingly unconcerned. "It could be prime real estate in a few years."

"That lot was someone's dream. My client had plans, I led them to believe it was a done deal."

"A mistake on your part, son."

Mom glowers at her husband before touching my shoulder. "Sweetheart, what your father did was beyond unsavory, but it *is* business."

Clenching my jaw, I fire the most important shot in this argument. "My client was Chloe Lockwood, Mom."

"Denton Harris." The shrill wail of a banshee fills the house as Mom lays into him. "How dare you? Why would you…" She goes on and on, her face turning red and her arms flailing.

For his part, Denton Harris plays the delay tactic. Delay speaking, delay explaining, delay apologizing. In business, it's handy. When you've betrayed your son, it's reprehensible.

Needing to tell the story, I turn to Mom and explain further. I need to know I'm not crazy. Confirmation that what he did was wrong, not because he cheated, but because it just was. "Chloe went to him the same week I came back to town and tried to talk him into selling the lot next door. He said no, of course." She presses her hand to her chest. "They need more land. Chloe wants to expand their business, they're doing well enough, but *someone* owns everything around the current fields."

She exhales long and slow. "You denied her land we don't use, plus you bought property we don't need, all to spite James?"

Or was it to spite me? A show of power to put me in my place? He told me we could find the Sullivan's a better deal if we gave it time. Did my feelings for Chloe overpower finding the best deal for our client? Maybe. Still doesn't absolve him for what happened. Melvin Sullivan wanted to sell to Chloe. He was excited about the flowers Marcie enjoyed so much growing on her family's property.

"Fix it." My words are filled with venom.

The room goes silent.

Taking a measured breath, I cross my arms. "Fix what you did, or I will leave. Plain and simple."

Lazy indifference gives way to the first spark of mindfulness I've seen since entering his office. "Is this about your hatred for me?"

I scoff. "As much as you want to think everything is about you, it's not. Not even close." I've never considered that he cares much about how I feel about him. He never spoke the words, never made an effort to mend the fences broken long ago. "Sure, maybe at one point in my life I made rash decisions based solely on pissing you off. I can admit my faults, but my staying in Tulsa wasn't about us. I had to establish myself without you or the Harris name hanging over me."

"You have pride, son. Where do you think it came from?" He squares his shoulders.

"Maybe you're right. Maybe I'm successful because you pushed me, but at what cost?"

His gaze moves from mine to Mom. "Is my wanting the best for my family really so bad?"

What a trick question. "When you don't ask your family what they want, it is," I answer for her.

"Okay, what is it you want, Kip? You want me to sell land I bought for you and your sister to our enemies? You want me to roll over?"

"Your enemies, Dad. Not our." I step closer to his desk, my hands fisted at my sides. "And no, I understand your reluctance to sell our property. I know you'd both like for Brynn and me to settle here someday. Not that we don't own plenty of acreage to do both."

"Then what do you want? What will make you happy, son?"

"I want my feelings for Chloe Lockwood to mean more to you than your pride."

His peppered brows snap up. "Feelings?"

"Oh, please." I bite my tongue hard enough to sever to keep the harsh laughter threatening to spill from my lips. "Don't pretend like you didn't know. You just didn't want to accept it. Really, how could your son fall for the enemy?" The ache of Chloe's earlier words lingers in my chest. *How can we be together when our families hate each other?* This is my last play. My way of proving she is more important. That I would choose her, regardless of her choosing me or not. Stealing my courage, I reaffirm my ultimatum.

"Get over yourself, Denton. Make what you did right, or I walk."

Too furious to climb behind the wheel, I head outside. My legs itch for the path to Chloe's. To our tree, to the gate. Instead, I collapse in a chair facing her property and fail at willing my eyes from searching for her.

"Something happened between James Lockwood and your father when they were teenagers. It made them into the men they are now, Kipling. Don't let their quarrel prevent you from finding happiness." The whisper-soft comfort of my mother's voice is the sympathy that sends me over the edge.

Dropping my head into my hands, I blink back tears while staring at the ground. "I'm in love with her, Mom. I'm in love with her, and Dad did the one thing he could to ruin it."

"Your father loves you more than that. He didn't know."

"Bull." My neck pops with the speed at which my head snaps her way. She cocks her head, her eyes are bloodshot. Her tears make my nose burn. "He knew I was working on a deal for her." I sniff.

She steps closer. "A deal for Lockwood Blooms, yes. Did he know his only son was in love with his enemy's daughter? No."

"Whatever." I wave her words away and push to my feet, walking to the lower garden patio. "It doesn't matter what he did or didn't know. In hurting Chloe, he proved to her we don't have a future."

Mom's hollow laughter follows me. "Does she have a clue how stubborn you are? You'll prove her wrong."

"She made her choice. She thought I used her. That this was all a game to me. I took her to Seattle this weekend, Mom. I…

we…" I swallow down the words, but she picks up on what I'm not saying. "We solidified everything we felt, and we came home to this. She said she couldn't pick a life with me if it meant a lifetime of hate between our families."

Chloe painted a picture of us together. Of kids and holidays. Of course the picture was smeared with hate thanks to our fathers, but the fact she saw our future says something. Doesn't it? I'm not naïve enough to assume one great night of sex combined with our flirtatious history and a few dates equals forever. But it's within our grasp. Or it was.

Mom's fingers brush the back of my hand, pulling me away from the bush I'm shredding. "It's funny how Chloe thinks she has a say in controlling something as strong as love."

I grunt in agreement. I returned to Seaside hellbent on staying away from her, and look what happened. If I couldn't control the pull, how will she?

Toeing the remnants of torn leaves from the stone patio, I study Mom's easy demeanor. "Why are you taking this so well? You're not surprised?"

A smile I've known my entire life spreads across her face. "Sweetheart, you've watched Chloe since you were a child. Do you honestly think I never saw?" She taps my chest with the tip of her manicured nail. "A mother knows."

Tipping my head up, I examine the cloud-filled sky. "What happened between them?"

How, in a town where gossip is a sport, has the true reason for Denton Harris and James Lockwood's hatred never been revealed? Everyone knows the family history. The impregnated cows and pranks. The battle for land and power as our town grew. There are eighty years of stories, but nothing about those two reaching the level we're at.

"I think that's a history your father and James Lockwood need to share."

Does she mean she doesn't know, or she isn't telling? Either way, I don't press. Scrubbing my palms over my face, I sigh.

"I need to talk to her." I peer through the flowers and landscaping at the property line, wishing against all hope for Chloe to magically appear. When she doesn't, I turn on my heel. "I can't trust Dad'll lift a finger to make this right. I can't lose her without a fight."

"Kipling?" She calls after me, and I pause at the back door. "I know your father hurt you, but your sister and I love you very much. He's not the only one you punish when you run from him."

Petty.

I've classified Denton Harris as petty throughout my life. Unable to rationalize the barbs he threw toward the Lockwoods, I likened him to a man who failed at rising above a myriad of minor altercations with his neighbor.

But he isn't the only petty man in the Harris family.

Hurrying back, I seize Mom into a tight embrace, my pulse racing as my personal faults with this family become abundantly clear. "I'm sorry, Mom. In order to prove I wasn't him, I became him. I had no intention of doing that."

"We all make mistakes," she says, returning my hug. After a beat, she pushes me back, her eyes scanning my face as he touches my jaw. "He is a good man, Kipling. *You* are a good man."

No longer sure if I agree, I lean into her hand. "If he doesn't rise above his hatred and fix what he's done, I'm not sure what I'll do, but I won't let my anger with him run me off again. I promise."

Inhaling a shot of strength, I swipe my damp palms over my backside and knock. I've never stood at the Lockwood's front door. There wasn't a need. Standing here now, I second-guess everything. Maybe I should go around to the farm? On a normal day, Chloe works later than this. What was I thinking walking up to their house? Thanks to Reid, James knows his daughter spent the weekend with me. I wouldn't put it past the man to open the door with a shotgun aimed below my belt. Chewing my lip, I retreat one step, then another. Maybe they didn't hear. Maybe I can—

The pale blue painted door swings open, and James Lockwood appears, a walking cane in hand instead of a gun.

His jaw tightens, his eyes narrowing. "Come to steal my daughter away again?"

"Is she home?" I ignore his jibe.

"And what makes you think I'd tell you if she was?"

"I'm sorry, James, is it me you have a problem with or my father?"

"Well, my daughter wasn't a liar until you came along, so you tell me."

I scratch the back of my neck. "Right. For the record, I'm not the one who pushed to keep us secret."

"That's beside the point, Mr. Harris. If she hadn't been ashamed to tie herself to you, she wouldn't have felt the need to lie to us about it. Somewhere along the way, you breathed your Harris lies into her head and made her believe you were worth tearing her family apart. You see the problem?"

Well, damn, I painted Denton Harris as the bad guy here. James might give him a run for his money. I didn't come here for a fight with Chloe's father. I want the man to like me—asking for world peace would be easier—but I won't let him push aside what Chloe and I have. She might have trouble standing up to him, but I sure as hell won't.

"Yeah, I see the problem. The problem is you don't respect your daughter enough to allow her to live her own life. I bet you pictured yourself walking her straight down the aisle into Reid

Pruitt's arms, didn't you? You control her job, her home, her future…" I'm talking with my hands, pointing at the man with each verbal thrust. "If anyone tears your family apart, it'll be you. Do you think Chloe will forgive you for driving a wedge between her and the man she loves?"

He straightens, his face reddening. "The man she loves? You've been back in Seaside for what, a month? She doesn't love you, Kip Harris. You bring excitement to her life, a thrill of the forbidden. This will fade faster than you've been here."

I smile because his reasoning is beyond false. "For clarification, I've been back for two months. And if you think this is going to fade, you're sorely mistaken because what you don't seem to realize is how your daughter and I have tiptoed around this attraction since we were teens." James's face pales.

"I'm not going anywhere, Mr. Lockwood. I'm in love with Chloe, and while I'd prefer you to accept our feelings, I can honestly say your opinion makes no difference in the end. I won't walk away from her because of a little opposition. I'm made of stronger stuff than that."

Silence.

"Also, besides loving your daughter enough to carry out a secret relationship with her because she was worried about hurting you, and maybe a few childish pranks, you have no reason to dislike me other than my last name." I lift my hands, palms up as if I'm showing all my cards. "Ask yourself if my name is reason enough to destroy your daughter."

The man gives me nothing. He isn't arguing, which may be a good sign, but he's not exactly softening either. I've done all I can. Chloe knows how I feel. Dad knows how I feel. James certainly knows. Now, I wait.

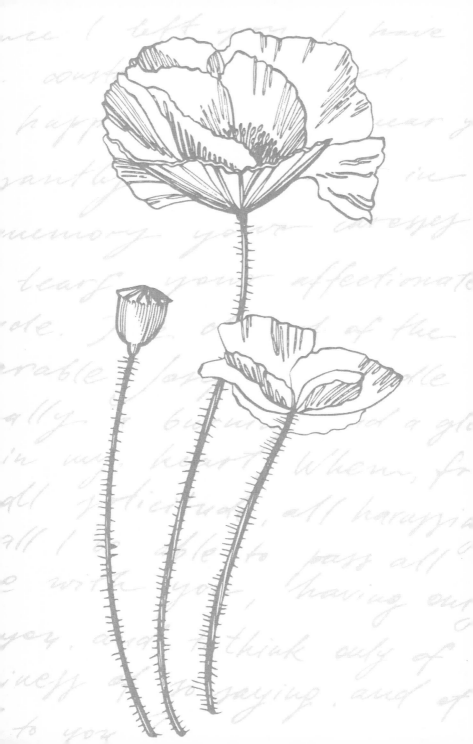

hloe

I'M SPRAWLED out on Grace's couch, my head in her lap, her fingers stroking my snarled hair. I've cried all the tears I can cry. My eyes are nothing but puffs of red and ache.

"And to think, all because of a Harris." She sighs.

"Do you want me to punch you? Because I will."

A soft chuckle surrounds me. "If that's what you need to feel better, I'd let you take a shot. But intuition tells me it's going to take something entirely different."

Yeah. Like being able to be with Kip without hate looming over us. Without families who can't get along for more than five seconds. How did we get here? How did I let it get this far?

"Eh," she says. "He wasn't so great anyway."

"Reverse psychology isn't going to work on me, Grace."

"Hey, you don't know that's not how I feel."

I laugh. "You've never given into the bad blood with Kip."

"Has anyone aside from the Lockwoods and Harrises?" Her

thighs jostle as she chuckles. "Because it was always obvious you two didn't actually hate each other. Was I going to back my best friend one hundred percent every time Kip struck? You betcha. But backing you doesn't mean I disliked him. I just enjoy a little bit of revenge." She flicks my ear, and a quiet, humorless laugh escapes me.

The destroyed look on Kip's face when he realized it was over is engraved into my brain. It's all I see. I don't think it'll ever fade.

"So, you're done?" Her fingers tug my curls, trying to comb through them. "You're going to let him go because of your dad?"

"It's not about going against my dad. I'm not some pliant child who needs to obey her father." Anymore. "It's more. It's Denton and what the future would be if our families can't work through their differences. Not to mention the future of Lockwood. If my dad and I are at odds, how could we possibly work together and keep the company running smoothly? I'm not saying I'd pick Lockwood Blooms over Kip. It's just I love the family business. The thought of losing it, too…"

"Well, he *is* retiring soon."

I sit up and face her. "Don't tell me you think I was wrong."

"Not wrong, just stuck in an impossible situation that has the potential to be made easier with the right mindset."

"What are you saying?"

"You love Kip, don't you?"

"Of course I do."

"So, let's put this into perspective. Ten years from now, when James has turned Lockwood Blooms over to you, who's by your side? Your parents? Or your husband?"

Kip. I hold her stare without responding. The answer in my eyes is obvious.

"I'm assuming husband is rolling through your mind, as it should be. So, can you picture it being anyone other than Kip Harris?"

No. I mean, of course right now I can't, but could that ever change? Or would we always be unfinished business?

"If you can't, who gets to control how you live your life? You? Or your families?"

"Do you think if I marry Kip, my dad will still give me Lockwood Blooms? Because after this morning, I'm not so sure."

"Then I guess you need to ask yourself one question. Which one can you live without?"

The answer slugs my heart like a bat to a baseball, but it doesn't mean losing the other wouldn't hurt.

Grace shifts, not pressing for an answer. "Remember when Kip came into Fig with Olivia?"

Ugh. Olivia. Thank goodness she didn't last long. But now, would he start dating her again? Will I have to watch them around town? Oh, I might throw up.

"I was trying to keep most of our conversation to myself to respect Kip's confidence in me, but I think he'd forgive me. Did you know he was considering staying in Seaside at that point?"

What?

"He said if you weren't so stubborn, it'd make his decision to stay a whole lot easier. I'm paraphrasing, of course."

My heart falters. That was right after the parade, before San Juan, before I broke up with Reid. Kip was already thinking of me as someone he could see as a permanent fixture in his life? He'd have stayed for me?

Grace leaves me with my thoughts as she heads for the kitchen. "You want to stay the night?"

I nod. "There's no way I can go home tonight. I don't want to see my dad's face."

"Then let's get in some jammies and watch a chick flick and gorge ourselves on junk food."

The breakup cure. "Now we're talking."

As I sort flowers for a large banquet order, the last person I ever expected to walk onto Lockwood soil appears in the doorway of my flower studio.

Denton Harris.

What he did to hinder Lockwood Blooms, his son's trust, and my relationship with his son comes barreling into my stomach, thrashing around. My mouth dries, hostility seizing my veins.

"Are you lost, Mr. Harris?" The pace of my lungs quicken. "Your property lies about fifteen acres west. Unless you're looking for Sullivan's land, then you're about ten miles off." I lower my eyes back to the flowers on the workbench, ignoring him as I spread out the foxglove.

"I suppose that's deserved."

I should feel guilty, but it's difficult to find it within me. And this is how the feud perpetuates. These vile feelings we can't seem to let go feed off of us. Soon, they'll eat us alive.

When he doesn't say more, I ask, "May I help you with something?"

"I was hoping I could help *you* with something."

"It's unlikely, but I'm all ears." I pause my sorting and meet his stare, crossing my arms over my chest, a feeble excuse for a shield against the man who has repeatedly wounded my family and me.

The creases at the corners of his blue eyes deepen as he steps into the studio in his pressed suit and tie, a white envelope in his grasp.

I drop my gaze to his outstretched hand like it's a serpent waiting to strike.

"Don't let your moxie die now. Take it."

Reaching across the wide table, I accept the envelope and untuck the flap. When I slip out the folded piece of paper, my forehead rumples as I read the typed letter.

"I'm selling Lockwood Bloo— you, the Sullivan property. It's all there in the agreement. Same price as the offer you originally made. No strings attached."

I blink, my hands dropping to the slab of wood, the letter clutched in my fingers. "You realize I'm a part of Lockwood Blooms, don't you?"

"And soon Lockwood Blooms will belong to you, and you alone."

"But why? Why would you do this for me?"

He slips his hands into his pockets, so like his son. "It should have been yours. The day I found out you were interested in buying, Kip went on and on about the great job you're doing managing Lockwood Blooms in your father's stead and how you needed more land to fulfill your potential. I had no right weaseling into the process."

Kip said that? Even then?

"I don't understand. Kip said you paid significantly more for the land. You'd be losing money selling it to me at this price."

"I'd be losing my son if I didn't."

I still. "What?"

"Have you not spoken with him?"

My head shakes on its own accord, words failing me. Not yet. I was going to go see him after work, with or without my dad's approval.

"It seems my son is in love with you, Miss Lockwood." Even though this isn't new information, his words bring chaos to my body, a riot in my lungs, and a hum in my veins. "When he found out about the sale, he tore into me."

Never has there been a man I want to cry in front of less, but alas, it's happening. A sheen of tears coats my eyes, blurring Denton, but I don't blink. They will not make an appearance on my cheeks.

"Kip didn't mince words," he says. "He gave me two options, but there was really only one."

"And what were his options?" My voice cracks.

"He demanded I make things right, ergo sell you the land. Or he would walk."

"Walk? As in...?"

"Leave Seaside Pointe."

No, he can't. Forget the land. Forget our families. I can't live without Kipling Harris. He doesn't belong in Tulsa. He belongs with me. However complicated our future might be.

"Believe it or not, I care very deeply about Kip's happiness. When he made it clear you were what he wanted, I knew I had to set aside the past." Denton clears his throat, stretching his neck to the side. "I love my son, Chloe."

I lose the battle. Tears slide down my cheeks, and I hastily wipe them away. "Of course, you do. I do, too."

He glances around. "I'm not sure a day has gone by in the twenty-two years since Mary and I moved into my family home that she hasn't looked out our windows and admired your fields."

Oh. "Here." I gather up some foxglove and cosmos, snipping and arranging them before snagging one of the metal vases off the shelving behind me. Moving around the table, I hold out the bouquet to Denton. "Give these to her."

With a crooked smile I'd recognize anywhere, he says, "Not a bad idea. I'm in the doghouse with her right now, too." We chuckle a little, and it's weird. I don't think I've ever heard Denton laugh. "Kip falling in love with you doesn't surprise me one bit. You have some fire in you, but you also have a kind heart."

I have the urge to hug him, but I hold back. Better to move one step at a time. "Thank you, Mr. Harris. Even if it took a little nudge from Kip." I smile good-naturedly. "Thank you."

He nods, turning to walk away, and stops. "Miss Lockwood?" I wait.

"I'm willing to work with you on financing. Whatever we need to do to make the purchase smooth for you. I'm sure things have been difficult lately with James being sick." He blinks away the bitterness in his eyes at the mention of my dad. "You're not your father, and I won't treat you like you are again."

Thank you feels like a weird thing to say in response while he's insulting my dad in the process, so I only nod, and he turns.

Seconds after Denton leaves the studio, Grace walks in with round eyes and her jaw dropped. "I was coming to check up on you, but I might need medical attention after my mini heart attack. Was that who I think it was?" Her thumb points out the door.

I grab her hands, the urge to twirl with laughter overwhelming. "You won't believe what happened."

39

Kip

I'VE SPENT two nights drinking and two days wallowing, so I'm not looking my best when there's a knock at my door late Wednesday afternoon. And obviously, I don't care since I roll off the couch shirtless and in joggers and drag my feet across the condo.

I swing open the door expecting Brynn, though why she doesn't use her key, I have no idea. Instead, I find Chloe.

My fingers grip the door frame for dear life. "Hey." My voice is so unused, I have to clear my throat and repeat the word as my hungry eyes drink her in. She's so damn beautiful, so damn mine. Except, maybe she's not.

"Hi." Her soft brown eyes travel the length of my body. A desire she can't hide darkening them. "Can I come in?"

Words clog my throat, so I step back silently, allowing her inside.

"Empty glasses by the sink and a pizza box on the counter.

Someone's having a rough day." Her lips part, a smile fighting to form, but her joke falls flat on this man's ears, and she sobers.

"The past forty-eight hours haven't been my favorite." Crossing my arms, I massage my shoulder for no other reason than I need something to do.

She rubs her arms and looks to the living room, no doubt noticing the jacket thrown over the couch and empty cans on the coffee table. *Yes, Chloe, I've fallen apart.*

"I had an interesting conversation with your dad today."

I tense, bracing for the worst. "Should I apologize now, or…"

With thin lips, she shakes her head. "Can we sit down?" She takes the lead without my permission, settling on the couch.

Chloe stares up at me, but I can't force my legs into action. I'm bolted to this spot by the door, my head refusing to catch up to her presence. Her lack of faith in me was a bigger deal than I cared to admit. I'm struggling to accept it. When I don't join her after a minute, she begins anyway.

"Okay." She takes a deep breath. "First, I want to say I'm sorry. The other day—from my dad finding out about us and losing Sullivan's—it was all a lot to process within a few hours, and I might not have handled it so well."

Digging my fingers into my stiff neck, I move closer. "Chlo, what Denton did…I can't fault you for being upset."

"Maybe not, but I'm still sorry for hurting you. I know you're not a liar, and you'd never do anything to intentionally hurt me. I shouldn't have let my feelings for Denton come between us." She fidgets with her hands in her lap, staring at them. "I say these things and want you to know I felt them before I talked with your dad, and I'm sorry it took me so long to get here."

I lower to the couch, and she faces me.

"I'm not going to lie, having you think those things was inde-scribably more painful than anything my dad did." My hands settle over hers. "Yet, I'm not surprised. We have a history of leaping without thinking things through, don't we?"

Flipping her wrist, she squeezes my fingers. "This all happened so fast. There wasn't much time to think, but I *have* been contemplating a lot these last couple of days. No matter what, this family feud shouldn't have a say in what happens between you and me."

Unable to resist the impulse, I cup the back of her head and touch my forehead to hers. "I can't tell you how badly I needed to hear that, Sunshine. I am so in love with you."

Closing the gap, her lips touch mine. One simple, soft kiss. "I love you, too."

"We don't have to figure everything out right away, you know? If this is too fast. If it's too much, I can set aside my lists and plans."

"That's some bold ambition." She laughs, and I swallow the sound with another kiss until she touches my cheek and leans back. "I don't care what the future looks like. I want to be with you."

"Are we crazy?"

"Totally insane."

"Are you really surprised we jumped into the deep end without a life jacket? We never do anything halfway, do we? All the bets, pranks, jibes. We could have stopped them at any time."

"Yet, clearly neither of us hated our little feud as much as we pretended."

Running my hand up and down her leg, I say, "So, I'm curious because I laid into him pretty hard. What did my dad say to you?"

"He told me you gave him a choice. That he either makes things right or you'd leave."

I swallow. "I meant it. I chose you. I'm not saying I don't share your fears about what a future between us would look like. Having a big family and raising them with nothing but love is important to me. If we get there"—she frowns—"*when* we get there, I'm banking on our dads loving us more than they hate each other."

"And if they don't?"

"Shhh." I touch my index finger to her lips. "Obviously, I'm an optimist. You know how much I love to win."

Kissing my finger, she pulls it away. "Well, Denton's selling us Sullivan's land, and he offered to help with financing. I'd call that a win."

My heart races. "He did? Chlo, yes, it's such a win. I'm so happy for you. It killed me to think your dreams for the farm were ruined out of spite."

"They weren't ruined, just stalled." She settles her hand on my thigh. "I would've found us another way. It just might've taken a bit longer."

"And I would have helped you however I could, but that's not the point. His screwing me over. His hurting you…" My teeth grind as frustration returns.

"It doesn't matter anymore. He waved the white flag, and he's selling us the land." I rein in my anger. "You should know he did it for you." She touches my jaw.

The kid inside me, who never stopped questioning his worth, dares to hope.

"He doesn't care about Lockwood Blooms, Kipling. He said he would not lose you over his pride."

If only I could believe him. Maybe there's a chance for true reconciliation.

"If Denton Harris can do it, James Lockwood better get his crap together." Her cheeks brighten. "*And* I'll tell my dad if he ever wants to see his grandchildren, he'll make nice with you and your family." She shrugs like it's no big deal, but the idea of a family and forever *is* big.

Chuckling, she smooths my mussed hair from my forehead. "I'm not going to let his bitterness control this. It's our life."

"And you know what, after we build the big house, you can

plant flowers all over the land you've always wanted since it'll be yours, too. All it'll cost is your marrying me."

"Sounds like a pretty steep price, but the flowers would be worth it."

"Don't get your hopes up, flower girl. I haven't asked yet."

Rolling her eyes, her hand captures my nape and draws me in for a kiss. "You will," she whispers into my mouth as her fingers skate over my ribs.

Yeah, I will.

"You know what the best part of fighting is, don't you?" I stand and extend my hand. A sexy grin tugs at her lips as she coyly glances up through her lashes. "Let's go make up, Sunshine."

Chloe follows behind me, peeling off her top before we've made it to my bedroom. "Just catching up with you." She tosses the cream shirt at my head.

"I'm not complaining, babe." I take her in fully in the light of day, admiring her curves and the freckles peppering her skin. Needing to taste and touch every inch, I crook my finger and sit on the edge of my bed.

She walks into my arms easily, standing between my thighs and running skilled fingers through my hair. I rest my face against her stomach. This is all I need. The warmth of her skin. The love of this woman.

I rub my cheek back and forth, loving the way her muscles flex and release beneath my touch. Stroking her spine, I knead the tension from her back and settle a kiss over her belly button.

Taking my time, I nose my way around her torso. She has a silvery scar on her side and a cluster of freckles crowning the top of her ribcage. My tongue traces them both, somehow relieved at finding minor imperfections on my otherwise perfect love, and I laugh against her skin when she yanks at my hair. Burying my face in her chest, I lavish her with the time and attention we didn't use Saturday night. We deserve slow and thorough. Wild and free. I want to give her everything I have; this beautiful woman whose natural floral perfume and delicate body drives me to distraction.

It isn't long before my patience wanes, the want in my veins for her physically painful. My hands dip around the back of her jeans, rounding over her backside and drawing her closer.

My name is breathless on her lips. Beseeching. Her craving as consuming as mine. Her nails tickle over my spine and shoulders, digging deeper with every passing moment. She presses her hips forward, searching for friction.

Smiling, I fall back, and she climbs onto the bed, straddling me. "Is this what you wanted?" I tease, running my palms over her hips.

"I want you." Her lust-filled voice sends all my blood south.

Breathing in shallow pants, I throw my arm over my eyes and pray for restraint as the little minx inches her mouth down my neck, over my pecs. Her fingers tease the waistband of my joggers, then tug, sliding them over my hips. Her hands and mouth taunt me.

"Who would have guessed this would be our fate," she says, nipping my collarbone.

Bucking at the pleasure-pain her mouth elicits, I seize her by the arms and flip, stealing her yelp with a kiss. "I need you now."

Together, we rid her of the last of her clothing. Struggling when her jeans strangle her foot. "This shouldn't be so difficult," I complain, and her musical giggle fills the bedroom.

Tossing her pants to the floor, I collapse in her arms—skin to skin. The melding of our bodies mirrors the meeting of our lips: exploring, soft, urgent, dipping and retreating the way lovers do.

She's everything. She's sass, and fire, and warmth.

I rip away from her mouth, my breathing harsh. "I love you."

Her smile is magnetic. "I love you, too."

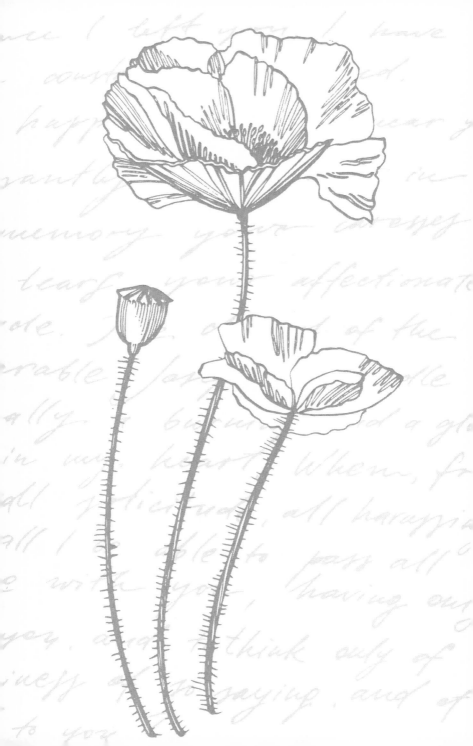

hloe

I'M BONE-TIRED, and it's not even six o'clock.

After getting little to no sleep last night staying over at Kip's, followed by nonstop weeding and harvesting today, I could go to bed now and sleep until morning.

I haven't entered my parents' house since leaving Monday morning after arguing with my dad. I've been at the farm every day, and he hasn't sought me out, so I have no intention of seeking him out. Especially since I've made my choice, it would only cause more contention.

When I open the back door of their house into the kitchen and head for the stairs for a shower, my mom is at the counter cutting lettuce. Oregano and garlic fill the air. She's making her famous spaghetti for dinner.

"Hey, Mom," I say, passing through.

She stops chopping. "Wait a second. Talk to me for a minute. I haven't seen you since you left for Seattle. I've missed you."

"Yeah, I missed you, too." How much does she know? I've been ignoring her calls, not ready to rehash things.

"Your father said you two had a fight when you got home. What happened?"

I shrug and give her the easiest, quickest answer. "I fell in love with Kipling Harris."

Her eyes soften like she knew.

"I'm sorry I lied to you about it."

She waves me off. "I understand why you did, but maybe we should talk about it."

"What more do you want? I chose Kip, and Dad isn't going to accept us, so. What's done is done."

Her arms open, asking for a hug. When I don't move right away, she waves me forward. "Don't leave me hanging."

A little snort slips out, and I step into her arms, resting my chin on her shoulder.

"You think I'd let something like falling in love with a Harris destroy my family? Think again, darling girl."

"I'd like to hear you tell Dad."

She withdraws, pursing her lips. "While I might let your father be when it comes to Denton, I have no ill feelings toward the Harrises. In fact, I like Mary. I'll even let you in on a little secret."

My head cants to the right.

"Sometimes we meet at the fence, and I give her bouquets of our blooms. The peonies are her favorite." Mom winks, and I chuckle.

"You're joking."

She shakes her head and opens her mouth like she wants to say more, but the front door opens and closes. We share a look. Dad.

"I really don't want to talk to him right now," I whisper.

"Then go on upstairs. I'll handle him." She kisses my cheek. "It'll all work out, Chloe Mae."

I rush as quietly as possible, but before I reach the stairs, Dad's voice stops me. "Loe."

With a deep breath, I say over my shoulder, "Dad, I don't want to argue. It's been a long day."

"Well, I think we have things to talk about, so come into the living room with me."

I fully face him, squaring my shoulders. "Are you going to take Lockwood Blooms away from me?"

His jaw tightens. "Loe, let's talk in the living room."

Not an answer, Dad.

"It's going to be a pointless conversation if it's going to be a repeat of Monday. I'm not ending things with Kip, and it saddens me how you can't see past your pride to give him a chance, but I'm not going to let you dictate who I love, who I will marry someday. And I will, by the way, so having a Harris as a son-in-law is something you should start getting used to."

"Loe," he barks. "Come sit down this instant."

Dad rarely yells. The only times I think he ever raises his voice is when a Harris is involved, but I'm not going to let his outburst deter me.

I shake my head and move toward the stairs. "I'm a grown woman. You don't get to yell at me like I'm a teenager breaking curfew. I'm only here because I'm grabbing a few things. I'll be staying at Grace's for awhile. She invited me to move in with her, and I'm seriously considering it." Even more so after this conversation.

"Kip came looking for you the other night."

My foot pauses on the first step, and I pivot.

"You were with Grace, so he got me instead."

Kip came back? Why didn't he tell me?

Oh no. What did Dad say to him? I'll never forgive him if he tore into Kip. Kip doesn't deserve any of his anger.

"Please tell me you didn't say anything I'm going to hate you for."

His brown eyes grow sterner. "That Harris is one of the most disrespectful boys I've ever met, and I will not allow him near any daughter of mine."

I shake my head. I can only imagine what Kip said after the day we'd had. Monday was brutal. "He's not a boy, and he's not disrespectful. If Kip said anything that bothers you, my guess is he was standing up for himself or me, as he should have. He's done nothing wrong."

"You're not going to date him."

I scoff, shaking my head. Who is this man, and what has he done with my kind, gentle father? Have I never given him a reason to lose his temper with me before? So eager to please him, hating to see disappointment in his eyes.

"You don't get a say, Dad. I'm an adult, and I don't have to let my father make decisions for me anymore. I'm not letting Kip go, and that's something you'll have to live with."

"If you chose him over this family, Lockwood Blooms is no longer yours."

Even though the possibility ran through my mind over and over, hearing the words come out of his mouth shove a knife through my heart and twist.

Gathering courage, I steel my spine, though tears fill my eyes. "Fine. I don't need it. You want to know why? I got Sullivan's land without your help, and guess who Denton Harris is turning the property over to?" Color recedes from his face. "Me. Not you, not Lockwood Blooms. Me. It was meant to be for our family, for Lockwood Blooms, but if you're going to kick me out…"

"You won't be able to get the bank to give you the kind of loan you need, not without the backing of Lockwood."

Every cruel word slung chips my heart. Who is this man? "Denton is willing to work with me on financing it. I think I'll be all right." It's as if Denton knew Dad would react this way. By offering me financing and putting my name on the agreement, he secured my future.

He shakes his head with a grunt. "Fine. Go and fail out on your own, but the Lockwood Blooms legacy stays and ends here. It no longer includes you, so don't even think about using the name."

"James!"

I whirl around, and through my tears, see Mom in the walkway between the kitchen and the entryway.

"Stay out of this, Robyn."

"I will not." With one step forward, she says, "She is your *daughter*, your only child. She's dedicated years to this family business and kept us afloat while you've been incapacitated. Don't you *dare* turn your back on her."

"It's my business, and I'll do with it what I damn well please!"

I remain silent, teeth clenched, my cheeks streaked in wetness.

Mom lifts her head, poised with a lethal glare. "If you take your family legacy away from our only daughter, you can kiss this marriage goodbye."

His head whips to Mom. "Robyn."

"I mean it. I've stood by you through your prejudice against the Harrises for thirty-eight years, but this charade has gone on long enough. If you're so consumed by this *ludicrous* feud that you can't discern what's most important, that your family should always come first, you're not the man I married. You're not the man I love. I will stand by our daughter, and I *will* leave your sorry behind in the dust."

Back and forth, his glare slides between his wife and daughter. A man I once thought hung the stars and moon. I'd have done anything to defend him and make him proud. And I have, time and time again, put this family and business before my happiness without even realizing it. Yet here he stands, ready to toss me aside all because I love Denton Harris's son.

"Fine," Dad snaps. "Make the biggest mistake of your life by choosing a Harris. Keep the farm for all I care, but you're no daughter of mine."

Drying my cheeks, one swipe at a time, I say, "The only mistake I ever made was admiring and respecting you."

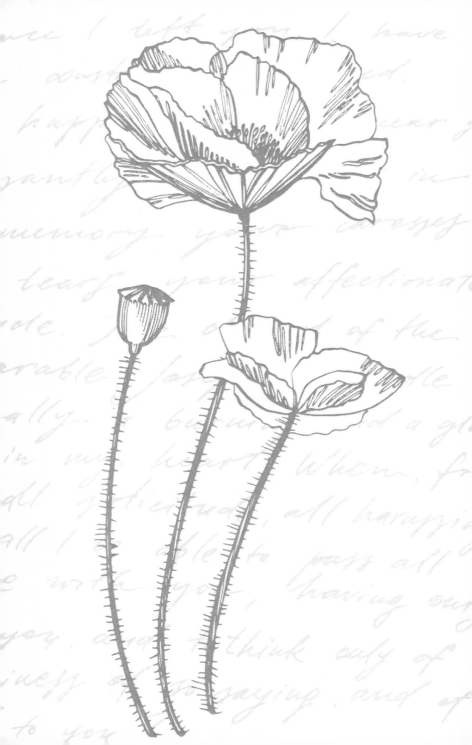

A NIGHT SPENT MAKING up with Chloe and confirming we would last through this mess made seeing Dad for the first time since Monday's argument less difficult. We're a long way from okay, he and I, but prioritizing my wants ahead of his feud with James changes things.

A phone conversation with Melvin Sullivan also helps. The idea of his lying about selling to Chloe left me hollow. Truth is, that wasn't the case at all. The poor, old man was confused. His son duped him. Led Melvin to believe the sale to Dad was for Lockwood Blooms in some roundabout way. I'm unsure how Joseph Sullivan managed his deceit, but at my urging, Melvin promised he'd look into his son's duplicity. Joseph has access to Melvin's bank accounts. What else could he have done not on the up and up?

I text Chloe when I arrive home from the office, telling her to get her butt to my place as soon as she's done with work. Our time last night wasn't nearly long enough. Will there ever be enough? Plus, with everything else, I didn't tell her the zoning for the Riverfront was approved. When Roger called yesterday, I was in the middle of my pity session for one. It was hard to find joy in what's to come with the one future I truly need on hold. Now we can celebrate together.

I'm finishing chopping vegetables when the door swings open, and Chloe's hollering my name before she sees I'm right here. Her teeth dig into her bottom lip as her puffy eyes well with tears. "I think my dad just disowned me."

"Wait. What?" Frozen, my mind replays and refuses her words.

Her face crumbles, and the knife clatters to the counter as Chloe rushes into the kitchen and throws herself at me. "Oh, Chlo. Babe, I'm sorry." I murmur, smoothing her hair back and tightening my embrace. "What in the world happened?"

"I told him I chose you. He threatened to take away the farm." Rubbing her cheek against my chest, she sniffles.

"Because of me." It's not a question because we both know the answer.

"Then my mom stepped in, defending me. It got so ugly. He's not kicking me out of Lockwood Blooms, but he said I'm no longer his daughter."

Taking her by the shoulders, I dip my head to her eye level. "Chlo, I love you, but I don't want to be the man who destroys your relationship with your father."

"You're not." Her hand rests on my waist. "He is. If he cared enough about me, he wouldn't let his hatred for your dad ruin our family."

"What can I do? I'll talk to him. I'll—"

She shakes her head, sniffling. "It won't do any good. It probably would only make it worse at this point. I've never seen him like this before."

My guilt compounds.

"Come here." Cradling her backside, I deposit her on the counter so we're eye-to-eye. "I guess we've passed the window of opportunity for me to tell you I spoke to him, huh?" Did he mention our conversation? Was it his tipping point?

Tilting her head, she runs the back of her sleeve under her nose. "Yeah, he beat you to it."

"I wanted him to know I wouldn't give you up without a fight. I never imagined he'd choose hatred."

One of her shoulders lifts. "Me, neither. I hoped it would blow over. That he might sling a few stones every now and then. But this? I don't know who my dad is anymore."

"I wish I understood our fathers. We'll make it better, I promise." I catch her fresh tear with my thumb and lock my arms around her once again.

We remain one, her face buried in my chest, her arms around my waist for a long while. My fingers brush through her waves, and my heart aches. This isn't how things were supposed to go. Eventually, her ragged breaths even out and her tears slow.

Tilting her head back, I kiss the tip of her red nose. "You know, I have a half-empty bed. You're always welcome here."

"While the idea is tempting." She kisses the edge of my mouth and reels me closer with her legs. "I'm moving in with Grace."

"Her bed is better than mine?" I cross my arms with an Oscar-worthy pout meant to coax her beautiful smile forward.

She flicks my stuck-out button lip. "No, she just has more than one. I much prefer yours."

Yeah, she does. "Her place sounds boring, but I'm glad you made the decision," I say magnanimously since I don't plan on her leaving my place often anyway.

"I should've moved out a long time ago. It'll be a lot less convenient, but I'm going to turn operations on my parents' land over to Reid for a while. I can't be there. And since your dad turned over Sullivan's land—which Grace is closer to—it works out."

Kneading her thighs, I tsk at her dilemma. "You're like a franchise now, Miss Lockwood."

Locking her hands around my neck, she aims for a smile, but it falls short.

"You're going to be okay, you know that, right? Whatever you need, I'm here."

Her tongue runs over her lips with a quiet sigh. "You're kind of stuck with me now, so you better not change your mind."

"Not a chance, gorgeous."

I'm steering for her lips when her gaze settles beyond me. "What's that?"

I glance at the coffee table where a flat, lavender-wrapped package with a white satin bow awaits. I can tell her about the Riverfront later. Tweaking her thighs, I step out of her legs. "Go open it and see."

Slipping off the counter, she moves to the couch, a little of her usual spark returning to her brown eyes. I make a mental note to never quit showering her with unexpected presents. As she removes the bow, I sit across from her on the coffee table, my legs locking one of hers in place. I cup my hands around her bent knee, and her eyes narrow.

"What? I want an unimpeded view."

She's careful with the wrapping paper, sliding her finger beneath each fold and popping the tape rather than ripping it open. It's exasperating, but I caress her knee and feign patience. When at last she lifts the box's lid and parts the tissue paper, her reaction is worth the wait.

She exhales a breathy, "Oh."

"I printed and framed them Tuesday. I had it in my head that I'd leave the box on your doorstep if you didn't change your mind about us by this weekend. Obviously, I didn't have time to give them to you last night."

"We had more important things to focus on." Her chin trembles. "This is a beautiful shot."

She picks up the framed picture, her fingers touching the glass as she studies the photo. It's one I snuck at the lavender fields while she was cutting her own bouquet. The sun was perfectly placed, and she was surrounded by a sea of green and purple. I couldn't help but think how I'd love for her to see herself the way I do—as the same sunshine flower girl who enamored me as a kid racing my bike through the backyard.

"That was a good day." She sets the frame aside and removes the second one. Her hand claps her chest, grasping her shirt.

Inching closer, my hands ride up Chloe's thigh as I lean in for a better view. "I had no idea Brynn took it until Monday night. After everything fell apart, she came over and watched me drink myself into oblivion. Then she showed me the photo on her phone."

"Look at us. Before Seattle, Grace and I were talking about you and me taking a picture together, and I was sad thinking about how we don't have any because we've been keeping things quiet." Her voice is so achingly tender, I struggle to contain my emotions.

In the photograph, we face one another, our bodies inches apart, our eyes locked. The entire world could disappear, and the two people inside this photo would never notice.

"Brynn wanted me to tell you this was the moment she knew we would be forever."

"We were arguing." She laughs and lifts her eyes to me.

"No. We were falling in love."

Removing the frame from her fingers, I set the box aside. "We almost lost this, Chlo." I take her hands in mine and kiss her fingertips. "I'm not losing us," I say with conviction.

"Good thing we know how to put up a decent fight for what we love."

Maintaining eye contact, my hands slip beneath her top,

bunching it in my palms as I pull the fabric up her body. Without a word, her arms lift, and her shirt disappears. Gripping her hips, I slide her to the edge of the couch and lift her onto my lap.

"What about dinner?" Her fingers untuck my shirt from my slacks.

Unhooking the clasp at her back, I meet her lusty gaze. "I'd rather have dessert."

CHLOE

I toss Alice a wave, carrying the empty buckets from earlier this week out of Flower Patch. "I'll see you Monday."

Since Reid is drowning in new responsibility, I offered to help with deliveries this week, and Alice couldn't make it through the weekend without another order.

When the glass door shuts behind me, and I head for Betty, I stop, my heart fluttering.

In the gray slacks and a freshly-ironed white button-up I watched him dress in only hours ago, Kip leans against the bed of my truck, twirling an Iceland poppy. The freckles across his face are more pronounced under the warm June sun. Not now, but when I can take my time, I want to kiss and memorize every one.

"There should be a billboard right outside town limits." He straightens from where he leans and lifts his hands like he's reading a sign. "If you want to find the prettiest girl around, look for the beautiful flowers."

A shockwave of goosebumps erupts across my body as one side of my mouth curves up. Even in my trusty overalls and work boots, he makes me feel beautiful. Will his compliment ever grow old? I think not.

"Kipling."

"My sweet flower girl." He continues twirling the poppy between his thumb and forefinger before offering it to me. "You still outshine all the other Lockwood blooms."

Shaking my head, I pinch my lips to hold back a chuckle at this reenactment we're playing. "And you still lay on the excessive charm."

"For you, Miss Lockwood? I'll never stop." Kip gives a crooked grin.

Accepting the pale orange flower from his outstretched hand, I yelp when his fingers close around my wrist and he pulls me into his chest.

"What are you doing?" My words are out of breath.

"What I wanted to do the first day I saw you here." His lips brush against my ear. "And what I plan on doing for the rest of our lives."

Kip dips me low, and I squeal, his lips inches from mine. "I'm kissing you in public."

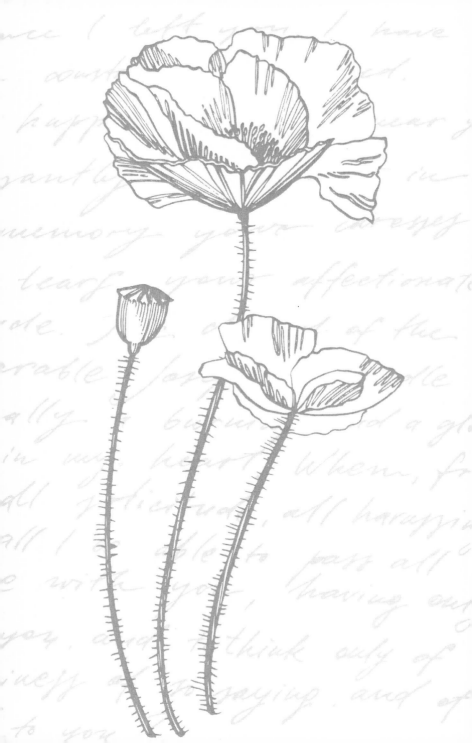

ayden

San Juan Island. One month prior...

"ABOUT THAT OFFER to look for the snake," Brynn says, stealing my attention from Bodhi and Chloe's conversation.

Resting my elbow on the armrest of my chair, I lean into her, unable to keep the building smirk from my face. "You don't want a new friend slithering into your bed tonight?"

I hadn't meant for the innuendo, but once it's out of my mouth, I can't say I want to take it back.

Brynn sweeps her heavy bangs from her eyes. "Do you think there's room for Chloe, me, and an extra body?" Her mouth quirks. "I suppose if it's small..."

A low chuckle spills from my mouth. Kip might cut off my left nut if he knew we were having this conversation a foot away from him. Knocking my head in the direction of our canvas cabins, I say, "C'mon. Let's go catch us a snake."

As we step away from the bonfire, I toss a comment to Chloe about asking for Bodhi's full name. Brynn slips her hand in mine, leading me toward their tent. Holding hands with my best friend's sister isn't something I normally do, but I let it happen, her small fingers so delicate in my large hand.

Before heading inside, we round the girls' canvas tent once, flashlight in hand, eyes peeled in the dark. "Where did you see it last?"

"It was on this side, right there. I watched it slither under like the little devil it is."

I get down on my hands and knees and shine the light under the raised cabin: dirt and dried leaves.

"Coast is clear."

After finishing the perimeter search, with no sign of devil snakes, we head up the steps. Inside, I kneel down, searching beneath the futon and bed, flipping up the covers to be thorough. When I come up empty, I slip around the corner into the small bathroom and snap back the curtain of the circular shower: nothing but a drain in a fiberglass floor.

"I don't know what to tell you, Brynn, but it appears your friend left."

"Are you sure?" She circles in place, rubbing at her arms, before sitting on the edge of the bed.

"I think your alleged snake sighting was nothing but an excuse to get me alone." I tuck my hands into my jacket pockets, lifting a teasing grin.

Her blueish-green gaze clings to mine as she toes her tennis shoes off. "There was definitely a snake earlier." Brynn scoots backward up the mattress, settling against the pillows stacked at the headboard. "But if there weren't, would you take issue with my lying?"

My head cocks to the side. Am I reading her right? Is she

coming onto me? We've been flirtatious all weekend, but her boldness surprises me. In a good way, piquing my curiosity. Though maybe it's the alcohol talking. We've had quite a few.

Lowering to the end of the bed at her feet, I say, "Not in the slightest." My tongue swipes along my smirk as I appreciate the length of her. From her skin-tight leggings over her shapely legs to the baggy sweatshirt hiding the rest of her figure. "Why are you so afraid of snakes?"

"Are you looking for something more than the obvious slithering reptile with fangs answer?"

"Is there another kind of snake you're familiar with?" Now that I ask, a few things Kip said in passing come to mind about a douchebag fiancé.

Tugging the cuff of her sweatshirt over her hand, she purses her lips. "As my brother's best friend, I imagine you know the answer."

I give a non-committal nod. Not a lot, but enough to know she was burned and hasn't gotten back out there since. "Only a thing or two." But since I do have Brynn alone, her douchebag fiancé is the last topic I want to discuss. "So, we're speaking in literals. Just can't handle the beady eyes, huh?"

"They're sneaky, and I don't like being startled." Her shoulders shrug. "I suppose that answer goes both literally and metaphorically, huh? They're creepy. I can't tell you how many garter snakes I came upon in our yard as a child."

I twist my body to face her, lifting my bent knee to rest on the mattress. "I had a corn snake growing up. My mom hated it. She wouldn't get anywhere near it. Lucky for me, that meant she stayed out of my bedroom. So, I guess you would've steered clear of my bedroom, too."

Her top teeth capture her bottom lip. "Is that a literal question we should be discussing?" She gazes toward the zippered doorway to the cabin.

My eyes zero in on her full lips. It's a risky topic to breach, but Brynn is gorgeous, and I'm buzzed enough not to care about how I *should* answer the question.

I kick off my boots as I lean back on my hands and slide up the bed beside her. Resting my head against my bent arm on the headboard, my eyes drift around her face, from her expressive eyes to her parted lips and back. "We could make it one."

"I want to." Her body rocks closer toward mine. Inches. "I want to tell you how very little would steer me away from your bedroom if given a chance. I want to tell you how very sexy I find you. How much I appreciate the way you do…everything." Her chin drops, and my will to keep my distance falters.

I hook my finger under her chin, lifting her eyes. "Don't lose your nerve now. What more did you want to say?"

"You're speaking of bravery, but I'm not brave. I'm terrified."

"Terrified of what?" I inch closer to her.

Brynn wets her lips. "I don't want to be hurt again, Hayden, but I don't want to feel like this anymore. I can't…there are things." Shaking her head against the pillow, she frowns. "I miss having a connection with someone. Would you think it crazy if I say I feel one with you?"

With a subtle shake of my head, I say, "There's something here, but you don't have to be terrified. There's no pressure, Brynn. I'm not the kind of guy who's going to ask for more than you're willing to give."

She leans forward and swipes her lips against mine, withdrawing enough to meet my eyes. "This means nothing, right? Just a moment of attraction. A weakne—"

Diving my hand into her chin-length hair, I cup the back of her head and smother her words. Brynn's whimper fills my mouth as I thrust my tongue between her lips. She matches my kiss, stroke for stroke, nibble for a nibble. The arousing glide of our tangled tongues has me groaning, and I allow my hands to roam along her hip beneath the hem of her thick sweatshirt. I need to feel more of her, all of her. My fingers grip her slender waist, clutching her thin T-shirt. When her fingers coast up my nape, along the trimmed hair at the back of my head, and sink into the longer strands on top, she fists the roots to the point of pleasurable pain. A low, deep grunt leaves me.

I roll Brynn onto her back, covering the whole of her body, pressing her into the mattress. Nothing exists outside of this canvas tent. My hand slides higher along her side over her shirt, my thumb stroking the supple flesh above her ribcage. With a quiet hitch in her breathing, she sucks my bottom lip between her teeth. Keeping some of my weight propped on my forearm beside her hand, my thumb caresses her soft jaw.

I'm not sure if it's the alcohol-induced haze, but this kiss is like none I've ever had before. The longer we go, the more I want, the more I want to devour Brynn. I never want to stop.

She writhes beneath me, and I rock my hips into her, sucking her tongue into my mouth. Needing less between us, I raise her bulky sweatshirt higher and higher. About to ask her to lift her arms, the rip of the zipper being undone breaks us apart. I slid off her as she rights her sweatshirt and sits up.

"Everyone decent?" Bodhi ducks into the cabin, a hand clasped over his eyes. "Please tell me you're decent." He mutters loud enough for our ears.

Some wingman. I run my hand down my mouth with a miffed exhale. "If I say we're indecent, are you leaving?"

"Are you saying I'm not invited to join in?" The zipper sounds again, testifying to his not leaving. He peeks through his fingers like a child. A heavy sigh releasing from his chest. "Phew, what a relief. I walked around before coming in for as long as possible. Do you know how stressed I was? Torn between two best friends. Protecting one's sister's virtue or ruining the other's sex life."

We weren't going to have sex. Or maybe we were. Hell. With my blood-drained brain, if Bodhi hadn't come, I might have ended my dry spell with her brother only a few yards away.

"Your loyalties are safe. We were just talking."

It's obvious we weren't just talking. Brynn's hair is tangled. Mine's probably disheveled from her eager hands. Her lips are perfectly red and plump, and not because of lipstick. But I don't want to put Brynn in that position if she doesn't want him to know.

Bodhi crosses the cabin and throws himself down on the futon, angling his attention toward the opening of the tent, away from us. "Hey, you're adults. I'm just gonna grab a little nap right here. Carry on, friends."

Without a single glance at Brynn, Bodhi drapes his arm across his face, trying to give us a slice of privacy. Though he could've gone to our cabin, with Kip right outside, it's better this way. I was thinking with the wrong head. Even if we are adults, and Kip's never threatened bodily harm for touching his sister, sleeping with her while he's right outside isn't ideal.

Peering over at Brynn, I almost groan. Dammit, Bodhi. I want to kiss her again so bad, but his presence douses me in cold water. Her longing eyes drift to me.

"I'm sorry," I whisper and run the pad of my thumb across her swollen bottom lip. Thoroughly kissed. I sink my teeth into my lips to keep from kissing her anyway.

"Don't be. I'm not. Wanna stay for a bit?"

I'd stay all night if Chloe didn't need a place to sleep. Though, if Kip had anything to say about it, they'd be sharing our cabin tonight.

"Come here." I slip my arm under her, drawing her closer. She nestles her body snug with mine. Her silky red head tucking under my chin and the flats of her palms against my chest.

Curled into my side like this, her tiny figure is dwarfed in my arms. It calms the ever-present storm in my chest, a storm that's been raging for years.

Huh.

Wrapping my other arm around her waist, I skim my hand up and down her curves, from her ribcage to her hips and back.

It probably doesn't mean much, but for a short while, I breathe it in.

"Thank you, Hayden," she sleepily whispers against my skin.

"For what?"

"For not being a snake."

When her breathing is even, I slip out from underneath her, careful to rest her head on a pillow. As I walk past Bodhi, he lifts his arm from his face, and I press my finger to my closed mouth to keep him quiet.

His eyes drift to Brynn tucked into the fetal position, fast asleep before he heads out of the tent in front of me. When I reach the opening, I glance back.

If I were a different man, a man with more to offer, I'd try healing her pain.

And mine.

What's the deal with James and Denton?
Want more Brynn and Hayden?
The stories continue in: *Seaside Pointe, book 2*

FROM THE AUTHOR

We began Kip and Chloe's story way back in 2017 then set it aside for various personal reasons, but in a year where the world shut down (2020), Seaside Pointe became a refuge. As with every book we write, there are so many little pieces of us in these characters and settings. Read our books and get to know us. We're inviting you in.

If you enjoyed this book, we'd love it if you'd take a moment to post a review at the site of purchase or any other book site you like using. We especially LOVE seeing TikTok and Instagram posts. Please tag us so we can share for you!

https://www.instagram.com/mindymichelebooks/
https://www.tiktok.com/@michelegmiller
https://www.tiktok.com/@haymind

ACKNOWLEDGMENTS

MICHELE

To my husband and kids, this Covid year has been crazy, but through it all, you four continue to be my rocks and true loves. Thank you for always asking about my stories and never making me feel bad for following a dream.

My amazing crew of readers, bloggers, and friends, you know who you are. The ones who like my posts and comment on my random musings. Those who encourage me when I'm pouting and help me when I ask. This world is so big, yet so small that I can have friends worldwide to share books with warms my heart. Thank you all for supporting my work and sharing it with your friends and family. I'm forever grateful for each of you.

MINDY

What a whirlwind the last year has been. I wouldn't have survived it without books and writing. Especially Seaside with Michele. What a sweet escape it's been to be in a world we created together.

My readers and friends, I see you and your constant cheering. I keep writing because of you.

To my people, Ryan and Zoey Sue, I know having a wife and mom as an author means having someone who isn't always present because my mind is in other worlds half the time. Thank you for loving me anyway and supporting this passion of mine. I love you most.

KEEP READING!

ABOUT THE AUTHORS

We're pretty awesome! We like singing in the car, eating white cheddar popcorn, and going on road trips together. You'll find us sharing a table at a few book signings each year. We have a love of romance, New York, anything sweet, and great books.

To find out more you can hunt us down on social media. We're all over the place!

Track down Mindy:
Email: mindy.hayes.writes@gmail.com
Website: www.mindyhayes.com
Facebook: www.facebook.com/hayes.mindy
Twitter: @haymindywrites
Instagram: @haymind

Connect with Michele:
Email: authormichelegmiller@gmail.com
Facebook: www.facebook.com/AuthorMicheleGMiller
Twitter: @chelemybelles
Instagram: @chelemybelles
Website: www.michelegmillerbooks.squarespace.com

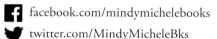

facebook.com/mindymichelebooks

twitter.com/MindyMicheleBks

instagram.com/mindymichelebooks

bookbub.com/authors/mindy-michele

Made in United States
North Haven, CT
21 December 2021

13504292R00250